RACHEL ABBOTT was born and raised in Manchester. She trained as a systems analyst before launching her own interactive media company in the early 1980s. After selling her company in 2000, she moved to the Le Marche region of Italy.

When six-foot snowdrifts prevented her from leaving the house for a couple of weeks, she started writing and found she couldn't stop. Since then her debut thriller, *Only the Innocent*, has become an international bestseller, reaching number one in the Amazon charts both in the UK and US. This was followed by the number-one bestselling novels *The Back Road, Sleep Tight, Stranger Child, Kill Me Again, The Sixth Window* and *Come a Little Closer* plus a novella, *Nowhere Child*, which was top of the Kindle Singles chart in the UK for over two years.

In 2015 Amazon celebrated the first five years of the Kindle in the UK and announced that Rachel was its number-one bestselling independent author over this period. She was also placed fourteenth in the chart of all authors. Rachel has now sold over three million books and her novels are translated into over twenty languages.

In 2018, *And So It Begins*, the first title in a new series featuring Sergeant Stephanie King, was published in hardback by Wildfire Books – a Headline company. It was named by *The Times* as one of the best crime novels of 2018.

Rachel Abbott now lives in Alderney and writes full time.

D0499353

ALSO BY RACHEL ABBOTT

DCI Tom Douglas Series
Only the Innocent
The Back Road
Sleep Tight
Stranger Child
Kill Me Again
The Sixth Window
Come a Little Closer

Novella
Nowhere Child

Sergeant Stephanie King Series
And So It Begins

For more information on Rachel Abbot and her books,
see her website at www.rachel-abbott.com

THE SHAPE
OF LIES

Rachel Abbott

black dot
publishing

The Shape of Lies

Published in 2019 by Black Dot Publishing Ltd

Copyright © Rachel Abbott 2019

Rachel Abbott has asserted her right to be identified as the author of this work in accordance with the Copyright, Designs and Patents Act 1988.

This is a work of fiction. Names, characters, places and incidents are a product of the author's imagination. Locales and public names are sometimes used for atmospheric purposes. Any resemblance to actual people, living or dead, or to businesses, companies, events, institutions or locales is completely coincidental.

ISBN 978-1-9999437-2-1

All rights reserved.

No part of this publication may be reproduced, stored in a retrieval system, or transmitted, in any form or by any means, without the prior permission in writing of the author.

Page design and typesetting by SilverWood Books
Printed on responsibly sourced paper

Find out more about the author and her other books at
www.rachel-abbott.com

Prologue

He's watching her. He knows where she's going, what she's doing, but still he watches. She's inside now – out of his sight – but she'll be coming out soon. It's been thirty minutes, but he doesn't mind the wait. He leans his shoulder against the wall of a shadowed doorway, a spot he has stood in many times before, and thinks about who she is and what she's become.

Finally the glass doors of the apartment block swing open and she strides out, her head high, blonde hair gleaming in the overhead lights of the entrance. Even from here he can tell she is wearing deep red lipstick and dark eye make-up, and the skirt of her short dress swings around bare, tanned legs. He can't see the expression in her eyes, but he knows they will be burning bright with the thrill of the night ahead.

And he hates her for it.

He watches as people turn their heads to stare at this captivating woman who walks with such confidence in her strappy stilettos. They are probably wondering why someone so beautiful is on her own on the streets of Manchester.

She only has to cover a short distance to her destination, and he doesn't need to follow her, but he does anyway. He wonders if she can feel his eyes burning into her back, despising her for who she is, for the pain she has caused.

He hopes she can, because then she might be scared. And he needs that. He wants to see her fear – taste it. But not yet.

Soon.

Monday

1

We all lie. To ourselves and to each other. We make excuses by referring to our untruths as fibs or white lies, trivialising them as harmless. Or we claim they are necessary to shelter others from hurt. However we try to justify them, whatever their shape or form, they are still lies.

Deception is a bigger word. Deceivers manipulate facts to create a false reality, like sleight-of-hand magic. There is nothing spontaneous about deception. It is carefully planned and skilfully orchestrated.

I lie to those closest to me every day, and each untruth plays its part in a greater deception. I am ashamed. I knew when I started on this journey that the path I had chosen was the wrong one, but the first lie slipped out easily and I convinced myself that I had no choice. I didn't realise then that a lie which I believed would harm no one would come with such a hefty price. I thought it was the only way to protect my family and hold it together. And as the deception increases in complexity, the pit I am digging grows deeper. I convince myself that it's nearly over, that soon I won't have to lie any more. Or at least not so often. But that's another lie – this time to myself.

Each morning as I wake up the first emotion to hit me is guilt, closely followed by shame. Today is worse than most. It's a special date for me, but I can't share its significance with anyone else. I have to bear the pain alone. My eyes fill with tears, and I allow myself a few moments to remember before I force myself from the safety of my bed. My chest feels tight, the urge to pull my knees up close and stay buried beneath the covers grows stronger, but my duplicitous nature urges me to paint a smile on my face and get on with the day.

I walk over to the window, pull back the curtains and look out over the golf course that lies at the back of our house. It's another beautiful morning, and on a day such as this the fairways will soon be full of men and women dragging their trolleys behind them, hitting a small white ball a hundred metres or so, only to trudge after it and hit it again. I don't get golf, but it's wonderful to see the beautifully cut grass, the artfully constructed ponds and the clumps of trees, which will be getting their autumn leaves before long.

We are lucky to have this house. It's a wreck, but when my husband inherited it from his uncle we could hardly refuse, and it allows us to be mortgage free. We will renovate it over time but it's taking longer than either of us expected, as no doubt these things always do.

I let the curtains drop back and head for the bathroom, squealing as a splinter goes into my foot from the floorboards that are waiting to be sanded back to their Victorian glory. The children aren't allowed out of their bedrooms without rubber-soled slippers, but I always forget. And it's my fault the floor is like this. In frustration at the lack of progress I ripped up the dirty old carpet two weeks ago, earning myself a rebuke from my husband, who has a plan that apparently I should have adhered to. He is a man who likes lists with items that can be ticked off in order as each one is completed.

The shower gives me time to take some deep breaths, and I stare into the mirror to reassure myself that no hint of my true feelings is showing. I see an unexceptional face: top lip slightly too long, a straight nose, and dark brown hair that waves to just below my chin. My oval-shaped navy-blue eyes are normally considered my best feature, but today they are puffy and I wish I could sink back into my bed with a couple of cold teabags on them for half an hour. But I can't, so I run a flannel under the tap and push it firmly against the offending skin in the hope that I will be able to work miracles with some make-up.

Finally I walk downstairs, picking my way past two bin liners stuffed with stripped-off wallpaper – another of my failed attempts to be helpful. I hear a giggle and look towards the open door to the kitchen, through which I glimpse the comforting scene of my children eating breakfast at a rickety Formica table under the watchful eye of my husband. He comes into the hall as he always does to make sure I have everything I need for the day ahead. I notice he is limping today, but I don't comment. I know he hates it.

I reach up an arm to wrap around his neck. 'You're so bloody *tall*,' I say, pulling his face down towards mine and resting my lips briefly on his. It's true – he is. And his wide shoulders look as if they are made to be leaned on. If only I could.

'Morning, short stuff.' He smiles and kisses me back.

I straighten the jacket of the smart new suit I bought for days like today when I have an important meeting and strike a pose. 'Do I look okay?'

'You look gorgeous – ready to conquer the world.'

Dominic always does his best to make me feel good. He hasn't worked for eighteen months, since the event we euphemistically call his 'accident', and is perfectly content to be a stay-at-home dad, caring for the children and gradually restoring the house. He says he has no desire to return to teaching, but I suspect he underestimated the time needed to care for two small children.

I used to be the polar opposite of my unambitious husband. When I was eighteen I wanted to fly, to jump every hurdle in my path, to be everything I possibly could be. But that lust for life brought me nothing but turmoil, and I learned to value stability and a life free from uncertainty. Sometimes, though, I strive to free a tiny portion of myself from the confines of a life constrained by the codes of others.

I step towards the kitchen to say goodbye to my children, and speak to Dom over my shoulder. 'You were up early this morning. Couldn't you sleep?'

'I was too hot. I think my next job has to be sorting our bedroom windows so we can at least open them and get some air in the room. It was stifling. Sorry I woke you, but I knew I wouldn't get back to sleep so I went for a walk – you know it helps in the morning.' He's following me, so I stop at the door and turn.

'I heard the car go. How's your leg feeling?'

'Not too bad, although I probably walked too far. I decided to drive to the park for a change of scenery. It was just before six when I got there and there was no one else around. It was perfect.'

'Sounds lovely.' I walk into the kitchen. 'Now, where are those gorgeous children of ours?'

Most of the time I find it easy to play the part of the perfect wife in a perfect family, but occasionally it feels hard to know which is the charade and which is my reality – this life, with the children I love dearly, or the secret life in which I play the starring role.

I hurry over to the table. It's time I was on my way, but I can't resist kissing Holly over and over on her cheek until she pushes me away with a giggle. I spin towards Bailey and lift his chubby little hand to lick the honey off his fingers before he smears the sticky goo all over my clothes.

'I'll see you kids tonight. Have a wonderful day,' I shout as I head for the front door.

I turn back briefly in the doorway, give Dominic a final cheery wave and walk towards my brand new raspberry-red car, groping in my handbag for the keys.

I'm about to reach for the handle when I stop dead. Just in time I've seen what's on the window, only inches from where I was about to put my hand. I want to turn and run, but I know I should stand still and wait until the source of my fear flies away. It doesn't look as if it's going anywhere, though, and I stare transfixed at the yellow and black stripes, the slender body pinched in just below the fine wings. I know where its stinger is, and I'm told that only female wasps can sting, but I don't know how to tell the difference and I don't care. They are all enemies to me.

For a second I think the wasp is about to leave as it lifts itself from the glass and buzzes around for a few moments. But it settles back down. I feel as if it's playing with me, waiting for me to swat at it so it has an excuse to attack.

I hear Dominic shout from the open door, 'Hang on, Anna.' I can't look at him, but he'll be glancing over his shoulder to check the children are still eating breakfast. I hear the irregular beat of his footsteps hurrying towards me and feel his fingers on my arm. He reaches out a hand holding a handkerchief. He pauses, and then he lunges and I give a little yelp of fear.

'Got it,' he says with a note of satisfaction. He turns and smiles. 'You're good to go, darling.'

I can breathe again, but somehow the sight of the wasp feels like an omen. I still haven't moved.

Dominic opens the car door for me. 'Do you need to come back in the house for a few minutes? Are you going to be okay?'

For a moment my mind turns blank, but then I shake myself. At least Dominic never laughs at me; he has even researched the problem. 'Spheksophobia – that's what fear of wasps is called,' he'd told me when he first saw the level of my panic.

I was stung three times as a child, and have hated and feared wasps ever since. But that doesn't account for the paralysing terror I feel now. I can never explain it to Dominic. The trauma of the moment I became truly spheksophobic was far worse than he could ever imagine.

Sadly not everything can be solved by Dominic with a

handkerchief and a bit of love and attention. Some things demand so much more, and the thought of the secret mountain I need to climb sneaks up on me. I feel my throat tighten. More lies, more deceit.

There are times I can't wait for it to be over, and at other times I never want it to end.

2

I sometimes ask myself which is the real me: the family person – mummy to two adorable small children and wife to a strong, dependable husband; the professional person – Anna Franklyn, head teacher, a woman with drive, ambition and genuine concern for the well-being of those in her care; or the other me – the one no one knows, the one whose pulse races with guilt-ridden excitement.

When I'm at school it's easy to shed my heavy cloak of remorse and slip on a public face, and during the half-hour journey each morning I transform myself into this better version of myself. I originally joined the small Church of England primary school two years ago as deputy head, but after the acrimonious dismissal of the head teacher just months after I arrived, I was promoted until they could replace him. They never did, so I was delighted and a little astonished when they offered me the permanent position.

As I drive, I glance out of the window at the people hurrying to work. A brief spell of weather too hot for early September has brought out the bright clothes that had been abandoned during a wet and miserable August. Girls in colourful short dresses and men in shirtsleeves walk with their heads up towards the sun, rather than stooping to shield themselves from the rain.

I force my shoulders to relax, the tension of the morning slowly seeping from my body. One wasp is not going to ruin my day, and I look at the other drivers, the pedestrians and bus passengers, and wonder what scares them. Everyone's afraid of something.

I can see there is heavy traffic up ahead, which is irritating but not the end of the world. I lean forward and switch on the radio. Above the chirpy voice of the presenter I can just make out the sound of a pneumatic drill so I turn the radio up a little, relax back into my seat and feel the sun warm me through the window as a 90s Take That song plays. I have a momentary flashback to my teenage self in Cindy Williams' bedroom, both of us trying to copy Jason Orange's dance moves. Life was simple then.

The music fades and the presenter's voice cuts through the final notes. 'Now it's the moment you've all been waiting for – the highlight of your week! It's time for "The One That Got Away!"'

I enjoy this weekly segment, so I tweak the volume higher as I draw closer to the roadworks. 'Today we've got Susie from Oldham on the phone, ready to tell us her tale of thwarted love. This is the story you voted for last week, folks. So tell us, Susie. Who was he – or she? Why was this person so perfect, and how did he or she get away from you?'

Susie from Oldham talks enthusiastically about a gorgeous man she'd met online and how some ill-judged images sent by text had abruptly ended their budding relationship. It's not the best story I've heard and I don't understand what possesses people to send photos of their body parts via SMS, but it brightens my journey a little. Sometimes the stories in 'The One That Got Away' are funny, sometimes sad, but it has become quite a talking point among my friends and colleagues. There's even a TOTGA Facebook group. The best bit, though, is the phone-in at the end of the feature. Callers pitch a teaser to tell their own tale of woe, and the one that gets the most votes is selected for the following week's programme.

'We've got three callers on the line ready to entice us,' the presenter says, his voice rising with excitement. 'Are you ready, listeners? Remember, you can vote for your favourite online or via text, and the winner will reveal the happy, sad or gory details of their story at the same time next Monday.'

I'm getting closer to the pneumatic drill now, which is annoying as it's becoming difficult to hear the radio. The first pitch is embarrassing, as they sometimes are. Some girl is crying because her boyfriend has gone back to his wife, and it's making me a bit uncomfortable. What if his wife's listening? The presenter thankfully cuts her short and moves on to the next caller.

'My name's Scott.'

My hands grip the steering wheel a little tighter. The name Scott always gives me a jolt – especially today – but it's an irrational reaction.

'Okay, Scott, you're on. Sixty seconds to tell us why we should listen to your story in detail next Monday. And…*go!*'

'My story is about a beautiful girl – I called her Spike.' I hear myself gasp. Scott is talking quickly and the drill is making it even harder to hear. There is something familiar about his voice, but there has to be more than one Scott with a Welsh accent, surely? But Spike…What a weird coincidence.

'Spike wasn't her real name, by the way,' he says. 'I'll tell you her real name if I'm chosen, but I loved her. She was everything to me. Sadly we did some stuff we shouldn't have, and everything went horribly wrong. It nearly killed us, one way or another. It was fourteen years ago today – one year after we met – that we made the devastating decision that changed our lives – well, mine anyway. If you're listening, Spike, I know you won't have forgotten.'

I can't believe what I'm hearing. My eyes sting and I lift a hand to brush away hot tears. I want to reach out and switch the radio off – I don't want to listen to any more. My hand hovers over the button, but I can't do it.

'It was a terrible time, and Spike decided that – for me, at least – it was all over. Next Monday is another important day – the day that I always think of as "*the end*". And that's when I'll tell our story.'

I swallow hard, my throat tight. It can't be *my* Scott. I know that. *But the dates!* Surely this is our story?

The man calling himself Scott seems to have ground to a halt, and the presenter chips in. 'You like to keep us in suspense, don't you, Scott? Tell me, when did you last see each other?'

At that moment I pull level with the drill, and its clattering deafens me. The radio is on full blast, but I can't catch what he says, and by the time I am past the roadworks, the moment has gone. Only the presenter can be heard, telling his listeners there is one more pitch before they must make up their minds who to choose.

'I think young Scott has got us all intrigued, though. Who is Spike? And what did the two of them *do* that tore them apart? The mind boggles, folks. Don't forget to vote, and if my guess is right we'll all be tuning in next Monday to find out what happened to end Scott and Spike's wonderful relationship, and discover what was so special about this day fourteen years ago.'

The rest of the journey passes in a blur. My eyes have glazed over and I am barely functioning. My hands are shaking, and I grasp the steering wheel as tightly as I can, forcing myself to concentrate on the road, to cut the ridiculous thoughts out of my head. *It's not Scott.*

But the date, the accent and the names.

A Welsh boy called Scott had nicknamed me Spike many years ago, after I had my hair cut painfully short to try to look cool – a word that was bandied about all the time back then.

I might manage to convince myself that there are many men called Scott, and that Spike isn't such an imaginative nickname, but I can't ignore the dates. No one other than Scott would know the significance of today. It's a day I've been dreading, as I do every year.

I realise I have arrived at school without consciously knowing how I got here. I drive through the entrance to the car park of the old red-brick building which looked so shabby when I first arrived, and I take no pleasure in the colourful garden that an enthusiastic group of children and staff have created. I see nothing, blind to all but the memories. My head is swimming.

The radio is still playing, but I haven't been listening. Until now.

'Text us with the word "Scott" if you want to learn what happened to Scott and Spike fourteen years ago in Nebraska.'

I hear myself gasp. That must have been what he was saying as I passed the drill. *It all happened in Nebraska.*

I gulp back a sob.

Fourteen years ago today I was with Scott in Nebraska, and it was the worst day of my life. No one knows that except Scott, but it can't be him on the radio because Scott has been dead for fourteen years. And I killed him.

3

'Becky!' DCI Tom Douglas shouted as he walked through the major incident team's office.

Becky Robinson was standing over by a whiteboard, talking to DS Keith Sims. She turned at the urgency in Tom's voice. 'What's up?'

'Come on – time we got you back in action,' he said as he drew close.

Becky had been on maternity leave, and despite how hard she was finding it to leave her baby, she was excited at the thought of a new case. Knowing Tom would fill her in en route to wherever they were going, she grabbed her bag and followed him out into the sunshine.

'It's too bloody hot for September,' Tom said, opening his car door. 'It's like an oven in here.'

'The last case I was on with you it was freezing – snow several feet thick, if I remember correctly – so I can cope with it being hot for a change.'

Tom put the car into gear and reversed out of his parking spot. 'How's Buster?'

Becky smiled. Her baby was called George, but her partner Mark had referred to him as Buster during the last months of her pregnancy and it had stuck. 'He's doing great. Chubby little thing. You'll have to call round and see him again. Bring Lucy.'

Tom's daughter, Lucy, loved babies and she had always got on well with Becky. 'I'll do that. Thanks.'

'So, where are we off to?'

'Not far – central Manchester. Body of a male found in a car in a multi-storey. The car park's been sealed off, but that's going to cause havoc and general grumbling unless we can get it sorted quickly.'

Realistically it could take hours for the crime scene to be thoroughly examined, so those vehicles already in the car park were destined to stay there for the time being, and those waiting to come in would be turned away until further notice.

Becky groaned. 'We'll have people moaning that we're stopping them from going about their lives when some poor bugger's lying dead only metres away. They seem to think we do it on purpose just to make their lives more difficult.'

Tom grinned. It was true that the general public seemed to be divided into those who accepted that occasionally things happen that cause some inconvenience, while others sought someone to blame for any disruption. And it was usually the police who were held responsible.

'Fortunately for us,' he said, 'some hapless uniform will have to deal with all that crap. We, on the other hand, will have to get up close to our victim, and I don't have the first clue what state he's in. It's your first body for some time, Becky – are you feeling okay about it or are you more squeamish since giving birth?'

Becky snorted. 'Less so, if anything. Although I've become a lot more safety conscious. Wait until the next time I drive. No more hanging on to your grab handle when I go round the corner. I'm the antithesis of recklessness these days.'

Tom gave her a glance that said he didn't believe a word of it. He often teased Becky about his first experience in a car with her – in central London – saying he had no idea how they had managed to get from A to B without causing a major incident.

But the light-hearted chat came to an end as they arrived at the multi-storey. Tom's face was serious as he spoke. 'Well, here we are. Let's go and see what we've got. You ready?'

She nodded and threw open the car door.

As Tom and Becky made their way up the stairwell towards Level 5 of the car park, their footsteps echoed off the bare walls. There was a smell of hot concrete mixed with overcooked vegetables, probably coming from the staff canteen of the adjoining offices. Becky wrinkled her nose. Lifting one end of the extra-long, brightly coloured silk scarf that she was wearing to – in her words – hide her still-podgy baby belly, she rather theatrically covered the lower half of her face.

'We can't expect car parks to be places of great beauty, but when you chuck in a bit of stewed cabbage it all gets a bit much.'

Tom smiled and pushed open a door leading to a poorly lit expanse of car park. It was eerily silent. No cars were coming or going up and down the ramps, and there was no one to be seen.

'Where is everyone?' Becky asked, her voice sounding unnaturally loud.

'We have to walk up the ramp to the next half-level. I understand the car's at the far end.'

They turned up a short slope and looked to the right where three arc lights illuminated the gloom. Crime-scene technicians were busying themselves around one of the cars, and Tom was relieved to see the reassuringly large figure of Jumoke Osoba, or Jumbo as he was more commonly known, standing with his hands on his hips, overseeing their efforts.

The focus of attention was a dark grey Mercedes S-Class saloon, and as they drew closer Tom registered that the car looked new, although it was impossible to tell due to the personalised number plate – CEJ79. Jumbo turned towards them, and his characteristic wide white smile lit up his black face.

'Morning, Tom. Good to have you back, Becky.'

Becky gave him an answering grin as she and Tom slipped on protective suits.

'What have we got, Jumbo?' Tom asked, approaching the car.

'Male victim, somewhere in his thirties at a guess. It seems pretty obvious how he died, although the Home Office pathologist will have to confirm it, of course. Take a look.'

The first thing Tom noticed was that the driver's window was down. Given the heat, this wasn't surprising. He reached out a gloved hand to touch the bonnet. It was cold. It seemed likely then that the victim had been here a while, or at least the car had. The parking ticket should give them an accurate answer to that. Had the driver left his window open after taking his ticket from the machine when he arrived, or had he lowered it to talk to someone? Had he known his killer? Was he arriving, or was he about to leave? Tom mentally sorted the puzzle pieces and considered how they might slot together.

All the car's doors were closed, and Jumbo moved his considerable bulk out of the way to let Tom peer in through the window. The car next to the Mercedes was parked extremely close on the driver's side. It was a tight squeeze.

Tom gazed at a man's face, swollen and dotted with ruptured capillaries. His eyes were wide open, the whites bulging and red with blood, staring at nothing.

As Jumbo had said, there seemed little doubt how the man had died. A nylon cable tie was still around his neck. It had been pulled tight – impossible to shift – and had cut into the skin of his throat. He had been strangled – garrotted – from behind.

'What do you think?' he asked Jumbo.

'Cable tie, doubled up so it was long enough to go around both the neck and the headrest. At a guess it was already prepared, the end threaded through. He would just have had to slip it over the head and pull. A job of seconds.'

'Do we know who the victim is?' Tom asked.

'We think so. The car is registered to Cameron Edmunds – or Cameron Edmunds *Junior*, as I gather he's better known. He doesn't have any identification on him and the mobile phone we found on the seat is locked. So until we can get at the SIM, that's no help.'

The name at least explained the registration plate, and Tom assumed the number was the year of his birth, although even in this state he looked younger.

'Jumbo, you might want to look at this.' One of the crime-scene team was kneeling between the two cars, examining the blue Ford Focus parked next to the Mercedes.

Tom and Jumbo crouched down next to the technician and looked where he was pointing. There was a deep dint in the door of the Focus, flecked with what looked like flakes of dark paint. They turned towards the Mercedes and Jumbo gently pulled open the rear door, lining up the marks.

'Someone either got in or out of the back of the car in quite a rush, wouldn't you say?'

Tom nodded. 'Or both.'

Becky strode across to the two men.

'Boss, I've been speaking to PC Khatri – he was the first responder. The person who called it in said he'd just parked his car on the far side of this level and decided to walk over to take a closer look at the Merc – his dream car, apparently. Thinking it was empty, he sneaked a peek inside. He's downstairs in the parking attendant's office being given a cup of tea for the shock. Shall I go and have a word with him?'

'Yes, in a moment. We'll also need to get what we can on Cameron Edmunds – get to his family before any word of this gets out. But before you do that, take a look at the scene and tell me what you see.'

Tom and Jumbo stepped away from the car to give Becky space, silently watching her.

She peered closely at the dead man's bloated face, conscious that this was someone's husband, father or son. The desire to win justice for the people who had lost him would drive her to seek answers so the killer could be caught. It was what made the job so rewarding, and it felt good to be back.

'The engine is cold so the car's been here a while, but there's no sign of rigor mortis yet, so he's not been dead long. That suggests he had returned to his car and was about to leave. So why would he open his window? Surely he'd have switched on the air con?' Becky looked around, turning full circle. 'What about CCTV?'

Jumbo pulled a face.

'Is there none at all?' Becky asked with a sinking feeling. It would have made life so much easier.

'It's one of the few remaining multi-storeys without, I'm afraid. But then I guess our killer knew that. There are cameras at the entrance and exit, but not on each floor,' Jumbo said.

'Bugger,' Tom muttered.

'Quite. There are several in the streets nearby, but it doesn't help unless we know who we're looking for.'

Becky stood back from the car and stared at it. The victim was attacked from behind, so had the perpetrator been in the car already? She returned to the driver's window and looked again at the dead man's face.

'Did either of you notice that the skin around his eyes and nose seems swollen, irritated? It could be anything – a cold, maybe, or an allergy. But I wonder if something was sprayed in his eyes to distract him, giving the killer time to jump in the back.'

'What, pepper spray – or Mace, maybe? Well spotted,' Tom said.

'I'll point it out to the pathologist,' Jumbo said with a nod of approval.

Becky wondered whether the window was already open, or did the victim wind it down to speak to his killer? Why would he do that? Did he know him? Maybe the killer had pretended to need help, or had signalled to the victim that there was something wrong with his car – a flat tyre, possibly – and he had lowered the window fully to take a look. Then the killer had sprayed something into his eyes, dived into the back of the car, whipped the cable tie over the victim's head and garrotted him.

Could it have been a random attack? A theft? There was no wallet, but his phone was still on the seat. Nothing about it seemed random to Becky, though. The spray and the cable tie suggested it was carefully planned.

It felt like an execution.

4

Monday is usually my favourite day of the week. We always start the school day with assembly, and I love looking at all the bright, eager faces of the children sitting cross-legged on the floor in front of me. Most are still untouched by any of life's harsh realities and they smile happily, their expressions glowing with innocence.

Today, though, I have struggled to focus and the hours have dragged. I smiled my way through an important meeting with the trustees, and no one seemed to notice the vacant expression behind my eyes as the words spoken by the man on the radio continued to spin round and round in my head, with one thought forcing itself to the surface over and over again.

If anyone finds out what Scott and I did, my life will fall apart.

I remind myself that Scott is dead – I *know* he's dead – and my fears are irrational. But my stomach is in knots.

If it's not Scott, does someone else know our story?

Throughout the day, memories of my time with him have been haunting me, and in the end I can't resist logging into the TOTGA Facebook group to see what people are saying. Inevitably Scott's story is intriguing everyone, and there are all kinds of theories.

'Do you think they killed someone?'

'Perhaps they robbed a bank! Maybe they were like Bonnie and Clyde!'

But no one knows. No one must *ever* know.

At the end of a long day I find myself unwilling to go home. However much I love my job, I always look forward to seeing my children. I can imagine them now, probably at the kitchen table drawing with their daddy, who will have picked them up from school and given them a snack so we can all have a meal together when I'm home. But I want to hide here, where no one can read the fear in my eyes.

It's so much easier since Dom has been looking after the children. I can remember when Holly was born and we were both teaching. Every day was a rush, dropping her off with a child-minder, dashing back to pick her up, trying to find time to do the shopping, the washing, clean the house. Bailey came along four years ago, and then we moved into a house that was falling apart. I don't know how we managed. Dom, a drama teacher at a secondary school, was involved in plays in the evenings and weekends as well as his classroom teaching, and I neither of us seemed to have a spare moment.

And then came Dom's 'accident'. He doesn't like to use the word 'mugging' because it reminds him of what really happened. He feels he should have done better than he did, but I don't know why. There were three of them, and he did well to get away with only the damage to his leg, although it still troubles him sometimes.

He was off work for six months while they broke and reset his bones to try to fix the leg, and in the end Dom admitted that he liked being at home with the children. As his inheritance had left us with no mortgage, he wondered if perhaps we could manage without his salary. I was happy to agree.

I would have done anything to make him feel better. Anything at all. Because it was my fault – all of it – but I can never tell him that.

The children go to the local primary, and it takes me thirty minutes to drive to my slightly larger school. By the time I arrive home each night Dominic has started the dinner, played with the children, and the world seems a calm, organised place.

At least, the world between the four walls of my home.

Nevertheless, tonight I need to delay my journey.

I quickly send Dom a text to say I'll be home by six, and find jobs to do to justify my late departure. Finally, when I can't put it off any longer, I walk out to my car, knowing I'm going to have to make a call. I've been putting it off all day, but there is one person who knows more than anyone should, and I need her to keep that knowledge to herself.

I pull my mobile from my bag, switch it to hands-free and start the engine.

'Hi, Mum, it's me,' I say unnecessarily as her phone is set to play 'Isn't She Lovely' when I call, and there's no persuading her to change it.

'Hello, darling. I'm so glad you called – I've been worrying about you all day. I heard the radio this morning and tried to speak to you a few times, but it went straight to voicemail.'

I know my mother will have heard the broadcast. She likes to listen to the same radio station and watch the same television programmes as I do. The truth is she's lonely, but she won't move away from the home she shared with my dad. I shudder when I think how close she came to losing it.

'I'm sorry, Mum. I was in a meeting and switched my mobile off.' It's a poor excuse, but I hadn't wanted to speak to her until I had calmed down. I needed to be ready because I know exactly what she's going to say.

'Did you hear Scott on the radio, Anna? What a turn-up. You thought he was dead, didn't you? I've been thinking of nothing else since this morning. I bet it was a hell of a shock for you.'

I slam the car into reverse. 'Not really, no. What's there to think about, Mum? Scott *is* dead. I went to his funeral – well, his memorial service anyway. His parents were there. This is someone else. There's more than one Scott in the world, you know.'

I have to convince her that it's nothing – that she's got it all wrong. If I don't, she will talk to Dominic about it, and I can't let that happen.

'Yes, but what about the Nebraska bit?'

I make sure my sigh is audible. 'You do know, don't you, that Nebraska is about one and a half times the size of England? You wouldn't think it strange if a man was talking about his girlfriend and said they went to *England*, would you?'

'No,' my mother says slowly. 'I suppose you're right.'

I don't mention the fact that Nebraska isn't exactly a popular destination for British tourists, and I'm hoping my mother has no idea. For a woman who thinks Manchester is a foreign country even though she only lives a hundred miles away in Cumbria, this seems a fairly safe bet. She has to think it's nonsense – nothing more than a coincidence. Thank God the date means nothing to her.

'Look, Mum, can we not talk about this again, please? I've never spoken to Dominic about that summer.'

'Why not?' My mother sounds bemused. 'You were nineteen years old. Surely Dominic wouldn't mind that you had a boyfriend? I'm sure he doesn't believe he's the first man in your life.'

Dom knows there was someone, although he has no idea how much I loved him, but he also knows I did a degree in English literature, and there is no way that would have included a two-month work-experience placement in Nebraska, which is what my mother believes.

'Of course Dom knows I had boyfriends before him. He even knows one was called Scott, but we've never felt the need to share any details, and I don't want to start now. Please, Mum, let's not talk about this again.'

It's my mother's turn to sigh. 'Well okay, if you say so. I never thought Scott was good enough for you anyway, but you were so far away, and me and your dad were just pleased there was someone looking out for you, although you were in such a state when you came back from America. He made you quite ill, didn't he?'

I close my eyes for a moment, remembering the pain, then I force myself to speak normally. 'Let's not go back there, Mum. It was years ago. I'm a happily married woman with a great job and two terrific kids now, so let's look on the bright side, shall we? I'll speak to you soon.'

I blow out a long slow breath as I disconnect, hoping my call has done the trick. I can't let her start digging up the past, and she always talks about my time at Manchester University as if it was an aberration on my part. She hadn't wanted me to leave home when I was eighteen, but the thought that she and my dad had – at least initially – been reassured by Scott's presence in my life is almost more than I can cope with.

'If only you knew, Mum,' I whisper.

5

15 years ago

'Mum, will you please stop fussing!' I whispered fiercely, horrified that someone might be able to hear every word through the open door to my room. The corridor was buzzing as all the other first-year students settled into their new home in the halls of residence without any of this nonsense. But my mum would not shut up.

'Listen, Anna, you're a long way from home, and I need to be sure you're going to be okay.'

I wanted to tell her it was actually only a hundred miles, but I was beginning to wish I had chosen a university on the south coast.

'Let's get you unpacked,' she said, bustling around the room, trying to open the bigger of the two suitcases.

'*No*, Mum.' I reached out an arm and put it around her shoulders. 'I know you're trying to help, but I honestly don't need you to. I haven't decided where to put my stuff yet.'

I couldn't tell her that this felt like my break for freedom. I had the best parents in the world, but they couldn't understand why I would want to leave the beauty of our home in the Lake District to come here, to Manchester. It was only a few years since the IRA bomb in the city centre, and Mum was convinced there would be another one – with me slap-bang in the middle. She wanted me to stay at home and get a job in a local hotel – maybe even the one where she worked – until I got married and started a family of my own.

A family was all she had ever wanted, although I was a major surprise – I hadn't come along until she was forty-two and they had given up all hope of having children. She couldn't believe that I wanted something different.

I turned to my dad, who was leaning against the wall with a faint smile on his lips.

'Don't look at me, Anna. You know she won't listen to what I have to say on the subject.'

I turned back to my mum, who suddenly looked lost. With no daughter to fuss over, cook for, drive around, it was going to be hard for her. It was going to be hard for me too. I lacked the confidence of other girls my age; I'd known everyone back at home since I was born, but no one else. We never even went on holiday because my mum's job was seasonal. But I had to learn to fend for myself.

I wanted to make my own decisions, and the first of those would be to do something drastic with my hair. I felt as if I needed to reinvent myself – kick-start the new me into life – so I was going to dye it blonde and have it shorn to a spiky cut. A brave decision, but nothing ventured...

'Come on, Iris, love,' my dad said, trying to ease Mum gently out of my room. 'Give the girl a bit of space. Let's get off home – you'll want to get back before dark.'

I could see my mum was trying hard not to cry, so I ignored the lump in my throat and gave her a hug. 'I'll miss you both, but I'll be home for the weekend soon, and before you know it, it'll be Christmas. It's an easy train ride, Mum – you can always come and see me for a day if Dad's working.'

That was true, but the life we led in the back of beyond was so quiet that a trip into Keswick four miles away felt like a major event. Taking a train to a big city like Manchester on her own was way outside Mum's comfort zone.

As they reached the door she turned back and reached out her hands to grip mine.

'We've had the conversation about boys and watching yourself, but there are some bad people in the world, Anna. Types that you have no experience dealing with. Be careful, love. I mean it. Be very careful who you trust. Bad things can happen to good people too, you know.'

I smiled, never thinking for a moment that she was right to warn me – that I might do something I would be so ashamed of that I would never be able to tell a soul.

I closed the door behind my parents and leaned against it, my heart beating a little faster with a heady mixture of excitement and apprehension. For a moment I wanted to open the door and yell, 'Come back! Take me home!' Instead I focused on the mental image of the exciting life I had been dreaming of for years and held it in my mind until I was sure my parents had gone. Then I slid down the door until I was on the thin carpet, knees hugged tightly, and allowed a few silent tears to drip down my cheeks.

'Stop it, Anna,' I muttered to myself, scrubbing at my face with a tissue. 'You can do this.'

6

Now

The house seems strangely quiet when I walk in. There isn't the usual cacophony of children playing, although I can hear the television and I wonder if, for once, Dominic has relented and let them watch some cartoon or other. It sounds like the news, though – something we rarely watch until Holly and Bailey are in bed. I push open the sitting-room door to find Dominic standing up, arms folded, staring at the screen. He switches the television off and replaces the remote on the table.

'Hi, darling,' he says, turning to me with a smile.

'What were you watching?'

'The news. Some guy's been found murdered in a car park in town.' Dominic shakes his head, as if in despair at what the world is coming to.

'Do they know who he is? Have they caught his killer?'

'Apparently not – in answer to both questions. Or at least they're not saying.' He steps closer and reaches out his arms to pull me into a hug and speaks to the top of my head. 'But on to more cheerful subjects – how was your day?'

'Okay. Nothing special. A boring meeting with the trustees, but they seem happy enough. Where are the kids? It's very quiet around here.'

I had been relying on the children to keep me occupied and to give me somewhere to focus my gaze so as to avoid Dom's penetrating eyes, worried he would read the turmoil this morning's radio programme has created. I'm safe at the

31

moment, with my head buried in his chest.

'Holly was invited to go and play with her latest best friend, Daisy, and Bailey kicked up such a stink about being excluded that Daisy's mother very kindly said he could go too, much to Holly's disgust. I'll go and pick them up in a couple of minutes.'

I push myself out of his arms and give him a grateful smile, turning away before he can study me too closely. 'I'll go and get changed out of this suit then. I won't be long.'

As I walk through the hall towards the stairs, the doorbell rings.

'I'll get it,' I shout, climbing over the clutter to reach the door.

I'm half-expecting to find that the children have been brought home early, and am surprised to see a man in black leathers with a red stripe down each side, his helmet visor pushed back so he can speak.

'Pizza for Franklyn.' He holds out a stack of four boxes.

Surely Dominic hasn't ordered pizza? He's obsessed with healthy food, especially for the children.

'Are you sure they're for us?'

'Well if your name's Franklyn and this is your address, then yes. They're for you.'

'Okay, how much do I owe you? I'll get my purse.'

'Nothing to pay. All paid for in advance.'

The delivery man pushes the pizza boxes into my hand and turns back towards his scooter. 'See you next time,' he says with a wave as he strides off down the path, belatedly remembering to shout 'Enjoy!' over his shoulder.

I carry the pizzas towards the kitchen, stopping at the door to the sitting room. Dominic has put the news on again and has his back to me.

'You didn't say you'd ordered pizza,' I shout over the monologue of the newsreader.

'That's because I didn't,' he says, turning to see me standing with the stack in my hands. 'You didn't pay for those, did you?'

'No. He said they were already paid for so I presumed you'd ordered them.'

'Nothing to do with me. I've made fish pie.'

I see Dominic's puzzled expression and know it reflects my own.

'How weird. Shall I call them and check it out?' I ask.

'Nope. If they've delivered them by mistake it's not our problem. You eat one if you like, but I'd rather the kids had the fish pie I made. A bit better for them than pizza.'

I hate wasting food. Surely it wouldn't hurt the children to eat pizza for once; the fish pie will keep until tomorrow. I carry on towards the kitchen and plonk the boxes on the table, lifting the cardboard cover of the first one to check what topping it's got. Under the lid is a handwritten note: *Enjoy the pizza – your third prize win in this month's charity raffle.*

I stand staring at the note, my heart thudding, not realising that Dominic has come up behind me.

'You won them in a *raffle*? Really?'

I swallow and force a smile onto my lips. 'It was probably organised by one of the teachers from school.' I slam the lid shut. 'I'll bin these, shall I? Your fish pie sounds much better. I'll go and have a shower while you collect the kids.'

I know my behaviour must seem odd to Dominic. We would normally joke that of all the things we could win in a raffle, it had to be something we didn't want. But all I can think of is how to get away from him before he realises I can hardly breathe. Because this is no coincidence. There has been no raffle. At least not for nearly fifteen years, and the only other person who knew about that one was Scott.

7

Then

The first five days after I arrived in Manchester passed slowly. I had thought it would be easy to make friends, but although everyone was chatty and pleasant, they all seemed so much more comfortable in their skins than I felt. I had never had to walk up to someone I didn't know and introduce myself before; in Cumbria I was surrounded by familiar faces wherever I went.

I did all the right things. I signed up for activities and tours, went to special film screenings and got involved in fundraising. People chatted to me, smiled at me, laughed with me. It was great. But no one said, 'Shall we go somewhere tonight?' or, 'Do you want to come to a concert with me?'

The students in my hall were always talking about what was happening that night. 'There's a great gig on tonight,' one of them might say.

That was my cue. I should have said, 'Yes, so I heard. Shall we go together?' But I didn't.

I had been so excited about my freedom, but I hadn't realised how hard it would be to make the first move. At home I had automatically assumed I was included in events – one of the benefits of long-standing friendships, I suppose – and I'd never realised before that I was shy and lacking in self-confidence. To make matters worse, the new haircut that was supposed to make me feel brave and independent was a disaster.

It took me a while to pluck up the courage to head to what I'd heard was everyone's favourite bar, where there was often live music. What if no one spoke to me? Nervous as I was, though, I had to do it.

'Okay, here we go,' I muttered as I locked my room. 'It's going to be fine.'

I wanted to reach for the sky, to soar above the clouds – and if I was going to fly, this was my first lesson. I needed to test my wings, however fragile they might be.

The bar was noisy, and there wasn't a spare seat to be had. Maybe I should have come earlier. Tempted to turn round and go back to my room, I forced myself to push through to the bar to order a half of cider, and then, drink in hand, wandered to the edge of the room and propped myself up against the wall, trying to look relaxed. I felt self-conscious about being on my own, but I couldn't see a single person I recognised.

'Oh, I love this,' a girl at a table nearby shouted as she leaped up from her seat and made her way towards a few dancers, joining in with people she clearly hadn't come with and possibly didn't even know. Even if I'd had the courage to do the same there was nowhere to put my glass, or my bag. Why I'd thought it necessary to take a bag I don't know. I decided to have my drink and then go back to my room. At least I had made the effort, and I convinced myself it would get easier.

I felt, rather than saw, someone lean against the wall by my side. My body was turned slightly towards the dancers, and when I glanced over my shoulder I saw I had been joined by a boy. He looked to be about my age and was grinning.

'Not dancing, then?' he muttered, close to my ear. The music was deafening and I wondered if I'd heard him correctly. I gave him a tentative smile in return.

'Are you a fresher? I'm a second year. Economics and politics. You?'

'English literature,' I answered.

I searched for something interesting to say. Fortunately the gap was more than adequately filled by the music.

'Are you enjoying this?' he asked.

'It's okay. I don't know anyone yet, so I didn't know who to ask about the best things to go to.'

I felt stupid. That was more information than he'd asked for.

'Do you fancy going somewhere that's a bit more fun – and quieter?'

I turned towards him. He was clean-shaven with a thick mop of dark curly hair and a lovely wide smile. Good teeth, as my mother would have said. I wanted to say yes, but I didn't know him. I didn't even know his name, so how could I go somewhere with him? I didn't want to be rude, though.

'Thanks for asking, but I'm meeting someone.'

'Thought you said you didn't know anyone?'

I felt myself blushing.

'It's okay. You don't know me from Adam. I get it. What's your name?'

'Anna.'

'Well, good to meet you, Anna. I'm Scott, and as you've probably noticed from my accent, I'm from north Wales. I wasn't going to suggest anything inappropriate, honestly. But maybe some other time.'

Scott pushed himself off the wall and sauntered back towards the bar, where he deposited his empty glass. He turned and waved as he walked out of the door, and I wondered if I would ever see him again. I had been an idiot for saying no. He seemed nice.

8

There was a hum of conversation in the incident room as everyone waited for Tom to open the discussion. He stood in front of a whiteboard, shirtsleeves rolled up in deference to the heat, and glanced around the room as the last of the stragglers found a seat.

'Okay, let's make a start. You all know the details of this morning's murder. It's a nasty one that feels carefully planned with all the hallmarks of an execution. The killer came equipped with a double-length cable tie and, although it's not been confirmed yet, probably something to spray into the eyes of the victim. So it's unlikely to have been random. If I'm right, someone wanted this man dead, and we need to know who and why. Let's go through what we've got. DI Robinson, can you kick us off, please?'

Becky stood up. 'All the evidence points to our victim being Cameron Edmunds. He usually appends the word "Junior", and as you might suspect, there is an Edmunds Senior, but I'll come back to him. We've been unable to get a formal identification so far. As it was his car, the victim is approximately the right age, and there is no sign of Edmunds at his home, we have no reason to suspect it's anyone other than him, but we have no fingerprints on file. Although we've done an online search for recent photos, we've been unable to find anything – no social media accounts, as far as we can tell.'

Becky referred briefly to her notes. 'Edmunds lives in Prestbury. Married with four children under ten. We finally managed to get hold of his wife, but she's not available to identify him until tomorrow. The children are being looked after by their nanny while Mrs Edmunds – Dawn – is taking a break at a spa in Surrey where mobile phones are frowned upon, so it's been difficult to get hold of her. The nanny, rather bizarrely, didn't have the details of where the mother of the children in her care was staying. Cameron Edmunds Senior is cruising somewhere in the South Pacific, according to his housekeeper.'

There was a murmur in the room – probably mutterings about how the other half live.

'We sent an officer from the local force to the spa to inform Mrs Edmunds that we believe the victim to be her husband, but she's not prepared to drive back from Surrey tonight. She's been detoxing all day and hasn't enough strength to face the journey, even though she wouldn't have to drive herself. According to the officer, she said, "I can't see it makes any difference whether it's tonight or in the morning if he's dead. I'll be home by midday." So I think that paints a picture for us.'

Becky raised her eyebrows at the assembled officers.

'Edmunds' car entered the car park at nine thirty p.m. last night. At the scene the pathologist gave a very approximate time of death as around six thirty a.m. Yes, he had been out all night, but apparently that's nothing unusual. His wife hadn't spoken to him since she went to the spa three days ago, so she didn't realise he wasn't at home.'

'Do we know where he went between his arrival and when he was killed?' DS Keith Sims asked.

'Not yet. Apparently he spent several nights a week away from home. If his wife knows where he was, she hasn't told us, and she didn't seem too perturbed by his night-time absences.'

'Did he have a mistress?' Keith asked, and Tom saw Becky's jaw tighten. She liked to get all the facts on the table before people started to throw random questions her way.

'Can I suggest that DI Robinson gives us everything we have up to now, and then we can open up to questions?' Tom said mildly. He didn't want to embarrass Keith, although it seemed from the sergeant's flushed cheeks that he had succeeded. But if it became a free-for-all, they wouldn't get anywhere.

Becky continued: 'The blue car parked next to his had been there overnight too. We've traced the owner, who had come into town for dinner and had too much to drink. He'd originally parked on the road but was scared the car would be towed if he left it there overnight, so he'd taken a risk and driven it into the car park – only a hundred yards away – and taken a taxi home. We'll be checking his alibi, of course. He doesn't remember seeing the Mercedes, which might be indicative of how much he'd had to drink, or maybe it wasn't there. It's something to think about.'

As Becky paused and consulted her notes, Tom pondered the Focus driver. The Mercedes wasn't an easy car to miss, particularly as it was parked so close. Did Edmunds leave and come back later?

'Finally,' Becky said, 'we'll also need to check the wife's alibi, although I find it hard to believe she drove all the way up from Surrey, whizzed into Manchester to kill her husband and then drove back to the spa without her absence being noticed. That's not to say she can be ruled out – she could have paid someone else to do her dirty work for her.'

Becky was looking around the room. For now there wasn't much to add.

'We have a phone,' Tom said, 'but it's not registered to Edmunds. It's a burner with a prepaid SIM. We won't call any of the contacts until we know what we're dealing with, but it may come in handy to trace where he's been recently. Any questions?'

'Are we going to search Edmunds' house?' a young detective asked.

'Not yet. I've talked to DI Robinson about this, and while the wife has to be a suspect – even if she didn't kill him with her own hands – there are four children in that house with no one but the nanny to explain to them what's happening. We'll wait until the wife is back and take it from there.'

Tom waited as a smattering of questions were asked and looked at the faces around him, all as eager to get cracking on the investigation as he was. It seemed Edmunds was well off, given his address in one of the most expensive areas of Cheshire and his fancy car, but they hadn't been able to find any evidence of employment other than a non-executive directorship of a casino in Manchester. Anyone who lived an extravagant lifestyle with no apparent income was a person of interest to the police, although apparently, when asked about her husband's job, Dawn Edmunds had answered that it was 'spending his father's money'.

Tom decided it was time to rally the troops.

'Right. We've got plenty to get on with, so let's focus and catch this killer! We don't want the good people of Manchester feeling terrified to go into a car park, so the sooner we crack this, the happier I'll be. Enquiries into our victim's history and finances are being pursued overnight, and two people have been tasked with trying to get hold of any CCTV from the streets surrounding the car park. First thing tomorrow we need to go and talk to the parking attendant who was in charge of the office overnight. I couldn't get anything out of him, and neither could DI Robinson, but he was clearly anxious, and I got the feeling it wasn't just to do with a body being found in his car park. Keith, you go, and take Lynsey with you.'

Lynsey was a young detective who had joined the team just before Becky left for maternity leave, and she was proving to be astute and focused – a good foil for Keith's pedantic adherence to protocol.

'For now, though, I suggest we all get off home. Come back fresh tomorrow and we'll see where we're up to,' Tom said. 'Either DI Robinson or I will attend the post-mortem, and by then Mrs Edmunds will be back to formally identify the body.'

Despite the fact that it had been a long day, there was a buzz of animated chatter as the incident room emptied except for the small team tasked with continuing the investigation overnight, and Tom made his way back to his office. He had to update his boss, Detective Superintendent Philippa Stanley, but he hoped to get away by nine o'clock at the latest.

He was about to put in a call to see if Philippa was still at her desk when his phone rang. It was Louisa. Even though they had been living together for several months, Tom still experienced a rush of pleasure at the thought of going home to her.

'Hi, Louisa. Sorry, darling, but I'm not going to be back for a while.'

'That's fine, Tom. And it's not why I'm calling. It's about Lucy.'

Tom felt his heart jolt. Lucy, his thirteen-year-old daughter, lived with his ex-wife, Kate. He saw as much of her as he could, but she was fast developing a life of her own, and he missed her. His job made him painfully aware of the potential threats to her safety, and he worried constantly that something could happen to her.

'Is she okay? What's up?'

'She's fine. She's here.'

'What, at our house?' That was unusual for a Monday evening.

He heard a brief mumbled conversation in the background, and the next voice he heard was Lucy's. 'Hi, Dad.'

'Hi, Lucy. Sorry I wasn't there when you arrived. Did your mum bring you?'

'No. I caught the bus. There's something I need to tell you, Dad. But it will have to wait till you're home. You are *coming* home tonight, aren't you?'

'Of course, and I'm looking forward to seeing you. Is everything okay?'

'Yes…well, sort of anyway. But I'm not going to say any more. I'll see you later.'

Tom didn't like the sound of this one bit, but he was unable to persuade his daughter to tell him anything. He just hoped he could get the meeting with Philippa over quickly so he could get home.

9

The kids have taken longer than usual to get to sleep tonight. They seem more than a little hyper, and I can't help wondering if the tension is rolling off me and onto them. Either that or they had too many fizzy drinks at Daisy's. I am staggered by the ease with which my children seem able to pick up on my mood, even when I'm trying so hard to be jolly, but Bailey decided to have a major strop after his bath and Holly shouted at him for being a baby. This was my time with them, and it had descended into chaos.

Dominic came up to see if he could help, but I found that even more irritating – maybe because I knew the children would calm down quickly for him. He rarely seems to get agitated by anything. Just as the children seem able to pick up my nerviness, Dom entering the room always has the effect of a warm blanket wrapped around them, holding them tight.

'Go away, Dominic. We're fine,' I said, hearing how tight my voice was.

He looked at me with concern. 'If you're sure.'

I knew he wouldn't argue. He reserves his fights for things of greater significance, only showing anger when people fall short of what he calls 'acceptable standards of behaviour'. Unbeknown to him I do that all the time, and tonight will be no exception.

Finally I manage to settle the children and go slowly downstairs. I feel stifled and stressed by the day's events and I need to get out of the house, to find space to think. Through the partially closed door to the sitting room I once again hear the

43

murmur of the TV, and as I push it open I see Dom is watching the news again. The screen is showing a car park in central Manchester, one that I know well.

'What's going on? Is this the murder you mentioned?'

'Yes. They still haven't named the victim.'

He stops talking as the newsreader gives his report.

'A man was found brutally murdered in a central Manchester car park early this morning. It is understood that he was in his own car, and that the assailant attacked him from the back seat of the vehicle. Police have confirmed that he was strangled, but as yet no other details have been released.'

'It's not safe anywhere these days,' Dominic says, turning towards me, his eyes on my face. 'Do you know where in Manchester that multi-storey is?'

'No. It's not one I recognise,' I lie, wishing my husband still had his back to me.

Dominic picks up the remote to turn the TV off, and his eyes move to the bag in my hand, then back to my face.

'You're going to the gym? You don't usually go on a Monday.'

I can sense the question in his voice. He doesn't like patterns to be broken, but I smile as if I'm unaware of his feelings.

'I know, but it's been a difficult day, and I could do with running off some of the stress.'

'Really? I thought you said there was nothing more exciting than a trustees' meeting?'

He's right. I did say that.

'That's true, but we're due an Ofsted inspection. It could come any day with practically no warning, and everyone's a bit antsy, as you might expect. You don't mind, do you?'

Dominic shakes his head, as I knew he would. 'Of course not. You go. You're the worker and you deserve some time to yourself. Will you be late?'

I hate it when he refers to me as 'the worker', as if I consider him to be a lesser being because he doesn't earn a salary. I make a promise to myself to be extra appreciative of everything he does for this family, but tonight I need to be somewhere else.

'I don't know what time I'll be back. I might have a swim too, so don't wait up. I want to wear myself out so I can fall asleep as soon as my head hits the pillow.'

'Do you think it's safe to go out with a killer on the loose?'

'Dom, I suspect there is *always* a killer on the loose somewhere in Manchester.' I walk over and drop a kiss on his head. 'Love you.'

Without another word, because I know my voice will shake, I pick up my gym bag and head for the door.

The drive only takes twenty minutes at this time of night, but every second is filled with thoughts of the man on the radio who claims to be Scott. *Who is he?*

Nothing that has happened today can be a coincidence. The timing – today of all days – the names, the mention of Nebraska. And, as if the radio show wasn't enough, the pizzas and the message. Taken together they can mean only one thing.

This is about me. It's a warning. But a warning of what? A warning that someone is going to reveal my past in order to shatter my present and my future? But who? Why?

Nobody except the two of us knows what we did and the depths – to my shame – that we sank to. And Scott's dead. Did he tell someone else? Who, though? We agreed no one must ever know, and I was with him until the very end. I would have known if he had told someone.

I can't make sense of it, so the only thing I can do is drive the fear of exposure from my mind for a few hours in the only way I know how.

I pull the car into my reserved parking bay next to the lift and get out, grabbing my gym bag from the back seat. The car park is quiet, and for a moment my mind is full of images of the multi-storey, less than a mile from here, where a man has been murdered. I used that car park regularly until recently, before I found this place. I shiver at the thought that it could have been me.

I dodge into the lift and press the button for the sixth floor. It's unlikely I'll stumble across anyone who knows me, but I can't take any risks. I have to be doubly sure.

Pulling my keys from my bag, I select the newest, the shiniest. As the lift doors open, I glance along the corridor to check it's clear then stride across to the door facing me and insert the key.

I quickly push the door open and slip inside, closing it firmly and leaning against it for a moment. The entrance leads to a short hallway. At the end is a tiny living room and kitchen, but I make my way to the bedroom, throwing my gym bag into the corner by the door where I won't forget it later.

I can feel the thrill of anticipation, the knowledge that the next three hours will drive every negative thought from my mind and make me feel so much better – more confident, more alive.

Stripping off my jeans and T-shirt, I fling open the wardrobe door and pull out a short black wrap dress. Next I open the drawer that contains my box of tricks and start to apply make-up – dark red lipstick, black eyeliner. Finally I twist my hair into a knot, select a blonde wig and slip on a pair of stilettos.

I am ready.

10

Tom had found it a struggle to get away from Philippa, who was in a chatty mood, but in a rare perceptive moment she realised she didn't have her DCI's undivided attention.

'I can see you're only partly with me, Tom, so whatever it is that's more interesting than solving this murder, I suggest you go and deal with it so we can have you with us one hundred per cent tomorrow.'

Tom stood up. He didn't need to be told twice.

'I'm off then,' he said and wasn't surprised when Philippa made no enquiry as to the cause of his distraction. If it wasn't to do with work, she wasn't interested.

What on earth could be the problem with Lucy? All she had told Louisa was that she wanted to talk to her dad first, and she would rather not say anything until he was home.

Now, as he pulled the car into the drive of his Edwardian semi, he could see the light on in Lucy's bedroom. He had been tempted to call Kate to find out what was going on, but having been assured by Louisa that Kate knew where Lucy was, he felt he should leave it to his daughter to explain.

'Hello!' he called as he pushed open the front door.

Louisa appeared in the kitchen doorway and smiled at him, indicating with her eyes that Lucy was upstairs. Just then there was the sound of a door slamming – it seemed impossible for his daughter to close a door quietly – followed by a clatter as she ran downstairs.

'Hi, Dad,' she said, flinging her arms around him.

Tom pulled her close but gave Louisa a puzzled look over the top of his daughter's head. They had always been affectionate with each other, but as she had moved into her teens Lucy had been a little more sparing with her hugs.

'This is a treat,' he said. 'To what do we owe the honour of a visit on a Monday evening? I'm told your mum knows you're here – is that right?'

Lucy pushed him away. 'You haven't called her, have you? Did you check up on me?'

'No, Lucy, I didn't. If you tell me that she knows, then I believe you. But I do think we need to let her know that you've arrived safely.'

Lucy gave him a look of incredulity and pulled her phone out of the back pocket of her jeans.

'Well, for one thing I've sent her a text. But if she doesn't believe me, she can check on the app she's put on my phone. She knows where I am, Dad. She *always* knows where I am.'

'Well, that's good.'

'Is it? If you say so.'

The mood had deteriorated slightly, and Tom wanted to get it back on an even keel.

'Let's go into the kitchen and have something to eat. Then perhaps you can tell me what's going on. And I'll need to call your mum, love. I know she knows where you are, but she's going to want to know that you're okay too.'

Lucy gave a deep sigh and headed for the kitchen without another word.

Louisa stopped at the door. 'Do you two want to be alone? I can eat in the sitting room if you need to talk.'

Tom was about to say that wouldn't be necessary when Lucy spoke. 'No, Louisa. It's better if you stay. This involves you too.'

Tom gave Louisa a look of surprise as he ushered her into the kitchen. This was a version of his daughter he hadn't seen before.

Yes, she had started to become more assertive as she reached her early teens, and that was the way it should be, but this sudden burst of apparent confidence was something else. Or was it bravado?

Louisa had already laid the table for three. She shooed Tom towards a chair and placed a glass of wine in front of him. 'I'll serve up,' she said. It was normally something they did together, but there was nothing normal about this evening.

'Okay, sweetheart. What is it you want to tell me?' Tom asked Lucy.

'I've moved out. I can't cope with Mum any more, and I've decided I'm going to move in with you and Louisa.'

Tom's momentary delight at the thought of seeing Lucy every day was quickly tempered by deep concern. Something had to be wrong, and he could tell from the determined set of her mouth that Lucy was expecting an argument.

'Lucy, darling, you know how much I – both of us, in fact – love you being here. This is your home too. But have you thought through all the implications of living here?'

Lucy folded her arms. 'Oh, here we go. I suppose you're going to come up with fifty reasons why I can't do what I want.'

'No, that's not what I'm saying. I just want you to consider everything carefully. For one thing you would have to change schools, and all your friends live close to your mum too. Perhaps it would help if I knew why you've come to this decision. Have you fallen out with your mum over something?'

Lucy stared at him and her eyes filled with tears. 'I thought you'd understand. I thought you'd want me here. I should have known better!' With that, she turned and ran out of the room. They heard her stomp back up the stairs.

'Oh Lord,' Tom muttered. 'Sorry, Louisa, but I'd better speak to Kate before we eat. Is that okay?'

Louisa gave him a sympathetic smile as she pulled a pan from the hob. 'Of course – dinner will keep. And I don't know if it helps, but I remember being thirteen. I'm not sure it's the same for boys, but I felt as if no one understood me and the world was against me. Maybe we should suggest she stays for a few days, and when she's had a chance to see how it's working out you can both make a decision.'

Tom reached out his arms and pulled Louisa towards him. 'Good idea. Thanks for that. She'll be okay in half an hour – she doesn't easily give up on a good plate of food. In the meantime I'll talk to Kate. That should be fun.'

Giving Louisa one last squeeze, he pulled his phone from his pocket.

Tuesday

11

'*Shit!* Bloody traffic.'

How had I managed to forget the roadworks? There are at least three other routes I could have taken to school if my head had been in the right place when I set off this morning. But it wasn't and I only have myself to blame. I had no more than a few hours' sleep last night, and I'd had to dream up an excuse to Dominic for getting home at two in the morning – an excuse I prayed he might somehow believe. He was sitting up in bed pretending to read when I finally crept upstairs as quietly as I could.

'Oh, Dom, you shouldn't have stayed awake for me. You'll be shattered tomorrow.'

'It's okay. I wanted to be sure you got home safely. Where've you been until now? That must have been a hell of a workout.'

I was about to try to explain when I heard a cry. 'Mummy! *Mummy!*'

Dominic started to get out of bed. 'I'll go,' he said.

'No, stay where you are. I probably woke him, so I'll go.'

Bailey's room is opposite ours and the door was ajar. An owl nightlight was casting a turquoise glow over the bed, and Bailey was sitting up, rubbing tears from his eyes.

'Hey, Bubbles,' I said softly, using the pet name he'd had since being obsessed with blowing raspberries at six months old. 'What's up, sweetie?'

I sat on the side of the bed and pulled my little boy to me, wrapping his warm body in my arms and rocking him.

'I had a dream about the man.' Bailey was no longer crying and his eyelids were already drooping.

'What man, sweetheart?'

'The man,' he replied unhelpfully.

'Did he say something you didn't like?' I asked gently.

'No. He was just staring,' Bailey answered, but I could feel him going heavy in my arms.

I rocked my son for a few more minutes and then gently laid him back down. 'Well, he's not here now, Bubbles, so there's nothing to be frightened of.' My words were wasted, though. Bailey – reassured by his mother's presence – was once more asleep.

I made my way back to our bedroom, leaving the door open so I could hear if he stirred again, hoping that Dominic had dozed off. But he was awake, waiting for me.

'Everything okay?'

'Yes, just a bad dream. He said it was about a man, but he's gone back to sleep now.' I leaned towards my husband and gave him a gentle kiss.

'I hope a nightmare is all it was.'

'What do you mean, Dom?' I felt a flash of concern.

'There's been some guy hanging around for the past couple of days. I've seen him on the road outside, and I saw him on the golf course close to the fence this morning. I hope he didn't speak to Bailey.'

My concern turned to something more solid, more tangible. Could this be my tormentor?

'What did he look like?' I asked, trying to keep my voice level.

Dom turned his back to me, clearly wanting to get some sleep. 'Ordinary. Average height, dark curly hair. No one we know. I shouldn't have mentioned it. I'm sure it's nothing. Let's just go to sleep.'

I turned off the light so Dom couldn't see my eyes and snuggled up to his back.

'You never said why you were so late,' he murmured.

The lie was already prepared. 'I'm sorry. I stupidly went into the relaxation room after my swim and fell asleep. Next time I'll set the alarm on my phone in case I doze off.'

Dominic grunted. 'I was worried, that's all.'

I kissed the skin between his shoulder blades. 'Look, I'll try to get back early tomorrow – today, now – and I'll cook something for us, for after Bailey and Holly are in bed. What do you think?'

He didn't respond, and there was no time to say more this morning before I left for school – if I ever get there.

I didn't feel like putting the radio on when I first got in the car. The memory of the voice claiming to be Scott is still with me. I forget about it for minutes at a time, and then it punches me hard as I think about what it might mean. I've done things that I'm deeply ashamed of, that I thought were buried in my past. It was another life, a different me. If the truth is allowed to escape from where it has been so deeply buried, I could lose everything – my family, my job, my carefully nurtured, unremarkable life.

I force myself to face a question, one I never thought I would have to ask: is there any way at all that Scott could still be alive?

I don't believe it. He couldn't have survived what I did to him. I remember his memorial service and how terrified I was that everyone would turn to stare at me, that they would know I had killed him. It wasn't the worst day of my life, but it was close. I was only glad it wasn't a funeral. I don't think I could have borne it had there been a coffin, knowing Scott's body was inside. I heard a friend of his parents say he had been cremated in America, and I thought how dreadful that must have been for the family.

Sitting here in the hot car I have too much time to think and a shudder runs through me as I balance my certainty that it can't be Scott against the terrifying thought that someone else knows the whole story. And if Dominic's right, maybe that person is watching me – and my family.

The traffic is now at a standstill, and despite the air conditioning, the sun's heat through the window is making me drowsy. I lower my forehead onto the steering wheel. I need distracting, so I reach out to switch on the radio. I take some deep breaths in time with Sam Smith's crooning, but the music comes to an end all too soon, and it is time for the presenter to chivvy his listeners along with his chirpy voice. It makes me tired just listening to him.

'Before we go to the news, I thought I'd give you all an update on next week's "The One That Got Away". We've had an *astounding* response this week. Scott – the guy who has promised to tell us all about the love of his life, Spike – seems to have grabbed everyone's attention. We have never had so many votes for one single caller, and the whole of Manchester wants to know what traumatic event brought about the end of Scott and Spike's relationship in Nebraska. I can't wait. I don't know about you!'

I stare at the radio as if it will somehow tell me what I want to hear – that this is all nonsense and the man on the radio didn't say Nebraska, he said Nevada. Or it wasn't Spike but Mike. Or anything at all that will demonstrate conclusively that none of this is about me.

The honking of horns finally pierces my trance-like state, and I jerk my head back, thinking they are hooting at me. But the traffic is still not moving; it's just drivers showing their frustration to no end whatsoever as far as I can see, and I feel the tension increase across my shoulders. I try to concentrate on the voice on the radio in an attempt to steer my thoughts away from the edge of the black hole they want to fall into.

Today there is another phone-in, this one on current news stories. It is usually dreadful, with ill-informed people stating their opinions as if they are fact, but at least it gives me something else to think about.

'I'm speaking now to Brian from Levenshulme. Which news item has you intrigued today, Brian?'

'That murder in the multi-storey. It's not safe any more, is it? Somehow you always expect lowlifes to be the victims of crime. But it seems that no one's safe.'

'What do you mean, Brian?'

'This guy was a class act! Drove a great big Merc, for God's sake.'

The presenter interrupts him again. 'Sorry, Brian, but the police haven't issued a name yet. I expect they want to be sure of their facts and inform the family before it's made public.'

There is a scoffing sound down the phone. 'Well, someone should tell bloody Twitter then. Hashtag MancMurder. His name's on there so I'm saying nowt I shouldn't. It's—'

The line goes dead.

'Sorry, listeners, we had to cut Brian off before he revealed a name that may, or may not, be correct. Now, who've we got on line three? Ah yes. Stacey. What do you want to talk to us about this morning?'

I stop listening when I realise the talker is moaning about recycling and reach for my phone – anything to distract me until the traffic starts to move. I open Twitter and type the hashtag into the search bar. There are hundreds of results, but they all repeat the same name. I feel as if the air has been punched out of me, and a groan builds in my chest. I check several tweets to be sure I'm not just seeing retweets of a single theory. No. And they all say the same – that the dead man is Cameron Edmunds Junior.

Cameron.

I think back to the night before. I had expected him to be there waiting for me, as he usually is. But there was no sign of him. I dismissed it, thinking it might have been because I had chosen to go out on a different night. But by last night he was already dead – murdered in a car park.

Cameron's death links everything – and ties it all back to Scott. But if by any remote possibility Scott *was* alive, do I believe he would kill Cameron? I don't know. Who can say whether he could have become bitter and twisted enough to do this? And if so, why now, after all this time?

I shake my head angrily at my futile speculation and ask myself which is the greater threat: exposure of my past sins or the revelation of my present-day secrets? The police will be crawling all over Cameron's life. Will they find out about me: how I know him and what I am to him? Will I be a suspect? I think that is inevitable.

One way or another, it seems my life is about to be shattered into a thousand razor-edged shards.

12

Then

'Hello again.'

I was sitting outside a café enjoying a bit of autumnal sunshine, sipping a Diet Coke while trying to study my notes on the morning's lecture.

I lifted my head at the friendly voice. 'Hello.' I recognised him immediately from the other night. Scott.

'Mind if I join you?' he asked, pulling out a chair. 'What are you reading?'

'"The Love Song of J. Alfred Prufrock",' I said with a smile.

'Ah, the wonders of T. S. Eliot.' I hid my surprise that a student of economics and politics knew about early-twentieth-century poetry. 'Are you enjoying it?'

'I am, actually.'

'Good. If you weren't enjoying it after a couple of weeks on your course it would be a bit sad. Did the gig the other night get any better after I'd gone?'

I dropped my eyes back to the page. 'I left just after you.'

Scott laughed. 'I thought you might. You should have come with me. I had fun. Do you want another Coke?'

'No, thanks. I shouldn't really be drinking this one. It's supposed to rot your insides or something, isn't it?'

He grinned at me. 'Most things that you enjoy are bad for you. Can I get you a coffee? Water?'

'No. I'm fine, honestly.'

Scott wandered off into the café and towards the bar to order his drink, and I sneaked a look at him through the window. Average height with quite a slender frame. A bit on the thin side, if I was honest, but it was his friendly open face and lovely smile that drew me to him. I lowered my gaze quickly as he turned his head in my direction and I wondered what his assessment of me would be. Short, skinny, with hideous dyed-blonde spiky hair, but when I risked another glance he was still looking at me.

A noisy group of five or six students walked past me and pushed into the café, laughing and joking with each other. Before the door closed I heard them hail Scott and saw them make a beeline for him. It was easier to watch him now because he was chatting with them and was no longer looking at me. I could see he was popular, and one of the girls in particular kept touching his arm and leaning against him. He had lost interest in me, and who could blame him? So I was surprised to look up about ten minutes later to see him standing by my table.

'Listen, Anna, a few of us are going out later – nothing special, but the film society is running a series of supposedly cult films, and tonight it's *Rosencrantz and Guildenstern Are Dead*. I thought you might like it, as an English lit student. There's a great cast. Have you seen it?'

I wasn't sure what to say. I hadn't seen it, but I didn't know the other students and felt a little uncomfortable gatecrashing their evening.

Before I had the chance to answer, a shadow was cast across the table. Someone was standing behind me, blocking out the pale sunlight, and by the look on Scott's face it wasn't someone he wanted to see.

'Are you going to introduce me, Scott?' The voice was deep and slightly husky.

The guy walked around the table so he was to my right. He was tall with dark blond hair, pale blue eyes and a thin layer of carefully maintained stubble along the line of his chin. I guessed he was about twenty-two – no more – but he had the air of someone much older.

He held out his hand to me. 'Cameron Edmunds Junior.'

I had never heard anyone outside of American films tag 'Junior' on to the end of their name, and for a moment I nearly giggled. Fortunately, Scott came to my rescue.

'This is Anna,' he said. Dark red stains coloured Scott's cheeks, and his eyes had changed from soft pools to hard pebbles. He was watching Cameron warily, as if he were a dangerous animal about to bite.

'You're new, Anna, aren't you? You look vaguely terrified and haven't yet adopted the air of indifference that will no doubt come to you in time. Watch out for this chap.' Cameron waved his hand in Scott's direction and leaned slightly towards me as if sharing a secret. 'He's like a vampire – not safe to be let out at night,' he said in a stage whisper.

Cameron grinned as if it was a joke and I returned the smile, but then I noticed that Scott's jaw was clenched tight, his lips pressed together. His gaze never left Cameron's face.

Two steps behind Cameron was another guy. Short and lean, with broad shoulders and slender hips, his body looked as if it was made of iron. His narrow, sharp features didn't alter, but his small dark eyes shifted from me to Scott and back again.

Nobody spoke for what felt like minutes, but it couldn't have been more than a few seconds. Then, with a chuckle, Cameron turned and sauntered away, lifting his hand in a farewell salute. I raised my eyes to look at Scott, who was staring down at the gap between his feet.

'He's a twat,' I heard him mutter, shaking his head. 'And Jagger's an evil bastard.'

I assumed Jagger was the young guy standing behind Cameron, and I had to agree that he made me feel uncomfortable, although Cameron had seemed amiable enough. Nevertheless

I felt deeply sorry for Scott, who had clearly found the whole encounter embarrassing for some reason. Fortunately I was spared the need to find the right words as two of the people Scott had been talking to at the bar dashed out through the door, full of life and laughter.

'Was that Cameron Edmunds?' a young girl with long dark hair asked.

The boy she was with frowned. 'I didn't know you knew him, Scott. What did he want?'

Scott let out a long slow breath, clearly trying to calm himself. 'Nothing. He was taking the piss, and I shouldn't let him get to me. Do you fancy grabbing a burger or something before the film? I'm starving.' The other two seemed enthusiastic about the idea, and Scott turned to me. 'You coming, Anna?'

I shook my head. 'No, I'm good, thanks. I'll just get on with some work.'

I could see he was disappointed. Perhaps he thought I had turned him down because of what Cameron had said, but it wasn't that. The others seemed friendly enough, but I didn't know how they would feel about me tagging along.

After what felt like too long, Scott nodded. 'Okay. I'll catch up with you some other time.' He grabbed his jacket from where he'd draped it over the back of a chair and walked away, a few steps behind the other two.

Trying to ignore the little voice in my head telling me I was a fool, I dropped my head to return to my book. I read Eliot's words. Prufrock's indecision and his fear of rejection felt so very like my own, and I was ashamed of my diffidence. I wasn't prepared to settle for a life of regrets, so I took a deep breath and lifted my head.

'Scott,' I shouted. He turned back towards me, his eyebrows raised. 'Would it be okay if I changed my mind?'

13

Tom's call to his ex-wife the evening before had gone about as well as he had expected.

'She shouldn't be travelling here on her own, Kate. I know it was daylight, but I didn't know she was coming. What if I'd been away overnight? What if she'd never made it? How long would it have been before we realised she wasn't where you thought she was?'

Kate sighed. 'You don't need to worry. I'm not an idiot. I monitor her all the time via her mobile.'

Tom wanted to point out that this was far from an infallible solution, and there was nothing to stop someone taking Lucy's phone and throwing it in the canal, but there seemed little point in causing an argument for the sake of it, so he let her talk.

'If she's decided that she's better off with you and your new woman, what can I do? Let's hope for Lucy's sake that this one lasts.'

Again he bit back his irritation.

'Louisa and I have been together for over a year, as you know. And we took things slowly. I would never have asked her to move in with me if I thought it made Lucy uncomfortable.'

'Well, maybe you've found your soulmate at last, Tom.' He could practically taste the acid dripping off her tongue.

Kate had frequently been petulant with him since she had walked out of their marriage nearly ten years ago, although they generally tried to get on for Lucy's sake. But this reaction was churlish even for her.

'Anyway, pleasant as this is, I don't have time to chat. Let me know when Lucy gets fed up and wants to come home.'

The conversation had told Tom absolutely nothing about why Lucy had decided to leave her mother's house, and he didn't know what to do next. He had long ago come to terms with the fact that living with Kate was better for Lucy – particularly when she was younger and Tom had lived alone. His hours were irregular, and Kate hadn't worked since the day he married her, saying he needed to support her so she could give their daughter the best childhood possible. And now Tom was in the middle of a difficult murder case and couldn't commit to being home at a sensible hour or to running Lucy back and forth to school. Louisa had offered to take time off work, saying she would take care of transport and make sure Lucy was never stuck in the house on her own, so it was a viable solution, but only in the short term.

As Tom walked into the incident room at the start of what he felt certain was going to be another long day, he could feel his irritation with his ex-wife returning. But a sea of expectant faces turned towards him, each member of the team knowing he had attended the early-morning post-mortem – a part of his job that he disliked intensely – so he forced himself to focus.

He made his way to the front, and the room fell quiet.

'The pathologist has completed the post-mortem, although as always some results will take a while to get to us. But just as we thought, our victim – who for now we should assume is Cameron Edmunds – died of strangulation. And DI Robinson was right – he had been sprayed in the eyes with Mace.'

This was met with little surprise, but Tom knew his next revelation would make the team sit up and take notice.

'Of more interest is the fact that when the pathologist examined Edmunds' throat, it was stuffed full of ten-pound notes. Ten of them – although whether the value is significant, we don't know. Yet.'

As he expected, there was a murmur as people turned to each other to comment.

'Thoughts, anyone?' Tom looked around at the faces. 'Yes, Keith.'

'We've tracked the victim's movements, sir. He was at the private casino in town where he's a director. His father used to own it, but he's retired now. I understand Cameron Junior went there most nights and he'd been losing heavily. Could that be related to the ten-pound notes? Anyway, he left the casino at around six a.m. Apparently he often went somewhere – not sure where yet – for breakfast, but clearly not yesterday.'

'If he was losing so much, where was his money coming from? Do we know?' Tom asked.

'We've looked at his bank statements, and money has been flowing in from his father. Enough to cover household expenses but nothing more – certainly not enough to cover his gambling losses. We're checking for other sources now.'

'Good. What else do we know? Yes, Lynsey.'

'According to staff at the casino, he was sometimes seen at the tables with a woman. She often stood behind him as he played, although they arrived separately. No one was inclined to give me a name, claiming they didn't know. We don't believe them – misguided customer confidentiality, at a guess. We're getting CCTV from the gaming hall to see if she can be identified.'

'Good. Any news from Jumbo on traces found in the car?'

Becky stood up. 'I've got an initial report, but they're still working on it. The man has children, yet the car interior is spotless. According to the wife, who's being driven home as we speak, the children aren't allowed in his car and he has it valeted every few days. The car park where he was found offers a wash-and-valet service, so we're checking if the Merc was cleaned by them, and how recently.'

'Edmunds' car entered the car park at nine thirty p.m. on

Sunday night,' Keith said. 'That's confirmed by CCTV at the entrance. We checked the arrival of the blue Focus, and it tallies with the time stated by its driver, just over an hour after Edmunds, at ten forty-five.'

'And let's not forget the fact that the Focus driver can't remember seeing the Merc, even though it was about as close as it could be,' Tom added. 'I know we've made a start on the CCTV from the surrounding streets and the car park entrance and exit, but we need to stretch the period of interest to cover the time from when Edmunds arrived to when we shut down civilian access. I can't say specifically what we're looking for, but basically anything that doesn't fit. And of course it goes without saying to check for any known villains entering or leaving.'

He could feel the buzz in the room as the intelligence was starting to come together, and it was at times like this that he loved his job. They would find this killer, he was sure. But now it was time for him to go and speak to Cameron Edmunds Junior's wife. Her apparent lack of interest in her husband's death could be a cover for her grief, or it could put her in the frame as his killer.

On the other hand, it could be exactly what it seemed to be. Total indifference.

14

By the time I arrive at school, my nerves are shattered. Not only has the traffic been horrendous, but memories of Scott – and now of Cameron – won't stop slamming through the meagre defences I have tried to build. No amount of persuading myself to think of something else, to prepare myself for the school day ahead, has stopped the flashbacks from following one another thick and fast. And when the police start to ask questions, which is surely inevitable, what will I tell them? What will I tell Dominic? How will I explain what Cameron was to me?

'Someone doesn't look very happy this morning.' The school bursar pulls a mournful face as I walk into my office. Jennie Lucas is the one person who can be guaranteed to beat me through the school door each morning, and I don't know where I would be without her. Shorter than me and slim to the point of being skinny, with an unruly mop of blonde hair, she exudes happiness and energy. I've never been great at making friends, but if I had to name them now she would be top of my list, so I try to force a smile.

'Sorry,' I say. 'I got stuck in a traffic jam that I could have avoided. I'm just hot and frustrated with myself. Ignore me.'

Jennie laughs. 'I'd never do that. Sorry for teasing you, but you're usually so cheery. How about a cup of coffee? And there's some mail that might put a smile on your face.'

Jennie always opens the post and filters out the junk, so I sit down and start to wade through the neatly stacked pile of anything she considers worthy of my attention. Invoices, flyers that she thinks might possibly be of interest, an invitation to join the local WI…and then I see it about halfway down the pile.

I feel my body tense as I pick up a card with a colourful picture of a stack of books on the front. I stare at it, my mind spinning. I am miles away, and it isn't until the smell of coffee hits me that I realise Jennie is standing in front of me, mug in hand. I look up.

'I didn't think you could still get those,' Jennie says, putting the mug on my desk. 'I thought everyone sent online gift cards these days.'

I don't answer, my gaze falling back to the ten-pound book token I am grasping in my hand, a tremor running down my spine. Inside are the words *You're a winner! Congratulations.* I say nothing for a moment and I can feel Jennie's eyes burning into the top of my bent head.

'Can you give me a moment, Jennie? There's something I need to do,' I say, without looking up.

'Sure.'

I hear a note of confusion in the single syllable, but Jennie turns away without another word and returns to her office.

I know what this is. Perfectly innocuous to those who don't know any better, to me it is a sign that someone knows too much about my past. The pizzas told me something else. Whoever this is, he knows where I live. Now I have proof that he knows where I work too. He wants me to know he's on to me. The radio programme, Cameron's murder and two innocent-looking gifts are all inextricably linked to one person.

Scott.

But that's impossible. So how has someone put all the pieces together? Who is he, or she, and why now, after all these years? Who is trying to frighten me?

I jump up from my chair and start pacing to ease the pressure building inside me. I no longer know what to believe, but I need to find out the truth – one way or the other – before the worst of my sins are exposed on the radio in a few days' time.

Ignoring the coffee, I march through into the outer office. Jennie looks up at me, her grey eyes widening at the tautness of my body and my scowling face. I try to relax, attempt to smile, but I can see she isn't fooled.

'Jennie, I don't know what I have in the diary for today, but everything has to be cancelled. I have somewhere I need to go. It's personal. Please can you cover for me?'

She nods slowly. I trust her, but not enough to tell her what is going on. I don't trust anyone that much.

I can feel her watching me as I hurry out through the door towards my car, and I imagine she must be wondering how something as innocuous as a book token could have caused so much agitation.

I could never find the words to explain.

I don't know if I'm doing the right thing, but if I do nothing my world will fall apart in less than a week. I can't allow that to happen.

I hit traffic again as the ring road clogs up, a delay I could do without. I'm anxious about being away from school for too long – it's irresponsible and impulsive – but what choice do I have? I need to find out if there is someone Scott was close to, someone he never told me about.

Finally I am on the M56 heading towards north Wales. I have no idea if Scott's parents still live in the same house; I've had no contact with them since their son's memorial service. Indeed, that was the first and only time I met them, but I had to go. I had to say goodbye to the boy I had loved so much.

Mr and Mrs Roberts had no idea who I was, or what my relationship had been with their son. They didn't speak to me or single me out from the other students who had travelled from Manchester on a September day not unlike this one, and

I remember the pain I felt that Scott had never told them about me. I had always believed we would be together forever.

I knew I was falling for Scott from the first time he smiled at me, and when he walked me back to my room after the trip to the cinema I remember waiting, hoping he was going to ask to see me again, terrified that he wasn't interested.

As he said goodnight he leaned towards me and kissed me lightly on my cheek. 'See you around,' he said. 'Tonight was fun.'

He lifted his hand in a wave as he walked away, and I felt his absence in a way I had never experienced before. The part of me that had been bubbling with happiness in his company suddenly felt like a hollow drum.

I had no idea if he would want to see me again. My experience with boys was so limited – the only boyfriend I'd ever had was someone I had known since I was five, and he didn't really count. For both of us dates had been a convenience, each of us being nothing more to the other than someone to go to parties with. But Scott was different. He was funny, kind, thoughtful. He made his friends laugh, and I felt in awe of the ease with which he chatted, joked and even touched them in a way that I never could have – a hand on the shoulder of a mate at the bar, a hug goodnight for one of the girls who was feeling a bit low.

I spent a week pining for him, hanging about where I thought I stood the best chance of bumping into him, acting like a thirteen-year-old with a massive crush. I thought about how it might feel to run my hands through his thick dark curls, or to kiss that wide smile from his lips, but there was more to it than his looks. He seemed to offer a passport to another world, to a life filled with friends and fun that I wasn't sure I would ever be able to achieve on my own.

A week after our cinema trip, I found Scott waiting for me as I came out of a lecture, sitting on a wall huddled into his coat as it had turned cold all of a sudden.

When he saw me, he grinned. 'I checked the timetable and saw there was a lecture on Samuel Beckett. I had a feeling you'd be there, and I wanted to catch you to see if you fancied a curry tonight.'

I thought he was asking me on a date, and spent the day flushed with excitement. But of course I was wrong. I felt like weeping when we walked into the restaurant to see we were part of a table for ten. I consoled myself with the fact that he had come looking for me, had arranged to travel on the bus with me and walked me home.

That night he kissed me on the mouth. I hadn't known how many nerve-endings there were in my lips until then, or that the lightest of touches could make every single one of them tingle. It was just one kiss, and it lasted no more than two seconds, but as Scott walked away, I was struggling to breathe.

I hungered for more, but it took another three evenings of saying goodnight with a single kiss before he held me, his hands moving slowly over my body. Finally he asked if we could go to my room.

I don't think I have ever, either before or since, wanted anything more. My body ached for him, but at the same time I was terrified. I was a virgin, and I thought he would expect so much more than I knew how to give. I didn't know if I should tell him or not, but in the end I didn't need to. He knew.

He was so gentle, so loving, and he took things slowly until he knew I was ready, lifting his head to look into my eyes, checking I was okay.

I was more than okay; I was in love. I wanted to tell him right then, but I managed to stop myself.

We saw each other regularly after that, but he still met his friends, sometimes with me, sometimes – and those times were unbearable – on his own. He encouraged me to go out and mix with other people, but I didn't want to. I used the time when he was out with friends or playing football to catch up on the work that I had let slide.

I think back to the sick feeling in the pit of my stomach the first time I realised he'd been lying to me. I'd decided to sneak along to football practice, to watch him in secret from behind the small stand. I wanted to see him play, to watch him enjoying himself with his mates, to see his legs in football shorts and think about the last time his thighs had touched mine. I remember scouring the field, back and forth, thinking I must have missed him. I waited until the teams filed back to the changing rooms in case somehow I hadn't recognised him on the field. But Scott wasn't there.

At first I hadn't been concerned. Maybe he'd changed his mind about playing. But the next day I asked how practice had gone, and he was enthusiastic about his part in the game. He even told me he had scored a goal.

Looking back on that time, I wish with all my heart that I'd had the confidence to ask him what was going on – why was he lying to me? But I was scared of losing him, so I said nothing and let the pain eat away at me from the inside.

And then everything changed. Just as I was working myself up to ask for an explanation, he told me he loved me. What could I do? Those words were everything to me, and if he had told me a tiny lie about a stupid football game, what did it really matter?

That was all so long ago, though, and today I need to face his family – to find out if he lied to me about keeping our secrets safe too. I push down hard on the accelerator. Now that I've started, I can't wait to get this over with.

15

As Tom turned off the busy main road onto a quiet lane bordered by hawthorn hedges, Becky stared out of the window. Even though they were only three miles from the market town of Macclesfield, it felt as if they had penetrated deep into the Cheshire countryside.

'Are we ready?' Tom asked quietly.

Becky could see how uncomfortable he was and knew he dreaded visiting the bereaved, especially when a loved one had been brutally murdered. But it had to be done. Cameron Edmunds' wife deserved to know what had happened to her husband.

'Yep, as ready as I'll ever be,' she answered, doing her best to give him a reassuring smile.

They didn't know what to expect. Was Dawn Edmunds' apparent lack of concern simply a cover for the fact that she was heartbroken? Or would she be angry? Or accepting? All they knew was that she had been in no rush to get back from her spa weekend.

'The house is down here, on the left,' Tom said. As Becky glanced down at her phone to see if there were any messages she needed to respond to, she was surprised to hear Tom mutter, 'Shit.'

She looked up. Several cars and vans were pulled over at the side of the road and a group of people, some with cameras, were standing expectantly outside the gates of Cameron Edmunds' home.

'Who in God's name leaked his name?' Tom muttered, knowing he wouldn't get an answer. In truth, it could have been anyone, including Cameron's wife.

He turned off the road and pulled up in front of the gates. The journalists moved out of the way of the car, but the photographers bent down to snap quick photos of Tom and Becky's arrival. Becky saw how rigid Tom's jaw was.

'I'll get out and ring the bell,' she said. 'You stay here and try not to frighten the press too much.'

She jumped out of the car to press the buzzer by the electric gates, nodding acknowledgement to the journalists who shouted a few questions, but not deigning to answer.

No one responded to the intercom, but a humming sound indicated that a motor was being activated, and the gates slowly began to move inwards, parting to allow Tom to drive through as Becky slid back into the car. A few seconds later they rounded a bend in the drive and there ahead of them was Cameron Edmunds' home.

'Jesus,' Tom muttered, trying to suppress a grin, his mood cheered by what he saw in front of him. 'It's a bloody castle!'

Becky smiled. She knew he wasn't a fan of the ostentatious, and this house had it all. A relatively new build, its low central structure linked two tall wings with steeply pitched roofs, each gable wall boasting a single huge window at least six metres high. The entrance was via a stone-built portico that looked to be something of an afterthought.

'Not exactly cosy-looking, is it?' he said, and he was right. It looked austere, forbidding – a place that might define a person's financial status rather than say anything about his character. 'Come on. Perhaps it's a bit less intimidating inside.'

Becky pushed open her door and got out of the car again. However unappealing its architecture, the house was situated in a peaceful spot with no sound other than the distant hum of traffic from the main road. But the warm air felt heavy, and Becky longed for a thunderstorm to break through the sticky atmosphere.

The front door was opened by a little girl in shorts and a

sparkly pink T-shirt who looked about nine years old. She spoke before either Becky or Tom could say hello: 'Mummy is in the lounge.' Without giving either of them the chance to reply, the little girl scurried off.

Becky turned to Tom and shrugged before moving into a vast marble-tiled hallway with two uncomfortable-looking giant black leather wing-backed chairs. Ahead was a wall-to-wall fish tank, separating the hall from whatever rooms lay beyond. Between the two chairs was a door they assumed led to the lounge. Glancing at Tom for his approval, Becky knocked softly on the dark wood.

'Mrs Edmunds? It's DCI Douglas and DI Robinson. May we come in?'

There was a murmur of assent, and Becky pushed open the door to reveal a gloomy room with three deep-purple sofas sitting on a black carpet. The walls were painted battleship grey, and to Becky it felt as if she was entering a cave. The only splashes of light to relieve the gloom came from a few empty white vases, evenly spaced on fitted bookshelves. There wasn't a book in sight.

A room to be depressed in, was the thought that sprang to Becky's mind.

Her gaze was drawn to Dawn Edmunds, curled up in the corner of one of the sofas, her feet tucked under her. She looked young – probably not much more than thirty – although the layers of make-up added to her years. Her long blonde hair was artfully waved and immaculate, but her eyes were bloodshot, and Becky had the feeling this was due less to tears than to the contents of the glass in her hand, filled with a clear liquid which she strongly suspected was not water.

'We're very sorry for your loss, Mrs Edmunds,' Tom said.

Dawn Edmunds smiled. 'Good. Because I'm not. It complicates things, but that's as far as it goes.'

Becky avoided looking at Tom.

'We apologise for disturbing you at this very distressing time,' she said, 'but we're going to need you to formally identify your husband so we can continue with our investigation. I know it's going to be painful for you, and I do wish it wasn't necessary, but I'm afraid it is.' She gave Dawn some time to absorb this, but there was no reaction so Becky continued. 'At some stage it would be helpful to us if we could also have a chat about Cameron – either now or, if you prefer, after the identification. Do you have someone who can look after the children while you come with us?'

Dawn Edmunds nodded. 'The nanny's here – they'll be fine. I'll answer your questions now, if you like. I can't help you much, I don't suppose, but let's get it over with.'

'Do you mind if we sit down?' Tom asked. Dawn waved a hand carelessly at the facing sofa. Becky perched right on the edge, sensing that if she sat back she would never get up again, so deep were the cushions.

'When did you last see your husband, Mrs Edmunds?' Tom asked.

Dawn bit her bottom lip and stared into her glass. Her voice was surprisingly steady. 'Friday night. I was watching the TV and I heard him, rather than saw him – he was jangling his car keys in that annoying way of his. Then I heard the front door slam and his car started. The kids were in bed. I left for the spa early on Saturday, and I didn't see him then, so I don't know if he came home or not.'

Becky assumed this meant that they didn't share a bed, but it was a thought to park for later.

'What did he say as he left on Friday? Did he give you any indication that the weekend ahead was going to be different from any other?'

Dawn gave a mirthless laugh. 'He didn't say anything; he just went. We didn't speak much, unless it was absolutely essential.'

'Do you know where he was going?' Becky asked.

'Not really. I know he went to the casino most nights, but

I never asked and he never volunteered any information.'

'Did you speak to him over the weekend, or did the nanny – or maybe the children – see him, do you know?'

Dawn shook her head. 'The nanny's terrified of him, so when I knew I was going to be away I arranged for her and a friend of hers to take the kids to Legoland for the weekend. They got back on Sunday night, but if Cameron had been here at all he'd have gone out by the time they arrived home.'

'Can you think of anyone who might want to hurt your husband – anyone who had a grievance against him?'

Again, the cold laugh. 'Just about anyone who ever met him, at a guess.'

Becky didn't know where to go with this and glanced at Tom, who gave her an almost imperceptible nod. He was going to take over again, thank goodness.

Tom leaned back on the sofa, as if this was a friendly chat. 'Tell me about your husband – where you met, how long you've been married. It would be helpful to get a picture of the man.'

Dawn said nothing for a moment, but as the silence lengthened she took a sip of her drink and started to speak hesitantly. 'We met when I was at university, here in Manchester. I got into a spot of bother and Cameron helped me. I hadn't quite realised how high the price would be.'

'What do you mean?' Tom asked.

'Cameron wanted a wife, but it had to be someone amenable, who would do what he said, give him children – he specified four – and basically apart from that the main requirements were to look ornamental when he needed to appear respectable in public, and otherwise to shut up and keep out of his life. That was the deal. He was very clear that those were his terms. So I agreed. I married him.'

'If you were so unhappy, didn't you think about leaving him?' Becky asked, unable to stop herself.

'Ooh, you don't know much about my husband, do you?' Dawn shook her head slowly, her lips turning up in apparent amusement. 'You'd think that would be a solution, wouldn't you? But no. I'd signed a pre-nup – my deal with the devil – and if I left I had to walk away from everything, including my kids.'

'I'm sure the courts would have been favourable to you with regard to your children.'

Dawn's eyes met Becky's.

'I don't think you understand, Inspector. There's the legal argument, and then there's the Cameron argument. There would have been so many ways to make me seem an unsuitable mother – faked drug or drink addiction, huge debts, or if push came to shove a few shattered limbs, maybe even a broken back to put me in a wheelchair for life.' Her eyes flitted back and forth between Tom and Becky as if imploring them to understand. 'I don't think you've quite got a handle on my Cameron yet, have you?'

16

The town where Scott had lived all his young life was small, I remember that – nestling between hills on the edge of the Snowdonia National Park. His parents' house was just off the main road but for the life of me I can't remember if it was on the right or the left. I was so distraught on the day of the memorial service – so terrified of being there, but even more terrified of not being there – that I barely noticed.

Pulling the car to a stop, I decide that the most likely place to find the answer is in the small shop proudly displaying a Post Office sign. I push open the door to the sound of an old-fashioned bell. A woman with a turned-down mouth is sitting on a stool behind the counter, knitting. She glares at me. Deciding she doesn't look like the type to volunteer information for nothing, I buy some chocolate and a bottle of water and approach the counter to pay.

'Hot again, isn't it?' I say with a smile.

'Too hot, if you ask me,' the woman says, putting her knitting down and holding out her hand for the money. 'It's September, for God's sake. Roll on the winter.'

There is nothing positive I can say to that, but I need to get this woman on my side.

'I've not been here for a while, but it's such a lovely part of the world. I once knew someone round here by the name of Roberts. Do you know if the family still lives here?'

The woman lowers her hand and stares at me. 'You do know this is Wales, don't you?' she says with a sneer. 'So which of the roughly fifty thousand people in this country with the surname Roberts might you be talking about then?'

I am no longer the young girl who was scared of her own shadow, but this isn't the moment to be argumentative.

'Oh, of course,' I say with a small laugh. 'I'm so sorry. I hadn't thought. They had a son called Scott.'

The woman nods slowly. 'Right.' She picks up her knitting again, and I wait. 'I don't normally like to gossip about people in the village,' she says, a statement I find difficult to believe, 'but you might as well know that Scott came to a bit of a sticky end. He's dead, so if it's him you're looking for, you're out of luck.'

The clacking of the needles stops, and for the first time the woman looks me in the eye, no doubt hoping to see shock or dismay.

'Yes, I know about Scott,' I tell her. 'A tragedy, although it's some time ago now. But it was his mother I was hoping to see.'

The woman gives a bark of laughter. 'Well, that's almost as bad. Sylvia Roberts is alive, but she's away with the fairies. She's been admitted to one of those posh homes in Colwyn Bay. They call it a hospice – a fancy name for what it is, in my opinion.'

I don't want to know what the woman thinks a hospice is, and I groan inwardly. Colwyn Bay is another forty minutes away. I will never get back to school this afternoon if I visit Mrs Roberts. I don't know what I will gain anyway, especially if Scott's mother is suffering from some form of dementia, as 'away with the fairies' might suggest.

'Is Mr Roberts still at home?' I ask.

'Ha! He didn't last more than two years after that boy of theirs died. They doted on that kid – thought he was their world. No one else in the family counted for anything. And when the father died, Ma Roberts went into even more of a decline. The house is up for sale now. It's up the road on the right – you'll see the estate agent's sign if you're interested. But it's a dark, dingy place that's had no one to care about it in many a year, so I doubt it'll sell quickly.'

I'm angry with myself for taking the impulsive decision to come here. Maybe deep down I was hoping that, despite everything, I would discover that by some miracle Scott is still alive. Of course he isn't.

Still, Mrs Roberts could hold the key to it all. Scott swore his family knew nothing about what we did, but maybe that was another of his lies. I have always felt safe in the knowledge that only two people knew our secrets, and one of them was dead. But what if I'm wrong?

The only person I can think of to ask is Mrs Roberts. It's a long shot, but I'm here now – or close enough.

I thank the lady in the post office and hurry back to my car. I can still make it to Colwyn Bay and back before the end of the day – just. I can use the journey to ring around the various care homes to find out where Mrs Roberts is living. At least I have her first name now, so it shouldn't be difficult.

As I pull into the drive of the hospice, I look around. This is not what I was expecting from the woman's description. The entrance drive to the stone building is overgrown, and tall trees deprive the windows of light. Should my mother ever need to be looked after by anyone other than me, it's not a place I would choose for her.

For a few minutes I sit and stare at the door, wondering if I should go in. What can I say to Mrs Roberts? What excuse can I have for my visit, and will I even be allowed to see her? Maybe I don't want to know the truth. But I haven't come all this way for nothing, so with renewed determination I get out of my car and head towards the building.

Inside the narrow hall I see a sign saying RECEPTION above a small hatch. A young girl with a pretty, smiling face is sitting on the other side, behind a desk.

'Hello. Can I help you?'

'I wonder if it would be possible to see Mrs Sylvia Roberts, please? I used to know her son, and I found myself in the area so I thought I'd call in. I don't suppose she'll remember me, though.'

The girl's smile widens further. 'I wouldn't worry about that too much. She doesn't recognise anyone. I'll check with the manager, but I'm sure it will be okay. Do you want to sign in, then take a seat in the lounge? First door on the left. I'll need to check some ID against your signature. Sorry – new regulations.'

The lounge is empty, and I perch on the edge of a chair, willing my brain to come up with a good excuse for being there.

The young woman is standing in front of me before I realise it.

'You can go through now. It's the third door on the right, down the corridor.'

I push myself up from the chair and head down the hall. I can hear a commotion in one of the rooms, and it's only as I get close that I realise the noise is coming from Mrs Roberts' room.

'Settle yourself down, darlin'. I'm going to bring you a nice cup of tea. Shush, now.'

I stand in the doorway, taking in the sight in front of me. A lady who can only be in her early sixties is sitting in an easy chair, and she is crying.

A black woman in a dark blue uniform turns her kind face towards me. 'Sorry. I should have told the boss no more visitors. She's got herself into a right lather. Can you give her a minute before you try to speak to her – let her calm herself? It's always the same when he's been. Maybe you should go back to the lounge. I can come and get you when she's a bit more herself.'

I want to ask her *who* has been, thinking whoever 'he' is could be another source of information, but I don't need to.

Mrs Roberts tells me herself. 'Scott! Where's Scott? Where did he go?' She pulls a handkerchief from her pocket and mops at her eyes.

I can't move. I feel myself begin to tremble as her words register.

She said, 'Scott'. She said his name twice. Oh my God, he's alive!

My eyes flood with tears, but I blink them away as the nurse turns back towards me.

'It's going to take a while. Best if you go, if you don't mind. You'll have to wait. I don't know why he winds her up so much, that son of hers.' She shakes her head and frowns, but I don't want to wait.

He was here – maybe just minutes before me, if she's in such a state now. Surely I would have seen him if he had walked right past me? I was watching the door from my car for at least ten minutes before I came in.

I have to find him, and he can't be that far ahead of me. I want to break into a run, but I force myself to walk quickly back to the reception area, where a man is leaning against the wall, talking to the girl through the hatch. Rudely, I interrupt.

'Sorry, but it's urgent that I catch Mrs Roberts' son. Did you see where he went?'

The girl looks a bit shocked at my lack of courtesy, but the man turns to me with a sympathetic smile. He's wearing a dog collar.

'He was leaving as I arrived, dear. He usually goes out of the back door and parks in the lower car park.'

I give the man a tight smile, and I know he can sense my rising panic. *Scott was here!*

I don't even pretend to walk now, but set off at a run, back down the corridor towards an exit that the kindly vicar has pointed out to me. I slam through the doors and race across a small terrace, only realising now that the home is built on the side of a hill. I can see stone steps leading down through a shrubbery. I head for those.

The path is narrow and the bushes rise tall on either side. I feel a shiver as the thick foliage blocks out the sunlight. The path twists and turns, with steps hewn out of the rock, and then I come to a fork. I stop for a moment, unsure which route to take.

All I can hear is my own breathing, so I hold my breath. There isn't a sound. I turn to look back at the hospice, but it's hidden by a bend in the path.

Suddenly there's a noise – a stone clattering down steps as if someone has dislodged it. I give an involuntary gasp. It came from the path on the right, but before I can collect myself I hear footsteps, speeding away from me. He's here, and he's running. I catch a glimpse of a dark head of hair, but it's gone in a flash.

I sprint down the steps, but they are too widely spaced for a single stride and too close for the double step of a runner. My feet suddenly slide from under me on a patch of loose gravel and I fall heavily into a holly bush, managing at the last moment to protect my face. I yelp in pain as the sharp leaves rip at the flesh of my bare arms.

And then I hear the sound of an engine firing up and a car skids out of the car park at speed. Did he know it was me chasing him? Why didn't he stop?

A sob bursts from me, and I drop my head onto my knees. Scott was here – almost within touching distance – and there are so many things I want to ask him.

How did you survive? How long have you been back? Why did you let us all believe you were dead?

I loved him so much, but he nearly destroyed me. Memories of the torture of the last few weeks we were together surge through me, and I wrap folded arms tightly around my head. *Why didn't he stop?* But if he had, would I have run into his arms or screamed at him for what he did and all that he's doing now?

Finally I scrub the tears from my face and force myself back to my feet to trudge back to my car. Sinking into the driver's seat, I lean my head hard against the headrest. *What is this? What does it mean? Why does he want to torment me?*

But I know the answer to the last question. For fourteen years I have believed that I killed him. Maybe he's decided it's time I paid the price.

17

Then

The six weeks that Scott and I had been together had flown, and Christmas was looming – too close for comfort. I had no idea how I was going to cope when we went home to our respective families, and I was already anticipating the emptiness I would feel without him. When he touched me I felt on fire, and I ached with longing for him on the nights when I slept alone. Four weeks without him would be unbearable.

With Scott I had learned to be a different person. I embraced life in a way I had never done before and took every opportunity to push back the boundaries of my childhood. I was eating food that I had never heard of, listening to The Verve and Catatonia, and making love with a passion and lack of inhibition that startled me. At last I was learning to fly, and Scott was my instructor. And he had a nickname for me – Spike. No one had ever called me anything but Anna before.

I had pushed his lies about the night of the football game to the back of my mind. I didn't want to be that person – the one who was always questioning, always prying. Next I would be searching through his pockets or checking his phone. I didn't believe he was cheating on me with another girl; he didn't hide me away and his friends had welcomed me.

I decided after our first few weeks together that I had to do something to take my mind off Scott when he wasn't around, so I volunteered as a charity fundraiser. My first task was to sell raffle tickets. The organisers had cleverly pitched the tickets to be cheap and the prizes focused on young people – food, books, entertainment, clothes, with the big prize being a holiday for four. Most students could be persuaded to part with ten pence for a good cause, and almost everyone had offered more. As someone who had been scared to talk to anyone just a few weeks previously, I had found selling the raffle tickets offered me the perfect excuse to approach strangers, and I was growing in confidence. I hadn't restricted myself to students, and I'd been out on the streets of Manchester. Suddenly, university life was everything I had ever hoped it would be.

I had just decided that my life couldn't get any more perfect, when it began to fall apart. The time had come for me to return any unsold raffle tickets to the charity and hand over the cash I had collected, and I was so proud of myself as I pulled the shoebox in which I had stashed the money from the top of my wardrobe. I had been regularly exchanging coins for notes, so I didn't expect the box to be heavy. But neither did I expect it to be empty.

I stared at the white void. There was nowhere for the money to hide. Had I put it somewhere else and forgotten? I pulled everything in my room to pieces, yanking out drawers, searching under the bed, under my mattress. But I knew where I'd put it. I hadn't hidden it because I thought it was secure. I always locked my room when I went out and there was no sign anyone had broken in.

I sat on the bed and put my head in my hands. *Where was the money?* There was nearly three thousand pounds missing. I'd been collecting for weeks, and several of the lecturers had been generous.

I was on my hands and knees, searching for a second time to be sure, when I heard a knock on the door. It was Scott. He would know what to do. I rushed over to the door, unlocked it and burst into tears.

Scott held me as I cried, stroking my hair, whispering

meaningless platitudes that nevertheless soothed me. When I calmed down we sat on the bed, Scott holding my hand as I told him what had happened.

'Look, you'll just have to tell them that the money is missing. It's not your fault, Spike.'

I turned to look at him, and he must have seen the incredulity on my face because he squeezed my hand and said, 'It's *not*. They can't blame you.'

'So who *can* they blame? I was responsible for it. I don't understand how anyone could have got into my room without me knowing.'

'Perhaps you popped out without locking it. It would have only taken someone a moment. Or perhaps you were in the bathroom and someone sneaked in. You don't always lock the door when you're in, do you?'

That was true. I had only locked it today because I was intending to count the money.

I reached for my phone. 'Well, there's only one thing for it: I'll have to call the police.'

Scott snatched the phone out of my hand. 'Don't do that. You'll make yourself very unpopular with everyone on this corridor if they're all questioned.'

He was right. No one would thank me if their rooms were searched. Some of them had a mild drug habit, or maybe not so mild in some cases. But I shook my head and held out my hand for the phone.

'No. It might make me unpopular, but I don't care. This is stealing, and if I'm going to tell the charity the money has gone, they have to know that I've reported it.'

Scott transferred the phone to his other hand – the one furthest from me. I looked at him and held out my hand.

He dropped his head and stared at the floor.

18

Now

I should leave Colwyn Bay. It's too late to go back to school and home is closer, but I can't go there either. Not yet. I have too much thinking to do.

I drive without knowing where I'm going, but I'm drawn to the beach. I've always loved the sea, and I park the car and stare at the blue-grey water. It doesn't soothe me, so after a while I get out, thinking a walk might blow away the cobwebs and ease the pressure inside. I lock my handbag in the boot and set off, the cool sand feeling good on my hot feet.

I must cut an odd figure in my smart work clothes, carrying my shoes in my hand, but if I get any strange stares I don't notice. The beach is quiet as the children are still at school – where I should be. But a few people are risking a dip in the sea, and I envy them as they laugh and shout about how cold the water is. I feel as if I will never laugh again.

Three words repeat themselves in my head. *Scott is alive.* I can feel my heart racing. I have always believed that part of me died with him all those years ago. I never wanted to love someone like that again, to feel such extremes of joy, fear and despair, and I have put barriers around my heart that only my children are allowed to penetrate. Maybe him being alive will free me from a tiny portion of the guilt that has been plaguing me for fourteen years.

I still don't know how he survived. When I left him he was all but dead and I believed he had drawn his last breath, but there is no relief, no elation at the fact that the man I loved is alive. I feel a complex cocktail of emotions. I'm bewildered by what he wants from me now, petrified that he might expose my past sins on the radio, shocked that he might be involved in Cameron's murder, and angry at myself for – despite my fears – wanting to see him.

Cameron's murder holds its own threat, should my relationship with him be discovered, and I don't know which shoulder to look over. Should I be more afraid of the repercussions of Cameron's death, or of Scott's resurrection? Either could blow my world apart – my job, my marriage, my family. I have so many secrets, both past and present.

Head down, I pace along the beach, no longer looking to the right or the left. It's a long time later, when I hear the voices of children shrieking as they run into the water, that I lift my head. The warm weather has brought families here after school, and I'm shocked to realise how much time has passed. I have been here for too long. I promised Dominic I would cook dinner, and now I'm going to be later than ever. The children will have been home for a while now, and I'm so far away. How could I have lost track of time?

My car is at the opposite end of the beach and I start to run, sand kicking up onto the legs of my trousers. It seems to be taking forever to get there, and the sand grows softer as I run, my feet sinking in. I fall to my knees, pick myself up and set off again, dismay at my own carelessness spurring me on.

By the time I reach the car I know I'm going to have to dream up some excuse for how late I am, and I brush frantically at my clothes to remove the sand.

I open the car door and jump in, shoving my key into the lock. I hear a beep from my mobile and remember it's in the boot, so with a groan of frustration I leap back out of the car to grab my bag and I pull out my phone. A text from Dominic, and below it I can see I have missed three calls – all from him, all in the last fifteen minutes.

He never calls or messages when I'm at school. What can have happened?

I hastily open the text.

Where are you? Holly's had an accident, and I can't get hold of you. I'm taking her to hospital, but she wants her mummy. Call me when you get this.

Oh shit! I ram the key into the ignition. *Holly!* What could have happened to her? It's going to take me two hours to get home. *How am I ever going to explain this? How could I be so far away? What's happened to my baby?*

I want to phone Dominic straight away, but if I do he'll know I've got the message and won't understand why it will take me so long to get to him. I need to get closer first.

I bite back a sob. I *need* to know what's happened to Holly but I can't ask.

I realise that Dominic may have called Jennie when he couldn't get hold of me, assuming I was in a meeting that she could interrupt. Maybe she'll know how my daughter is, and it's easier to lie to her than to Dom.

I quickly make the call.

'Anna, where *are* you?' she asks immediately.

'Never mind that now. What's happened to Holly? I haven't been able to get hold of Dominic.' It's amazing how quickly lies come to me these days – they burst, fully rounded, from my lips.

'She's fallen over. She's hurt, but it's not critical so don't worry. I don't have all the details. Once he knew you weren't here, Dominic hung up. I presume so he could call you again.'

She hears the break in my voice as I thank her and she tries to calm me, thoughtfully refraining from asking me any more questions. Finally we hang up, but not before I've promised to call her later to let her know how my daughter is.

Tears are streaming down my face as I drive, but I can't lose it now. I have to get back safely.

Thoughts of Scott and Cameron flee from my mind. Right now the only thing that matters is my family.

19

After Dawn Edmunds' revelations about what might have happened to her had she decided to leave her husband, Tom decided the sooner they got the identification over with the better it would be. Then they could focus on digging further into his background. If he was as evil as she said, he was a man who would have enemies. On the other hand, she could just be a disillusioned wife.

Dawn had come along to the mortuary with them amiably enough, although she was slightly unsteady on her feet, which she blamed on the starvation diet she'd been on for the last few days. Tom thought it more likely to be due to what he imagined was the neat vodka in her glass.

'Now Cameron's dead, I'm going to pig out on chips,' she said with a hint of glee. 'He said I was getting fat, and either I did something about it or he'd lock me in a room and starve me until I was fit to be seen in public,' she'd told them with a shrug. 'Hence my trip to food hell – three cups of clear broth per day. Whoopee-do!'

After that pronouncement she had slumped against the door in the back of the car with her eyes closed, and neither Tom nor Becky had tried to engage her in further conversation.

In the mortuary car park Tom switched off the ignition and turned to her. 'I'm afraid your husband might look a little different to how you remember him due to the way he died. I'm sorry about that.'

'Let's get it over with,' she said, swiftly reapplying lipstick to her plumped-up lips with the aid of a small mirror.

Tom and Becky walked with her along the corridor, their footsteps the only sound. Tom had made this journey many times with relatives, but it was unusual for them to be apparently unconcerned about the outcome. He couldn't work out whether Dawn would be glad to see Cameron dead so she knew he was out of her life, or whether – despite everything – her husband had offered some sort of security and without him she might be lost.

Tom and Becky stood either side of Dawn as the mortuary technician pulled back the sheet covering the deceased's head and shoulders, and Tom felt himself wince slightly. Cameron's face was badly discoloured. At least his eyes were closed so she didn't have to see the signs of haemorrhaging as a result of the strangulation.

Dawn had been looking down – the first sign that she was feeling anything at all about the experience. Tom didn't push her, waiting for her to feel ready, but when she finally lifted her head she gasped. Tom glanced at her and saw her frown.

'*Shit!*' she said with some force.

'I'm sorry. It's never a pleasant experience.'

Dawn gave him a puzzled glance. 'What? No, no, you don't understand. It's not him! That's not Cameron. This guy – even with his face looking like that – looks far more pleasant than my bastard husband.'

Tom gave Becky a concerned glance. Had they put this woman through more than twenty-four hours of stress – of one sort or another – believing her husband was dead, only to find it wasn't him?

'Are you absolutely certain, Mrs Edmunds? We won't rush you. Take as long as you need.'

'Oh, I'm sure all right. It's not him. *Shit!*'

Dawn's revelation that the body in the mortuary wasn't that of her husband left Tom both embarrassed and concerned. There were all sorts of implications, not least where the hell *was* Cameron Edmunds? Having said she couldn't believe the 'bastard' wasn't dead, Dawn had become quiet, standing head down, deep in thought.

'Mrs Edmunds, we're going to have to ask you to come back with us. We need to ask some more questions, I'm afraid.'

Her head shot up. 'Why? I don't know anything.'

'You're sure your husband hasn't been in touch since Friday?'

'Of course I'm sure. Look, he'll probably come swanning in at some point as if nothing's happened. All he'll care about is whether the guy leaked bodily fluids onto his leather seats as he died – and somehow it will be my fault if he did. It's not him – he's not dead – so what more do you want from me?'

The words came out in a rush, and Tom sensed she was more than disappointed it wasn't her husband. She seemed dismayed.

'It's not that simple, Mrs Edmunds. If you could come back with us for a short time, I can explain what we're going to have to do now, and why. We won't keep you for long, then I'll arrange for someone to take you home.'

She bit her lip. 'Okay. But I need to tell the kids. I'd told them he was dead, you see. That's why I kept them home from school. They're going to be confused.'

An interesting choice of words, Tom thought, although the children weren't the only ones who were confused. If the victim wasn't Cameron Edmunds, who the hell was he, and why had he been killed so brutally? What was he doing in that car? Had he simply been in the wrong place at the wrong time? Was Cameron Edmunds the killer – although to murder someone in your own car seemed a little far-fetched? Or was Cameron the intended victim, and had he gone into hiding? Whatever was going on, he needed more information from Dawn Edmunds and they needed to find her husband.

'Let's get you out of the mortuary at least,' Tom said, lifting an arm as if to guide her from the room. They made their way outside into the fresh air. 'I do understand your children need to know as soon as possible, but we won't be releasing any information to the press just yet.'

'Why's that? Do you think Cameron killed that guy?' She shook her head. 'Not a chance. He doesn't do his own dirty work – he'd have got Jagger to do it for him.'

'Jagger?' Tom asked.

'His minder, hard man, all-round bastard.' She almost spat out the last word.

Tom already had concerns about Cameron Edmunds' apparent wealth and lifestyle in view of his lack of income, but hearing that he had a minder only increased his suspicions.

'We don't know what happened, Mrs Edmunds, but if your husband was the target and it becomes known that he wasn't the victim, he may be in danger. It changes the nature of our investigation, and that's why I need to ask you to neither confirm nor deny that the dead man is your husband to anyone beyond your immediate family – especially not to a journalist.'

She nodded. 'Okay, I get that. Although it's tempting to give the killer a chance at another shot at him.'

The bitterness in her voice couldn't be missed, but Tom chose to ignore it.

'Do you have any idea where he might be?'

Dawn slowly shook her head. 'It must be obvious that we're not exactly a close and loving couple. He tells me nothing, and I don't ask.'

He felt sad for this woman, who – on the face of it – had an enviable lifestyle. But he bet she would swap it all to be with someone who cared about her.

'I'm afraid we're going to have to search your house. We need to find your husband, and there may be something that tells us where he is. Rather than ask you to come back with us now, I'll let you get home to the children. We'll arrange transport for you and a team will be with you very soon. They'll explain the search process in more detail and I'll follow within the hour. We can talk then. Is that okay?'

'I don't know,' Dawn answered, a frown between her eyebrows. 'If Cameron finds out I've let you in…'

'You're not "letting us in" – we'll have a search warrant, and I'm sure he'll understand.'

She lifted wide eyes to Tom's and gave a small shake of her head.

20

I can hardly see the road as I crawl along the motorway, which is crazy with early-evening traffic. Every time I wipe away the tears of anger and self-disgust they return to blind me.

I'm frantic with worry for Holly. How could I not have been there for her when she needed me? Whenever I try to convince myself that, as a working mother, I could have been even further away – on a course or in some meeting where I couldn't be reached – I let in the other fear and I make bargain after bargain with myself. *If Holly is okay, I'll tell Dom everything. Or If Holly's okay, I'll go to the police and tell them how I know Cameron.*

I called Dominic as soon as I could, when I was about an hour away. He said she'll be fine, but despite my begging for more, he was sparing with detail. It felt as if he was punishing me.

Finally I arrive at the hospital and race through the automatic doors into the Accident and Emergency Department, spinning round and round, trying to spot Dominic. He is sitting in a corner, clutching a plastic beaker of something that looks vaguely like tea in hands hanging low between his knees. His trainers are covered in blood and his head is bowed. I feel a thump of fear.

'Dom,' I shout, running towards him. 'Where's Holly? Is she okay?'

Dominic raises his head slowly. 'Where the hell have you been? It's hours since I called you.'

He never questions me, always trusting me to do my best. His tone speaks volumes about his disappointment in me, and that hurts, even though maybe it's justified. I sit down heavily and reach for his hand, but he pulls it away.

'I'll explain later,' I say. 'Just tell me how Holly is and what happened.'

Dominic shakes his head. 'She's okay. She's had a head CT because she passed out. But they think it was the sight of the blood that made her faint, so they're waiting for the doctor to sign her off and we can take her home. She's already been stitched.'

His voice is low and controlled, and for the first time I can remember I realise Dom is angry. With me.

'Can I see her?'

'She's asleep. She exhausted herself, mainly by crying for you. The nurse said she'd call me when Holly wakes up.'

'What happened, Dom? How did she get hurt?'

Dominic stands up and walks over to the bin to throw away his tea. He has his back to me, and I feel a beat of unease, as if the solid foundations of my marriage are shaking. Whatever else is wrong in my life, he and the children are the rock I have been clinging to, the part of my life that makes sense. They are the reason I do what I do. Everything is for them.

'She was playing in the garden with Bailey,' he says finally. 'I was in the house. I heard her scream and I ran to the window. She was running away from the hedge – the back hedge where it borders the golf course. She ran into the old store where I keep my tools. I've no idea how she got in – the door's always locked. But she did. She tripped and fell on a chisel that was lying on the floor, cutting her leg and hitting her head on the workbench. I don't understand that either, because I always put my tools away.'

I feel sick. My poor baby.

Just then a nurse walks towards us. 'Mr Franklyn, your little girl is waking up. Do you want to come back in?'

Dominic turns towards the nurse. 'Yes, I'll be right there.'

I stand up.

'No, Anna. Stay here. We haven't worked out an excuse for you taking so long to get to her, and until we do I don't want her upset any more than she already is.'

I grab his arm as he starts to walk away. 'No way, Dominic. Whatever you're blaming me for, Holly is my child too.'

I push past him and follow the nurse.

Holly is drowsy, and I lean down to kiss her, whispering that I'm here, she's safe, I love her. The doctor says she's going to be fine, and there is nothing to worry about, but nevertheless my chest is tight with guilt and I can't shake it.

Dominic's disappointment is almost as hard to bear as Holly's pain. From the start of our relationship he has been unequivocal about the importance of truth, and yet I'm going to have to lie to him about where I was this afternoon. He has such a strong sense of right and wrong, and it was this steadfastness that attracted me to him. He is unwavering in his belief that family has to come before everything, and I understand why he feels like that.

As I sit by my daughter's bed, stroking her hand, I think about the time I met Dom nine years ago. After Scott I had always believed I would neither find nor want anyone else. I was certain I would never again experience the exhilaration and euphoria of being in love – the racing heart, the trembling, the loss of appetite. But was that what I wanted? Did I want to suffer the anxiety, panic and feelings of despair when things went wrong? I had begun to realise that perhaps I needed a love that was gentler, easier to live with, maybe even predictable.

After my first year at university and that summer in Nebraska, I didn't go back to Manchester, switching instead to Lancaster University, which was nearer home. My mother was happy, if no one else was. I muddled through somehow, my body aching for all I had lost, comforted by the warmth and security of my childhood home. On the side of a hill overlooking Derwent Water, the tiny cottage my parents had restored stone by stone in the long years before I came along kept me safe while my battered heart healed.

When I finally forced myself to break free, it was to teach in a school in north Lancashire. Working with the sweet children, I recovered some of my confidence, and when a tall young man called Dominic Franklyn came over from the local secondary school once a week to teach drama, I felt stirrings of interest in a man for the first time in years. I was comfortable around him from the start. The word that described him best was 'unthreatening'. He seemed kind, level-headed and thoughtful, and whenever he was around I felt calm.

We became lovers, and it wasn't long before I realised he wanted more. And perhaps, at last, so did I. I knew, though, that if I wanted Dom to be a permanent part of my life, there was one thing I was going to have to tell him, sooner rather than later. I didn't want to lose him, but the longer I kept my secret the more difficult it would become. The moments after we made love were always the most precious to me, when we lay face to face in semi-darkness, noses almost touching, legs entangled, baring our souls and allowing each other to get as close mentally as we had been physically. I chose my moment well. I knew he was in love with me and he deserved my honesty.

'Dom, there's something I need to tell you,' I said, my voice low and gentle.

Dominic put his finger on my lips. 'Me first.'

That's when he told me about his childhood: about how his mother had walked out on him when he was two years old, and how his father had struggled alone to bring up both him and his four-year-old sister.

'I can't tell you how it felt – how it still feels, ridiculous as that sounds,' he said. 'I spent most of my childhood wondering what was the matter with me – what I had done to drive her away when all I wanted was to be loved. My father was shocked when she left, but it wasn't until I was an adult that he explained to me what had happened.'

I wrapped my arms around him, pulling him as close as I could while he talked.

'My father was a man who believed in trusting the people you love. He trusted my mother and never questioned her, but it turned out she had a vice, one he knew nothing about.' Dominic paused, and I could tell he was finding it hard to tell me. 'My mother, it seems, liked having sex with strangers. When my dad found out it nearly killed him. He told her she either had to stop or get out. She chose the latter and I've never forgiven her. What sort of a person does that – thinks her kicks are more important than her children?'

There was no answer that I could give. But Dominic hadn't finished.

'I'd love us to have children one day, Anna, but only if I can be sure your values are the same as mine. I don't want any secrets between us. I couldn't stand that because I don't want to end up like my dad. I'll do whatever it takes to keep my family safe, but I have to be sure my wife feels the same way, that I can trust her.' He paused for a moment and lifted one hand to stroke the back of my head where it lay next to his on the pillow.

I knew that this whole speech was his way of proposing – I was sure that for him it would be marriage or nothing – and for a moment I was silent.

'Have I said too much?' he asked. 'I had to tell you how I feel before things go any further because this is one area in which I can't compromise. My mother lied and cheated, then walked away from her children without a backward glance. That must never happen to a child of mine.'

I remember feeling the tension in his body as he willed me to say what he wanted to hear. Finally, perhaps sensing that I was struggling, Dominic broke a silence that had lasted too long. 'What were you going to tell me?'

I knew that if Dominic and I were to have children together, there was one thing he would be almost certain to find out. He would know that his child wouldn't be my first.

'I had a baby, Dom. When I was nineteen. It wasn't planned, but I never considered a termination even though I was at university at the time.'

He pulled his head back and looked at me. 'What happened to him, or her?' he asked, a puzzled expression on his face.

I dropped my head to rest on his shoulder. I didn't want him to see my eyes. 'It was a boy. He was stillborn.'

'Oh, my darling, I'm so sorry,' he said, pulling me closer. 'What about the child's father?'

'He was called Scott. I loved him, but he died too.' A sob shook my body as I remembered Scott's last moments, and I cried then as I hadn't done for years. Dominic held me tightly until the tears dried up. Then I asked him not to mention it again, and he never has.

Now here we are, waiting to find out if our first-born child is going to be okay, and I have let him down. I had allowed something to take priority over our children, and I can't tell him what it was.

I wipe a tear from my cheek and look up. Dominic is watching me, and his face softens. He walks around the bed, holds out a hand to pull me from my chair and slips his arm around my shoulders. It feels as if it weighs a ton.

One lie, so long ago. I didn't think it mattered; he never needed to know the truth. But once I lied about that, I had to lie about everything else, and if I don't find Scott and stop him, everything I have done will have been for nothing. Because I know it is the one lie that Dominic will never forgive.

21

Then

I didn't sleep a wink the night the charity money went missing. I knew by then where it had gone, but I had no idea what I was going to do about it.

'I borrowed it,' Scott had finally admitted. 'That's all. Just a loan. I'm sorry, Anna. I know I should have asked you first, but I thought I would be able to put it back before you noticed, and then it wouldn't matter.'

I shook my head. 'But it *would* matter. You took something that wasn't yours, or even mine.'

He had hung his head even lower – knowing, I'm sure, that I wasn't going to be persuaded that this was acceptable.

'When can you get it back?'

'Tomorrow. Honestly, just trust me. Okay?'

I wanted to. More than I could ever say. My hunger for him, my need to be with him hadn't diminished, and after I agreed to have faith in him – for a few hours, at least – we made love with an urgency driven by the intensity of our emotions. But I felt a shadow of doubt about Scott, and it was like a dull ache at the heart of my happiness.

After a final lingering kiss, Scott leaped from the bed saying he had to go. He wasn't going to stay the night – he had to 'see about' getting the money back. I didn't know what he meant, but he was pulling his clothes on, and I didn't want to delay him. I had to pay the money over within thirty-six hours or have a very good excuse why not.

I spent the next day lying on my bed staring at the ceiling, wiping away the tears that slithered down my cheeks, jumping up whenever I heard footsteps outside the door, expecting it to be Scott. But it never was, and time was running out.

Just when I had given up hope, there was a soft knock on the door.

I yanked it open with a welcoming smile, expecting Scott to hold out an envelope or a bag, or *anything* as long as it was stuffed with notes.

His hands were empty.

'Where is it?' I gabbled, pulling him into the room, my eyes darting to his pockets and back to his face. 'Where's the money?'

His eyes wouldn't meet mine. 'I couldn't get it. I'm so sorry, Spike.'

'Don't call me that,' I spat, as if using my pet name was the worst of his sins.

'Look, I don't have the money, but I do have a solution.' His words were eager, and he reached out to grab my hands. I pulled them away and folded my arms. 'Do you remember I introduced you to a man called Cameron Edmunds a few weeks ago?'

I did remember. I thought he seemed a nice guy, but Scott had acted as if he were the devil's spawn.

'He can be really generous with people he likes. His dad's loaded, and sometimes Cameron can be persuaded to lend money to friends.'

'But I'm not his friend.'

Scott shook his head. 'It doesn't work like that. If he likes you, trusts you, he'll do it – I know he will. You can just borrow it for a few days until I can pay it back.'

I stared at him. 'Why do *I* have to be the one to borrow it? You're the one who took it, Scott.'

He shook his head. 'Don't be like that, Anna. I told you – I thought I would be able to pay you straight back. I've said I'm sorry, and I meant it. Anyway, he's far more likely to lend to you than to me. He likes girls, and he doesn't seem keen on me for some reason.'

We argued back and forth for an hour. In the end I had two choices: borrow the money, if Cameron would lend it to me, or report it stolen. If I chose the second option they would discover Scott had taken it. I would lose him, and despite everything I didn't want that to happen. He had made a mistake – an error of judgement.

I considered asking my parents, but they didn't have that sort of money. Both of them were on minimum wage, and between them brought home around two hundred pounds a week. Three thousand would have meant borrowing against the house. And how would they repay it? I couldn't do that to them.

My throat was tight with stress and unshed tears, but I managed to speak.

'Where do I find Cameron?'

I had hoped Scott would come with me, but he was adamant that it would be counter-productive, so I made my way to a smart-looking bar on Oxford Road with tall smoked-glass windows where Cameron 'held court', as Scott put it. I stood outside for ten minutes, trying to muster the courage to walk in.

'Stop being so wet, Anna,' I muttered under my breath. 'Get on with it.'

I pushed open the door and tried to look confident, wondering if I should buy a drink and act casual, or if I should scour the room for Cameron. In the event I heard a burst of laughter from my right as I entered the bar and glanced over to see him with his friend Jagger at a table full of people, all of whom seemed to be laughing uproariously at a story Cameron was telling.

I watched him for a moment, his eyes dancing as he leaned forward towards his enthralled listeners, and I envied his confidence and ease. I couldn't break into this circle, though, and I was about to turn to leave when I heard him shout above the rowdy students, 'Anna? Come and join us.'

I was staggered that he remembered me, not knowing back then that one of Cameron's specialities was never forgetting a face and a name. I didn't want to join them in spite of his welcoming grin; what I needed to say to Cameron had to be said in private.

He must have noticed my hesitation, because he said something quietly to Jagger, who got up from the table and came towards me, his pinched features showing no expression. He seemed an unlikely friend for Cameron, who exuded charm and self-assurance and appeared to have a smile for everyone.

'You here for a drink, Anna, or is it business?' Jagger had a scratchy voice that seemed too deep for his lean body.

'I…' I didn't know what to say. I looked wildly around me, as if someone was going to come to my rescue.

'Okay, come with me.'

It seemed I didn't need to say any more. Jagger nodded at the barman, who gave him a solemn nod in return, and we walked through a door at the side of the bar into a small dark storeroom with a table and two chairs in the centre.

'Sit,' he said.

I was wishing I hadn't come and was about to tell Jagger it was a mistake when the door opened again and Cameron strode in. My tension eased as he smiled at me.

'Sorry about this grotty little room, Anna, but we got the impression you'd rather talk in private than in front of the others. You look worried, but don't be. We're all friends here. What can I do for you?'

It was kind of him to understand. He was trying to make it easier for me. I wanted to come straight out and ask him, but I felt so uncomfortable.

He sat down opposite me and leaned casually on the table.

'Listen, Anna, people usually come to me because they're in some kind of trouble and need help. I like to help where I can, and I can see something's upsetting you. Do you want to tell me what it is?'

I hesitated for a minute, but he was looking at me with such understanding that I told him everything – or almost. I lied about one thing: I said I had lost the money, not that Scott had taken it.

'The thing is, if I tell the charity I've lost it they won't believe me. They'll think I've stolen it, and I haven't!' I could feel tears stinging my eyes and prayed that I wouldn't cry.

'It's not a problem. I like you, Anna – you seem honest enough. I can lend you the money – as a friend – but I'm sure you understand that we'll need you to sign an agreement.' He looked at Jagger. 'We can sort that in the next couple of days, can't we, Jagger?'

'Oh, will it take that long?' The words burst from me before I had time to think.

Cameron raised his eyebrows. 'Urgent, is it? Well, I'm sure I can trust you. I can give you the money now, if you like, and then we'll sort out the agreement later. How does that sound?'

I felt as if a huge burden had lifted from my shoulders. 'Thank you so much. Scott said you'd help me, but I didn't really believe him. It's such a relief, and I'll pay you back as quickly as I can.'

I knew there were questions I should ask, but it seemed rude when he was being so helpful and I had never met anyone quite like him. How he and Jagger must have laughed at my naivety.

'You'll be wondering about the terms, no doubt,' he said, as if reading my mind. 'Even though we're friends, it's best for both of us if we recognise it's a business transaction, so I charge a very reasonable ten per cent interest. It's all in the agreement. I don't mind too much when you pay back the lump sum, as long as you meet your interest payments. How does that sound?'

Once more my eyes flooded with tears. Cameron reached over to touch my hand lightly before nodding to Jagger, who walked across the room and picked up a duffel bag. He reached inside, extracted three envelopes and handed them to Cameron.

'Each of these contains a thousand. Are you happy walking home on your own with this amount, or would you like Jagger to come with you – make sure you're safe?'

I felt a flash of concern. If he already had the money, had he known I was coming?

'Don't look so worried, Anna. People often come here to borrow from me, so I always have a bit of cash handy. It's all perfectly normal. And Jagger's been collecting some interest today, haven't you, Jagger?'

I didn't like the sneer on Jagger's face, and much as I didn't feel comfortable walking around with that much money, I knew I didn't want his company. There was something unnerving about the man.

'Thank you, but I don't need anyone to walk me back – you've done enough for me. I can't tell you how much I appreciate it.'

We stood up. 'We'll see you in a day or two to sign the agreement. Jagger will track you down, and if you're stuck again, you know where to find me. I'm usually here until about nine o'clock each evening before I move on.'

I looked away from his pale blue eyes, wondering if I would see him again or whether it would always be Jagger. I felt as if he had saved my life, and I would always be grateful for that.

22

After putting Dawn Edmunds into an unmarked police car to take her home, Tom and Becky returned to the incident room, where he was told Philippa Stanley wanted to see him immediately.

Tom knocked on her door, and as he entered she looked up expectantly, one hand holding a pen suspended above a stack of papers, as if she was giving him time for a single short sentence before she got back to whatever she was doing.

'Confirmed our victim, have you?' she asked.

'Confirmed that it's not who we thought it was, yes.'

'What?' Philippa laid her pen down. Clearly this was going to take more than the twenty seconds she had allocated. 'Sit, Tom. Tell me.'

'Dawn Edmunds swears it's not her husband and seems genuinely disappointed by the fact. So that leaves us with some difficult questions. Who is the victim? Why is he dead in another man's car? Is Edmunds still in danger – if he was the intended victim?'

'Damn it,' Philippa said, strong language for a woman who prided herself on having risen through the ranks without swearing. 'I thought you were going to tell me it was all sewn up. I was hoping for a result for the crime figures.'

Tom bit back a riposte. There was no point; it was her job to demonstrate the success of the team on every possible occasion.

He didn't have to spell out to Philippa all the ways in which the investigation had just become trickier. With an unknown victim, they would normally put out an appeal for information.

But they had to bear in mind that this may have been a case of mistaken identity, and Edmunds might still be in danger.

'So what's the plan?'

'We've got a search warrant for the house, and I'm following the team out there when you and I have finished here. Although we didn't release a name, it's all over social media that Cameron Edmunds is dead, and we're hoping that will work in our favour. No one will find it odd that we're at his home.'

'I presume you've discounted the other option – that Edmunds was the killer of the unknown victim?'

Tom laughed. 'I can't believe he's daft enough to have killed someone in his own car. That would be the double bluff to end all double bluffs, but obviously we can't entirely rule it out. The search team should be at his home now. Meanwhile, we need to find out who the dead man is and decide whether he was the intended victim or not. I've said it before, but there was nothing random about this attack. It was vicious and carefully planned.'

Philippa studied Tom for a moment, then nodded and looked back down at her paperwork. Tom knew he was dismissed.

Dawn Edmunds was clearly an intelligent if somewhat disillusioned woman, but when Tom arrived at the house he sensed a change in her. She greeted him in the hall, another glass of clear liquid in her hand from which she took a few deep gulps, swearing she had no idea where Cameron might be.

'I can't contact him. His mobile's switched off, as no doubt you know. He's probably flushed the SIM down a drain somewhere.'

She was right – they had checked his phone and its records thoroughly.

'Why do you think he hasn't contacted you?' Tom asked.

There was a slight tremor in her sharp laugh. 'Chief Inspector, you have to understand that he doesn't care what I think. He knows I would dance on his grave. But if he's alive, that's a whole different ball game. He'll blame me for the fact you're here, whether it's my fault or not, so do what you need to, but I'm not giving my consent to anything.'

The almost celebratory mood had gone. Instead, Tom saw an anxious woman afraid of making a wrong decision, or at least afraid of the potential repercussions.

'Look, I'll tell you this much. The only place you're likely to find anything of interest is in his study. He wouldn't leave anything incriminating in his bedroom in case the cleaning staff found it, but they're not allowed in the study. Jagger comes in twice a week to clean it.'

'Tell me about Jagger.'

Dawn screwed up her face. 'Nasty little weasel of a man. He's got the fine features of something that lives underground, if you know what I mean.' She shuddered. 'If anyone knows where Cameron is, it's him – but I didn't tell you that, okay?'

'What's his full name, and do you have an address?'

'I've no idea where he lives – in some cave in the hills, at a guess. His first name is Roger, which he hates and never uses. He's been my husband's minder since they were at university, doing all his dirty work. Kneecapping is something of a speciality, I believe.'

'What do you mean, dirty work? What does your husband do that requires someone like Jagger as a minder?'

Dawn's eyes flickered. 'Christ, I've said too much. God help me if he finds out. I don't know what he does, okay? I overhear stuff sometimes. He forgets I'm there most of the time. We don't talk about what he does – I don't want to know – and the money for the kids and running the house comes from his dad. I don't ask. What I don't know can't hurt me.'

Tom was prevented from pushing her further by the appearance of one of the search team.

'Sir, we've found a safe.'

Tom turned to Dawn. 'Don't look at me,' she said. 'I don't

know if it opens with a key, a combination or a fingerprint. Not a clue. I'm not allowed in there – no one is, except Cameron and Jagger – and what's more he has a camera pointed at the door so that if anyone goes in, he'll know about it. He says he's not having locked doors in his house, just rules, and we'd all better obey them. He's a real shit, you know. But I guess you're getting the picture.'

'If he has a camera, the feed must go somewhere. Do you have any idea where?'

Dawn shrugged and chewed a thumbnail. 'I have no idea how this stuff works, but at a guess it will go to Jagger somehow.'

'Do you want me to get a locksmith for the safe, sir?' the officer asked.

Tom thought about it for a moment. 'I'm guessing it's a high-end safe, not a B&Q special?' The officer nodded. 'Maybe leave it for now. Opening it could cause all sorts of issues with legal privilege, so unless we know there's something in there that's vital to the investigation, we'll put a hold on it.'

Tom excused himself and left Dawn to top up her glass while he went in search of Becky.

'We've not found much yet,' she said. 'Why don't you get yourself off home and see how things are going with Lucy? If you stay much longer she'll be in bed by the time you get back.'

Tom had told Becky that his daughter was staying with them but hadn't given her any details. She was right, though. He didn't need to be there for the search.

He took his leave and drove home slowly, going over in his mind what they knew – which wasn't much – and twenty minutes later he was pulling into his drive, ready to face the other puzzle in his life. What on earth was going on with Lucy and her mum?

Opening the front door, he called out, 'Hello,' making his voice more cheery than he felt.

'Hi, Tom. We're in the kitchen,' Louisa shouted.

He could smell something delicious, and walking into the room he was pleased to see Lucy at the hob, stirring the contents of a large casserole dish. She turned to smile at him. Tom felt instant relief that there appeared to be an air of calm, and for now no teenage tantrums. He reached towards his daughter, kissed her on the cheek and turned to give Louisa a hug. 'I got home as quickly as I could. Sorry I wasn't back earlier. This case is getting more and more complicated.'

'We saw it on TV,' Lucy said. 'Those poor kids, losing their dad like that.'

Tom couldn't tell Lucy and Louisa that the dead man wasn't who everyone believed him to be, so he changed the subject. 'What are we eating?'

'Louisa and I have made a Moroccan chicken thingy and some couscous with lots of roasted veggies.'

'Excellent. When will it be ready?'

'Fifteen minutes,' Louisa said.

'Good. So, Lucy, shall we have a quick chat?'

Lucy turned around fully, waving a wooden spoon in the air. 'Do we have to, Dad? I picked up some clothes today so I don't need to go home for a while.'

'Come and sit down for a minute,' he said. 'I just need to find out what's happened, so whatever we decide, we can make sure that you and your mum have resolved your issues. She's an important person in your life, love. You can't shut her out.'

Lucy put the wooden spoon down with a clatter and stomped across the room to sit at the table. 'So it's my fault?'

'I didn't say that. I don't think arguments are usually the fault of one person. They're generally a combination of circumstances and personality. So what caused you to argue?'

Lucy tossed her head. 'If you must know, we argued about you. To start with I was mad at you, but then I realised it was all her fault. And she lied to me. You've always told me not to lie,

114

Dad, and so I try very hard not to. That's why I was so mad at her.'

Tom noticed that Louisa had turned down the heat under the food and quietly slipped from the room.

'Explain.'

'I asked her why you split up, and she said she'd been stupid. You weren't paying her any attention, always thinking about work and stuff, and she met someone else who she thought she could love better.'

There was nothing there that Tom could argue with. He had been working his way up the ladder as a detective, and they were forever short of money. Kate wanted the best of everything, and the only way they would be able to afford the lifestyle she craved was for Tom to be promoted to a senior position. He'd had no choice but to work hard. And, he had to admit, he was ambitious back then. Kate had been tempted away by a young London trader called Declan, who was making a fortune. She had taken herself and Lucy to the other end of the country and it been the worst time of Tom's life.

'I think your mum's being fair, Lucy. I did work very long hours, and I should have realised it was making her unhappy. I'm not going to make excuses, but when she took you away I was devastated. I need you to know that.'

Lucy nodded. 'That's why I know that the next bit she told me is a lie. She said she offered to come back to you. She said it would mean you could spend every day with me, but you refused. How could she tell a lie like that?'

Tom felt the muscles across his shoulders tense. What was he going to say to his daughter? He reached for her hand. 'Sweetheart, she wasn't lying. It's not exactly the way it seems, but it's not a lie.'

Lucy stared at him for a moment and then yanked her hand out of his. 'So you didn't want me? She was telling the truth? She made one mistake, but even for me you wouldn't let us back into your life?' She pushed back from the table.

Tom wanted to stop her. He had to make Lucy understand how it had happened without sounding as if he was blaming her mother. In fact Kate's interest in Tom had only revived when he inherited a fortune from Jack, his brother, but their daughter didn't need to know that.

It was too late, though. Lucy's eyes had filled with tears. 'I didn't believe her. You've always told me that losing me from your life when I was so young was devastating. But you could have had me back, and you didn't want me, did you, Dad?'

And with that she turned and ran from the room.

23

It's such a relief to be home, to have Holly asleep in her own bed and an overexcited Bailey finally settled. My son doesn't really understand what happened, but he'd had his routine disturbed and it had made him anxious, not least because once more he could probably feel my tension. I still haven't spoken to Dominic about where I was and what kept me, but the moment is coming, and I can't bear to see that look of disappointment in his eyes again. Whatever I tell him, I have to be convincing. He'll believe me because as far as he knows he's never had any reason to doubt me. All the bargains I made with myself in exchange for Holly's safety have been forgotten. I can't tell him the truth, and I feel tears stinging the back of my eyes as I walk downstairs.

I quickly blink them away as I step into the kitchen, where Dom is pouring us both a glass of red wine.

'I thought maybe we could do with this,' he says, his face solemn. 'I'm sorry if I was hard on you earlier, Anna. I should have listened first before jumping in with both feet.'

I shake my head. 'You were worried, in shock. Our daughter had been hurt in our own back garden and on your watch. You were bound to be upset.'

I feel a stab of self-disgust. I didn't mean to hint at blame, and no one cares more about our children's safety than Dominic. It was an automatic response, intended to deflect any accusations that he might be about to make. But it was unfair, and I grab the glass and take a large gulp, not wanting to look at my husband's face.

'Do you think it was my fault?' he asks, his hurt tone making me furious with myself.

'I'm so sorry, darling. I shouldn't have put it like that. Of course it wasn't your fault. I know you weren't neglecting them.' Another word I shouldn't have used – one that would inevitably make him feel even more guilty. 'Are you any clearer about what happened?'

'Not really. Holly was dreadfully upset and kept saying she was sorry for going into my shed, although I told her it was my fault for forgetting to lock it. Did Bailey tell you what happened?'

'No. Just that Holly was running away. But when I asked him what from, he said he didn't know.'

There is a pause, and the unasked question hangs in the air, making the room feel claustrophobic. I walk over to the back door and open it as if to let some air in, but I need to have my back to Dominic as I speak.

'I'm sorry you couldn't get hold of me, Dom. I had to go out to visit a difficult family today. The child has been missing a lot of school, and when she does turn up she looks terrible. I'm going to have to talk to social services about them. But before I start something that might be difficult to stop, I wanted to know if there was some problem I could help with.'

'And was there?'

'No. I don't think so. It's simply a very unhappy household with two parents who struggle to find the will to get out of bed each morning. I'll spare you the details. Anyway, I left my phone in the car. I didn't want any interruptions, and I was with them for much longer than I anticipated. When I left I felt depressed by the whole thing so I went for a drive. Stupidly I didn't check my phone. When I saw your message I headed straight back, but there'd been an accident and I was held up for ages. I'm so sorry. As soon as I knew, all I wanted to do was get to Holly.'

The last sentence at least is true.

I stare sightlessly into the shadowy back garden, but as I begin to relax now that the worst of my lies are done with, my attention switches to the door to the shed, softly lit by the light spilling from the back door and the kitchen window. *Why was Holly in there? How did she cut her leg?* I take a step outside.

'Where are you going?' Dominic asks.

'I want to see where my little girl hurt herself.'

I hear the sound of Dominic's glass going down on the worktop and know he is going to follow me. I walk quickly towards the shed.

'Bugger,' I hear him say. He had kicked off his blood-soaked trainers as soon as he came into the house and now he will have to go and hunt for something to put on his feet. I don't wait.

The garden is shrouded in darkness. The heat of the day has left a veil of heavy air, and there is a smell of damp earth, as if a storm is coming. I can just make out the path in the borrowed light from the open door.

I reach the shed and push against the wooden door.

'Ouch!' I snatch my hand back, putting my finger into my mouth and sucking. A fragment of wood has buried itself deep in the soft flesh of its tip. I peer down to see where it has come from, ever conscious of ways my children might get injured, and give an involuntary gasp. The edge of the door is splintered, as is the door surround. It looks as if something has been inserted between the two to force the door open.

It's clear what has happened. The shed has been burgled and that is how Holly managed to get in. I should have known Dominic wouldn't have forgotten to lock it, and in his panic at the sight of Holly's injury he can't have noticed the evidence of the break-in.

Assuming the burglar is long gone, I reach out a leg and kick the door open. The long narrow space is pitch black at the far end, but I am sure there is no one there. I would feel it if someone was lurking in the shadows.

Reaching out a hand for the light switch, ready to flee if I am proven wrong and someone rushes at me, I press it down. The old fluorescent tube splutters into life, lighting the interior of the shed for a second, then plunging it back into darkness, repeating the pattern until it finally stabilises. I wasn't wrong. There is no one here.

I hear a footstep behind me and my body freezes, as for an irrational moment I believe the burglar is behind me. The footsteps grow closer and at the exact moment I realise that it's Dominic, following me from the kitchen, I see a photograph propped against his toolbox. My hand flies to my mouth. *How did that get there? Who put it there?*

I step quickly inside and grab the photo, pushing it into the pocket of my jeans.

'Are you okay, darling?' Dom says quietly behind me.

'No. Not really. Look what I found.' I lift a finger and point to the door. 'We've had burglars. You'd better check what's missing.'

'What? God, what a pain,' Dominic says with a sigh. 'I suppose I'd better call the police.'

'*No!* Not the police.' I don't think before I speak, but my reaction is instantaneous. I don't miss the look of surprise on Dominic's face.

'Why not? If we're going to claim on the insurance we've got no choice.'

I think quickly. 'The children have been upset enough. If they wake up to see flashing blue lights and find a policeman sitting in our kitchen, they'll be terrified. Maybe leave it to the morning and see if anything has been taken before we decide. If nothing's gone, it's probably not worth it.'

'Do you think it's the man who's been lurking around the place for the last few days? The one I told you about?'

I switch off the light before I turn to Dom so he can't see my face, edge past him and head back up the path. 'I don't know, but

I need that wine. Come on. We've had enough to deal with for one night. Let's have a couple of glasses and try to relax.'

But I'm not going to relax until I've had a chance to hide the photo. It feels as if it's burning my skin through the fabric of my jeans. I didn't have the chance to look at it closely, but I know who it is.

24

Then

Relieved as I was that I didn't have to confess to losing the charity money, I couldn't rid myself of the heavy despondent mood that had been with me since I had discovered it was missing. It was only when Scott finally explained to me why he had taken it that I felt my mood lighten. It seemed his parents were no better off than mine, so when they suffered a small fire in their kitchen they couldn't afford to replace even the basics, and Scott had wanted to help.

'My dad's not well, and as the insurance pay-out was due any day I told them I still had some of my loan left, and I'd been earning a bit of cash so I could lend it to them. I didn't want them to worry, and I thought I'd get it back quickly. But the insurers are now claiming it wasn't an accident – you know what they're like, trying to wheedle out of coughing up. It's been hell for my parents, but I will get it back, Anna. I promise.'

I felt sorry for them – and for Scott, who was deeply embarrassed – but I was just glad the nightmare was over and I silently thanked Cameron as I handed over the money to the charity. And when the insurance came through I would be able to pay him off.

The following day, Jagger was lying in wait as I came out of a lecture.

'He wants to see you,' he said and walked away. I presumed I had to follow.

Cameron was sitting in the back room of the bar again, and

he gave me a friendly smile when he saw me.

'Hi, Anna. I don't have long, I'm afraid, but I thought we should get the paperwork done. Here's the agreement, and if you could sign on the last page we're all done and dusted.'

I looked with dismay at a three-page document, the typing small and closely spaced in two columns on each page.

'I probably need someone to look at this for me,' I said, about to fold the document and take it away.

I looked up at Cameron. The smile had dropped from his face.

'You don't trust me?' He looked over my head. 'What do you think of that, Jagger?'

'Ungrateful, if you ask me. You trusted her with the money and no agreement, but she doesn't trust you.'

Cameron reached for the contract. 'Don't worry, Anna. Just give me the money back and we'll forget all about it. I thought you'd agreed to the terms – see, on the first page in big letters it says ten per cent. What more do you need to know?'

I panicked. I didn't have the money to give back to him. I saw him look at his watch – he was obviously in a hurry.

'I'm sorry,' I said. 'I didn't mean to offend you, but I've always been told it's important to read contracts.'

Cameron smiled at me, his head on one side as if he understood my concerns.

'Okay, not to worry. I'll be straight with you about the terms, and then you decide whether to sign or to give me the money back. Either is fine, but I don't have long. We agreed the interest, right?'

I nodded warily.

'I like to be fair, so the other thing in there you need to be clear about is the charge I have over your assets in the event that you don't pay me any interest or repay the capital sum.'

My heart was beating faster. I didn't have any assets – I didn't own anything other than my books, clothes and my laptop.

'I appreciate you probably don't have much in the way of assets right now, so don't let that bother you. The charge says that future assets are good too. In other words, you can pay me back when you can afford it. Does that seem fair?'

There was something about this I was uncomfortable with, but I couldn't put my finger on it, and I was feeling so agitated that I simply nodded. The thought of Jagger standing behind me, out of my sight, wasn't helping my nerves either.

'And, again to be clear, the agreement states that you came to me and asked for money. I didn't approach you, and I agreed to the loan on the basis that you are a friend in need of help.'

He was right.

'Okay. Pen, please, Jagger.'

Cameron scrawled his name and the date, and then passed the pen to me. Every instinct told me not to sign – that I was being rushed and needed to read it – but I didn't have the money to give back to him and I could cope with the interest payments. I'd worked out how I was going to do that. I didn't think I had any other option.

I took the pen and added my signature.

Cameron handed the document to Jagger and walked towards the door, squeezing my shoulder as he passed.

'Well done, Anna. We'll see you soon.'

It wasn't long after I had signed the contract – three days, maybe four – that I came to understand everything in the cruellest way possible.

Scott and I had been to the students' union bar that night for a half of cider for me, a half of bitter for him. I told him it was all we could afford until I had paid Cameron back. He had looked slightly startled but hadn't argued.

We took the direct route back to my hall of residence – using the back streets even though it was dark, because I felt safe with Scott. I remember we were talking about me getting a job for a couple of evenings a week. I had forgiven Scott for taking the money. He loved his parents; I understood what he had done, and I loved him.

I realised after a few minutes that he had stopped talking and wasn't really listening to me either. His head was darting from side to side, then he twisted to look behind him.

'Shh,' he whispered.

He could hear something that I couldn't, so I fell quiet and walked on the balls of my feet. Then I heard it too – the sound of heavy breathing, as if someone had been running – but there was no one on the street either in front of us or behind.

I glanced anxiously at Scott, wondering if we should head back to the main road. My heart was beating fast, and I started to walk more quickly – but it was too late. As we passed the cobbled back alley that ran behind the bars and offices of Oxford Road, three figures leaped out of the shadows.

One came for me, grabbing me from behind, clamping a gloved hand over my mouth. I tried to cry out, but I could barely breathe and felt sick with fear. The other two men seized Scott and dragged him into the alley. I felt a knee in the small of my back and a voice said, 'Move.'

I tried to swivel my head in shock. I was sure I recognised the voice but I had to be wrong. I was pushed into the alley. I struggled, trying to kick out, but the arms holding me felt like steel. I groaned in horror as Scott was thrown to the ground. He brought up his arms to cover his head and curled into a ball. One of the men grabbed his legs and pushed them backwards, leaving his chest and belly unprotected. That was where the kicks landed, one after another. It was the sounds that would haunt me: the hideous thud of boots hitting Scott's unprotected body; the groans of anguish that burst from his lips; the grunts of exertion from his assailants.

I tried again to break free, but my legs seemed unable to bear my weight, and without the man holding me I would have fallen to the ground. I moaned in despair into the gloved hand.

'Shut the fuck up, Anna,' the voice said, and I almost passed out. I was right. I did recognise it. *Jagger.*

Suddenly it was over. The kicks had stopped and Scott had gone quiet. I thought he was dead. The two men ran back up the alley. Jagger shoved me away and followed them. I collapsed onto my knees on the cobbles, crying out with pain. But my only concern was Scott.

I crawled towards him, sobbing, shouting for help. But no one came.

I reached his side and touched his face. 'It's okay, Scott. I'll call an ambulance and the police. I know who it was. Don't worry. The police will get them.'

I was struggling to my feet when Scott stretched out a hand. 'No police, no ambulance. No, Anna. Don't!'

I couldn't believe what I was hearing. Why wouldn't he let me call the police? Those guys were animals.

Slowly he pushed himself up. 'I'm fine. It was only a kicking – a warning. I'll be okay.'

'What are you talking about? Scott, it was *Jagger*! I recognised his voice.'

'I know,' he said, resignation in his voice.

'Wait till I tell Cameron about this – God knows what he'll say.' Even to me my words sounded empty.

Scott's head turned and his eyes glimmered in a stray beam of moonlight. 'Who do you think sent him?'

I wanted to be surprised – shocked, even. But strangely I wasn't. The image of those pale blue eyes that had charmed me flashed into my mind, and they suddenly reminded me of icicles. I felt a rush of shame for my gullibility.

After a moment's silence I bent towards Scott, putting out a hand to help him to his feet, but he waved me away; he just sat on the cobbles staring at the space between his bent knees.

Finally he raised his head and looked up at me. 'Do you love me?'

'Of *course*.' And I did. He was my boyfriend and he was hurt. All I wanted to do was take care of him, make whatever was wrong in his life go away.

'You're my world, Anna. You know that, don't you? But I need your help.' His voice broke on a sob as he wiped cheeks wet with tears with the back of one hand. 'Please, Anna, I need your help so badly.'

There was no question in my mind. He loved me. He needed me. He was mine – I could feel it – so I listened as he told me the truth about why he had taken the money, and how deep the hole he had dug for himself really was.

Wednesday

25

I can't remember ever taking a day off due to illness, either real or – as in this case – fake. Dominic looks at me with concern when I return to our bedroom after a shower to say I am staying at home to be with Holly.

'Whatever for? She's okay and I'll be here. If I'm even slightly concerned about her I'll call you. Honestly, we'll be fine.'

But Dominic doesn't know about the photo, evidence that whoever broke into our shed wasn't there to steal a few screwdrivers and an electric drill. In fact, Dom has already checked and nothing at all seems to be missing, so he now assumes that the burglar was disturbed before he'd had the chance to take anything.

I try to smile as I perch myself on the edge of the bed. 'The doctor said Holly needs a day in bed, so who's going to look after her while you take Bailey to school?'

I put my head down and rub my wet hair with a towel, not wanting my husband to see the expression in my eyes. It's now only five days until Monday's 'The One That Got Away' radio broadcast and I may only have a short time before he discovers I'm not who he thinks I am. Where will we all be one week from now if I do nothing?

Dominic takes the towel out of my hand and pulls my head against his hard stomach, rubbing the back of my hair. 'Bailey having a day off to stay at home with his sister is infinitely more sensible than you pretending to be sick. It's not like you, and Holly's fine, you know.'

But I can't face the day ahead. I've brought danger to my

family, and Scott has been watching the house, has been in our shed. That's too close for comfort. I lift my head and go to sit at the dressing table, my back to my husband.

'I need a few hours of calm after last night. I'll go in this afternoon. It'll be fine, honestly. And anyway, Bailey's only just started at the "big school", as he calls it. Keeping him home will upset his rhythm. You know that.'

I watch Dominic in the mirror – his brows knitted together, a finger scratching his chin. He looks bemused, but he won't argue. Instead he comes over and wraps his arms around my shoulders from behind. 'Whatever works for you. Sorry you're stressed – it's a crap way to feel.'

I have to give him more than this. 'It's because I wasn't there for my little girl.' That part is true. 'If I'd taken my phone with me, or if I had come back a different way, I could have been there for you both.' And that part isn't.

We're tiptoeing around each other and it feels strained, uncomfortable, as if there is a sheet of glass between us – allowing us to see, but not to touch. He can sense there's something going on in my head, but he won't ask. It's not his way.

'I'm going to go and get Bailey up,' Dom says. 'Take it easy for a while. Holly's still asleep so you can lie on the bed and relax until you feel a bit calmer. I'll take Bailey to school and come straight back.'

There are times when I wish I hadn't chosen to marry a saint. It's as if his virtue shines a bright light on my imperfections. His one failing, if you can call it that, is that he can neither understand nor tolerate what he sees as weakness in others.

Sometimes this irritates me, and I try to make him understand that people are not perfect – everyone is capable of making a mistake or doing something they are ashamed of. But deep down I know that my attempts to make him more tolerant are a corollary of my own failings.

Inevitably, my mind strays back to Scott and all that he could reveal. The thought of Dominic's inevitable disgust at who I used to be and what I have done terrifies me. His eyes will lose their light as he looks at me, and the peace and security that I found in him will be shattered.

I stifle a sob and reach into the dressing-table drawer where I have hidden the picture. I haven't had the opportunity to look closely at the photograph yet as Dominic has been close by all night. But now I can hear him talking to Bailey, explaining why Holly isn't going to school.

The photograph is lying on top of the detritus in my drawer, face down, and I turn it over. It is a close-up of a young teenage boy. I first met Scott when he was nineteen, nearly twenty, but the eyes staring back at me are the same dark brown, the brows heavy and black, the perfect cupid's bow of his upper lip and thick lower lip just like when I first met him, permanently set in a smile. Less so by the end. There is only one person this could be.

I jump when the doorbell chimes, and I remember Scott is not the only danger. I have been waiting for this since yesterday. It must be the police, here to question me about Cameron's murder. I didn't think it would be so soon.

I push the photo back in the drawer. I can feel my heart pounding and listen as Dominic goes downstairs to open the door. I hear his voice. He sounds surprised but I can't hear what he says. Then the door closes. Have they come in? I hear his footsteps coming back upstairs, but he goes back into Bailey's room.

I wait for a beat. 'Who was that?' I shout.

'Oh, the postman. I ordered some hinges and they've arrived already. I only ordered them yesterday.'

I let out a breath, long and slow. The danger is past, for now. But they will come soon. It's inevitable.

I have been worrying about Scott's threatened revelations, which for a while have masked my other fear – that my relationship with Cameron will be revealed. However many excuses I might try to make about the past, about who I was when I was with Scott and the terrible secret that I thought no one need ever know, I can't make the same claims about Cameron. Dominic will know this is not about who I *was*. It's about who I have *become*.

Moving to Manchester was a huge mistake. Cameron found me, and I owed him. He was never going to let me forget that.

26

Eighteen months ago

When I first arrived as deputy head teacher at Monks Lane Primary School, it was a dreary place. But when I walked into the school at the start of my first term as head, the place looked so much more cheerful. I looked proudly at the children's paintings in their brightly coloured frames on newly painted white walls. I was loving my job, and any reservations I'd had about moving back to Manchester – a city which didn't hold good memories for me – were gone. Everything bad that had happened was so long ago. It couldn't touch me now. At least, that's what I believed.

The school is part of a multi-academy trust, and the trustees decided that I personified their core values, so I was rolled out to talk to journalists, speak on the radio and generally spread the gospel. I was less than happy about being interviewed on local television, but I was young to be a head, and someone on the board of trustees obviously had influence with the BBC, so I had made my television debut the night before. I had felt very uncomfortable, but the ordeal was over and I was feeling relaxed as I made my way into my new office.

Jennie followed me, smiling brightly and juggling a pile of files in one hand with a cup of coffee in the other. She is one of those people who lights up a room as she enters.

'Thanks, Jen.'

'You're seeing the governors this evening, Anna, so you should watch the video of your interview,' she said. 'They're bound to want to talk about it, and it's good, you know. You've nothing to worry about.'

The idea didn't thrill me.

'I thought I might lace your coffee with something to help you deal with the shock of seeing how brilliantly you performed. It was shown again on the late news.'

I groaned.

Jennie edged round the desk and navigated to the clip, dragged the video control along to the right point in the programme and hit Play.

I saw myself on screen for the first time, and it took me a while to get used to it. I'm short and slender, and next to the tall, well-built presenter I almost looked like one of the children. Then the camera homed in on my face as the presenter asked a question.

'Monks Lane is a faith school and I know the trustees are keen on your vision and values, so what can you tell us about those and what they mean to your pupils, Anna?'

'The core values of the school underpin the whole of our community and inform our aims and ethos.' *God, I sounded pompous.* 'Christian values need to be embedded into our daily lives, with the family at the heart, and we believe that truth is at the centre of everything. We encourage our children to strive to always tell the truth and to be true to their word, to take responsibility for what they think, say and do, and to treat each other honestly and fairly.'

As I talked about our behaviour policies, behind me was a picture of the school, with the five value words running across the top: TRUTH, JUSTICE, RESPECT, HONESTY, RESPONSIBILITY.

I wanted to turn it off. I wasn't sure I could look at myself and listen to the person spouting those words, given who I had been and what I had done, but Jennie's eyes were shining as if she believed every word, and I felt such a fraud.

There was a deserted feel to the school after the governors' meeting ended. I had seen the last of them out of the building and was the only one still there apart from the caretaker, Barry, who refused to leave before me. He saw it as his responsibility to make sure the school was locked up properly at the end of the day, and while I found it slightly irritating that he thought a mere woman wasn't capable of following procedure, I had to admit that I was grateful for his presence when the building was empty.

Knowing my children would both be fast asleep by the time I got home, I decided to call Dominic to ask him to defrost the chilli I made at the weekend. There was no answer on his mobile, but he had an early-evening rehearsal for a drama production at school and maybe it was running late.

I stood up from my desk and looked out of the window. It was dark, and the mist that had been hanging around all day had thickened and settled. I got my things, headed towards the front door and found Barry hovering in the foyer. 'I'll see you out, miss, then I'll lock up behind you and go out the other way. My car's out back.' I had told him it was okay to call me Anna but he always chose to ignore it.

'Thanks, Barry. I'll see you tomorrow.'

I heard the door slam behind me and the clunk of the locks shooting into place. Hurrying towards my car, I felt a thin drizzle on my face, or maybe it was the mist hanging in the air. Whatever it was, it wasn't pleasant.

I was about to open the car door when my phone rang. Thinking it was Dominic returning my call, I answered without checking the screen.

'Mrs Franklyn? This is the Accident and Emergency Department at Salford Royal Hospital. I'm afraid your husband has been admitted.'

My mouth went dry, and I grabbed the door handle with my spare hand.

'What's happened? Is he okay?' I managed to ask.

'The police are with him now. He's conscious but in some pain. Are you able to get here? He's asking for you.'

Relieved that he was at least conscious, I leaned heavily on the door, oblivious to the weather.

'Of course, please tell Dominic I'll be with him as soon as I can.'

With that I hung up, quickly called the babysitter to ask her to stay on and jumped into the car. With shaking fingers I thrust the key in the ignition and slammed the gear stick into reverse. I saw the last of the lights go out in the school as I turned the car towards the gates.

What had happened to Dominic?

My brain felt foggy, confused with shock, and for a moment I thought I was seeing things. There appeared to be a car parked between the gateposts of the exit from the school yard, blocking my way. I cried out with frustration. I couldn't afford any delays.

Suddenly I was dazzled by headlights. I lifted an arm to shield my eyes from their glare. The beams were broken by the silhouette of a man, standing legs apart, arms folded. Somehow I knew he was waiting for me.

I glanced over my shoulder. *Where was Barry?* Then I remembered he was leaving by the back way. The school was in darkness. He'd gone.

I pipped my horn at the man to signal him to move, but I knew I was wasting my time. I wondered if I should call the police, but my car door was locked, so he couldn't get to me. My heart beat faster. I needed to get to Dominic. What was this man doing? What did he want?

He started to walk towards me and I double-checked the locks. He moved to within two feet of my front bumper, and I saw his face illuminated in my own lights. It was an eerie sight, the glare from below casting shadows, his eyes black hollows. Despite the fact that it was over twelve years since I'd seen him, I knew exactly who this was and I felt the urge to jump out of my car and run back into the school, locking the door behind me.

Jagger.

I had been afraid that my return to Manchester would lead to revelations from my past, but I had been back for a while now and thought I was safe. I had a new surname and was nothing like the student who had studied at the university for just one year.

He lifted his hand and flicked a finger. He was telling me to get out of the car. That wasn't going to happen; he was dangerous and I had no idea what he intended to do to me. But now I knew who he was, I couldn't call the police.

He got tired of waiting and strolled round to my door. '*Out!*' he shouted. 'Out, Anna, or I'll smash the fucking window.'

I knew he would, and I had no doubt that he had some weapon handy.

'I'm not going to hurt you, you stupid bitch. Not yet, anyway.'

I wanted to scream at him to get out of the way – I had to go – but I knew enough about him to realise that the more difficult I was, the longer he would delay me, and I told myself that I could deal with him. I wasn't an innocent eighteen-year-old girl any longer, scared of her own shadow. I was a woman with a responsible job, a husband – an injured husband – and two children. I didn't believe he was going to attack me. All I could think was that I had to get this over as quickly as possible so I could get to Dominic.

I undid my seat belt but left the engine running, then inched the window down until the gap was wide enough to talk through but still too small for his hand to reach in.

'What do you want, Jagger?'

'Oh, remember me, do you?' He laughed nastily. 'I thought you might. Get out of the car, Anna. We're not playing games.'

'How did you know where to find me?' But I knew the answer: the TV coverage.

Jagger wasn't listening, and I saw him reach behind and pull something from the back of his jeans. I jerked sideways, sure that it was a gun, and lunged for the door. I was literally a sitting target in the car. I got out quickly, my eyes on his hand. But it was a hammer, no doubt to smash a window had I not complied with his demands. At least, that's what I hoped it was for.

'You're big news, girl!' Jagger had a sick grin on his face. 'Your face appeared right in front of my eyes on the telly. I grabbed a shot on my phone and showed Cameron. I'd know those eyes of yours anywhere, and we were mighty impressed with the bullshit too. The school's trying to show they've got a good 'un this time, it seems. If only they knew, Anna. If only they knew. Maybe we need to enlighten them.'

I forced myself not to react.

'I loved the bit about truth and honesty. And let's not forget respect for others. I guess that means not treating them like fools. Oh, and your non-stealing policy. That was good too.'

'I've never stolen,' I said, mustering up what defiance I could.

'That's just semantics, I'm afraid.'

It was easy to forget that Jagger wasn't your average thug. He had graduated with a first in economics the year I left Manchester, and I had mistakenly assumed he would have used his undoubted abilities to move on, and I would be safe. It seemed I was wrong. Clearly being the minder of one of the cruellest men I had ever met was more appealing or lucrative than becoming a banker or an accountant.

'Cameron wants to talk to you.' He nodded his head towards the other car, but I couldn't see inside. 'Go on. Don't make me force you.'

I hadn't seen Cameron since the end of my first year in Manchester, and I had hoped never to see him again. And yet here he was.

I walked slowly towards the car, and Jagger opened one of

the back doors. There was no point in arguing, so I got in. Jagger slammed it shut, then stood with his back to it.

The interior light briefly illuminated Cameron's face. Older, as I would have expected, but he looked the picture of a successful, confident man, and the added years suited him. For a second I had a vision of what I might see if the perfect exterior was stripped from his body to reveal the devil beneath.

'Anna! Such a pleasure,' he said with the fake charm that had sucked me in all those years ago. I didn't answer. 'Jagger and I had forgotten all about you until last night, so what a surprise it was to see you, all grown-up and successful, appearing on the television.'

I still didn't speak. I didn't trust my voice.

'How's your husband doing? Do you know?'

For a moment I just stared at him. *What did he mean?* He sat silently and watched as I worked it out.

'You see, Anna, you took my money and never paid me back. You promised to – several times, in fact – but then you disappeared. Did you think I would forget?' He shook his head and tutted, his tone one of fake disappointment. 'You let me down, Anna. You asked me to have faith in you, but you weren't to be trusted. So take this as a warning. You let me down again, and I'll hurt you. You're hurting now, aren't you, worrying about your husband? Well next time Jagger won't be quite so gentle.'

I lost all control and started to scream. Jagger yanked the door open, wrapping one arm around my throat and a gloved hand over my mouth. Memories of that night in the cobbled alley flooded back. He didn't have to speak to make his message understood.

Cameron leaned across and patted my arm. 'Think about how you're going to pay me back, Anna,' he said, smiling. 'We'll be in touch.'

27

Becky pushed open the door to Tom's office with her foot and walked in bearing two mugs of tea. 'Door shut? That's not like you,' she said.

'I know, but I'm dealing with some personal stuff right now, and I don't want the whole team knowing what's going on.'

Becky frowned. 'Anything I can help with?'

Tom was silent for a moment. 'Maybe. It's Lucy.'

Becky handed over the tea and sat down, listening as Tom explained why his daughter was staying with them and what had happened the previous night. He had followed Lucy upstairs to try to explain why he had decided that he and her mum shouldn't get back together, but she hadn't wanted to listen and had refused to come down from her room to eat the food she had so carefully prepared. She wouldn't come out of the bathroom to talk to him that morning before he left for work, so he'd sent her a text saying how much he loved her, and that he would talk to her properly that evening.

'Anyway, enough of my problems. I'm sure they'll sort themselves. Let's get back to our investigation, which is now looking a hell of a lot more complicated. What's your general feeling? No one's heard from Edmunds or seen him, and we still don't know the identity of our victim. As you said, it had all the hallmarks of an execution, but who died, and who was supposed to die?'

Tom was about to suggest they head to the incident room to catch up with the team and stress the urgency of finding Cameron

Edmunds when there was a knock on the door and Keith Sims marched in. 'Sir, I think we may have something.'

Keith was obviously not going to tell them what it was without being asked, so Tom obliged.

'As we noted, the car was immaculate, and we finally managed to check with the valeting company. It was valeted as soon as Cameron Edmunds arrived on Sunday evening. They're generally not busy at that time, but the company always leaves one person on duty.'

'On a Sunday night?'

'Yes, it seems that as Mr Edmunds was a regular, there was one bloke who was happy to work because he always got a fat tip. Anyway, they key thing is that the valet was completed by ten thirty that night, and in theory the car was returned to a parking bay. But Lynsey spent most of yesterday going through the CCTV and spotted the Mercedes leaving the car park at ten thirty-six.'

Tom sat up straight. 'So Edmunds came back and went somewhere during the night? That explains why the Focus driver didn't see the Mercedes. Do we know where he went? Have we been able to track his mobile activity?'

'We don't believe it was Mr Edmunds driving the car, sir. Inspector Robinson said the attendant in the office had seemed very uncomfortable when she spoke to him. That's correct, isn't it?' he added, looking at Becky.

'Cut to the chase, Keith,' Tom said. 'Who was driving, why, and when did they get back?'

Keith jumped slightly. 'Oh. Right. It seems the bloke who volunteered to valet the car on Sundays didn't just do it for the tip. After Edmunds went to the casino, he borrowed the car and went off – to use his mate's phrase – "on the pull". He said it was easy to pick up women in a flash car like that. He always returned it in the early hours and then slept in the car until his morning shift.'

Becky knew where this was going.

'And where's this guy now?'

'Missing. The car park attendant didn't say anything because he said it never occurred to him that his mate was the one who had been killed. He believed what everyone else did. Then, when he didn't turn up for work, he wondered if he might be the killer.'

'And he still didn't say anything?'

'Seems that way, sir.'

'Stupid bugger,' Tom muttered. 'Okay, Keith, get back to the incident room and you and Becky brief the team. We need a name, and then we need someone to identify him. But – and this is critical – we do not release this information to the press. It's possible this guy was the intended target, but we don't know. And until we do, Edmunds' life could still be at risk, if he's not dead already.'

After Keith and Becky left the room, Tom sat back in his chair and forced his shoulders to relax. At least it sounded as if they might have found out who the victim was, and hopefully that would give them a new set of leads. He was about to head to the incident room when his mobile rang. He groaned when he saw who it was, but tried to put a friendly smile into his voice.

'Hi, Kate. Sorry, it's a bit hectic here right now, so unless it's anything vital I'll have to be quick.'

'Well, it depends on your definition of vital, I suppose. It's about the happiness of our daughter, but if you think your latest murder investigation is more important then I'm sure it will wait.'

Tom silently counted to ten.

'What's up?'

'She sent me a text this morning to say that she wanted to talk to me, so I called her before she went into school. She said you'd had words.'

'We did. Well, she had words with me. I told her the truth, or at least the part she allowed me to tell her before she stomped off, and she didn't like it.'

'The truth about what?'

'She asked if you'd suggested we should get back together for her sake when she was five. Apparently that's what you told her, and she didn't believe you. I confirmed you were telling the truth.'

For once Kate was silent. Tom waited. Finally she said softly, 'I didn't think you would do that.'

Tom chose not to respond, and Kate's appreciation of his honesty didn't last long.

'Anyway, she's coming home to me tonight, Tom. You can stand Louisa down. I'll pick Lucy up from school.'

'Is that her choice or yours?'

'I've told her it's the right decision, and now she knows I didn't lie to her she no longer has any reason to move out.'

'So where does that leave us all?' Tom asked.

'She'll stay with me. I've persuaded her that this is her home, and although I'm sure you make her welcome, she must be able to see that she's an inconvenience.'

Tom felt his face flush with anger. 'She is not, and never has been, an inconvenience. You know that. Don't you think she deserves to understand? We both know that your offer to come back had nothing to do with any love you might have felt for me. I came very close to saying yes, but it would only have been for Lucy, and what sort of a life would she have had with two parents who had lost not only their love, but their respect for each other?'

He heard her tut. 'You are such a romantic, Tom. How many marriages do you know that exist on nothing more than a little tolerance thinly disguising a shedload of resentment?'

'That's cynical even for you. We may both know people like that, but there are also some great marriages, with couples supporting and loving each other. I wouldn't want our daughter brought up in anything less.'

'So if she came to live with you and Louisa, she would bear witness to this utopia, would she? Well, maybe at some point she will, but for now I've convinced her this is where she has to be.'

Tom had never known his ex-wife to be so hard. 'What's going on, Kate? You sound bitter.'

'Goodbye, Tom. I've said all I want to say.'

She hung up.

28

I hear the front door slam as Dominic leaves to take Bailey to school. I watch him from the window and see that he's limping. Sometimes his leg is fine, but today it seems to be troubling him, and as always I feel a heavy beat of guilt.

There have been so many times I have wanted to tell him about Cameron, Jagger and my debt. But how could I, knowing that everything about our life together is in jeopardy and it's my fault? If it had only been the threat of violence, I could have turned to the police. But there was more, so much more, and if Dominic knew it all – who I really am – I would lose him.

Not for the first time, I wonder if everyone's life is composed of a series of roles, and I am not alone in striving to play each one to the best of my ability. Which of them is the real me? The head teacher – reliable, honest and assertive? The mother – gentle, loving, affectionate? The wife…?

I stop trying to think of adjectives for that role. I want to believe that I'm a good wife, but I'm fooling myself, because when I consider the other role – the clever, artful, disciplined, emotionless persona that few people know – I am forced to evaluate different words to describe my role as a wife: deceitful, duplicitous, scheming… I could go on, but I stop.

It would be better if I went to school. If I'm busy I will have something to focus on that might take away the gnawing anxiety that threatens to suffocate me. If I stay here with Dominic all day, his tolerance and good humour will paradoxically aggravate me.

I stand in my daughter's bedroom doorway and watch her.

She's still asleep, her little body worn out by the events of the previous evening. I'm about to creep over and drop a gentle kiss on her forehead when she stirs.

'Mummy?'

'I'm here, darling.' I sit down on the edge of her bed. 'How are you feeling?'

'Okay.' She sounds a little forlorn as if she's trying to be brave, and I stroke the hair back from her forehead. 'The man won't come again, will he?'

There is a prickle at the back of my neck. 'What man, darling?'

'The one Daddy says has been spying on us.'

I try to disguise my shock at the thought that Dominic has told Holly this. The poor child is terrified.

'Did you see him? Is that what scared you?'

'No, but I heard a man talking on the golf course and I thought it might be him. Daddy said not to tell you because you might be worried.'

I feel a stab of regret. Dom must have seen how concerned I was when he mentioned the man watching the house, and in his efforts to protect me from further anxiety, he's made the children his co-conspirators. They are the ones that should be protected. Not me.

'Oh, I'm sure no one's watching, Holls. I haven't seen anyone, so don't worry. Okay?'

She gives me a shaky nod, and after a few minutes I tell her I'll go and get her a drink.

Poor Holly. Is Dominic right? Is Scott watching us? He had plenty of time yesterday to get back from Colwyn Bay and break into the shed to leave the photo while I was wandering up and down the beach, but I can't let him frighten my children. He might think I'm fair game, but they are not.

My thoughts are interrupted by the sound of voices from the sitting room and I realise Dom has left Sky News running.

Walking through the door to switch the television off, I stop dead. On the screen is the face of Cameron Edmunds. It's an old picture, and a bad one, captured as he was leaving the casino, but it's definitely him. I've been scouring the Internet for updates on his murder but have heard nothing new. I'm still waiting for the knock on the door, and the threat of the police questioning me in front of Dominic is hanging in the air above me, blocking out the sun and darkening my world.

I reach for the remote and turn the volume up.

'Police are still refusing to confirm or deny that the body found in the Manchester city-centre car park is that of Cameron Edmunds, but earlier this morning his wife stepped out of their Cheshire home to give a statement to the press.'

The screen cuts to a young woman standing outside open high wrought-iron gates. Her blonde hair is elegantly styled, and she is so thin that even her immaculately applied make-up can't disguise how haggard she looks.

'The police have asked me not to speak to you, but I'm fed up with you all hanging around my house. You're upsetting the children, and I'd like you to leave, please.' She swivels her head from side to side, leaving no one in doubt that she means all of them.

The shouts of the journalists can be heard, asking if it's true that her husband is dead. Not for the first time I wonder how they can steel themselves to ask such insensitive questions.

She looks from side to side, as if deciding which journalist to talk to, and it seems she has chosen Sky News, because she turns to face the camera.

'I was asked by the police to identify the body, and I'm here to tell you that it wasn't Cameron. So please can you get yourselves away from my house, away from my children and stop bothering us.'

There are more questions, voices shouting in the background, but Cameron's wife turns and walks back down the drive, lifting her hand and pointing what appears to be a remote control, and soon all that can be seen is the disappearing back of Mrs Edmunds through the bars of the gate.

The studio anchor questions the reporter at the scene: 'So, David, what do we make of Mrs Edmunds' statement?'

'It's hard to say. We know that police have been at the house and several boxes have been removed, so it's clear they've undertaken a search, but as it seems certain that the victim – whoever he was – was killed in Mr Edmunds' car, they could have been searching for evidence that Edmunds is a suspect in the crime, if not the victim. The police have refused to comment, so we have to wonder if Mrs Edmunds simply wants to get the press away from her gate.'

I tune out of the rest of the report. Is he dead or isn't he? Was she lying, as the reporter suggested she might be? I feel torn. Half of me desperately wants Cameron to be dead. The other half needs him alive to keep the police from my door. He has ruined enough of my life already.

29

Then

The sound of laughter drifted through the door of my room from the corridor. There was a big party that night and the other girls were pretending to be cool about it but were rushing into each other's rooms, trying on clothes, testing out make-up. No one knocked on my door. I had told them I wasn't going. They knew something was wrong, but I couldn't tell them what; I was too ashamed. So I lay back on my bed, hands clasped behind my head, and listened to the music spilling from an open door and voices screeching along to Tom Jones singing 'Sex Bomb'.

Scott was due to come round that evening while everyone else was at the party. I was going to tell him what I had decided to do – what my plan was. I hadn't seen him in the two days since he had told me the whole sorry story, and the situation was far worse than I could ever have imagined. There was more than the missing three thousand pounds of charity money to worry about.

Once I'd got him up off the cobbles that night I made him tell me everything.

'No more secrets, Scott. I can't help you if you don't tell me the truth.'

'I do love you, Anna,' he repeated for about the third time, his arms wrapped tightly round my shoulders as I half-carried him back to my room.

Finally the words came, his voice quiet.

'I lied about my parents. I'm so sorry, but I was too ashamed to tell you the truth. My family are so proud of me, but they don't understand that when I leave uni I'm going to have a whacking great loan to pay off. My dad's been off work on the sick for years, but Mum keeps saying, "It'll be okay when Scott's finished university. You'll be able to take care of us, won't you, love?" They have no idea. They expect me to be making a fortune, not to be saddled with debts, and I didn't want them to be disillusioned.'

'Go on,' I said.

'Last year one of the guys suggested we should go to one of the casinos in town. Maybe play on the slots or even have a bit of a dabble at roulette, so I went along – for a laugh.' His eyes met mine for the first time. 'Lots of students are doing it, you know. It's not just me.'

I knew this was true. There were posters all over campus, offering help to people addicted to gambling, but I said nothing. If I'd stopped him talking he might never have started again.

'I became fascinated by the blackjack table, and one guy kept winning. He wasn't just lucky, Spike; he knew what he was doing. The idea of winning big time using skill – like the guy that night – appealed to me. So I learned everything I could about blackjack – how to play the odds, how to be a winner.'

Scott looked at me, a feverish glint in his eye, and I could see how much this meant to him. To my mind they were all games of chance, but there was no point saying so.

'To start with I won a few, lost a few, and I wasn't losing much but it felt like *too* much. The plan was to make money, so I decided to ignore all the strategies I'd researched and follow my gut instinct – same as most people, I guess. That's when I started to get into trouble.' He paused and took a deep breath. 'Things spiralled out of control. I lost too much, and the more I tried to recover my losses by playing dangerously in an attempt to win big time, the more I lost.'

I thought about the lie he had told me about football practice and now it all made sense. He hadn't wanted me to know that he was at a casino. I felt a paradoxical wave of relief that it wasn't because he was seeing another girl.

Scott turned his big, sad eyes on me, and I swam down into them and was lost. How could I let him down when he needed me so much? He dropped his gaze, and I knew there was more to come.

'That's when I made my biggest mistake. I borrowed money.'

'Who from?' I asked. But of course I knew.

'Cameron. I started by borrowing a thousand pounds, just so I had enough to pay for stuff plus a bit on the side to try to win back the money.' I stifled a groan. 'I thought I could win a few games and pay him off quickly, but I couldn't. His interest rates are massive, Anna. And I haven't paid him for two months, so this week he demanded money. But all I could give him was the three thousand I borrowed from you. It wasn't enough. I'm so far behind.'

'Three thousand in *interest*? His rates aren't bad. Ten per cent these days is good, isn't it?'

Scott stopped walking and turned to look at me. 'It's ten per cent, but that's per *month*. On the three thousand that you borrowed he's going to want three hundred handed over to Jagger every single month until you can pay back the three grand. If you miss a payment, he charges interest on that too.'

I stared at him, a sick feeling in my stomach.

'Why in God's name did you send me to him? *Why?* You know I can't pay that much. *Jesus*, Scott!'

'It was just a quick fix to get us out of the mess we were in so you didn't have to say the money was gone.'

'You mean it got *you* out of a mess. I was never *in* a mess.'

He dropped his head. 'This is all my fault, I know. Look, I promise I'll find a way to get you the money.'

I wasn't listening to his promises. All I could think of was my debt.

'What will happen if I don't pay?'

'I've told you not to worry,' he said, pulling me close again. 'You don't owe enough for him to do you any damage.'

But Jagger had beaten Scott up that night, and I felt sick at the thought of what he might do to me.

'How much do you owe him?' My voice sounded surprisingly calm. 'No more lies, Scott. It's all I can do not to walk away from you here and now, and never see you again. So how much?'

Scott spoke the words so softly I wasn't sure I had heard him properly.

'Twenty grand.'

I swallowed hard, resisting the temptation to yell at him again, to tell him what an idiot he was. Instead I tried to come up with a way out of the mess. He needed help, and more than I could give him. But every suggestion I put forward about involving the university, his parents, the police, fell on stony ground, and there was no disguising the terror in Scott's eyes.

'You don't get it, Anna. If Cameron's confronted or even arrested, Jagger will still be out there. He'll kill me. You've seen what I got for being behind with my interest. I can't risk exposing them.'

Maybe that would have been the time to tell Scott it was his problem, not mine, and walk away. But I loved him. I loved every moment I spent with him. I'd been happier and felt more alive in these few weeks than ever before. I couldn't give up on him now.

Furious as I was at the position he had put me in, anger wasn't going to help. We needed to work together to put this right. He had made a mistake. I would help him. I would come up with a plan.

As I lay on my bed waiting for Scott, I realised the corridor outside my room had fallen silent. Everyone had gone to the party. But I stayed where I was, eager to tell him my plans – my idea for how to save him. And myself.

By the time he arrived, I was sitting at my desk poring over my calculations. He slid through the door silently as if expecting someone to be waiting behind it and walked across to me, wrapping his arms around my shoulders.

'I've missed you,' he whispered.

I could hear the emotion in his voice and knew he was asking me, in his own way, if I felt the same. I stood up and turned to hug him. We clung to each other as if we were drowning, which perhaps we were, saying nothing, drawing comfort from the warmth of each other's bodies, until finally I gently pushed him away and turned back to my computer.

'What've you come up with?' he asked, peering at the screen.

'I have an idea, but it's risky and will only help with this month's payments. We'll have to think of something else after that.'

I had no idea what – even in my wildest dreams I couldn't keep coming up with something month after month. I hated what I was about to suggest, but we were out of options and I needed to meet my interest payments.

The back of my throat ached and I swallowed hard.

'We're going to do a parachute jump. I've printed sponsorship forms – one for each of us – and we can do it next weekend. We just need to get people to sign up for whatever they're prepared to give, and then collect the money when we've done it.'

I knew it was fraud and felt sick as the words tumbled from my mouth.

'I've found where we can do the jump, and it's not too far from where I live. You could come up for the weekend – stay with me. My mum and dad would love to meet you. Then we could do the training and everything together.'

Scott turned horrified eyes on me. 'I can't jump out of an aeroplane! Sponsorship's a great idea, but not that.'

I felt my eyes fill with tears. I thought he would be thrilled with my ingenuity.

He groaned. 'I'm sorry, Spike. I know you're trying to help, but I'm not sure I can face your parents either – not until I'm out of this mess. We're too stressed, and they're bound to feel it.'

He was probably right about that, but I couldn't help being disappointed. I was sure they would love him.

'What about a sponsored walk, or a run or…something?' he suggested.

'No one's going to pay big money for you to walk a few miles, are they? It needs to be something brave.'

'I get that. But don't we have to pay to do the jump?'

'We'd take the expenses from the money we raise. The rest would be ours.'

I was trying to kid myself that it really would be for charity because the money would be used to replace the cash I had collected and Scott had lost, but I knew it was wrong.

Scott scratched the side of his face as he thought. 'So why do the jump at all? Why not just say we've done it?'

'Because people need evidence. We'll need to show them our certificates.'

He shook his head. 'Come on – you know that's not true. Have you ever signed a sponsorship form and afterwards asked to see evidence that the person has completed the task? Anyway, we could find photos. No one's going to know it's not us, are they? They'll just see bodies floating down to earth. *And* we save the money it would cost us to do it, plus my train fare up to yours. We'd be much better off.'

I understood the logic, but to raise enough money I would have to rely on the support of people I had known all my life. Friends, family, maybe even some of the regulars at the hotel where Mum worked. And wherever in the country I said I was going to jump, I knew my parents would insist on coming to watch and cheer me on. I hated lying about where the money was going, but I had to cover the first payment, and I needed their help. And somehow doing the jump made it all seem slightly less wicked.

'I'll have to do it,' I said. 'We'll need separate forms, so if you don't think anyone will come along to support you, I suppose it doesn't matter whether you do it or not.'

Scott sighed. 'I'm sorry, Spike. Another of my many shortcomings is that I'm scared of heights.'

The thought of the jump terrified me too, but how difficult could it be?

'How much do you think we might make?' Scott asked.

'I'd hope to make at least five hundred pounds. Do you think you could do the same?'

Scott looked crestfallen. 'Is that all? It still won't be enough. We need to think of something else – something bigger.'

He was right. I would be able to pay one month's interest with a little to spare, but it wouldn't touch Scott's. We sat in miserable silence for a while, until he leaped up and punched the air.

'I've got it. Why don't we replicate the raffle – the one you raised the three grand for? We'd need to offer prizes, of course – probably a big win for someone.'

'Won't the prize take all the money?'

'Yes, if we actually declare a winner and *give* them the prize.'

'Won't people want to know who's won?' I asked.

He started to pace, hands behind his head, thinking out loud. I didn't like the sound of it.

'We'd have to go to other universities, different parts of Manchester, because you've been selling tickets here for weeks, so we could go to Salford Uni, Manchester Met, local colleges.' He spun towards me, clearly excited by his idea. 'Then we could produce a sheet with the winners on – fake names from different universities – but we'd make sure someone on each campus won something. That way everyone would know of a winner, even if they didn't know them personally, and hopefully no one would query the big prize.'

'What sort of prizes?'

'Something cheap, affordable. Things that students love. Maybe free pizza delivery, book tokens, cinema tickets, a Tesco voucher – things like that. Look, I'll email you some ideas. Can you design the tickets and get them printed? If you made three grand just around here, we could run it for – say – two months and easily get five. With that and the sponsorship for the parachute jump, we might keep Cameron off our backs until after Christmas.'

I knew this was only a temporary fix. We would have to come up with something bigger and far more profitable if we were to find enough money to cover the interest and start to repay both loans. But however sick I felt at what we were about to do, it was nothing to the fear of what Jagger would do to Scott, and very possibly me, if we failed to make our payments.

But I should have listened to the voice in my head, telling me that what we were about to do was wrong. Terribly wrong.

30

'What the hell does Dawn Edmunds think she's playing at?' Tom shouted as he stormed into the incident room. 'Becky, have you spoken to her?' He marched towards her desk and stood there, hands on hips, as if he was about to blame her for Mrs Edmunds' statement to the press.

'I've been trying to get hold of her since the news went out, but she's not answering her phone. I thought I'd go out there and explain that she might be putting her husband's life in danger. Do you want to come?'

'No, I bloody don't. I wouldn't be able to keep my temper. We've got officers there in case her husband comes home or someone decides to come looking for him. What the hell were *they* doing when she was chatting to the press? Having a cup of tea? Give them hell, Becky.'

Becky stayed silent. Tom was in a rare bad mood, and she could only assume it had something to do with the problems with his daughter.

'Keith, where are we with the details of the victim?' Tom stomped off towards the whiteboard, to which Keith was sticking photographs in perfectly straight lines.

Becky breathed a sigh of relief and turned to Lynsey. 'Do you want to come with me to see Mrs Edmunds, Lyns? Get out of here for a while? The house has to be seen to be believed.'

Lynsey leaped up from her desk, clearly as anxious as Becky to escape. But their getaway was thwarted.

'Becky, come and take a look at this.'

She winked at Lynsey, who was looking slightly terrified. The young detective sat back down abruptly and Becky made her way over to Tom.

'The victim in the car – the valet – is Derek Brent, we believe, so before you go off to read Mrs Edmunds the riot act, can you liaise with Keith and set up an investigation into Brent, as quietly and subtly as we can? All we say is that he appears to be missing and he might be vital to an ongoing investigation.' Tom tapped his finger on a name on the board. 'Next we have Roger Jagger. Tell Becky what you just told me, Keith.'

Keith pulled a piece of paper from below Jagger's name on the whiteboard and read from it. 'He isn't on any electoral register that we can find. He doesn't pay tax and isn't registered for National Insurance. We can't find any bank accounts in that name, nor can we find a driving licence. We have a Roger Jagger with a police record, but no address that is still valid, and we don't know if it's the same man.'

Tom turned to Becky. 'Is Jagger his real name or a pseudonym? We need to find him. It sounds like he's our best lead to track down Edmunds, who's been missing for a couple of days now. We need to make sure he's alive and safe.'

He turned back to the board. 'There was nothing of any use in the Edmunds' house, and for now we can't get into the safe. We've requested CCTV from the casino, and we've had officers there seeing if they can identify the woman he is sometimes seen with. A picture would be helpful, so see if we can grab a still from the CCTV when we finally get it. Get someone to check ANPR to see where he's been in the last week – anywhere that his wife might identify as out of the ordinary, if she knows what that is. I want to know where his phone went to sleep each night and where it woke up each morning. Whether he was the intended victim, the perpetrator, or is entirely irrelevant to our investigation, we need to know.'

Becky decided not to mention to Tom that most of these tasks had already been assigned. There was no point, so she merely nodded.

'I'll make sure everything's in hand before I go to see Mrs Edmunds,' she said evenly.

'Well, let me know when you're ready because I've decided I'm coming too. Her husband is now a missing person, flagged on PNC as locate/trace. We need to know everything about him – every last little sordid detail that she has implied but hasn't told us. Ring ahead and tell the officers on duty there that we would appreciate it if she's bloody sober when we get there.'

With that, Tom strode out of the room.

Becky ignored Keith's slightly shocked expression, turned to Lynsey and winced.

'I guess you wouldn't want to come now even if I suggested it, would you?'

'Err...no, I don't think so. Plenty to be getting on with here.' Lynsey grinned.

Becky laughed. 'Wish me luck.'

31

In the end I decide I can't stay at home – not even for the whole morning, let alone the whole day. Dominic is watching me with concerned eyes, and I have to get away so he can't see my confusion.

If Cameron's wife was telling the truth, it wasn't her husband's body in the car park. And, whatever the reporters think, I find it hard to doubt her. There was something depressingly indifferent about her, as if she didn't much care whether her husband was dead or not as long as the reporters moved away from her gate. Knowing Cameron as I do, that makes perfect sense.

School feels like a safer, calmer option, although Jennie can be uncannily perceptive too. I switch the radio to a music-only channel for my journey. I don't want to hear anyone's opinion on any subject at all right now, least of all on whether Cameron Edmunds Junior is dead or alive.

I still sometimes feel a tremor of fear as I drive through the school gates, scanning the car park for any vehicles that I don't recognise. Today it hits me hard as I remember the morning shortly after Dominic was hurt eighteen months ago, when I walked through the main entrance to find Jagger sitting on one of my new red chairs in reception, looking respectable in a suit, white shirt and tie.

'This gentleman would like to talk about his daughter, who's moving to the area,' Jennie informed me.

I wanted to scream at him to get out, to leave me in peace, but I couldn't, so in a shaky voice I politely invited him into my office.

I'd spent the days after Dominic's 'accident' looking over my shoulder, waiting for the inevitable moment when Jagger would strike, but I never expected him to have the audacity to march into my school.

I asked him to take a seat because Jennie could see through the glass window in the door between our offices, and with a charming smile, as if we really were chatting about his daughter, he cut straight to the chase.

'Your debt is off the scale, Anna. You're smart, and I imagine you've checked it out. Three thousand at ten per cent per month compound interest for – what – over twelve years? Billions, Anna. Billions.'

He was right. I had used an online calculator and nearly passed out when I saw the total. Three billion, give or take a million or two.

'Funny how it adds up, isn't it?' He gave me a sick smile. 'Cameron's not unreasonable, though. He knows you can't pay that, and it would be foolish to ask. So we've assessed your assets – looked at your house, both your cars, and we have a rough idea of their value. No mortgage, I understand. That's good, isn't it? Makes life easier.'

I didn't answer, the tightness of my throat making words impossible.

'Oh, and of course there's your mother's house!' He rolled his eyes. 'How could I forget that? How thoughtful of her to transfer ownership to you.'

I closed my eyes. How had he found that out? But he seemed to know everything. After my dad died, Mum thought it might help avoid inheritance tax if she transferred her house to me, as she was in her seventies. Although I told her repeatedly that the value of her home was below the tax threshold, she wouldn't change her mind.

'Governments switch these things around, so better to be safe than sorry,' she'd said.

Jagger was clearly waiting for me to say something, but there was nothing to say. The agreement could well be binding, but demanding repayment using threats of violence was definitely illegal. What would happen if I went to the police? Who would he hurt next? Dominic again? My mother? My children?

Jagger nodded as if my silence signified compliance. 'Cameron has decided that on the basis of the value of these two properties – around £450,000, we reckon – he'll settle for that. We expect to see sale boards up in the next two weeks.'

He stood with a further smile and walked towards the door. He turned, one hand on the knob. 'Oh, and Cameron asked me to mention – if you're thinking of stalling for time or seeking third-party advice – that he has some photos your husband, or indeed the trustees of the school, might be interested in. And of course we know where you live. Be seeing you, Anna.'

That was eighteen months ago, and I don't know how I made it through the next few days or how I managed to convince everyone that I was fine. When Jennie asked if there was something worrying me, I said I was concerned about Dominic's leg, which was true. In fact, it became a useful excuse for my erratic moods while I tried to figure out what I was going to do. How could I deprive my family and my own mother of their homes?

But I learned a vital lesson in those few days. I discovered that I was able to lie without blinking, and I taught myself to hide every emotion other than those I wanted people to see. I taught myself to become the other me.

There are no unknown cars outside school when I arrive today. It's one less thing to worry about, and so, pasting a smile on my face, I walk through the front door and head towards my room, giving a cheery wave to Jennie as I pass the window to the general office. The look I get from my friend and colleague is difficult to interpret. It's a smile but one that tells a story. A story that hasn't yet been shared with me.

With a frown I close the door to my room, expecting Jennie to come bounding in behind me with a cup of coffee, eager as ever to say hello and talk about the day ahead. But she doesn't appear. Maybe after my absence yesterday, and then again this morning, she is beginning to wonder if I am as reliable as I should be. I need to offer some explanation for yesterday, and I should do it straight away if I want to retain her trust, so I push back from my desk and walk through to the outer office.

Hanging onto the doorknob, I lean through the opening. 'Hi Jen, have you got a minute?' I give her my brightest smile.

Jennie looks up, and I'm shocked to see tears in her eyes.

'Are you okay? What's the matter? Come into my office and tell me what's upsetting you. Let me see if I can help.'

Jennie gives me a look that I can only describe as puzzled, but she stands up and follows me, grabbing a couple of tissues from a box. I guide her towards the sofa in what I call my 'cosy area', where I chat to parents and children in an informal way.

'I'm sorry for my absence yesterday and this morning. I know it was unprofessional, but there was something I had to do that I don't want to talk about. It's tricky, but I'll try not to make a habit of it.'

I smile as if I have cracked a small joke, but Jennie looks down at the tissue she is twisting in her hands. 'You don't have to tell me,' she says quietly.

'I know, but you're my friend and I don't like keeping things from you unless I absolutely have to.'

Jennie lifts anguished eyes towards me. 'I understand why you need to keep it a secret – we all do. You've been very specific about not wanting to talk about it, but it's impossible for me to say nothing, to act as if there's nothing wrong.'

I stare at her. What on earth is she talking about?

'Look, I don't know what you mean, Jen, but everything's fine. Really it is.'

'It's *not*, though!' Jennie is practically shouting. 'This is when you need your friends, so don't shut me out. I don't know how long you've got, but for God's sake, Anna, we can't ignore that it's happening. We care about you, you know. All of us.'

Now I'm totally bemused.

'Jennie, love, tell me what you're talking about. Please.'

Jennie raises her eyes in apparent frustration. 'Stop messing with me. You've posted it on the Internet, so it's not exactly a secret. You say you don't want to talk about it and that's fair enough, but can we just acknowledge it and then never mention it again?'

This is becoming weirder by the moment. I no longer know what questions to ask.

'And before you say another word, Anna, we're all chipping in. We'll get you the money. We've already been talking about ways we can help, and everyone's putting their minds to jumble sales, sponsored events, anything we can think of. We'll get you there.'

'Jennie, help me out here, please. Tell me what you mean.'

'Did you think we wouldn't see it? You can't put up a crowd-funding page and expect word not to get around. Look, I'm going to go and make us both a cup of coffee and then you need to tell me when you were diagnosed and what's going to happen. Then I promise that unless you want to talk about it, I won't mention it again.'

With that Jennie leans forward and wraps both her arms around me. Then with a choked-back sob she stands up and goes through the door, back into her own office.

I rest my elbows on my knees and cup my chin in my hands. My fingers feel cold, my throat dry. This is worse – far worse – than I thought. I know I'm going to have to look, but the idea makes my stomach turn over. Feeling like an old woman, I push myself slowly up from the sofa and go back to my desk. I stare at the screen for what feels like minutes before I can bring myself to open a browser and load the most popular crowd-funding site. I search on my name, and up pops a large picture of me, taken recently and without my knowledge. There are other photos of me, with Dominic and the children. These I recognise. They have been copied from my Facebook page.

I read the text with mounting horror. It describes – in first person as if I am speaking – how I have been diagnosed with a rare form of cancer and how I don't have long to live. I tell the world that I have one final wish – to visit family in Nebraska before I die.

'Oh, dear God,' I whisper.

I can't draw my gaze away from the screen. I can feel the panic rising in me. I'm horrified that someone would do this, and the fact that Nebraska is mentioned again makes my stomach turn over and I wonder if I will be sick.

I swallow hard, knowing I need to deal with this – and now. Scrolling to the bottom of the funding page, I see another photo. This time it isn't from my Facebook page; it's a picture of me going into the hospice in Wales, head down, deep in thought. And it is date- and time-stamped. Yesterday at 13.08 p.m.

I feel dizzy and grasp the edge of the desk, slumping in my chair. I have to take this page down. What if Dominic sees it? How can I explain it – any of it? But most of all, how can I explain my lie to him yesterday? How can I justify my visit to a hospice in north Wales?

My vision fragments as if I am looking at the world through a kaleidoscope. A sense of helplessness washes over me and I drop my head in my hands and try to control my breathing.

32

As I pace my office, waiting to hear back from the crowd-funding site about having the page removed and getting any donations refunded, I remember how I had thought our sponsorship scam was such a good idea. Now it haunts me.

Some people on the staff have already made contributions, and I know I will have to call a staff meeting for the end of the day. I'm still praying that Dominic hasn't seen the page. I can't think why he would, unless someone pointed him there, and that raises a question – how did the staff find out about it?

Once I have managed to calm myself a little, I call Jennie back into my office.

'Jen, I'm so sorry that you've been upset by what you read online. I have no idea how or why it happened, but it's not true. None of it. I'm going to explain to everyone later. And I'll tell them what's going to happen about getting their money back.'

Jennie stares at me as if she doesn't believe a word.

'It's true, Jen. Honestly, I'm not ill. I feel sick right now that someone would play such a trick on me, but I'm okay.'

'But what about that photo of you – taken yesterday, leaving that place? There was a huge sign right next to you with "hospice" on it.'

I stifle a sigh. 'I went to see someone. It's a long story and not relevant, but it was a wasted journey. How did you find out about the page on the funding site, though? It's not the kind of thing that you look at unless someone asks you to, is it?'

'No, there was an email sent to the school inbox. It said it was from a "concerned parent" although it wasn't a name I recognised. Do you want me to check?'

I nod, and she scurries back into her office, returning with a pink Post-it in her hand.

'It's not helpful,' she says with a shrug. 'It's a Gmail account – blackjack1981.'

I look away from Jennie. I can't let her see the shock that even I might not be able to disguise, although why I am surprised, I don't know. Blackjack – the cause of all our problems, and 1981 – the year of Scott's birth.

'What did the email say?'

'Nothing much. Only that he or she – it wasn't signed – had been very upset to see that you were so ill. That you were exactly what the school needed, and so on. And there was a link, so I clicked on it. And you saw where it took me. Why would I ever have doubted it? Especially as it opened by stating that you didn't want to talk about it. I nearly didn't say anything, but in the end I couldn't let it go.'

'Well, thank God for that. People could have been contributing for days before I realised.'

One thought fills me with dread. If the school has had an email, Dominic might have had one too. I need to know. There is a good chance he won't have seen it because he rarely gets email, and with Holly at home he has probably spent the day amusing her. I have to get Jennie out of the room, so I make some excuse about having phone calls to make, and with a watery smile she leaves me to it.

Fortunately I know Dom's password, because in our house we're not supposed to have secrets, so I log into his account and skim through the junk. And there it is, still unread, thank goodness. I quickly bin it, then go to his deleted folder and remove it from there too. I have been promised that the funding page will be taken down this afternoon, but until then I am going to keep the browser window open and check every few minutes in case a follow-up email is sent.

For a moment I think about the sponsorship drive I devised all those years ago. I feel nothing but disgust for the younger me and I have never forgiven myself for what I did. I was so desperate to get out of trouble and keep Scott safe that I persuaded people I knew and cared about to sponsor me – but at least I did the parachute jump, terrifying though it was. I can still hear the instructor's voice as he told me to climb out of the plane and hang on to the wing strut with both hands; I can feel the wind buffeting my cheeks as I waited for his signal to fling myself backwards and away from the plane, praying that my parachute would open.

Scott had more friends at university than I did and got a lot of sponsors, but he never did the jump, showing photos he had found on the Internet to anyone who asked for evidence. One man jumping from a plane looks much like any other.

Between that and the raffle, we got enough money – just – to cover our interest payments until after Christmas, which was a huge weight off my mind. I'd arranged a bar job in Keswick over the holiday to raise more money, and we rarely went out anywhere any more – saving every penny – although there were nights when Scott said he needed to catch up on his work, so I didn't see him.

I thought we were fine, and Scott made love to me with a passion and urgency that left me breathless. He seemed so confident that things were going to work out, and for a few weeks it was easier to believe him, to try to forget what we had done and the laws we had broken.

I realise now, with the benefit of hindsight, that I should have known it was a mirage, and that Scott's absences told a different story.

It was only when I got a phone call to say that he was in hospital, this time unconscious, that I admitted to myself what I had suspected all along. The realisation that I could have prevented it haunted me. I should have taken Scott's interest payments to Jagger along with my own. I should have recognised that he was addicted to gambling – that he believed he could win back all he had lost and turn the hard-earned hundreds we had made into thousands. Instead he failed to make his payments, and Cameron's revenge had been swift.

33

Then

I didn't eat or sleep for the five days that Scott was in hospital. I tried to talk to him about what had happened, but he turned his head away from me, although not before I saw the shame in his eyes. The police hadn't been able to get anything out of him either and said they had no viable suspects.

His injuries were worse this time, his face a mass of cuts and bruises. And that was only the damage I could see. His body had suffered, as it had before, but his spirit seemed to have died too. He barely spoke to me, and I could tell he was tortured by guilt.

Scott went back to his parents in north Wales as soon as he was discharged from hospital, the doctors saying he needed bed rest. I headed to Cumbria for Christmas but felt under the weather the whole time I was there. I was worried to death. My mum was overjoyed to have me home and fussed over me constantly. She made all my favourite meals, but I struggled to eat them.

'I'm sorry, Mum. This lasagne is delicious, but I've probably got used to eating a bit less while I've been away.'

'You do look a bit peaky, love.'

She looked so worried that I felt guilty fretting about Scott, but the nausea wouldn't go away and I lost weight, although I had precious little to lose.

Finally, the time came to return to Manchester, and the thought didn't fill me with joy. I couldn't wait to see Scott, but there was the dull weight of dread in my chest, not knowing if his beating was a precursor to more trouble. When he walked into my room that first evening, I was shocked by what I saw. The bruises on his face had faded, but the light had gone out of his eyes.

He hugged me tightly, both of us unable to speak. He smelled the same – clean, salty skin mixed with the old leather of his well-worn jacket – and I didn't want to let him go. We had spoken on the phone over the holiday, but it hadn't been easy. There had been so much left unsaid when we had parted and our conversations had felt stilted, so I had resorted to emailing him, telling him over and over how much I loved him. It was easier than saying the words out loud. I was scared that things between us might have changed, but feeling his arms around me, I forced myself to believe they were the same.

'I love you, Anna. I've missed you so much,' he whispered.

I squeezed him tighter, my eyes filling with tears at the sadness in his voice.

He led me towards the bed, and I thought we were going to make love, but I was wrong. We sat side by side and he grasped both my hands. He pulled me round to face him, but he didn't meet my eyes.

'Cameron's been in touch. He has an idea. I don't know what you'll think.'

I was fairly sure that if it was an idea of Cameron's I wouldn't like it.

'He says it's the way lots of people get the money to meet their payments – it's quite a common route for students to go down.' He took a deep breath and rushed out the next part of what appeared to be a prepared speech. 'It seems people will pay a lot of money for a bit of company – someone attractive to go with them to dinner, or the theatre, or to a party.' He tried to smile. 'It sounds perfect – going to some terrific places, eating the best food in Manchester, and getting *paid* for it – doesn't it?'

I didn't know if he meant him or me. I was afraid to ask.

'I could do it – lay on the charm,' he said, the enthusiasm in his voice not matching the dull expression in his eyes. 'There are some older women out there who like to be seen with a younger man. But the biggest call apparently is for young women to spend time with businessmen who fly in from all over the world and don't want to spend their evenings alone. I reckon you could do it a couple of times a week and easily clear five hundred a month – more if you were flexible.' He risked looking me in the eye. 'That's not so bad, is it? What do you think?'

I pulled my hands back sharply. 'You want me to be an *escort*?'

Scott hung his head. He didn't like it, I could tell, but I could feel his fear.

'You only have to be nice to the men.'

'Have *sex* with them?'

He reached for my hands again. 'No, no!'

I'm sure Cameron wanted me to do more than smile and flatter, which was probably what being 'flexible' meant.

Scott's voice dropped to a murmur. 'I wish I hadn't mentioned it. I'm sorry.'

I wanted to cry, scream, tell him he was a bastard for even considering it. But I couldn't. Desperation was rolling off him in waves, and I needed him on my side. I hadn't been planning to tell him that night, but now I had to.

'We have another problem, Scott.' I paused and took a deep breath. 'I'm pregnant.'

34

Tom had decided to let Becky take the wheel for their trip to Prestbury to see Mrs Edmunds. He needed the fear induced by her fast and furious driving to dislodge the hard ball of tension in his chest, so was slightly disappointed when she kept to the right side of the road on every corner and drove at a sensible speed. He closed his eyes and forced his shoulders to relax. Becky left him to his thoughts.

'Sorry about earlier,' he said finally.

'That's okay. You're the boss – you're allowed to lose it from time to time.'

'Not really, but it's just been one of those days.'

'Lucy?'

'Kate as much as Lucy. I don't know what's happened to her. We've always managed to be civil with each other; Lucy's the one that matters and she needs a good relationship with both her parents. But Kate seems to want to drive a wedge between us now.'

Becky was silent, and he wondered what she was thinking.

'How did Lucy say her mum's been?' she finally asked.

'Weird, I think was the word.'

'Could it be another man?'

'I don't know, and right now I don't want to think about it because I don't have the answer. Let's focus on Dawn Edmunds, shall we? Because here we are.'

The gates were standing open and deserted, the press having apparently decided that there was nothing of interest here now the victim wasn't Cameron Edmunds.

Becky's phone pinged as they were about to get out of the car. 'Keith's sent some images of the woman at the casino – the one who was with Cameron.'

'Good. Maybe Dawn will know who she is.'

'Doubt it – in the closest shots she has her head turned away from the camera. There are couple of long shots of her face, but they're pretty grainy.'

'Bugger. Well, we can ask, I suppose. I hope she's sober. I know our guys can't stop her drinking, and I shouldn't have suggested otherwise, but we need to get some information from her – some *real* information.'

They got out of the car and started towards the door, to be greeted by a young police officer in uniform. He looked at Tom warily.

'I'm sorry about what happened, sir. I had no idea she was going out to talk to the press. I'd gone to the bathroom, and PC Tinubu was talking to the nanny.'

Tom nodded. 'It's done now. We're here primarily to ensure that she and the children are safe if someone is still after her husband, and also so that we know immediately if he comes home. But bear in mind she's strong-willed and maybe impulsive, so keep an eye on her.'

Dawn was curled up in a corner of one of the sofas, looking totally different from the woman they had met only one day before. The perfect make-up was gone; the hair was tied back in a ponytail. She looked years younger and much more vulnerable.

She didn't wait for Tom to speak. 'I'm sorry. I shouldn't have gone out to talk to the press, but the whole thing was upsetting the kids.'

She had taken the wind out of Tom's sails and there was little point in showing his irritation.

'Mrs Edmunds—'

'Dawn, please. Just Dawn.'

'Dawn it is then. I need to ask you a question. I'm sorry if you find this upsetting, but we've been told that when your husband went to the casino he was sometimes accompanied by a woman, and we're trying to find her in the hope that she'll lead us to him. The CCTV shows her standing behind him as he places his bets, but we have no evidence that he either arrived or left with her.'

Dawn looked Tom in the eye. 'You're treading carefully as if I give a damn. I don't. He could have been shagging her senseless for all I care.'

'Right,' Tom said, there being no appropriate comment he could think of. 'Do you mind taking a look at a photo to see if you recognise her? We can't see her face, but if it's someone you know well, you might be able to recognise something about her.'

Tom nodded to Becky, who pulled up one of the images on her mobile and passed the phone across. Dawn looked at it for a couple of minutes, enlarging the image and moving it around.

'I don't, but she's a surprise.' She shrugged. 'Not his type at all, I'd have said. Doesn't look tarty enough. And she's got red hair, which he claims to hate.'

Tom was disappointed. He had hoped there might have been something about the woman that she recognised. They had drawn a blank at the casino too, although he was certain someone knew more than they were saying. They would try again when the night staff came on duty.

'When we met you, Dawn, you said that you had effectively been forced into marrying Cameron. What did you mean?'

She shuffled about a bit on the sofa, as if trying to find a comfy spot, and it now seemed she could no longer meet Tom's eyes.

'I was in my third year, studying history. I did something stupid, and Cameron found out. A mistake I've been paying for ever since.'

'What did you do?'

Dawn lifted her gaze to his. 'You're a police officer. Why the hell would I tell you?'

'Because anything we can find out about Cameron might be useful. He's still missing, Dawn, and a man has been killed.'

She frowned. 'Are you recording this? Because if I tell you, I don't want you to use it against me.'

Tom shook his head. 'We're here to try to find your husband. We're not after you, so unless you're going to admit to a major crime, you can relax.'

Dawn looked at her hands, playing distractedly with her fingers as she considered whether to speak.

'Okay. You can't prove anything, and it will be your word against mine if you try to arrest me.' She lifted her eyes and gave Tom a fierce look. 'I was involved in a carding scam when I was at uni in Manchester. I worked weekends at a hotel. Whenever I saw an opportunity I would call up to a likely-looking guest's room after he'd checked in and tell him the credit-card reader hadn't worked, but there was no need to come back down to reception; he could give me the details over the phone. It always worked – no one ever questioned it. Then I sold on the details for cash.'

Credit-card fraud had been one of Tom's focuses early on in his career as a detective, and Dawn was talking about several years ago when carding was much less sophisticated than it was now.

'Cameron was one of my victims. I'd heard stuff about him, but I was a cocky kid who for some bizarre and totally senseless reason thought it would be funny to get one over on him. I believed I was smarter.' Dawn gave a mirthless bark of laughter. 'I wasn't. He worked it out and came for me – with Jagger. I was terrified, but Cameron decided he liked the look of me, and having a wife and kids would make him appear more respectable. So he offered me two options – a criminal record or marry him. If it wasn't for my children, I would definitely think I'd made the wrong choice.'

'You said you'd heard stuff about him. What did you mean?' Tom asked.

'Cameron's dad vindicated the lack of attention he gave his son by ensuring he wanted for nothing. So Cameron was loaded, and he decided to use his father's money to make more for himself. He became widely recognised as the university loan shark – "helping" students and then fleecing them. I knew that, but nobody talked about what happened to the kids who failed to pay up. Nobody dared, and I didn't find out until after we were married. At least one kid committed suicide because of him. I eventually learned – too late – that he has no boundaries.'

Tom sat forward. If Cameron had hurt so many people, could one of them be seeking vengeance? Was he still in the same business? Tom knew that hundreds of thousands of households were in debt to loan sharks and for one of them this could be payback.

35

Nowhere feels safe to me any more. Scott has left a photo in my shed, and now that he's infiltrated my school with his emails and the sponsorship campaign it feels as if he can get to me wherever I am. I'm so ashamed of what we did, and terrified of what he is going to reveal on the radio on Monday. Even more petrifying is the thought that he might try to get to me through my children.

I still don't know how he survived, or how he managed to fake his own death. Why would he have done that? All I know is that I have to find him before he tears my life apart.

The staff meeting I called at the end of the day had gone as well as could be expected, and the staff had responded with shock when I told them that the page on the website was a complete fabrication – someone's idea of a joke. A few of them were bewildered by the idea that someone would want to pull such a terrible stunt, but I apologised profusely and promised to make sure every single one of them got their money back. If the site wouldn't refund it, I would give them the cash out of my own pocket.

I kept an eye on Dominic's inbox too. It seems I managed to catch the email in time, but my body feels as if it's trapped in a vice and someone is turning the screws, tightening the jaws inch by painful inch, minute by agonising minute. I will be crushed if I don't do something. I have to find Scott, to stop him, and I only have a few days left before every detail of my past life is revealed. I keep imagining the headlines and seeing the shock on people's faces. Most of all I picture Dominic's reaction to all I haven't told him and see nothing but disgust in his eyes.

Is that what Scott wants? There have been times recently – even before the radio programme – when I sensed eyes watching me. Has he been following me? It doesn't matter now. I need to draw him out so I can confront him. Anything is better than trying to anticipate what he's going to do next.

When I reach home I know Dominic can sense my tension, but I'm hoping that spending half an hour with Holly, telling her stories until she falls asleep, might soothe me as well as her. I kiss Bailey goodnight, and his eyes are already closing by the time I take myself into my daughter's room and lie down beside her on the bed to weave fantasies of far-flung beaches and painted elephants. Gradually I see her drift off to sleep, a smile on her face, and I kiss her gently.

'Love you,' I whisper against her ear.

Quietly I slip out of the room and into our bedroom. I can't stay up here all evening. It's only a couple of days since I last went out alone, but I'm finding it hard to breathe. I quickly undress, pull on my gym kit and make my way downstairs.

Dominic turns his head towards me as I walk into the room, and I see an expression in his eyes that I don't recognise. There is something sad in his gaze, and for a moment I wonder if I've pushed him too far. But he holds out a hand to me and I take it.

'You off?'

'Do you mind?' I ask, and he shrugs.

'I miss you when you go, but you're the one with the stressful job, so I understand it's what you need to do. Don't fall asleep again though, will you?'

He tries to smile, but it doesn't quite reach his eyes.

I'm not sure if I should go. There's something in the air – a sense of disquiet. I glance towards the window. Our lights are on, but the curtains are open. What if he's out there, looking in, watching us? I shake the feeling away and grab my car keys.

I could drive this route into Manchester with my eyes shut, I'm sure. For eighteen months I've been making the same journey at least twice a week – more frequently if I can find a plausible excuse. What started as a necessity, though, has become a part of my life that I keep telling myself will end soon. However, I'm not sure I believe that.

I drive into the underground car park and head towards the bay reserved for my apartment, right next to the lift.

'Shit!' I mutter, when I see someone has taken my spot. I slam the car into reverse and back into the one remaining spot in the furthest corner.

The car park is quiet, as it always is at this time in the evening. Thick concrete pillars cast shadows from the few ceiling lamps, some of them flickering, creating a strobe effect. My trainers make no sound as I walk. It is eerily silent.

I hear a dull bump, as if a soft object has hit something hard, then a rustling sound coming from the other side of one of the pillars, like fabric brushing on fabric, maybe two legs rubbing together as someone moves.

I stop dead. 'Who's there?'

Nothing. The silence returns.

I wait a moment and then start to walk again, faster this time. I want to run, but then I wouldn't be able to hear. I force myself to stay calm and look around – to the left, to the right, over my shoulder. I squeeze between two cars and stop dead. A man has stepped out from behind one of the pillars and is standing facing me, hands held loosely at his side.

There's no point screaming. No one will hear me. I think of running for my car, but he will catch me. I know he can move quickly, and I know how dangerous he is.

'What do you want?' I ask, swallowing the lump that's threatening to choke me.

'We need money. It's time for a payment,' Jagger says. 'A big one.'

'Cameron gave me until Christmas.' It's true, but there are no rules in this game.

Jagger slowly shakes his head. 'Things have changed. He needs cash, and he needs it now.'

He's had cash, lots of it, from me. Usually I find Jagger waiting for me in the street, lurking at the mouth of a dark alley – just where he belongs. He rarely speaks. He simply holds out his hand, and I pass him an envelope stuffed with notes.

'So Cameron's wife was telling the truth. It wasn't him in the car.' I try to keep the disappointment from my voice, but Jagger scowls and I rush to say something else. 'Do you know who tried to kill him?'

'I'm working on it.'

I have to ask, and the words tumble from my lips before I can stop them. 'Do you think it was Scott?'

Jagger looks at me as if I'm deranged. 'Scott *Roberts*? He's dead, Anna. I know you were besotted, but don't go imagining things. Just get me the money.'

I move to Jagger's left to pass him, but he reaches out a hand that feels as if it's made of steel and wraps his fingers around my arm.

'Don't fuck with me. *Tonight*, Anna! No excuses.'

I struggle to break free of his grasp, anger and an explosion of panic making me reckless.

'Go screw yourself, Jagger.'

He laughs at my boldness.

'You owe him. Twenty-five grand. Tonight. I'll be waiting, and if you don't have it I'll be taking a little trip to see your mum. So isolated, her house, isn't it? She must get scared from time to time.'

I feel my T-shirt sticking to my back, but I can't let Jagger know how he's making me feel.

'I'm sick of your threats. It can hardly come as a surprise to you that someone wants Cameron dead. Maybe you'll be next, and frankly I don't give a shit.'

Jagger grabs me by the throat and pushes me against the pillar. This time he's not laughing.

'You might think you can evade me tonight, but tomorrow and every day after until we're paid I will be in your face. At home, at school. You can't hide, Anna. I'll see you very soon.'

36

I flee from the car park into the lift, whimpering with relief when the doors close, then rush into the apartment, slamming the door, leaning hard against it. My legs are shaking so much that I need to sit down. The anger I felt as I stood looking at Jagger's weasel-like features has gone, the adrenaline fading with it. I dart into the bathroom, knowing I need to shower the cold sweat from my body.

I didn't need this tonight. Isn't it bad enough that Scott is promising to destroy the safe, stable parts of my life? Just as I am three people, I have three lives: home, school – both of which have felt calm, steady and secure – and my secret life; precarious, thrilling but until tonight carefully under my control.

I still don't know what Scott intends to do, how he plans to make me suffer. I pause as I remember Jagger's conviction that Scott is dead. Until recently I believed that too, and I still have no idea how he survived what I did to him, or why he would fake his own death and allow his family to mourn him. But I saw him with my own eyes, fleeing from the hospice. And who else would leave his photograph in our shed? Who else knew about the scams, the fraud and Nebraska?

Of course it's Scott. Jagger is wrong.

Jagger. I don't want to think about what happened in the car park, but however brave I felt then, the danger hasn't gone away. I know what Cameron will do if I don't get him his money. He'll start with the photos – the ones he took of me all those years ago – then he'll get Jagger to pay Mum a visit. I *can't* let that happen. If

I don't fix this, we'll lose our house, Mum's too, and my family will fall apart. I have to get him the cash, and I have to do it tonight.

I dry myself and hurry to the mirror to start the remodelling of Anna Franklyn into the other me. My hands are shaking as I put on make-up and clothes, then deftly arrange a blonde wig and apply an extra layer of dark red lipstick.

Saskia Peterson is ready.

I stare at the face in the mirror and stop shaking. Saskia is scared of no one. She knows no guilt. She is true to herself and she's good at what she does. More than good. Saskia moves confidently – her stride long, her hips swaying as if there is a beat in her head that no one else can hear.

If I manage to pay Cameron the money he is demanding, maybe it will be enough and Saskia can fade into obscurity. I have always thought that would be a good day, but she is part of me now, a part I don't think I can let go. Because while Anna has kept her feet firmly on the ground, Saskia has learned to fly.

I pull a handbag from the wardrobe and make my way out of the door, down the staircase to the main entrance of the building and out onto the street.

I don't have far to walk, and tonight I am glad. Once again I feel as if eyes are watching me, and I glance across the street to a dark doorway. I'm sure I can see someone there. But maybe it's a shadow, or perhaps Jagger is checking that I'm doing as he demanded.

My work is about to begin. It's an easy way to make money, and one that I enjoy more than I can say. And I have Cameron to thank for that.

And Scott, of course. It all started with Scott.

37

Then

Two weeks after our return to university following the Christmas break, I decided I had to do something. Scott seemed to be falling apart. He looked lost – as if he was in a huge hole and didn't know how to climb out. He was gambling again, I was certain, using the latest instalment of his student loan in the belief that he would get lucky. I wanted to beg him to stop, but then the last of his hope would crumble and the remaining morsels of bravado that were holding him together would disintegrate.

I can still see his expression the night I told him I was pregnant – the horror on his face. Was he simply shocked that I was pregnant, or was he dismayed because it scuppered his plan for me to work as an escort?

'Have you made arrangements?' he finally asked. He didn't say what for, but I knew.

'You mean an abortion?'

He nodded.

I burst into tears. 'No. And you haven't even asked me how I feel about it.'

He pulled me to him, stroking my hair as I sobbed.

'I'm so sorry, Spike. I'm such an idiot. I was just surprised. I'm so focused on getting that twat Cameron off my back that I rarely think of anything else. How *do* you feel?'

I looked at his face and could see the panic in his eyes. To him this was just one more problem – but that wasn't how it felt to me.

'I don't want a termination, Scott. I know some people

think it's nothing and other girls do it as soon as a pregnancy is inconvenient, but to me it's a baby. *Our* baby. There's a life growing inside me, wanting to be loved.'

We talked for hours, Scott giving all the logical reasons why an abortion would be best, while I tried to explain why I didn't think I could do it. In the end I said we should leave it for a couple of weeks – let the idea settle, rather than make a snap decision.

But I knew I was going to have the baby.

The more immediate problem was how to keep Jagger off our backs. Scott had no chance of complying with Cameron's demands, and I couldn't even afford my own interest payments. I had no idea what punishment would be meted out to me if I failed to pay. There was only one thing to do. I was going to have to speak to Cameron.

I hadn't seen him since the day I had signed the agreement. All interest payments were made via Jagger, just as all penalties were imposed by him. I had no idea if Cameron still hung out in the same place, but I thought it likely given the set-up in the back room.

Going there that night was the hardest thing I had ever done, but as I walked into the crowded bar I thought only of my unborn child. If Jagger hurt me, it could harm my baby. And that couldn't happen.

My spiky hair had grown out a bit by then, and although I had kept it blonde, it suited me as it waved over my ears and the back of my neck. I dressed with care in the new jeans my parents had bought me for Christmas and a black V-neck sweater. I didn't want Cameron to realise how badly he was hurting us.

He was seated in exactly the same spot as last time, facing the door, surrounded by what I now recognised as his usual bunch of sycophants, hanging on his every word, laughing at whatever he said. Cameron spotted me immediately and raised his eyebrows. Jagger followed his gaze and, without a word, got up and walked towards me.

'What do you want?' he asked without preamble.

My mouth turned dry, and I struggled to get the words out. 'To see Cameron,' I finally managed.

'He's busy.'

I didn't know what to say. I couldn't deal with Jagger. I didn't know if I could deal with Cameron either, but at least his corruption was concealed under a layer of fake respectability.

I was about to leave when over Jagger's shoulder I saw Cameron stand up. He was coming towards me. 'Anna!' he said, as if we were old friends and it was a happy reunion.

'I wondered if I could have a few minutes of your time.' I sounded like a supplicant, and hated myself for it.

He beamed. 'Of course.'

Like last time we went into the small back room, where Cameron and I took the seats while Jagger stood behind me. It was supposed to intimidate me, and it worked.

'How's that boyfriend of yours doing? Someone told me he'd had a bit of a mauling. Football thugs or something, wasn't it?'

He was smiling as if showing his concern, but there was neither humour nor sympathy in his eyes. They glittered with something that looked like amusement.

'He's fine.'

My stomach was in knots, but I tried hard not to sound nervous, reminding myself that Cameron wasn't much more than a boy. He was only a couple of years older than I was. Jagger was something else entirely. Young as he was, he looked like a man who'd had a hard childhood in a rough neighbourhood, but he was clever. It was a dangerous mixture.

Cameron's head was on one side, waiting for me to speak.

'I misunderstood the terms of the loan agreement.' I couldn't put the blame on him; I had to be the guilty party here. 'I'm going to struggle to meet the repayments, and I'd like to help Scott too, if I can, so I was thinking that maybe I could work for you to cover the interest. I don't know what you need. Cleaning, ironing?'

He smirked. 'I'm rich. I have a housekeeper. Think again, Anna.'

I swallowed hard. 'Is there nothing I can do?'

I could hear the pleading note in my voice and wished I could be stronger.

'We made a suggestion to young Scott. Did he not pass on the message?'

Scott had told me the idea of being an escort had come from Cameron, but he couldn't force me to do that, surely?

'I'm not prepared to be a prostitute,' I said quietly.

I saw Cameron raise an eyebrow at Jagger, who sniggered. 'A word, Cameron?'

Cameron nodded, stood up and went to the far end of the room with Jagger, who spoke quietly, Cameron lowering his head to listen. I had no idea what they were talking about and clasped my hands together to stop them shaking. Then Cameron sauntered back towards the table, pulled out the chair again, and sat down.

'Okay, missy.' His condescending tone grated on me, but I was in no position to object. 'Jagger, who among his many talents is a very wise man, has made a suggestion that might well work. There is a naivety to you that we think some men would like.'

I shivered. He wasn't going to give up, but neither was I.

'I've told you: I'm not prepared to be a prostitute.'

'We got that, and frankly I don't think you'd be much good at it. Tell me, have you ever been to a casino?'

I shook my head, trying not to shudder at the thought of all the problems gambling had caused me.

'I need someone to work for me four nights a week – possibly long nights. My father owns a casino in town, did you know that?'

I didn't, but now it made perfect sense. Cameron would know who was losing and then offer them loans. *Bastard.*

'We often have visitors from out of town, and they get lonely. They need company at the tables – roulette, blackjack, poker. Someone to encourage them, to keep them at the tables for longer, persuade them to place higher bets to impress the girl by their side.'

I didn't want to set foot in a casino, but if it was the only way, I would do it.

'Do I have to play?' I asked.

'No. Never. You don't have to fuck the men either, so there's a bonus for you. In fact, you never have to leave the premises with them.'

The thought of how I would have to behave, the falseness of it, was almost more than I could bear. I wanted to walk away, to say no, to find some other way. But I was out of ideas.

'Okay,' I whispered.

I worked for Cameron for three months, and he was right about the sex, although it was frequently suggested. But it turned out I was expected to lean against the clients and smile up into their faces, to let them touch me, put their arms around my shoulders and fondle my knees. What I didn't know was that every encounter, every inappropriate touch, every fake smile, was being recorded by the secret cameras hidden in the lights, making me appear to be exactly what I had refused to be. A prostitute.

And then it was over. I was out, and the interest started to mount again. But that was okay because by then we had a solid plan. We knew how we were going to repay our debts.

38

Now

I push open the elaborate glass doors and stride confidently into the building, remembering that misty night eighteen months ago when Jagger and Cameron accosted me as I was leaving my school. It's because of them that I'm here now – in a place I swore I would never return to after Cameron sacked me all those years ago. Yet here I am. I broke my promise to myself because I believed I had no choice. I didn't want to return, but it seemed there was no other way.

As I step onto the balcony and look at the vast room below I immediately feel a pulse of energy. I breathe in and out slowly, drinking in the atmosphere, listening to the clatter of the chips as they are scraped from the tables, the pinging of fruit machines and the occasional cry of elation or dismay from one of the punters.

I no longer come here because I need to. I'm here because it's where I want to be, where I come alive. It doesn't matter that my winnings all go to Cameron. It's the thrill of the game that has me hooked – and he knows it. He has a sixth sense where I'm concerned, because within seconds of my arrival his eyes always lift from the gold-topped blackjack table to the balcony where I'm standing now.

I remember my shock when I realised that there was a reason that only one table – the one he plays at – has gold-coloured baize instead of dark red. It is the high-stakes table, where a player can stake up to fifteen thousand pounds on one hand, betting on unseen cards. That's where Cameron plays. And he seems to lose far more than he wins.

It was strange not to see him at his usual spot on Monday night, but sometimes he arrives after I leave. Other times Jagger is waiting to tell me that Cameron wants me by his side at the table, and his wish is my command. He believes my presence brings him luck, although there is no evidence of that.

When Cameron demanded that I put our house and my mother's up for sale, I knew I had to do something desperate, something I would never have dreamed of doing under normal circumstances. But there was no longer any such thing as normal. There was only one way I might be able to get that amount of money. I had to win it.

Thoughts of Scott tortured me during those first weeks. It was because of his gambling that I was in this mess, but finally I understood the feeling of euphoria he experienced when he won, even if I couldn't forgive him for persisting when he lost. I wasn't going to follow in Scott's footsteps, though. I wasn't going to play blackjack. It relies too much on luck, and I needed to feel in control.

I had learned a lot in the months that I worked for Cameron, hanging around the men who paid for my company, watching them play, encouraging them to take chances, and I always thought I could do better. But there was only one game I ever considered playing – the only one with a human element that relied on the ability to read a situation, calculate the risks and analyse the strengths and weaknesses of other players.

Poker.

I had no idea if I could do it, but I had to try. I didn't want Cameron to know what I was planning, so while Dominic lay in his hospital bed I went straight from visiting him to a casino – one where I knew no one and which held no memories of Scott.

My mother had come to help with the children and she thought I was spending all my time with Dominic. I prayed she would never say a word to him, but I was doing it for us. How could I tell him that I had run up debts when I was at university, and they were the reason he had been attacked? I couldn't tell him that without telling him the rest, and I wasn't prepared to do that. So it was my responsibility to fix this.

Walking into a casino alone for the first time eighteen months ago, knowing I was going to be playing for money – my money – was the most terrifying thing I had ever done; worse by far than jumping out of an aeroplane, because my home, my family, depended on my success.

I remember moving towards the poker lounge slowly, as if delaying the moment, then walking blindly to a seat, almost stumbling as I pulled it out to sit down. My mouth was dry, but I hadn't brought a drink with me, scared I would spill it on the table despite the special glass holders.

The other players seemed focused and barely registered my arrival. Some had huge piles of chips in front of them, and mine looked paltry in comparison. But I had enough for the buy-in, and I had to believe in myself.

At first I played cautiously, trying to recall how it worked. I remembered that two cards were dealt to each player – the hole cards. I lifted the corners of mine to sneak a look. A king and a four. I was either going to have to put some money on the table or fold. Nerves got the better of me and I decided to fold.

As the five community cards were dealt into the centre of the table – first the three flop cards, then the turn and finally the river – I could see I would have had two pairs and would have won the hand. But the odds had been against me, and I could never have predicted that outcome.

After four hands I still hadn't placed a bet. I knew I either had to do this or get up from my chair and go and tell Dominic that we had to sell our house. And then have the same conversation with my mum.

It was time to be brave. I had to be much more ambitious.

Maybe the moment to be daring was misjudged. I was dealt two spades. It seemed worth the risk, so I bet. At the flop there were two more spades and I felt a flutter of excitement. I needed one more for a flush – a good hand – and there were two more cards to be laid down.

Neither was a spade.

I felt sick. The betting had been high throughout the hand, and I had put in too much. It was time for me to do the sensible thing – fold – but if I did that, I would never have the nerve to play for higher stakes. And I had to, if I was ever to repay Cameron.

Something happened to me at that moment. I forced my shoulders to drop, my head to lift and I placed my bet. Fifty pounds on a hand with nothing. I gazed confidently around the table. The player on my left raised to one hundred. He was fiddling with his chips, lifting them and dropping them. Was he nervous?

He lifted his eyes and I saw what looked like a hint of defiance. Was he bluffing?

The player to my right folded. There were two of us left, and my opponent's last bet was for a hundred pounds. I was certain, based on his betting and his body language, that if we went to showdown, I would lose.

That was the moment I became Saskia Peterson – the woman I had always believed I could be – a woman with confidence who apologised for nothing, who was every bit as good as everyone else, maybe even better.

As Anna I would have folded, choosing the sensible path and cutting my losses. But I was Saskia, so I raised to two hundred, my mood defiant, hoping my opponent would think he was beaten. It was make-or-break time.

The man stared at the table. He had lost a few hands earlier and he was down on the night, but if he raised again I couldn't match him. I had just fifty pounds left. If he called, I was certain I would lose.

I stared straight ahead, my face expressionless, until I heard a grunt of annoyance as he pushed his cards into the centre of the table. 'Fold.'

At that moment I felt a burst of elation as the tension that had gripped me exploded into a million glittering fragments. I had won! I wanted to dance, to sing, to shout – even to cry. And that feeling has never left me. But the part of me that people could see remained impassive, my eyes blank.

No matter how often I play, my muscles tense as I take my seat at the table and my heart speeds up. But no one can tell, and that's the way I like it. To this day I don't know who had the better hand that night. He had folded so there was no showdown, and I had no obligation to reveal my hand. But I am certain his cards would have beaten mine.

One week after my first success at the poker table I got a message that Cameron wanted to see me. The venue was the casino where I had worked for him all those years ago – the casino I am standing in right now.

I knew what he wanted, and I could only hope and pray that he would listen. He met me on the balcony, looking down on the scene below.

'Jagger's been checking,' he said without preamble. There was no hint of a smile on his face. 'The houses are not on the market. You've been warned, Anna.'

'I know. But I have another plan, Cameron.'

'Don't fuck with me, lady,' he said. 'Sell the houses – and quickly. There's no other plan. Where else are you going to get the sort of money you owe me?'

That was when I glanced towards the tables below me. 'I'll win it.'

Jagger barked out a laugh, and Cameron narrowed his eyes. 'Do you know how much money I lose on these tables each week? And I'm good at it. Don't be so fucking stupid.'

'Not blackjack. Poker.'

Cameron was shaking his head. 'I'm not prepared to wait another twelve years while you piss around winning a fiver here and there. You'd have to be winning thousands each week, and have you even got the buy-in for the big games?'

I couldn't admit that I had no idea how much that was these days; I'd been playing small stakes.

'Give me six months to get you the first payment. If you'll take a hundred grand then, I'll make the rest within a year after that. Will that do?'

'Why would I agree to this?'

'Maybe because you like taking risks.' I couldn't believe my own bravery as I said the words.

He stared at me long and hard. 'If you fail on one single payment, you will immediately sell both houses, and you'll pay an additional one year of interest.'

I remember gritting my teeth, knowing how massive a gamble this was. 'Let's worry about that if it happens, shall we? Watch me, Cameron. Then you'll see I'm good enough.'

With that I'd headed downstairs and into the poker lounge, walking with a confidence I wasn't feeling. To show him I was serious, I was going to have to play to win and risk every penny I'd won the previous week.

Cameron watched me that first night, certain I would lose – but I didn't, and he walked away without another word. He will never know how I felt, how close I had come to falling to my knees, begging him to let me find another way. Whatever confidence I had managed to exude was fake. I didn't know if I could do it, but I had to try.

It was so difficult for me at the beginning, lying to Dominic about the gym, telling him I had a sudden desire to get fit and learn self-defence after what had happened to him, getting changed and putting on my make-up and wig in the back of my car, living in fear of him checking the contents of my 'gym bag'. I knew Jagger continued to watch me play and reported back to Cameron, so I wasn't completely surprised when after two weeks he was waiting for me, barring my way into the poker lounge. I thought he had come to tell me it was over, that I'd lost because I wasn't winning enough to satisfy Cameron.

He held out an envelope. 'What's this?' I asked, suspicious of anything to do with Jagger.

'From Cameron.'

I opened the envelope and peered inside. Money – lots of it.

I looked up at Jagger. 'Why?'

'You're pissing around winning a few hundred here and there. Time to get serious, Anna. If you lose it, we add it to your account.'

I wanted to push it back in his face, but I couldn't. He was right. I needed to be playing for more, upping the ante, risking a raise when I thought I had a good hand and the odds were in my favour, bluffing when I thought I could get away with it. I had been playing too safe, scared of losing my meagre resources.

I became increasingly successful, never missing one of Cameron's payments, and I realised I needed to look the part. The more professional I acted, the higher my winnings seemed to be, so I reinvested, renting the apartment with its parking spot close to the lift so no one saw Anna Franklyn sneak in through the car park. I didn't care who saw Saskia Peterson walk out of the front door.

Now, eighteen months later, I feel the adrenaline rush of the game without the fear. The occasional bad night isn't the end of the world, and I always hold some money back so I can play again.

Tonight is different, though. It feels like that first time – as if I have everything to lose. As I stand here on the balcony, I am conscious that Cameron isn't in his usual position at the blackjack table, following me with his eyes. Maybe it's better that he's not here, because I need to focus. Jagger wasn't bluffing. Cameron needs cash if he wants to avoid being found by whoever wants him dead.

I can only believe it has to be Scott. It's too much of a coincidence that the man Scott hated more than any other was targeted at the same time as the threats to reveal my past and ruin my life have been aired.

For a moment I feel a flash of white-hot anger and I grip the balcony rail tightly. How dare Scott do this? Everything I have suffered at the hands of Cameron and Jagger – the attack on Dominic, the lying and cheating of which I am so ashamed – all of it is down to him. Those intense feelings of first love blinded me, and I made mistakes. And I've been paying for them ever since. None of this would be happening if it hadn't been for Scott's weakness. How dare he torment me now?

I breathe slowly to calm myself. Tonight I have to play to win big, and to do that I need to control my breathing, focus my mind. After a few moments drinking in the familiar sight of the gaming hall below me, I feel ready to make my way downstairs to the bar.

'The usual, Saskia?' the barman says, and I nod with a smile of thanks. He squeezes some fresh lime, adds soda and ice and passes it to me. I never drink when I'm here; I need all my concentration. I pick up my glass and make my way through the hall, hearing shouts of delight and groans of despair as I pass the tables. I can't understand why roulette is so popular; the odds are not good enough for me. I walk to the back of the hall, to the glass wall on which are engraved the words POKER LOUNGE.

It's quiet in here. People concentrate, hide their true feelings, and I'm good at that. Deception seems to be something of a forte of mine, and I often wonder whether poker has led me to hide my true self, or whether I am a natural liar.

39

Tom spent a quiet evening at home, trying to work out what was going on with Lucy and Kate. He had sent Lucy an affectionate text, simply asking her if she was okay, rather than making her feel under any pressure from him. It sounded as if she was getting enough of that from her mother.

Louisa was working, and so, having knocked up a quick bowl of pasta for his dinner, he switched on some music and sat back, trying to empty his mind, hoping that inspiration would come to help him solve either the problems with his daughter and ex-wife, or the puzzle of the car park murder.

Keith had called Tom on his way home to say they now had all Edmunds' bank information, but he suspected it was only half the story. Money for household expenses appeared to come from an account in the name of Edmunds Senior, who had refused to return from his holiday now he knew his son wasn't dead. There was nothing in the accounts that reflected any money won or lost in the casino, though, and it had been confirmed that Cameron had been known to lose half a million in a bad week. It didn't take many bad blackjack hands at the top table for that to happen. Similarly, he had been known to win – and win a lot. But there was no sign of any of this cash.

So where was it? Where did his stake money come from and where did his winnings go? And was this related to what Dawn had hinted at? If Cameron had loaned money to students when he was at university, was he still doing that now? Illegally, Tom had to assume. There was certainly no record of him on the Financial Services Register.

The only bit of news they had was that one of the team had gone back to the casino earlier that evening to ask more questions about the redhead seen with Cameron, this time speaking to the dealer at Cameron's favourite blackjack table.

'I always assumed she was a tom,' he'd said with little interest.

'A prostitute? So Cameron Edmunds was her client?'

'Nah, I don't think so. He just liked having something pretty by his shoulder. She probably made more money massaging his ego than she did massaging any other part of him.'

Tom wasn't sure if this helped or not, but it sounded as if Cameron might have been a source of funds to the woman, so even if they traced her she was unlikely to bite the hand that was feeding her. It was probably another dead end, but she seemed to be the only lead they had.

He had just decided it might be worth risking a whisky as it was doubtful he would be called out again, when his phone rang.

'Tom, it's Becky. Sorry to disturb your evening, but there's been another murder. I'm at the scene, and I've got a feeling it's related to the Derek Brent/Cameron Edmunds case.'

Tom tucked his phone under his chin as he walked out of the kitchen to pick up his keys from the table in the hall. Thankful he hadn't started on the whisky, he headed towards the door.

'I'm on my way. Where are you?'

'Believe it or not, in another car park. This time it's under a posh block of flats off Whitworth Street. I'll send you the address.'

Tom slammed the front door behind him and hurried to his car, switching his phone to the car's speaker system. 'What do we know?'

'The victim is another man in his mid-thirties. No identification on him.'

'What else?'

'It looks like he was hit with a blunt object. Jumbo's here with his team, and they found a broken exhaust pipe under one of the cars, which looks like it could have been the weapon. That suggests it might have been opportunistic, rather than planned. The car park's fairly quiet at this time of night apparently. The victim looks as if he could handle himself, but even the toughest guy can be felled with a heavy bit of pipe.'

'Why do you think it might be related?'

'The location – we don't get many bodies in car parks – but also the state of the body. Jumbo says it looks as if he was hit from behind first, and once he was on the ground his head was beaten to a pulp. Then – probably after death, although the pathologist will have to confirm that – another injury was inflicted.'

'Go on.'

'Both of his kneecaps were shattered. It's a completely different MO, but what does it remind you of?'

What had Dawn Edmunds said? That Roger Jagger's speciality was kneecapping. Although typically that form of injury was from a gunshot to the knee, when he had pushed Dawn she had said she thought Jagger's weapon of choice was a hammer.

Had Jagger done this? Was this one of Cameron Edmunds' loan shark victims? Or had Edmunds and Jagger worked out who had tried to kill Cameron and sought retribution?

Maybe. Maybe not. Right now, though, Tom was more concerned with the fact that two bodies had turned up in different car parks within a period of three days. Was this the start of a killing spree? Would there be more?

40

By the time I take my place at the poker table, I feel in control. I wipe all other thoughts from my mind and concentrate on the game. I know what's at stake. I need to be devoid of feeling. Only the game matters.

I am relieved to see that Ju-long is playing. He is possibly the worst player I've come across at this casino, but he is clearly wealthy. He raises when there is no chance of him winning, and he is responsible for about thirty per cent of my income. Maybe I can do this – win Cameron his money – if I keep my concentration.

There are five of us. Ju-long is two places to my left and between us is a man I haven't seen before. He's sweating and keeps wiping his face with a handkerchief. I'm hoping that's a good sign. To my right is a young man, probably no more than twenty. He seems relaxed and confident, and I don't like that. He's been here a few times recently, but not at my table so I'm not sure what to expect. To his right is a woman, late middle age, who looks as if she has smoked too much over the years. Her dark red painted lips have deep lines above and below them, but she's gone for a buy-in to match Ju-long and has a big pile of chips. It's a no-limit table, and I guess the stakes are going to be high. Just what I need.

One advantage of competing against poor players is that they often raise on weak hands, bluffing in the hope that other players will fold. I'm usually prepared to call their bets or even raise if I believe my hand has a reasonable chance, and it means the pot grows quickly.

I'm certain Ju-long has no idea how to calculate the odds

of winning, but the others at the table are unknown factors, so unless my hand is strong, I'm going to take it carefully. I have too much to lose – probably more than them. The downside is that I can't bluff Ju-long. He rarely folds and will bet high on a weak hand, but I can't risk doing the same.

The woman places the first bet – the small blind – and the young man follows with the big blind, and the hole cards are dealt. I lift the corners of my two to peek without risk of anyone seeing what I have. The jack of hearts and a four of spades. Nothing special. I could fold now, but the blind is low and it's not much to lose, so I call. The man to my left leans back with a sigh of frustration and folds. Ju-long, as expected, calls. He never folds before the flop. But he hasn't raised either.

Only one player has folded. The three flop cards are dealt. They do nothing to improve my situation. I'm not going to bluff. I don't know some of these players, and I want them to believe I play straight and only bet when I think I can win. That way it will be easier to bluff later – if Ju-long takes a break. The odds of me winning this hand are too low, so I fold and watch the others as the rest of the cards are played. The young man folds on the turn so it's between the woman and Ju-long. He has a glint in his eye and I know he has a good hand. Not brilliant, though – he fidgets when it's anything better than a straight. There is a pair of sixes on the table, so I guess he could be hoping for two pairs. As could the woman.

He raises, and the woman calls. The final card – the river – is dealt. It's a king, and I see his shoulders drop. It's not what he was hoping for. I watch the woman carefully. I need to understand her body language, but she doesn't give much away. She bets, and despite the fact that I know Ju-long hasn't got a good hand, he doesn't fold. He raises, and she folds. She's exactly the kind of player he likes – she adds consistently to the pot but doesn't have the nerve to go all the way. She will lose a lot tonight.

As play continues, I stick to my policy of watching and learning, remaining conservative with my bets. I'm winning, but not enough. I'm up about five thousand in the last hour, but it's time to push ahead. I decide to play one more hand and then take a break to centre myself again, to make myself believe I can do it.

The cards are dealt. I have two aces and I feel a shiver of excitement. I focus on holding my hands still, my face neutral.

I bet high, hoping my show of confidence will encourage some players to fold and increase my chance of winning. The man on my left shuffles in his seat for a minute or two then takes a sip of his drink, but finally he calls.

Ju-long raises, but it tells me nothing because his betting is erratic and unpredictable. The man on my left groans, and I'm sure he's going to fold next time round. That's good.

The woman calls, as does the young man. That's a disappointment – I would rather be rid of one of them before the flop – preferably both of them – but it adds to the pot, and I need that. Without hesitation I re-raise. As expected, the man on my left lets out a grunt of irritation and folds.

I have a feeling that this is my moment and it's all I can do not to lean forward eagerly and rest my elbows on the table. But I don't. I sit back and force my shoulders to relax.

It's Ju-long's turn to bet. He looks at his cards, and then round the table at each player, one by one. I don't know what he's going to do. He narrows his eyes as he stares at me, but I don't blink, and I don't look away.

Finally he calls, as does the woman. She must have two good cards, although at this stage of the game there is no such thing as a sure-fire winner. The young man folds. We are down to three players, and that's better odds for me.

The pot stands at £7000. I need more. Much more.

At the flop the three community cards don't improve things for me – the jack of hearts, seven of diamonds and king of hearts.

I don't react, but Ju-long's eyes have lit up. There are two hearts on the table, and I wonder if that is what's exciting him. Or maybe he's made a couple of pairs. I watch him carefully.

The woman checks, as I was sure she would, waiting to see if I make a continuation bet. I push chips to the value of £4000 onto the table. I am certain Ju-long will match me, but I don't want the woman to make it to the turn without at least adding substantially to the pot. If she folds, it will just be me and Ju-long.

Despite his apparent excitement, Ju-long only calls. With any other player, that might tell me something, but in his case it doesn't. To my surprise, the woman calls too. One of them, I'm sure, has hearts and I feel a beat of alarm. I can't lose this hand. I'm running out of time.

The turn comes. It's the ace of hearts, so I now have three of a kind. It's okay, but tonight I feel certain it won't be enough, especially as there is now another heart on the table.

I sense disappointment in Ju-long. He didn't want that card and he's fiddling with his chips, lifting them and letting them drop, clattering together. The sound sets my nerves on edge and I wish he would stop.

The woman checks. Maybe she has a flush or a straight. Either would beat my three aces. I check too.

To my surprise, Ju-long bets £5000. Is he trying to bluff us? I know he didn't like the card at the turn. I have to trust my instincts, and I have beaten him many times before in similar situations. I concentrate on my breathing. In, out, slowly. I can do this.

If I'm to have any hope of winning the money needed to meet Jagger's demands, I have to take a chance. A sudden image of my childhood home flashes into my mind to remind me what I'm playing for.

Focus, I repeat over and over in my head.

The woman calls. I've not seen her be this rash with her

betting before, and I still haven't got her measure. She is sticking with us but I'm starting to see an edge of unease in the way she is clenching and unclenching her fingers. There is no certainty of a win in her mind, and if pushed far enough, I'm sure she'll fold. Ju-long is a different matter.

Looking at the cards on the table, I attempt to work out what he might be hoping for. Thank God he's so transparent. He was excited by the flop but not by the turn, so it can't be hearts, which is good as a flush would beat my three of a kind. Maybe he too has three of a kind. But I have the aces. All I know for sure is that he is confident, but not so confident that he has gone all in.

I'm already in for six grand on this hand. If I call, I will be in for eleven. I'm going to have to push this as far as I can, or quit while I still have enough money to carry on playing.

It's a risk I'm prepared to take so I push my chips forward.

There is now over thirty thousand in the pot, and only the final card to go.

The silence round the table is intense. Even the two men who folded are riveted.

The card is dealt.

Not one muscle in my face or body reacts as I try not to stare too long at the table. The river card is the seven of spades! There's already a seven on the table, so together with the three aces I have a full house. Only three hands can beat me. My heart is hammering in my chest, and I can't believe that no one else can hear it.

Ju-long is fidgeting, and that's not a good sign. Does he have a straight flush – maybe even a royal flush? An unbeatable hand. He could have been bluffing with his lack of excitement at the ace of hearts, but I doubt it. Maybe he too has a full house. But I remind myself that I have the aces.

I glance at the woman. She's watching Ju-long, perhaps by now understanding that he won't fold. I think she's deciding how far she's prepared to go, because he will keep pushing. Can she trust that she has him beaten? She checks, biding her time.

It feels like anyone's game, but I don't believe her hand is as good as mine. I'm guessing she has a flush, but not a straight flush. A good hand, but she's wondering if it's enough. It's not, and I'm no longer worried about her. But Ju-long is a different story.

It's my turn to bet. The odds of anyone having better cards are slim. There is only one thing for me to do and I must do it quickly, before I lose my nerve. Because this is all or nothing for me.

'All in,' I say, as I push the whole of my remaining stack forward. Eight thousand pounds.

There's a gasp from the man on my left, who really needs to learn to be less vocal. Ju-long doesn't take his eyes from my face, and for a moment he looks puzzled, as if he can't imagine what I'm thinking. There is a flash of doubt and in that moment, I am certain I have won. He hesitates, then pushes his chips forward.

The woman shows her feelings for the first time. This is a step too far for her, and her face drops as she folds. She has lost eleven thousand pounds.

The winnings will give me the money for Cameron and my fund will be there for the next time I play. Because I know there will be a next time. If I lose, I'm finished.

It's time for the showdown and I pray I haven't misread Ju-long as our cards are flipped.

41

The scene in the car park was exactly as Becky had described it, the attack on the victim every bit as vicious. It was going to be hard to identify him from his face alone.

'What do you think?' Tom asked.

'Someone hated this man with a passion. Whoever killed him didn't just want him dead, he wanted to vent a lot of pent-up anger on him.'

Becky was right. The victim would have probably been dead after one or two of the blows to the head, but the assault had continued long after that.

'And then they had a go at his legs.'

Tom leaned against a pillar that had already been processed for evidence and folded his arms. Becky said her first thought had been that this could be one of Jagger's victims. But if this was someone who had failed to make a payment, what sense did it make to kill them? Unless this was a message to someone else.

'No identification on him?'

'Nothing – not even a phone, a receipt or cash. Maybe it was all taken by the killer, but you'd have thought they'd leave the normal rubbish people have in their pockets. Clean as a whistle.'

Jumbo walked over, and unusually for him, he was frowning.

'What do you make of the legs, Tom? We'll need it confirming by the pathologist, but I'm fairly certain the injuries were inflicted after he died. One of the bones has broken right through his jeans, but there is no blood at the site, which suggests his heart had stopped beating.'

'I was wondering about that. It seems a strange thing to do after death, doesn't it?'

'Unless it's a message, yes. I agree.'

'Ah, but what kind of message? Two murders – both in car parks. The first was execution style, and the ten-pound notes suggest it was some form of retribution. This appears to have been more spontaneous, but equally violent, the broken limbs suggesting either a revenge attack or – as you say – a message.'

Becky turned to look at the body again. 'I know the only slightly tenuous link is the fact that both murders were in car parks, but I can't get away from the idea that both are connected to Edmunds.'

Tom pushed himself off the pillar. 'It could be dangerous to assume a connection right now. It might blind us to other possibilities. Having said that, it should be one of our lines of enquiry. I assume we're checking that this guy isn't one of the residents?'

'Yes,' Becky said. 'Lynsey's up in the foyer with some uniforms. It's all in hand. And obviously any of the residents could be a suspect too.'

'Okay. If Dawn Edmunds is to be believed, Roger Jagger is a vicious bastard with a particular fondness for smashing people's kneecaps. Let's take a look at victims of unsolved attacks in the last couple of years, with particular emphasis on injuries to legs or knees, see if we can link any of them to either Cameron Edmunds or Roger Jagger. Also, check if any of them didn't make it home last night. And let's get a fuller picture of those two bastards. Whether Dawn's assessment of her husband is accurate or not, there's a lot about Edmunds that doesn't stack up, and he or his sidekick could be responsible for this poor guy's death.'

42

It takes me a few moments to take in what I am seeing in front of me. Now I understand why Ju-long wasn't excited by the ace of hearts. He wasn't making two pairs, a flush or even a full house, as I was anticipating. I would have beaten any of those with my ace-high full house.

He had something else. He had been dealt two sevens, and with the cards on the table he has four of a kind.

Ju-long has won.

I struggle to take it in. I can feel the other people at the table watching me. They know I have lost a lot of money, but they have no idea what it means to me. Jagger will be waiting. What will he do when I can't give him anything – not a single penny?

Finally, after what seems like minutes but is probably only seconds, I push my chair back from the table and stand up, my movements jerky. I hold the edge of the table for support for a moment before raising my head and walking from the room. More than anything I want to disappear, to run away and hide so I don't have to face what is to come.

I have no money left. I have a strict policy of always leaving half my money safely locked away, so that even after a bad night I have enough to play the next time. I have never strayed from this in the eighteen months I have been playing, but tonight I broke my own cardinal rule.

I feel detached as I walk through the dark Manchester streets, as if I'm floating high above my own body, staring down at this sad woman who has made one of the worst mistakes of her life.

Or maybe not the worst. Maybe just one of many. I think back to the eighteen-year-old girl who arrived at Manchester University with a thirst for excitement, filled with the belief that she could achieve great things.

Without knowing how I got here, I find myself in front of the apartment building, and I come down to earth with a crash. Through the glass doors I can see two uniformed policemen and one woman in a trouser suit standing in the foyer. For a moment I think they have come for me, and once again I want to run.

But I can't. I have to get back into my apartment, change my clothes and go home to face Dominic. It's time to tell him the truth.

Painting a smile on my face, I push open the door and feign surprise when one of the two uniformed officers stops me. 'Excuse me, madam. Can I ask if you live here?'

'I do, yes. I live in Apartment 624.'

He consults a list, flipping over the pages until he comes to the names for the sixth floor. 'And your name is?'

'Saskia Peterson. Can I ask why you need to know?'

'We're not at liberty to divulge any details, I'm afraid. Do you have any identification on you?'

I flash my keycard at him, hoping that is enough but doubting it. I have no identification in the name of Saskia Peterson, and I'm about to panic when I hear heavy breathing. Around the corner trundles the concierge, moving at an unusual speed for a person of his bulk. He is red in the face, his pupils dilated as if he's had a shock.

'Ooh, Miss Peterson. I'm glad you're safe,' he pants. 'Have they told you?'

'Mr Baldwin, if you remember, we asked you not to talk about the incident,' the young woman says, a hint of frustration in her tone. I presume by her clothing that she's a detective.

'Oh, sorry,' Mr Baldwin says. 'This is one of the residents.

You weren't questioning Miss Peterson, were you? She's been out. I saw her go. It was well before everything kicked off.'

He earns himself another irritated look, and the older of the two uniformed officers turns back to me.

'It's okay, Ms Peterson. Mr Baldwin has confirmed your identity. Thanks for your time.'

This is my dismissal. I'm relieved to get away, and I'm about to head towards the lift when the detective speaks: 'Will you be staying home for the rest of the night, Ms Peterson?'

How can I tell her I'm just coming in to get changed so I can go home to my husband?

'I expect so, yes,' I lie, knowing that I don't have to come back through the main entrance. I will leave through the car park and hope the police presence in the foyer has frightened Jagger off. Maybe all this will buy me some time.

I quickly shower away the perfume and make-up and pull on some tracksuit bottoms and a pair of flip-flops for my drive home. Moving as quickly as I can, I head for the lift, anxious to get back to my children. Their pull is so strong it makes my heart turn over. I have no idea what the consequences of my mistakes will be for my family, and I want to spend every precious moment close to them.

The doors to the lift open into the car park, and I immediately realise my mistake. There are more police officers down here – many more. And some of them are dressed in white suits. This is a crime scene.

Jagger. He was here. Who has he hurt this time? It can't be Dominic – he's at home with the children. Perhaps some poor unfortunate guy looked at him the wrong way and paid the price. Maybe someone witnessed our conversation. I have always thought this apartment block was a safe place. Until tonight.

'I'm sorry, miss,' an older officer says. 'If you've come to get your car, I'm afraid that won't be possible. Nothing is coming or going from here for a while. Give me your registration number and we can check where the car is and when we might be able to give you access. If you let me have your apartment number, we'll make sure you're kept informed.'

I'm about to agree when I realise that the car is registered to Anna Franklyn, but the apartment to Saskia Peterson. How will I explain that?

I turn towards the officer, who must be approaching retirement age, and paste on my best smile, trying to disguise the shake in my voice. 'Oh, don't worry. I was only going to stick my bag in the boot.' I hold up my gym bag and shrug. 'It's not a problem and I won't need the car for a day or two. What's happened?'

I ask because it would feel unnatural not to. But I just want to get out of there.

'There's been an incident, but there's nothing to see. If you're not going out, I suggest you head back to your apartment. Can I see your keycard?'

The keycards give residents access to the lift down to the car park. It's supposed to make it secure, but given my earlier encounter that doesn't seem to be the case. I flash the card at him, keeping my thumb over the blonde lady in the picture, give him another smile and turn to leave.

Inside the lift I lean heavily against the side and wonder if this nightmare will ever end.

How am I going to get out? I can't go through the entrance lobby. They are questioning everyone who comes and goes, and I am clearly not Saskia Peterson any longer.

I close my eyes. I have no idea what I'm going to do.

Thursday

43

I'm almost surprised when I wake up to find that I am in my own bed, at home with my husband sleeping beside me. I can't believe I slept, but emotional exhaustion must have taken over.

I can still feel a flutter of panic following the events of the previous evening – the disastrous poker game, a foyer full of police and my car inaccessible. In the end I had decided that the only way I was going to get out of the apartment block was to change back into Saskia, albeit without the full make-up which I had already scrubbed off, and go back out through the main entrance.

I kept on the joggers and flip-flops, but put the wig back on and a bit of lipstick. Then I tried to settle my screaming nerves, knowing it was going to be after 2 a.m. by the time I arrived home.

'Ms Peterson,' the uniformed police officer said when I reappeared in the lobby. 'I thought you were staying in?'

'So did I, officer. As you can see, I was about to settle down to a bit of late-night television.' I indicated my relaxed outfit. 'But I never got a chance to eat tonight and I'm starving, so I'm going to pop along to a late-night restaurant in Chinatown and feast on dim sum and crispy duck.' I licked my lips and gave him what I hoped was a suggestive smile. I could feel the eyes of the young female detective on me, but I didn't think my failure to return to the apartment later would arouse suspicion. Saskia had the air of a flirtatious woman, and they would no doubt assume I had found some other, more interesting place to stay the night.

'Be safe,' the officer said quietly as I left.

I dumped the wig in a bin. I couldn't risk stuffing it into my handbag. Dominic and the children have no concept of my bag being anything other than communal property, and it would have been discovered all too quickly. I found a black cab without too much of a problem but was dismayed to find I had chosen one with a chatty driver. I muttered monosyllabic responses so as not to appear rude as I scrubbed off the residue of the lipstick and tried not to cry with despair at all I had lost that night. I had no idea what I was going to do – I didn't even have enough money to join another game to try to win it back. I was going to have to admit everything to Dominic and the thought left me feeling weak.

It was only as the one-way system took us back past the entrance to the apartment block's car park that the driver's chatter broke through my reverie.

'…another murder,' he said, his tone one of disgust at what the world was coming to.

'Where?' I asked, my voice hoarse.

I knew the answer, of course I did. I had seen for myself the crime-scene team in their white suits, but I hadn't realised it was a murder. I had assumed an assault and been certain Jagger was behind it, perhaps as he waited for me. He'd done some evil stuff, but I'd never heard that he'd killed anyone. Now there would be a full-scale hunt for the killer, and Saskia Peterson would almost certainly be questioned as someone who used the car park.

The driver continued to rattle on about what he had heard on the news, but there was one question that I had to ask: 'Have they said who was killed?'

'Not yet, but the press are coming up with all kinds of theories. Another bloody car park too. It's not safe to set foot outside your own door any more, is it?'

I tuned out. There would be CCTV footage of me driving in. How much of my altercation with Jagger would be on film? Not much, I suspected, because Jagger would have chosen the spot carefully, but would the police want to question Saskia Peterson, or Anna Franklyn? I sat back in the cab and tried to think, but my brain was like pea soup and in the end I gave up.

By the time I got home Dominic was in bed, asleep, but now that it's morning I can't avoid the questions any longer.

As he rolls over towards me and gives me his early-morning smile, he reaches out an arm to pull me closer.

'What time did you get back last night?'

'It was late, I'm afraid. I'm glad you were asleep.' I've got to tell him, but I'm putting it off for as long as possible.

'I'd have waited for you but I got bored with the television. There was nothing to watch, so I came to bed early. Are you sure you're not overdoing things at the gym, darling? I know it helps relieve stress, and I'm all for that, but you need your sleep too.'

The stab of guilt at leaving my husband to a boring evening alone is nothing to the shame and horror I feel about what I will have to tell him sooner or later.

'I would have been home earlier, but I had a bit of a disaster with the car, so I had to get a taxi.'

Dominic opens his eyes fully. 'What happened? You didn't have an accident, did you?'

'No, nothing like that. Some idiot blocked me in – double-parked behind me – and although I went back into the gym and they put out the details over the tannoy, no one came forward. I waited for ages, thinking they would come back. But they didn't. In the end I shoved my bag in the boot and got a cab.'

'Thoughtless bastard.'

He rolls over and starts to get out of bed. I look at his broad naked back and ask myself how I'm going to save this secure life of ours.

'Give me your keys,' he says. 'I'll go and get the car later, when the kids are at school.'

Shit! The car park is nowhere near the gym.

Fortunately I hear Bailey shout, so I jump out of my side of the bed and go to him without responding to Dom.

'Hey, Bubbles, are you okay?'

'My throat hurts, Mummy.'

I sit down on the bed next to him and tell him to open his mouth wide and say 'ahh'. His throat does look a bit red.

'When did it start, poppet? This morning?'

'No, it hurt last night too. I was having a bad dream about the man.' Bailey rubs his eyes with his fists, still not fully awake.

'What man, darling?'

'The man who Daddy said is watching the house.'

The back of my neck feels as if someone is brushing a feather over it. I wait, not wanting to pump my child for information but knowing he won't be able to stop himself from saying more.

'Daddy says we have to be very careful, but we haven't got to worry you about it. He says it's all under control and you have enough to think about.' His eyes seem to get rounder and rounder – he's worried he shouldn't have said anything – so I smile encouragement and stroke his cheek with the back of my fingers, but the feather is now running right down the middle of my spine.

'Don't worry, Bubbles. I'm sure it's nothing. But what about your throat? Did Daddy give you something to make it feel better last night?'

'No. I went downstairs to look for you, but Dippy Della was there, and she was snoring.'

Della is our neighbour and is always happy to look after the children on the rare occasions we both go out without them. I should tell Bailey not to call her Dippy, but right now that's the last thing on my mind.

Why was Della there? Did Dominic go out?

I go back over his words this morning. Had I misunderstood him? I don't think so.

Why would he lie to me? Where did he go?

44

I've delayed my journey to work by half an hour and ordered a taxi. Holly's going back to school and I need to drop her off so Dom can stay at home with Bailey. But before I leave I need to talk to Dominic about where he went last night.

I've just followed him into the kitchen when the doorbell rings. Thinking it must be the taxi, I hurry to the door to ask him to hang on. When I open it, I find a woman of about my age with a dark bob and a pretty face standing on the doorstep. She is holding out some form of identification but before I have time to read it, she introduces herself: 'Good morning. I'm Detective Inspector Becky Robinson from Greater Manchester Police. I wonder if we could have a word, please?'

I can see my hand shaking where it's holding the door. I need to pull myself together.

Have they come for me as someone who knows Cameron Edmunds? Or have they made a connection between me and the incident in the car park last night? I quickly dismiss that. They can't have done. This has to be about Cameron.

I glance over my shoulder. Dominic is standing in the doorway to the kitchen, Holly by his side. She's gripping his hand as if she knows something terrible is about to happen.

I take a deep breath and paste a smile on my face. 'Yes, of course, Inspector. Come in.'

As she moves to one side, I see another officer behind her – a younger woman – and, barely resisting the urge to gasp, I realise it's the detective from the apartment block last night.

Have they come for Saskia?

She is unlikely to recognise me. She saw me with blonde hair, false eyelashes and bright red lipstick, then later with my face scrubbed clean; very different to Anna Franklyn, head teacher, with dark wavy hair and subtly applied make-up.

'Dom,' I say, turning towards him, 'why don't you take Holly to school? I need to speak to these two officers. I'll be here for Bailey until you get back.'

By now the police are inside the front door and I turn back to give them my most relaxed smile. I'm not a poker player for nothing.

'Actually, Mrs Franklyn – I'm assuming you *are* Mrs Franklyn?' I nod before she continues. 'It's not you we want to talk to. It's your husband.'

I spin round to stare at Dom, my brow furrowed. All of my self-control has flown out of the window. *Why on earth would they want to talk to Dom?*

'Holly,' I hear him say softly, his voice giving no hint that he is troubled by our visitors. 'Why don't you go up and keep Bailey company for a while – see how he's doing. Perhaps you could look at a picture book with him? We'll come and get you when it's time for school.'

She looks up at him with trusting eyes, lets go of his hand and skips upstairs, apparently reassured and unaware of the tension that surrounds her.

'Shall we go into the sitting room?' Dom asks. 'Would you like a drink – tea, coffee?'

I don't understand. What can they possibly want with Dominic?

'No thank you, Mr Franklyn.'

They follow Dom into the room and I trail behind, unsure whether I'm needed or not. Everyone takes a seat and the inspector leans forward.

'I'm sorry to resurrect what I'm sure was a painful time in your life, Mr Franklyn, but as a result of an incident last night we're trying to find links between victims of attacks that have taken place in the last couple of years.'

Two deep lines appear between Dom's eyebrows. He hates talking about that night.

'Why me?' he asks. 'There must be hundreds – thousands, probably – of attacks in Manchester every year.'

'Sadly that's true. But we're looking at assaults that specifically involved injuries to legs – particularly knees – and those in which a hammer was used. Our records show that the offence against you matches that profile.'

Dominic's brow clears and his voice breaks on his words. 'Have you caught him? Thank God for that. All I've ever wanted was to know that no one else would be hurt like I was.'

I reach out a hand to touch Dom's shoulder, knowing that night still haunts him.

'No, but we're hopeful that we're getting close to an answer, so we're interviewing everyone who has suffered a similar attack to see if we can pull together a clearer picture. Can I run a couple of names past you? Let me know if they mean anything. Roger Jagger?'

I don't flinch at the name, but I don't meet the eyes of the detective, focusing my concerned gaze on my husband.

Dominic shakes his head slowly. 'It doesn't mean anything to me, no.' He turns his eyes to mine. 'What about you, Anna? Have you heard that name before?'

All eyes are on me, but I force myself to remember that I am good at this. I shake my head and give a small shrug. 'Don't think so.'

'Cameron Edmunds?'

Dominic lifts his head. 'Now that name rings a bell. Why would that be? Is he a parent of one of the children's friends, darling?'

I wish he would stop looking to me for support. Each time he does, I feel the young detective's gaze on my face.

I have to respond, or they'll think we've been hibernating for the last few days. 'Isn't he the guy who everyone thought had been killed in Manchester?' I ask tentatively.

'Of course!' Dominic rubs the side of his head. 'I knew I'd heard the name. But it wasn't him, was it?'

The inspector shakes her head. 'No. But as far as you know, you have never met or had any dealings with either of these two men?'

It's Dominic's turn to shake his head. 'No. Unless either of them have children at the school where I used to teach, I can't think of any connection.'

'Thank you for that.' She pushes herself to the edge of the sofa, as if she is about to stand up. 'Just so we have everything, would you mind telling me, Mr Franklyn, where you were yesterday evening?'

Before Dominic can answer, the younger officer who hasn't spoken until now says, 'And you, Mrs Franklyn?'

The inspector barely blinks but I can see she is surprised at the question. I'm not. Her colleague must have recognised me. I am about to start on some lengthy explanation when Dominic speaks again.

'We were both in all evening. We've rather belatedly got ourselves hooked on *Game of Thrones*, so when the children are in bed we tend to gorge ourselves on chocolate and bloody battles. Last night was a three-episode marathon.'

Inspector Robinson looks at Dom, her eyes blank, and then glances at me. I give her a small, almost guilty smile – as if we are too old for such self-indulgence.

She stands up and nods at us both. 'Thank you for your time. We'll be in touch if we have any further questions.'

I almost want her to stay, because while she is here I can't ask

Dominic the questions that are burning me up. Why did he lie? Until today I would have said that Dominic never, ever lies. His personal code forbids it. But he said he stayed in all last night, and he lied to the police about where I was. Why would he do that?

45

Becky had originally thought Tom's suggestion that they interview victims of similar assaults was a bit of a long shot, but decided to do the first couple of interviews with Lynsey to form a judgement. Tom may have been on the right track, though, because there was definitely something in the air in the Franklyns' sitting room.

'What did you make of that?' she asked Lynsey, pulling the car over to the side of the road just around the corner from the house.

'Something didn't ring true.'

'I know, but we can't find any link between Dominic Franklyn and Cameron Edmunds.'

'It wasn't him I was worried about,' Lynsey said.

Becky looked at her colleague. 'I wondered why you asked where his wife was.'

'I can't be one hundred per cent certain, but there was a woman at the apartment building last night. She was called Saskia something. I can't remember her surname but I have a note of it. She's nothing like Anna Franklyn in many ways, but there's something similar about the way she holds her head when she's listening. And those eyes of hers are quite unusual.'

Becky twisted further in her seat and stared at Lynsey's slightly anxious face. 'Go for it, Lynsey. Let's have your theory. As Tom has told you before, it doesn't matter how daft it seems.'

Lynsey nodded. 'A woman came into reception. Blonde, glamorous, walked with a real swagger. Nothing like the Anna Franklyn we just met. She wore heavy make-up but somehow managed not to look tarty. She looked foreign, and when I heard her name was Saskia I assumed Russian, in spite of her surname – Peterson, I've just remembered. It stuck with me because of how she behaved.'

Lynsey paused as if getting her thoughts together, and Becky didn't prompt her.

'We asked for some identification, and I thought there was something in her eyes that hinted at alarm. She didn't open her bag to try to find proof of who she was, and then the concierge arrived and she left without showing us anything at all. She seemed relieved. A bit later she came back down. The make-up had gone and she was dressed casually. Said she was going out for something to eat, even though it was very late. That was the face that looked like Anna Franklyn, although still with blonde hair.'

'Did she ask what was going on?'

'No, although we later learned she had been down to the car park. The officer there kept a note of everyone who came so they could let people know when they could get their cars. When we did a debrief later, I referred to her as the blonde lady and he said I was wrong. She had dark hair. But she was definitely blonde when I saw her – both times.'

Becky thought for a moment. 'No cars have been allowed in or out of the car park yet, so her car must still be there. Let's check it out.' Becky reached for her radio.

As she expected, every car had been checked against the block's list of registration numbers, and it seemed they had done a thorough job.

'The parking spot assigned to Apartment 624 is close to the lift,' she was told. 'However, the car parked there last night belongs to the owner of 437. He said the spot is nearly always empty – only used once or twice a week – so sometimes he nabs it.'

Becky frowned. If you live in an apartment block, why would your car only be there one or two nights a week?

'Go on,' she said.

'So then we checked to see if we could find the car registered to 624 anywhere else in the car park, and we did. It was at the far end, well away from the lift.'

'Can we run a PNC check, please, on the registered keeper?'

'Sure,' the officer said, sounding slightly surprised given that the car registration had been matched to the owner of an apartment.

It didn't take long. 'Oh,' he said. 'That's interesting. The apartment to which the car is linked is in the name of Saskia Peterson, but the car's registered keeper is—'

'Anna Franklyn,' Becky said, smiling her congratulations at Lynsey.

She ended the call and sat back in her seat. Anna Franklyn certainly wasn't at home last night, so why had her husband lied? Anna Franklyn was a small, slight woman. It was hard to imagine she had been directly involved in the murder, but maybe she knew who was.

Before she had the chance to voice those thoughts to Lynsey, her mobile rang. It was Tom.

'Becky, we have an update. We got it wrong last night. Our victim's prints *are* on file; he got six months for ABH ten years ago. This isn't Roger Jagger's doing, though. Our victim *is* Roger Jagger.'

46

The police left ten minutes ago, but I still haven't had a chance to talk to Dominic. Holly heard the front door close and came bounding downstairs.

'Bailey's asleep, so I can't read him a story. When are we going to school? Is that a taxi outside? Is that for us?'

Dominic seems happy to keep her in the room with us, and I know why, but for once I'm going to have to send her away.

'Holls, can you go to your room, sweetheart? I need to talk to Daddy. The taxi can wait.'

'Why have I got to go? Is it a secret? I thought we weren't allowed secrets in our family.'

My poor Holly. If only she knew that my life is one big secret.

'It's not a secret, sweetheart, but it's about a problem I have at work and so it's not *my* secret. It's someone else's that I can't share.'

She looks totally bemused, as well she might. But she's a good girl and with an exaggerated sigh she leaves the room. That's another lie told in this house today.

I walk over to the door and close it, leaning my back against it. Arms folded, I look at Dominic, who raises his eyebrows as if to say, 'What's all the fuss about?'

'Why did you lie, Dom?' I can't think of a way to wrap this up nicely. 'You never lie.'

He nods slowly. 'That's true. I don't.' He doesn't say any more for a few moments but picks at a non-existent loose thread on his jeans. 'I lied for you, of course.'

I can feel my brow furrowing as I look at the man I thought I knew so well.

'Why, though? Does it matter if I was out?'

He shrugs. 'I didn't think you would want them coming to school to ask questions. The first whiff of scandal – even if totally unfounded – and the trustees will have you out. You know that.'

'But they weren't interested in me; they were interested in you – or rather any connection you might have to those men they mentioned.'

'Look, on the spur of the moment it just seemed to make sense to say we were both here.'

'But you weren't, were you?'

I am appalled at the tone of accusation in my voice and move across the room to sit next to him, but he jumps up and turns to face me, thrusting his hands in the pockets of his jeans.

'What do you mean? Of course I was here. Where else would I be? I'm *always* here.'

'Bailey came downstairs, and Della was asleep on the sofa. I presumed you'd gone out.'

Dominic scowls at me. 'Did you? Well you presumed wrong. Della called round to see how Holly's doing since her accident, and I asked her if she'd like a drink. She's lonely, Anna – which you might notice if you were ever here – and she does a lot for the kids. I gave her a large gin and we watched a bit of telly together. Then she dozed off – apparently she does that every night. So I went into the kitchen to make her a hot drink. That was presumably when Bailey came downstairs. Della likes cocoa last thing. Did you know that? No, of course you didn't. If I'd told the police she was here, they would have interviewed her and she would have panicked. Go and ask her, if you don't believe me.'

I feel ashamed of my suspicions. He's right about Della – she's always there for us – and he was trying to protect me, as he always does.

At that moment I feel a strong urge to tell him everything, but the waiting taxi driver beeps his horn. It's not the right time. I don't know if it ever will be.

I have never felt so isolated, as if I'm marooned on a sandbank and the sea is approaching from all sides, the wind whipping the surface into angry peaks of white foam, ready to engulf me.

'I'm going to be late,' I say. 'The taxi has been waiting ages. I'll get Holly.'

I know I should apologise to Dom. He deserves so much better, but the air around me seems charged with stress. He must be able to feel the sparks, just as I can feel the fabric of this family tearing apart.

47

Becky hadn't been totally surprised by Tom's news about Roger Jagger, but it was now even more urgent that they find Cameron Edmunds. Although it was tempting to head back to the incident room straight away, she wanted to follow up on Anna Franklyn first. When someone lied to the police, there had to be a reason.

She was about to turn the car round and go back to the Franklyns' home when the taxi that had been waiting at the end of the drive raced past, a woman and child in the back.

'She's taking the daughter to school. I'm guessing she'll carry on to work after that, given that she's not got her car. Let's see where she works, Lynsey.'

'I'll google her first, see if anything comes up. It might save time.'

Becky heard the clicking as Lynsey typed into her phone.

'She's a head teacher. She's been in the press quite a lot because she's turned the school around from underperforming to good. It's definitely her. There's a picture.'

'We'll go to her school and talk to her there, or ask her to come in for questioning,' Becky said. 'Let's find out what she's hiding.'

Tom knew they needed to find some answers soon. Two young men, both mid-thirties, both murdered in car parks. They had found nothing to suggest that Derek Brent had enemies, and Tom was more convinced than ever that Cameron Edmunds had been the intended target of that first killing, especially as Roger Jagger was now dead. Who next? Was this the start of a serial killing spree, or had these two men – who by all accounts had been close associates for over fifteen years – been specifically targeted? If Dawn Edmunds was right, Cameron had all the hallmarks of a modern-day gangster – no obvious source of wealth other than the money from his father and some relatively low directors' fees, and a life that he wasn't prepared to share with his wife, which seemed to involve causing injury to others. There could be little doubt he was involved in some form of criminal activity, so was there a vigilante out there, intent on eliminating the criminals of Manchester? Or was this more personal?

'Where are we up to with finding an address for Roger Jagger, Keith?' Tom asked.

'As we already discovered, there's nothing current on file. We did a thorough check when we were trying to locate him in regard to Cameron Edmunds.'

All Tom wanted to know was what they had now – not what they hadn't had yesterday.

'The good news is that we found a car that appears to have been abandoned close to the car park where Jagger was found. It was left on double yellows down a little-used alley, so it was only reported at the crack of dawn when a lorry couldn't get through to make a delivery. The registered keeper of the vehicle is a Robert Jackson, and initially we thought this might be Jagger's killer, but we pulled up the photo from Jackson's driving licence and, hey presto, up popped a picture of Roger Jagger. And an address. Obviously given his record, a fake identity might have proved useful – kept the same initials, though.'

'So what are we waiting for? Keith, you're with me. Let's see if anyone's home at Mr Jagger's house. How far?'

Keith looked slightly flustered. He was generally confined to the office because his manner didn't help with interrogation, but as Jagger was well and truly dead, Tom thought this was a good opportunity to let the sergeant smell some fresh air.

'Right. Erm, I haven't actually fed the coordinates into a map, sir. But I would say we're looking at forty minutes? It's a couple of miles away from the Edmunds' house.'

'Okay, you can check the finer details as we drive.'

'I'll just straighten my desk and I'll be right there.'

'Stuff your desk, Keith. It can wait. Come on. Let's go.'

48

My journey to school is proving to be a nightmare. To start with I kept asking the driver if he could go faster, find another route, anything to get me there quicker. But he became more and more irritated, and I'm sure he's now driving deliberately slow, so I've stopped asking and phoned Jennie.

'Sorry, Jen, I'm running a bit behind. My car was blocked in at the gym last night, and I ordered a taxi this morning but it was late.' I ignore the cold stare of the taxi driver in the rear-view mirror. He slows down even more. But I can't admit the police were at my house.

When we finally arrive I am tempted not to tip the driver, but my bad mood is not entirely his fault so I tell him to keep the change. He doesn't seem impressed.

I rush in through the main doors. The children are all in their classrooms, which reinforces my guilt at how badly I've been doing my job this week. I'm usually here at least an hour before the first child arrives.

As I close my office door behind me, I gaze around, remembering the weeks after I took over here, the fun Jen and I had reorganising it into a friendlier place, and I have to wonder if this time next week I will still be here – if I will still have a job at the school that I have grown to love. I don't know what truths will be exposed – either by the police or through the dreaded radio programme, which is getting forever closer. Whatever Scott says on the radio, there is one thing that I hope and pray he never reveals. If my marriage isn't over before Monday after I admit to

Dominic the extent of my deception and explain why we must sell the house, I know for certain there is one secret that would never be forgiven.

I've barely had time to sit down before Jennie pushes open the door. 'There are two women to see you, Anna.'

I stand up, about to ask who they are and whether they have an appointment when the truth hits me. I know who this will be. For a second I feel dizzy and have to grasp the edge of my desk.

'Are you okay?' Jennie asks, and I wonder for a moment if she thinks I was lying yesterday and if I really am ill.

'Fine. Sorry – not much sleep.'

She stares at me for a moment too long. 'Your visitors are from the police,' she says, bending to pick up a pile of papers from my desk.

I nod as if this is nothing out of the ordinary. 'Thanks, Jen. I wonder which of our lovely children they want to talk to me about. I hope nothing terrible has happened.'

'It's not about a child. They said it was a personal issue.'

But then I knew that. Her eyes don't meet mine as she turns to leave the room.

'Mrs Franklyn, thank you for seeing us.'

Becky looked at the face of the woman in front of her, who must have realised something was wrong if they had followed her to work to talk to her, but Anna's expression was pleasant, unruffled. Becky found that disconcerting.

'Have a seat, Inspector.' Anna nodded at the other detective to show she was included in the invitation. 'Would you like coffee?'

'No, we're good, thank you. I'm not sure if I introduced my colleague to you – Detective Constable Maltby – but you may recognise her.'

Anna turned her head slightly to look at Lynsey, a slightly confused smile on her face.

'I'm not sure I do. Should I?'

'I think so. You met last night.'

Anna must have known the game was up, but she managed to maintain the puzzled look.

'Okay, Mrs Franklyn, it would be great if you could stop playing games. Can you tell me where your car is right now, please? It may be worth you knowing – before you dream up some elaborate story – that we know exactly where it is, so perhaps you could just confirm it.'

'It's in the car park of an apartment block in central Manchester.'

'What were you doing at that apartment block last night?'

'I sometimes visit a friend there. She doesn't have a car, so we registered mine against her parking bay so I can come and go whenever I need to.'

Becky could feel her irritation rising. How long was this going to go on for?

'Your friend's name?'

'Saskia Peterson. You can check – she has an apartment there.'

Becky nodded. 'We know that, or at least we know that someone using the name Saskia Peterson has an apartment there. But last night you told DC Maltby that *you* are Saskia Peterson. Not only that, the concierge confirmed it.'

Becky watched as Anna bit the corner of her bottom lip and shook her head as if embarrassed.

'I know. I'm sorry. The thing is, Saskia isn't well, so she's given me her keycard so I can get in and out. The concierge made an assumption, and it's always seemed easier to run with it.'

'So Ms Peterson will confirm this, will she?'

Anna's eyes opened wide. 'Of course she will.' She paused as if remembering something. 'Well, she will when she gets back. She's been feeling a bit better and I managed to persuade her to go and stay with some friends in Scotland. She was leaving first thing.

Before you ask, I don't have the details of where she's staying.'

'No, but no doubt you have her mobile number.'

Anna nodded enthusiastically. 'Of course. I'll write it down for you, although I suspect reception up there isn't great.'

As Anna scribbled some numbers on a Post-it note, Becky marvelled at her ability to conceal her feelings while wondering at the same time how she expected them to believe she had memorised a friend's mobile number. Everyone stored them in their phones these days so they never had to worry about remembering anything.

'Why the wig?' Lynsey asked, alluding to the blonde hair of the woman she had met last night. 'And all the make-up? You were all glammed up. Why was that?'

Anna looked up from the note. 'Was I looking glam? That's very kind of you. I sometimes like to be blonde – makes a change. Here's the number, and if I hear from Saskia I'll ask her to get in touch.'

Anna stood up as if this was their signal to leave, but Becky and Lynsey stayed in their seats. For the first time Becky saw a moment of doubt flash in the other woman's eyes. Anna slowly lowered herself back into her chair.

'Why did your husband say you were at home all night?'

Becky got the impression that Anna had anticipated their first questions but not necessarily this one.

'He was asleep when I got back. He probably thought I'd only been out for an hour, so it wasn't worth mentioning.'

Becky resisted the temptation to groan. Did Anna expect them to believe that?

'Really? You didn't tell him that when you went to visit your friend you couldn't get to your car because it was at a crime scene? Did you know that someone was killed there last night – the second murder in a car park in a matter of days?'

Anna had gone very still, the smile no longer on her face.

'Who was the victim?'

'A man by the name of Roger Jagger. Did you know him, Mrs Franklyn?'

She shook her head, but her eyes wouldn't meet Becky's and Anna's skin had lost its colour under the thin layer of subtly applied make-up.

'No. Should I?'

'You tell me. We've been looking into all the people who have any connection with these crimes, and it seems you went to Manchester University. Is that correct?'

'Yes, but only for a year.'

'Both Cameron Edmunds and Roger Jagger were students there at the same time.'

Anna attempted at a laugh. 'I could hardly be expected to have known every student in a university of that size.'

'Of course not, although these two did have quite a reputation. So, to be clear, until today you had heard of neither Roger Jagger nor Cameron Edmunds? Is that correct?'

Anna appeared to be thinking.

'Look, I can't say for certain of course, but I don't think so. The names don't ring any bells.'

Becky knew they were getting nowhere. They had nothing other than the fact that this woman had an apartment under another name in the building where Jagger was brutally murdered. It was hard to imagine that she was the killer, and without anything to link her to either of the victims, there was little more they could ask.

But there was no doubt in Becky's mind that Anna Franklyn was lying about more than her name.

49

I didn't think the two detectives would ever leave, but finally they have gone. More than anything, I want to drop my head onto folded arms and sob, but I can't let Jennie know their visit upset me, and I push my shaking hands below my desk in case she glances through the window.

For a moment I had been tempted to tell them everything – admit to every mistake I've made – but I seem to be programmed to play the game to its conclusion – to showdown.

I thought they must have discovered my connection to Cameron. But I was wrong. They were here because my car was in the car park where Jagger was killed.

Jagger! I don't know how well I hid my reaction when they told me about his body being found, and I can't thrust from my mind those last few minutes as he pinned me against the pillar. Will they know about that? Is there CCTV? I had been there with him – arguing – in the very spot where he was killed.

I'm shocked at his death, but even more shocked at how I feel. I remember the steel of his grip as he held me while two of his thugs attacked Scott, the fear I felt when I found him waiting for me outside school to tell me they had put Dominic in hospital, the horror of him coming into school to threaten me, the chilling way he would appear at the entrance to an alley to demand money. I thought of him every day, wondering when he was going to turn up, what he was going to do to me, to my family, if I failed to make a payment. It should be a massive relief that he's dead. It *is* a massive relief, and yet there was a predictability about it all.

I knew what I needed to do and I felt in control of the situation. But maybe Cameron will find another minder now, and I won't see him coming.

Many people will be happy to know Jagger is dead, but I have to ask myself, *Did Scott do this?* The timing cannot be a coincidence, so if Scott is behind the murders, will he come for me next or will it be enough to expose me for who I am, or who I was?

Perhaps if I told the police the truth I could ask for protection against Scott and beg them to keep my relationship with Cameron and Jagger a secret. Then Dominic need never know that I have been playing poker to repay a debt and lying to him for all this time. But I know how this works. I can imagine them saying, 'We cannot promise to keep confidential the information you give us if it in any way impacts on the investigation.' And of course it will. I will be investigated because of my relationship – if you can call it that – with Cameron, and I may have been the last person to see Jagger alive. There is no way I will be able to hide everything I've done – who I am – from either the school or from Dominic. However vigorously I insist that I did it all to protect my family, everything will be exposed in all its ugliness.

My head is bursting with doubts about my choices and questions about the decisions I've made – I simply don't know what to do – but for the moment I need to paste a smile on my face, because Jen is hovering at the window. I give her a wide smile, and she comes in.

'Everything okay?' she asks.

I give a slightly theatrical sigh. 'For me, yes. But not for some poor soul who was apparently killed last night. Another car park death. I don't know if it was on the news this morning. I didn't get a chance to listen.'

Jen looks shocked. 'Good God. It's getting dangerous to go anywhere these days. But what did that have to do with you?'

'I went to visit a friend and parked in her car park. That's where the man was killed.'

She looks horrified for a moment, and then puzzled. 'I thought you said your car was blocked in the gym car park?'

Shit!

'Did I? I left my car in her car park while I went to the gym. It's not too far away and it seemed easier than moving it. Maybe I confused you.'

Her brow is still puckered, but I can see her relax slightly.

'So why did they want to talk to you?'

'My car's still there. They wanted to know if I saw anything.'

'Blimey. That's going to keep them busy if they're interviewing everyone who used the car park,' Jennie says with a laugh. But she has a point.

'I think there's a camera at the entrance, and they know what time people came and went. They said I arrived about half an hour before the body was found, so they thought I might have seen something. Anyway, it's done now. Let's hope they catch whoever it was.'

I shuffle some papers on my desk and jiggle my mouse around to bring my screen to life.

'Before we go through what's on today, would you mind making me a cup of coffee, Jen? Sorry to ask. I should be making you one really, but I've got a heap of emails to respond to, and thanks to everything going pear-shaped this morning I'm running behind.'

Jennie gives me a cheerful smile, as I knew she would. I answered her questions, and she trusts me to tell the truth. After all, one of the school values that I bang on about to staff and pupils is honesty. Maybe they would have a better understanding of the importance of the truth if I admitted how one dark lie had caused such untold havoc in my life.

50

Cameron Edmunds' wife hadn't been far wrong when she said she thought Jagger might live in a cave. It was actually a cottage, which could have been quite beautiful if the woods surrounding it hadn't been allowed to encroach on the garden and shroud the building in darkness. The walls and paintwork were stained with green mould through lack of light, and the windows were thick with years of grime. There were old net curtains at the windows, grey with age. There was a dead feel to the place.

No vehicle was parked on the weed-covered drive, but that made sense as they had found Jagger's car in central Manchester.

As Tom and Keith got out of the car, the silence struck both of them. The trees masked the sound of nearby roads and Tom would have expected birdsong. And yet there was none. Both men closed their car doors quietly and walked softly up the path to the front door, looking around almost as if they were expecting someone or something to appear from the dense undergrowth.

'We don't know if he lived alone or not,' Tom reminded Keith, 'and we don't have a search warrant, so we can't barge straight in. It doesn't look much like a family home, but you and I have both seen infinitely worse.'

Keith nodded, apparently unwilling to cut through the silence with his own voice.

They approached a once-white front door. Tom nodded at Keith to knock, stood back and gazed at the windows. He would have expected lights to be on, given the gloom created by the trees, but he couldn't tell as beyond the tatty curtains were what appeared to be wooden shutters.

He heard a dull thud from inside the cottage.

'Keith, there's someone in there. Knock again.'

No one came to the door. Tom pointed to the letterbox, and Keith bent down and put his mouth close to it, pushing the flap open with his fingers.

'Greater Manchester Police. Can you open the door, please?'

Silence.

'Can you see anything?'

'No, sir. It's blocked on the other side.'

Keith was still holding the flap open, and Tom could have sworn he heard a creak inside, as if someone was creeping downstairs.

He signalled to Keith to stand aside.

'My name is Detective Chief Inspector Douglas. We need you to open this door, or we are going to have to force entry.'

There was a definite scuffling sound, but it was moving away from the door.

Tom stood back. Could they get around the house to check for another way in – or out? Thick bushes abutted the house on either side, so even if there was a door at the back, they couldn't get to it.

'We're going to have to kick the door in.'

He looked at the shocked face of his sergeant.

'Look, whoever killed Roger Jagger could be here now, in his house. It's a reasonable assumption if someone's in there and they won't let us in. Especially as we can't get round the back to make sure they don't get away.' It was a risk, but Tom would take the flak if it came to it. He'd done worse.

Keith was about five inches shorter than Tom, who at over six feet probably carried at least two or three stone more in weight than his lean, narrow-shouldered colleague.

'Stand back,' Tom said.

Keith held out an arm. 'No sir, it's fine. Leave it to me.'

Tom tried not to look surprised and said nothing, hoping he wasn't going to have to step in and take over if Keith failed. To his amazement, Keith leaped at the door, one leg bent, and then extended it as his foot made contact. The door burst open.

Tom stared at his sergeant.

'Kickboxing,' Keith said, straightening his jacket.

There was no time to applaud, however, and Tom merely muttered, 'Well done,' as they strode into the house.

Immediately they felt the draught from two doors being open at the same time.

'Bollocks,' Tom shouted. 'Back door!'

Both men set off at a run towards an open doorway. They had no time to take in the kitchen as they sped through and out of the gaping door at the back.

They both stood still for a second, getting their bearings and looking about to see if they could spot movement or identify a place for someone to hide.

'*There!*' shouted Keith, lifting a hand to point. A man had broken cover and was heading deeper into the trees.

Keith was off like a shot, surprising Tom once again, but the man they were chasing seemed younger than either of them, and although Tom had been quite a runner in his time, he could see the man was getting away from him.

Keith had disappeared, but Tom ran on.

Suddenly the man stopped and grabbed the trunk of a sapling barely strong enough to hold him upright, and it took a few seconds for Tom to realise that Keith was barring his way. He must have cut back through the woods and round to the track, surprising Tom for the second time that day.

The man had his back to Tom, but he had no doubt who this was. He spun round, his eyes black with fury. 'Why the fuck are you chasing me?'

'Why the fuck did you run?' Tom responded, instantly understanding Dawn Edmunds' antipathy towards this man. 'Cameron Edmunds, I presume?'

The man stared at Tom without acknowledging the question. 'Who are you?'

'Detective Chief Inspector Douglas, Greater Manchester Police. So I ask again, why did you run?'

Tom was rewarded with a cold hard stare. 'When two men appear at the door claiming to be police, I would have to be more than a little naive to take them at their word.'

Tom was tempted to say that most people would never doubt it, but he let that lie.

'We need to go back to the house. I want to talk to you.'

Edmunds blew out a long breath and, without another glance in Tom's direction, set off back towards the cottage. He marched into the kitchen, closely followed by the two detectives. As they had run through, Tom hadn't taken in their surroundings. But in stark contrast to the outside, the inside of the house was immaculate. Every surface of the kitchen was either white or stainless steel, and the only things out of place were a dirty glass, a plate covered in crumbs and a mug of half-drunk coffee sitting by the sink, presumably waiting for someone other than Cameron to wash them. It appeared Jagger was the tidy one.

Cameron had recovered his air of confidence. He turned to Tom and put his head on one side as if to say, 'Well?'

'I'm sorry to tell you that Roger Jagger is dead. He was killed last night in the car park of an apartment block in central Manchester.'

Edmunds looked puzzled, as if he had heard something that couldn't possibly be true. He shook his head slowly. 'Jagger's dead? Are you sure?'

'I'm afraid so.'

Cameron said nothing, his eyes unfocused as if settling on some distant image in his mind.

He's a cold bastard, Tom thought. By all accounts Jagger was Edmunds' greatest friend, but other than looking slightly pensive, there was no sign that the news had distressed him.

'What was Mr Jagger doing in Manchester last night? I'm sure you know, and it would help us to catch his killer if you would cooperate.'

Edmunds gave Tom an icy stare and said nothing.

'Why are you hiding here?' Tom asked.

He was rewarded with an irritated grunt. 'Because someone was murdered in my car, so I assumed that whoever killed him was after me. I wanted to find the shit who did it before he – or she – found me.'

'Who are we talking about?' Tom asked. 'Who do you think was after you?'

'I don't know.'

Whatever Tom thought of Edmunds, and despite his suspicions that the man's life was far from clean, there was one thing the police were obliged to do.

'We need to keep you safe until we understand who might want you dead and who killed Jagger. It may or may not be the same person, but it's best if we take you home and make sure you're not seen.'

Cameron gave a derisive snort. 'Dawn will be disappointed. I suggest you don't tell her until we get there. She can't keep her mouth shut about anything, as you've probably gathered.'

Tom scratched his head. 'Regardless of that, your home is probably the best place for you. We can protect you there, and you have good security systems. Plus, we need your cooperation. We obtained a warrant to search your property when you were missing. There's a safe in your office—' Cameron's head jerked towards Tom, two lines etched between his brows '—and when we couldn't find the combination we left it alone. I have two choices now. I can, if I wish, get another search warrant, and this time we will force your safe open. Alternatively, you can open it yourself.'

'But as I'm alive and well, why the fuck do you need to get into my safe?'

Tom was struggling to hide his contempt for this man. 'Two men are dead, one of them possibly because the killer thought it was you in your car, the other perhaps as a result of his association with you. So we have to investigate you – every aspect of your life – to determine why someone wants you dead and why someone killed Roger Jagger.'

Cameron's jaw was clenched, and Tom was certain he was worried about the contents of the safe being examined.

Good.

'If I open it, you have to let me remove some personal items first.'

Tom looked him in the eye. 'Not a chance.'

51

I can't concentrate on anything. Over and over I run through all that's happened, starting with Monday and the radio programme. It seems this was Scott's way of throwing down the gauntlet, showing me that he was coming for me. Then came reminders of our past sins – confirmation that he was behind it all. And the murders. Scott had every reason to hate Cameron and Jagger, but the Scott I knew was gentle. What could have happened to him in the last fourteen years to make him so vengeful, and why now?

Then a thought hits me. If the radio programme was intended to warn me, how could Scott be certain I would be listening? It would all have been a waste of effort if his intention was to scare me but I never heard it. Cameron's murder wouldn't entirely have been a surprise, given his history; the arrival of the pizzas would have been confusing but nowhere near the warning that I believed it to be, and the rest I might have put down to some prank. It was the broadcast mentioning Scott and Spike that made the threat feel real. Somehow he had to have known that I would hear him; that the threat of revealing the scams would hurt me. He talked about the significance of the dates too, so I know he intends to expose me to the world for the worst of my sins. None of it would have worked if I hadn't been listening.

Even without Dominic's assertion that someone is watching the house, I am certain Scott has been spying on me. He stole the photos for the crowd-funding page from Facebook, so he must have been stalking me online too. How easy it is to forget how much of our lives we display for the world to see without a thought as to who might be watching. He could have joined public groups that I belong to as well.

That's it! The TOTGA Facebook group. Of course.

I reach for my mouse and log in to my timeline, certain what I'll see. I'm confident he hasn't faked a friendship with me, but there are several hundred members of the group that religiously follow 'The One That Got Away', and every week – until this one – I have taken part in the chat. Anyone reading the comments would know that I am a regular listener, although I haven't participated since Monday, when I first heard Scott's story. But he must know that I heard him this week, because why else would I have suddenly decided to pay a visit to his mother?

I never doubted he was dead until this week. Jagger seemed certain of it too, but it's true that I left him before he took his last breath. I can see his face now, contorted with pain, gasping for air. I knew he was dying, but I had walked away. In the moments before I turned my back on him, his eyes had watched me, begging me to stay, to help. But I didn't. I couldn't. And for that reason I believe there is only one person Scott could hate more than he loathed Cameron and Jagger. Me.

I drop my head into my hands. I have to do something, stop him from hurting anyone else. I can't just sit back and wait to see what happens next. I lift my head and pull my keyboard towards me. If I'm right, there is one way that I can contact him.

I log into the Facebook group and I start to type.

I've not had a chance to comment this week – it's been a busy one! But like the rest of you, I would LOVE to meet Scott and hear what he has to say for himself. I wonder why he's decided to talk about this now, after so long? Any thoughts? Won't be able to check in until later – I have to go and see an old lady in a hospice. Poor soul is so confused she keeps seeing her son who's been dead for years. As I said, a hectic week.

I decide not to wait to see if he responds. He will understand that I'm going to Wales and want to see him. He knows where to find me. No matter what he thinks of me, no matter what he intends, I can't live like this, waiting for the axe to fall.

I hate lying to Jennie again, but I tell her the police have called to ask me to pick up my car. I look at her trusting smile and wonder if she is the one person who might understand. But I can't risk it.

'They're interviewing everyone who was in the vicinity at the time of the murder and they want me there. They're doing a reconstruction, hoping that being in the car park will jog memory. It's likely to take a fair chunk of the day to get through everyone, and they wouldn't give me a fixed time.'

I shrug with an air of hopeless resignation, and Jen tuts at their lack of consideration. As I turn away I bite my lip and keep it clamped between my teeth so it won't wobble, telling myself that I had no choice but to make up this convoluted story. I take a deep breath and call a taxi.

I ask the driver to drop me off at the car park entrance. I'm scared to go through the foyer in case the detectives are there, so I walk down the ramp and use my keycard to get through the gate. Memories of the night before hit me and I shiver. It may be warm outside, but here – underground – it's always cold. And dark. I glance warily over my shoulder, as if I'm expecting Jagger to be lurking there. I can't believe he's dead, and I'm balancing an intense feeling of relief with one of uneasiness about what Cameron might do next.

I thought Jagger was invincible, and I'm sure he did too. I picture his narrow features and the mean look in his eyes when he crept up on me last night. I used to think he was a psychopath, but I was wrong. He was just a thug with a brain.

Who killed him? Was it Scott? It would make sense. Maybe he's taking revenge on all those who hurt him, but what does that mean for me? I stop and lean against a pillar for support, my knees suddenly incapable of bearing my weight. He loved me once though, and despite all that happened, all that I did, I can only pray it means something to him.

A police officer in uniform is standing at the bottom of the ramp, clipboard in hand. My instinct is to turn and run, but he's seen me and I can't let him realise I'm nervous. I can see figures moving around, searching under the cars, the gloom illuminated by bright arc lamps. They must have been at it for over twelve hours now.

'Can I help you?' the police officer asks.

'I wondered if I could collect my car,' I ask, pushing my hands into my pockets so he can't see them trembling.

'Registration number?'

I give him the details.

'You're in luck. Fortunately your car's about as far away from the scene as it could be, and we've already searched that area.'

He walks me to the car, and within minutes I'm clear. I'm not sure how I will be able to drive into that car park again, but I don't doubt I'll be back.

I can't face school until all of this is over, and if I'm going to be absent for the rest of the week, I need a good excuse. I'm going to have to lie again, but I'm hoping my slightly shouty voice over the sound of traffic will help convey a sense of urgency, and any quiver in my voice will be attributed to my distress at the news I'm about to share.

'Jennie, it's Anna. What a dreadful week this has turned out to be.' I make a sound that hopefully will come across as a sob. 'My mum has had a fall. She's been taken to hospital in Cumbria and I'm on my way there now. Tim Brighouse can take over from me – that's what a deputy is for after all – and there's nothing so important as my poor mum right now.'

Jennie is full of concern, as I knew she would be, and my sobs become real as I hang up. If I can't fix this, it will break my heart to admit how I have betrayed her.

The thought of betrayal brings Dominic sharply into focus. He won't be so easy to fool. I wipe my tears away to call him, and I'm relieved when it goes straight to voicemail.

'Dom, I've picked my car up from the car park and I'm on my way to a meeting with the trustees. I'd completely forgotten, with everything else that's been going on. I should be home at the normal time. I'm supposed to switch my mobile off in meetings, but after last time I'll check it at every break in case you need me. See you later.'

I'm so glad he didn't answer. After this morning and the visit from the police I'm not sure what to say to him right now.

I think back to the message I left on the Facebook group under the thread 'Who are Scott and Spike?' I wonder if it will be enough to spur Scott into action. There's no chance that Dominic will see it. He thinks social media is the work of the devil, and Jen isn't a member of the group. I checked.

More than anything, I'm hoping that Scott will read my words. I need to see him, flush him out of wherever he's hiding, stop him in any way I can from doing what he's promised to do. I have four days until he's back on the radio. Four days in which I hope he will take the bait and reply to my message.

I'll be waiting for him.

52

As Keith drove, Tom turned towards the back seat.

'Get down below the window, please, Mr Edmunds. We're nearly at your house now. Once we're through the gates we can get you inside without being seen. We already have a policeman on guard outside, and he can stay there until this is over one way or the other.'

'I assume there's no doubt that the first guy was murdered because the killer thought it was me in the car?' Edmunds asked, his voice muffled by the back of Tom's seat.

'We haven't ruled him out as the intended victim, but with Roger Jagger dead, it does seem more likely they were after you. Who wants you dead, Mr Edmunds?'

'Plenty of ungrateful bastards, I expect.'

'Ungrateful?'

They turned off the road and pulled up in front of the gates.

Cameron lifted his head. 'It's funny how appreciative people are when you bail them out of trouble, and how quick they are to turn on you when that debt needs to be repaid, don't you think?'

'You know that to lend money you need to be licensed, don't you, Mr Edmunds?'

'When has it ever been illegal to offer a friend some money? I've helped a few people out, but I've not broken any laws.'

Tom turned back to the front. He had no evidence of criminal activity yet, but he was certain he soon would have.

Becky pulled up behind Tom's car at the gates of the Edmunds' mini-castle just as Keith leaned out of the driver's window to press the buzzer. The gates quietly swung apart and both cars drove through and parked at the front of the house.

Dawn Edmunds opened the door herself, but stood back, a frown on her face. She had to be wondering why there were two cars, so Becky got out of hers to warn her what was about to happen. But just then the back door of Tom's car opened and she saw Dawn's face change to one of dismay. Becky glanced towards the man she presumed to be Cameron Edmunds. He was glaring at his wife, his eyes cold and black.

Neither of them spoke. Dawn stared at Cameron for no more than two seconds, then disappeared into the house, but not before she had given Becky a look of desperation. There was no doubt this was the worst possible outcome for her.

Tom gave a small shrug as he followed Cameron, who was already marching into the house. Becky sighed and signalled to Tom that she was going after Dawn, who was obviously intent on disappearing as she thundered up the stairs.

Becky knew which was Dawn's bedroom, and she knocked gently on the door. Getting no response, she pushed it open. Dawn was curled up on the bed, her mouth a tight line, her cheeks flushed. When she looked up at Becky, her eyes were bloodshot.

'Why's he back?'

'It's his home, Dawn. Did you think he was gone for good?'

'One can live in hope. I'm surprised that little shit Jagger's let him come back on his own. I thought he'd be standing guard at the very least.'

'Ah,' Becky said, sitting down on the edge of the bed. 'It's not been made public yet, but I can tell you that Roger Jagger died last night. He was murdered.'

Her mouth dropped open. '*Jagger? Dead?*' She paused, her eyes never leaving Becky's. 'Maybe there *is* a God after all. What happened?'

'It seems he was attacked from behind. The element of surprise – no one is immune to danger in those circumstances.'

'Well, when you find out who did it, please let me know. I'd like to say thank you. Or maybe kick him in the nuts for failing to get Cameron too.'

Dawn suddenly grinned, and Becky found herself liking this woman. Horrified as she clearly was by her husband's return, she had a dark sense of humour, and Becky smiled back, determined to find out the worst about Cameron Edmunds and free this family from his clutches.

53

I reverse my car into a spot in the hospice car park so I can watch people come and go. I wonder if Scott will take the bait. If he comes, I want to see him before he sees me. If I'm right and he's been tracking my activity on the Facebook group, he'll be checking to see if I comment and he'll know I'm here. I have sent him a clear invitation.

As I watch the door, I think about the Scott I knew when he was barely more than a boy. He made mistakes – we both did – and we were so scared. But our fear wore different faces. In Scott's case, the threat of physical violence hung over him like a black cloud. He tried to hide his addiction to gambling from me, and I turned a blind eye because it played to my own anxiety. I don't know what frightened me the most – losing Scott, not being strong enough to support the person I loved, or recognising that I was an idiot who didn't have the guts to run when she should have.

How many of us can look back to the days before we were fully formed emotionally and say that we didn't make mistakes? For most, those mistakes remain in the past. Mine first came back to haunt me eighteen months ago, in the shape of Cameron Edmunds and Roger Jagger, but I had that problem under control. I was repaying the debt, saving my family from losing everything we had and my mum from losing her home. I hated the lying, but I loved the thrill of poker. It was such a heady mixture – the deception, the fear of failure, the ecstatic relief when a bluff worked, and the joy at a big win.

I was Anna Franklyn by day – a model of decorum – and by night Saskia Peterson – the exciting, sexy, audacious woman I had dreamed of becoming since I was eighteen years old.

And now this. Scott wants to hurt me – either emotionally, physically or both – and I bang the heel of my hand on the steering wheel. *How dare he?* If it hadn't been for Scott and my desire to help him, my life would have been so different. If I'd reported him to the police for stealing the charity money, I wouldn't have defrauded my friends and family, borrowed money from Cameron, put my home at risk. The thought of all we did never leaves me. It's a heavy load that sits on my shoulders, weighing me down, and it's all Scott's fault. He has no right to make me suffer again.

I have to stop him before he does his worst. I can see the headlines now:

PRIMARY SCHOOL HEAD DEFRAUDED HER PARENTS AND FRIENDS.

I feel a fresh moment of shame because, scared as I am, *furious* as I am, I have to admit to a tiny frisson of excitement at the thought of seeing Scott again. Whatever else happened – however I felt by the end – he was my first love, and the trepidation that constantly threatened to derail us only served to heighten our passion. It was a time of intense emotion, so fierce that I have never experienced anything like it since, and have never wanted to, happy to settle for security and predictability.

I feel my eyes flood with tears as I acknowledge that I have chosen to replace the fiery heat I've fought shy of in my marriage with the thrill of the poker table. Dominic is a good man, but if ever there was a time to recognise the truth, it's now, and I have to admit that sometimes I feel stifled. The warm blanket that he wraps around us all sometimes threatens to suffocate me. I began to play poker because I needed to save myself, my marriage, my home and my mother's home, but now I don't want to stop. It's the only time I soar to the heights of excitement that I crave.

I quickly brush my tears away with the back of my hand as a man gets out of a car and walks towards the door to the hospice. He is about forty, too old for Scott, and I feel a pang of disappointment. Whatever logic tells me and however much he is scaring me, deep down I can't deny that I'm hoping to see him. Surely he will turn up?

My thoughts are disturbed by a ping from my phone and I glance down. A Messenger notification. The name of the sender is one I don't recognise, and I know without looking that his profile will tell me nothing.

Swallowing the tightness in my throat, I open it.

Spike! How lovely to hear from you. I know that FB post was meant for me, but sadly I can't get to Colwyn Bay to see my wonderful mother today, so I'm going to miss you. I hope you've not been waiting long! I'm surprised you managed to get away, especially with your little boy home from school. Is he not well?

My body tenses. How does he know about Bailey? He must have been to the house. I need to call Dominic. Without reading the rest of the message, I call home. There is no answer. *Has Scott hurt my baby?* I try Dominic on his mobile. It rings once, twice, three times. Any moment now it will switch to voicemail and then I'll panic. But Dom answers. I can tell he's in the car – I can hear traffic.

'Where are you, Dom?' I practically shout down the phone.

'Calm down. I've just popped to the supermarket for something to eat. Why? Where's the fire?'

'Where's Bailey?' My voice is fast, urgent.

'Christ, Anna, what are you all worked up about? He's with me of course. He was feeling a bit better so I decided to risk taking him out, but he's fallen asleep.'

'Let me speak to him.'

'I'm not going to wake him. He's fine. What the hell's the

262

problem, and where are you?'

Once more I lie. 'I'm sitting outside the trustees' office about to go in for a meeting. I left you a message.'

'So what's the Bailey anxiety all about then?'

I try to slow my breathing. 'Sorry. I heard something on the news about a little boy who's been abducted, and it frightened me.'

'Really? I've had the news on and I didn't hear it.'

'You must have been on a different station. Just give him a kiss from me, won't you?' Dom must think I have lost it altogether, but now I know my son is safe, I need to avoid further questions. 'Oh crap. They're watching me from the window. I need to go in. See you later,' I say, and end the call.

Taking another deep breath, I go back and read the rest of the message from Scott.

> I'd love a chance to reminisce, talk about our days at uni and especially those last days in Nebraska. Remember my old home? Course you do. You've already been to my town, haven't you? Nothing gets past me! Let's meet there tomorrow. 10 a.m. suit you? At the house. I'm "dying" to see you. Love Scott xx

My mouth is dry, my hands shaking. I stare at the message for minutes. I feel as if the world has gone silent around me, the buzzing in my ears drowning out the birdsong. Putting 'dying' in speech marks says it all. That has to be why he's here. It has to be revenge for what I did to him – for leaving him to die.

For a moment I wish I hadn't started this, but there's no way I can refuse to meet him now. He's been watching us and he feels like a constant threat to my children. Unless I deal with him now, I will forever be looking over my shoulder, scared to allow Holly and Bailey out of my sight.

I briefly think about the police. But what would I say? I have no evidence that Scott has been following my family or that he was the one to break into our shed. And his messages say nothing

263

that would look odd to anyone other than me.

But whatever he has planned, there is one thing that Scott knows about me that nobody else must ever know. He knows what happened to our baby. So I take a deep breath and force my fingers to be steady as I type my response.

I'll be there.

54

'Right, Mr Edmunds,' Tom said. 'Could you please either give me the combination to the safe, or open it yourself, and then stand back so that we can remove the contents?'

Cameron gave Tom a hard stare. 'Why would I do that?'

Tom wasn't having a great week, and his tolerance was in limited supply. He slammed the folder he was holding onto the desk.

'Because if you want us to catch Roger Jagger's killer, you will save us all some time and just bloody well do it.'

Tom saw Keith quickly disguise a startled expression, but Cameron must have realised he had little choice so pushed himself up from his chair and strode over to the safe.

Tom didn't know what he was expecting to find, but he wasn't particularly surprised to see stacks of notes, mostly fifties by the look of things, piled at the back of the safe. In front of the money was an old-fashioned leather-covered ledger that looked like the kind of book companies used to keep their accounts before computers took over the world, and a large brown envelope.

Pulling a forensic glove from his pocket, Tom lifted the ledger and envelope from the safe. 'You can close the safe again, for now,' he said.

He wasn't interested in the money as such, only in its source, and he was hoping the ledger would give him that information.

'Sit down, Mr Edmunds, while I take a look.'

He opened the unsealed envelope and pulled out about thirty photographs. Every picture had been taken in a casino, mostly at the blackjack table or by the roulette wheel, and each showed a different male player. The photos had one thing in common: a smiling girl at the centre of each image, her arm draped over the shoulders of the man or leaning over to place chips with his arm around her waist. There were six different girls, and most of the images had faded slightly, suggesting they were several years old.

'What are these?' Tom asked.

'Just photos.'

'I can see that, but why are they in your safe?'

'What do they look like? They're some of the prostitutes who hang out at the club, okay?'

Tom wondered if they had been taken in order to blackmail either the men or the girls – some of whom looked no more than eighteen – but there was no evidence of that, so he put them to one side for now.

He flipped open the ledger, which had been maintained beautifully. The writing was neat, and a couple of summary pages referenced individual detailed pages further into the book.

'Explain this ledger to me, please,' Tom said to Cameron, who had returned to his chair, rocking back as if indifferent.

'It's a list of people who at some time or another came to me as a friend to ask if I would lend them money.'

'Why would you lend money to so many *friends*?'

'What the fuck has this got to do with who killed Jagger? Isn't that the priority?'

Tom raised his eyebrows. 'It seems to me that someone was seriously pissed off with either one or both of you, and, looking at this, money has to be high on the list of motives. We'll be investigating every single one of these so-called "friends" to see what they have to say. It would save us a lot of time if you talked us through the list so we can prioritise.'

Keith pulled out his mobile phone and placed it on the desk.

'You are not under arrest, but we would like to record this

conversation, so I need to caution you. You do not have to say anything. But it may harm your defence if you do not mention when questioned something which you later rely on in court. Anything you do say may be given in evidence.'

Cameron shrugged. 'Look, the ledger was Jagger's province. I've told you what it is. I've always had money. I've tried to help people where I can.'

'And do you always get the money back?'

'Some fail to find the funds to repay me, but most, generally speaking, manage it.'

'What happens to those who fail?'

Cameron stared at Tom for a moment, and it seemed he had finally realised that Tom wasn't going to give up. He sighed and shook his head as if it had nothing to do with him.

'Jagger could be quite persuasive.'

'And I'm sure you know that any form of harassment used to recover a debt constitutes breaking the law.'

'I never asked him about his methods.'

Cameron's mouth twitched, as if he knew Tom couldn't touch him now that Jagger was no longer available to be questioned. With a minimum of two hundred names in the ledger, Tom's team had a huge task ahead of them. Their first job was to either implicate or eliminate each person from the two murders, but all they needed was just one of them to give evidence that the money had been demanded back with threats, and Cameron Edmunds would be finished.

Tom pulled up a chair to the desk and sat down to skim through the ledger, knowing it would require a much more detailed look but hoping something would leap out at him. Most of the entries seemed straightforward, showing what appeared to be an initial sum borrowed, the rate of interest – which had increased substantially in recent years – and the date of each payment.

There were gaps in some of the payment schedules, but

almost all of them recommenced within a few weeks. These people should be questioned first and it would be interesting to find out how they had been persuaded to start paying again. One entry stood out. The initial date of borrowing was fifteen years ago. Repayments were sporadic, and then a note had been made: '*Hold until September.*' After September, two thick black lines had been drawn across the page, and there was no more income recorded.

A couple of pages further on was a second entry, also with a hold notice. Under that was a question mark, and then – seemingly from nowhere – repayments had started again eighteen months ago, over twelve years since the hold notice was added. And the repayments were substantial.

The first name was S. Roberts. The second was A. Osborne.

'Tell me about "S. Roberts", Cameron,' Tom said, having dispensed with calling him Mr Edmunds as it showed a level of respect he didn't feel the man deserved.

'Scott was a friend at university. He begged me to lend him some money. I believe he had a girlfriend with expensive tastes. I was happy to help out. He asked for a repayment break, which I granted him, but he died – many years ago now.'

'And "A. Osborne"?'

'She helped out at my father's casino for a while, so I gave her a break too. She never came back to university but turned up again not long ago and was happy to repay her debt.'

Tom stared hard at Cameron, who returned the look without wavering. Tom found it hard to believe that the woman had sought Cameron out with the intention of paying off her debt after all that time, and the repayments seemed out of all proportion to the original loan, so she had to be high on the list of people to interview. And he had no intention of taking Cameron's word that Scott Roberts was dead either.

He closed the book with a thud as Becky poked her head

round the door. 'Boss, I've just had a call from Lynsey. We think we've got something.'

Tom felt a burst of energy at the thought of a breakthrough and pushed himself out of the chair.

'Keith, can you stay here with Mr Edmunds, please? Give him a receipt for the ledger – and Cameron, please answer DS Sims' questions about Jagger's movements yesterday. And yours on Monday. We need to know where you were between leaving the casino and the body being found in your car. Don't mess us about. The sooner we know who killed Jagger and possibly tried to kill you, the sooner you'll be able to return to your normal life.'

Tempting as it was, Tom didn't add 'until we lock you up'.

He followed Becky out of the room.

Tom left Edmunds Towers – as he privately thought of the house – ahead of Becky, who despite her claim to be driving more slowly these days still managed to beat him back to the incident room. She was bending low over a monitor with Lynsey when he walked in.

'What've we got?'

Lynsey turned to look up at him.

'When we looked at the CCTV close to the car park where the first body was found, it was impossible to identify any suspects. The streets weren't busy, but they weren't deserted either, and no one stood out as looking particularly suspicious. I did notice one guy wearing a hoody with the hood up and his head down, though, which seemed odd given how hot it was even at that time in the morning, but there was nothing more than that to attract my attention.'

Tom stared at the CCTV and watched the man walk down the road for a couple of seconds. 'And?'

'I picked him up again on a street close to the car park where

Jagger was killed.' Lynsey split the screen to show the two images side by side. 'The walk is the same. Head down, not running but certainly not strolling. He looks like a man on a mission.'

Tom could see she was right. This was way too much of a coincidence.

'So where does he go?'

'Ah, there's the rub. He disappears into the car park under Manchester Central. He could have got into a car there, or he could have walked out through one of the many exits.'

'Bloody car parks,' Tom muttered.

'We've got as many people as possible scouring CCTV from both before and after Jagger's murder, and from Monday as well. We'll get him, sir.'

'Have we ruled out all the residents?'

'Not entirely. We've got some interesting intel on one of them. I was at the apartment building last night, and a woman gave a false name. Anna Franklyn. Claimed to be Saskia Peterson.'

'Does that make her a suspect in your view, or is she just some woman leading a double life?'

'I don't know. I can't find any connection between her and either of the victims other than a very tenuous link: they briefly attended the same university. And the fact that she – together with about a hundred other people – has an apartment in the building above the car park where Jagger was killed. I don't think she's physically strong enough to have killed him, given how he died, so I don't think she's a suspect, but she's lying about something.'

Tom's mobile phone rang. He looked at Lynsey and shrugged.

'Yes, Philippa. What can I do for you?'

He listened as she asked him to come straight to her office. The assistant chief constable was with her, demanding to know if they were looking at a serial killer.

He hung up. 'Anything else, Lynsey?'

'Not really.' She nodded at the screen. 'I've written up the report, so I'll email it to you.'

Tom smiled his thanks and hurried towards the lift.

55

I'm dreading going home. I don't know what to say to Dominic. It feels as if every word that comes out of my mouth is a lie, and I'll have to lie to him tomorrow too, because nothing is going to stop me from going to see Scott.

I need to be the hunter, not the hunted. I am much stronger than I was all those years ago, and I must summon every scrap of my strength to deal with whatever comes, to protect my family even if it means risking my own safety.

Whatever it takes, I will win this battle.

My new-found determination fades a little as I pull into our drive. Dominic's car isn't here, and that's a surprise. He should have picked Holly up from school and he hasn't called to say that he was going out. *Where are my children?*

I fling open the car door, but before my panic has a chance to build, my question is answered. 'Mummy!'

I hear the shout from next-door's porch and I sag with relief. I can just make out Holly's head over the hedge, and I assume Bailey – too short to be seen – is with her.

Della pokes her head around her front door, drying her hands on a tea towel. 'Hi, Anna. Holly collected from school, as promised. And Bailey's perked up a bit, haven't you, sweetie?' Della looks down towards where I assume my son is standing. 'Is everything okay with you, Anna? You look a bit peaky. Dominic said you were at the gym again last night when I popped round. Don't go overdoing it, love.'

Della's brow is furrowed and I wonder what Dominic has told

her. And where is he?

'Everything's fine – thanks, Della. I really appreciate you picking Holly up.' I smile as if I knew all along that she had been asked.

'Come on, kids,' I say, and I walk to the end of Della's drive so they can run to me, Bailey with his arms out to be picked up. He's still such a baby. 'Are you feeling better now, Bubbles?'

'I'm okay,' he says slightly mournfully, as if he'll get more fuss if he's not quite well.

'Have you had anything to eat at Della's?'

'She gave me a sandwich after school,' Holly says. 'It was yucky egg, though.'

'I hope you didn't say that, Holly. It was very kind of her to look after you.'

'I had soup for lunch,' Bailey says. 'Della said it would make my throat feel better.'

Lunch? Why was Bailey at Della's for lunch? So he wasn't with Dominic when I spoke to him. *Why did he lie?*

'Did Daddy say where he was going, Bailey?' I ask, my voice as nonchalant as I can make it.

'No.'

He doesn't offer any more than that, and much as I want to quiz him, I don't want the children to feel my concern. I'm desperate to phone Dom, but I force myself to take deep breaths and acknowledge to myself that I'm probably overreacting, given everything else that's been happening.

Holly is in a chatty mood and I can't just ignore her, but although I check my mobile every few minutes, there is no message from my husband. Finally, breaking all my usual rules, I give them both another sandwich and as a treat I sit them down on the sofa to watch a cartoon. I take my phone into the kitchen and call Dominic.

To my surprise, he answers after the first ring.

'Dom, where are you?' I ask.

'Ah, sorry about this. I thought I'd be back by now. Busted, it seems.' He chuckles.

'That isn't an answer. Where *are* you?' I repeat.

'On a wild-goose chase,' he answers unhelpfully.

'Where?'

'Do I have to tell you?' He pauses, and I wait. 'Okay, I suppose I do. I'm in Lancaster.'

Whatever is he doing there? It's where I finished my degree and did my teacher training, but we don't keep in touch with anyone there, and my mum is much further north.

'Anna,' he says, a question in his voice, 'are you okay?'

'No, not really. Why Lancaster?'

I hear a sigh. 'You've caught me red-handed. It was supposed to be a surprise.'

'What do you mean?'

'I'm sorry, darling, I'd hoped to be home by now so you'd never find out, but life is never simple, is it?'

I have no idea what he is talking about.

'I don't really want to tell you, but you're sounding all suspicious so I suppose I've got no choice. What's coming up in the next couple of weeks?'

I know what he means. It's my birthday.

'I can tell by your silence that you've guessed. Look, I would really like this to be a surprise, so can we leave it there?'

What can I say? I know where he's been. There's a wonderful antique jewellery shop in Lancaster, and Dom caught me looking at their website recently. What he doesn't know is that I was thinking of something for Saskia, not for Anna, but I'm certain that's where he's been.

'Why did you tell me Bailey was with you?'

'Because you were in a state of panic over something. I knew he was safe, but if I'd told you he was with Della you'd have phoned her, told her to lock her doors and windows and all kinds of stuff. And you'd have demanded I go straight home. And I checked, Anna. I phoned Della as soon as you hung up, just to be sure he was okay.'

There's not much I can say to that. He's right. I was panicking, but I couldn't tell him why.

'How long before you're home?'

'It looks like the weather's about to break, and when it does, there's going to be a storm, so I guess I'll be about an hour and a half. Sorry, darling. It wasn't supposed to be like this.'

I look out of the window. The air has been getting heavier and heavier as the week has gone on, and I see a flash of lightning against the dark sky.

'Drive safely,' I say softly.

By ten o'clock I'm pacing up and down, frantic with worry. I've tried Dom's mobile at least twenty times, but he hasn't answered. Where is he?

It's hours since I spoke to him, and he was only in Lancaster. The weather is dreadful, and I pray he's not been in an accident. Why doesn't he call me?

I feel this is punishment for my earlier thoughts about the mundane nature of my marriage. I remind myself that I consciously chose my husband for his reliability and consistency in preference to the thrill of danger and uncertainty, and however confused I am right now, I want him home and safe.

56

Tom pulled up outside the modern detached house that he had visited so many times in the last few years and was relieved to see lights on inside. It was still early, although the sky was becoming blacker by the moment, but at least it seemed someone was in.

As he stepped out of the car, the first heavy drops of rain splattered onto the pavement and his head, so he ran for the shelter of the small porch and pressed the bell.

He heard footsteps on wooden flooring and the door opened.

'Oh! I wasn't expecting you.'

'Hello, Kate. Can I come in?'

Kate turned her head to glance over her shoulder and up the stairs. Tom guessed that Lucy was in her room and, if she was running true to form, would probably have headphones on, listening to something on her phone or Snapchatting with friends.

'I suppose so,' Kate said ungraciously.

She set off down the hall towards the kitchen without another word, and Tom followed, watching as his ex-wife headed straight for the fridge and pulled out a half-empty bottle of white wine. Tom wondered if it was the remnants from another night, or whether she had already started drinking. She splashed some of the wine into a glass.

'Don't look at me like that, Mr Holier Than Thou. You know how to drink too. Don't forget, I've known you for a long time.'

She was right. There was a period after Kate left him and took Lucy to live two hundred miles away when Tom had drunk far more than he should have, but it was no longer true. He enjoyed a glass of wine and an occasional whisky, but that was it.

'I'm not judging you, Kate. It's not like you, that's all. You've never been a heavy drinker.'

'You haven't lived with me for ten years, so you no longer have any idea what I get up to in my own time.'

This was true, although throughout those ten years Tom had been picking Lucy up and dropping her off regularly, and in the spirit of making things as normal for their daughter as possible, he had often popped in for a friendly-ish chat with his ex-wife. She had found it difficult initially, resenting the fact that Tom had been able to resist her charms when she had offered to come back to him the minute her new relationship had fallen apart. But despite their history he had never wanted to hurt her, sensing she struggled to deal with the consequences of the decisions she had made, and over the years their relationship had become easier. Until now.

'Do you want to tell me what's going on? We've always agreed that for Lucy's sake we would be civil and never use her as a bargaining tool. We also agreed that neither of us would blame the other for the break-up of our marriage. So what's changed?'

Kate gave him a hard glare, as if he had done something wrong. If he had, he had no idea what it was.

She turned her back, took a swig of wine, filled her glass again and slammed the bottle down on the worktop. He waited.

Finally she turned back towards him, but her gaze was fixed on the floor. 'Do you remember I asked you for some extra money to fund a trip Lucy wanted to go on to London a few weeks ago?'

Tom nodded.

'Part of that trip was to the Stock Exchange.' She lifted her eyes. 'Guess who was giving the talk?'

He knew the answer just from looking at her face. Declan. The man she had left him for when Lucy was three years old.

'Surely Lucy didn't remember him, and he couldn't possibly have recognised her.'

'You'd have thought not, but he had a list of all the pupils – he had to have their names to get passes for them. And it turns out he has been checking out my Facebook page. Lucy is on my profile picture. He put the name and the face together, and hey presto!' She took another gulp of wine.

'So what? Kate, it doesn't matter if she knows about Declan. We never lied to her.'

She looked at him over the rim of her glass. 'No?'

'We told her all along that things between us hadn't been good for a while, that you found someone you thought would make you happier, but that it didn't work out.'

'Yes, but we omitted to mention that you were perfectly happy and didn't actually *know* that things weren't too good.'

For a moment Tom wished he didn't have to drive because he would have quite liked a glass of wine himself.

'This is stupid. How does this matter now? Yes, I was hurt, angry, all of those things. But neither of us is blameless. The fact that I didn't know something was wrong says a lot about where my head was. What did the idiot say to her?'

Kate smiled for the first time. 'You were never a fan, were you?'

Tom just gave her a look.

'He asked if her mum was called Kate, and then – according to Lucy – he smirked and whispered, "Did your dad ever forgive her for doing the dirty on him?" or something equally foul. We had always made out that our marriage was effectively over before I left you for Declan, and he blew that wide open.'

Lucy would have been mortified if any of her friends had heard and would have come back ranting and raving at Kate.

'Why didn't you tell me? We could have talked to her together. You know I wouldn't have let her believe that. And why did you think it would help to tell her that I refused to get back together?'

'Why not? It's true.' Kate's mouth turned down at the corners, and for a moment Tom thought she was going to cry.

'I don't get it. I'm sorry, but I can't see why we couldn't have dealt with it properly, instead of putting a child in a position where she has to take sides.'

'Maybe I wanted her to take sides.'

'Why, though?'

This time he could see that Kate was definitely hanging onto her composure by a thread. She shook her head, but her eyes were full of tears.

'Kate?' he said, his voice gentle. He could feel her pain, but he had no idea why she was so upset.

Kate swallowed hard. 'I wanted her to love me most. Just for a while. She's always told me that I'll never find anyone half as good as you, and when Declan told her it was all my fault I knew she would hate me. She would have got over it, I'm sure, but I don't know if she would have got over it in time. So I told her I'd offered to come back and you'd turned me down.'

There was something wrong – there had to be. Even though Kate had always felt Lucy loved him more, needing *all* of Lucy's love was new.

'What is it, Kate? Tell me. Let me help. What do you mean, "in time"? In time for what?'

This time she let the tears fall.

'I've got cancer.'

Friday

57

The weather broke with a vengeance last night, the storm raging as I waited by the phone for news of Dominic. I called the local hospitals, checked to see if there had been any accidents on the M6, tried his mobile again and again, while simultaneously trying to persuade the children that all was well and Daddy would be home soon.

Eventually I managed to get them to bed with a promise to send him straight up to see them when he got in, knowing that Bailey at least would be asleep by then.

In the end I heard his car at just before one in the morning and rushed to the door.

'Thank God, Dom. What happened? Are you okay?' I said, following him as he stomped into the sitting room and flung himself into a chair. 'I was so worried about you.'

'I'm fine, no thanks to the moron who forced me off the road. The bastard didn't even stop.'

He sounded livid, so I went to sit on the arm of the chair and reached out to him, but he was in no mood to be soothed.

'With all the rain, maybe he didn't see you.'

'Bollocks. Course he did.'

'Surely you don't think he did it on purpose?'

'Either that or he was a bloody blind idiot. It said on the radio that cars were aquaplaning on the M61, so I came off the motorway. The stupid bastard was right behind me, his headlights blinding me, and then he edged out as if he was going to overtake. I drove as close to the side of the road as I could to let him past, but then he cut in front of me and I skidded off into some bushes. Bumped my head, scratched the front of the car too. Wait till you see it.'

'Oh, Dom, I'm so sorry. Why didn't you call me? You must have known I would be frantic with worry.'

'My bloody mobile couldn't get a signal – must have been a black spot. I was standing out there in the pissing rain, but the few cars that passed weren't interested in being flagged down by some sodden guy at the side of the road, and it took ages before someone stopped to help.'

'What did they do?'

'Called the rescue service to tow me out. But they were busy and took forever to get to me. I should have called you as soon as I was back on the road and had a signal, but all I could think about was getting home.'

'Never mind that. You're here now. Have you reported it?'

'What's the point? I didn't get a number.' Dominic looked away from me.

'What? What are you not telling me, Dom?'

'I don't want to scare you, but I think I recognised the car. I've seen it around here for the past few days. I told you someone was watching the house, but I'm not sure you believed me.'

Scott, you bastard. I knew then that I couldn't back out of going to see him, even if I wanted to. I had to get away from Dominic before he saw the rage behind my eyes.

'Can I get you anything – a drink, painkillers?'

He pushed himself out of the chair. 'No, but thanks. My head's not too sore. I'm just furious. I'd prefer just to go to bed, if that's okay. I'm sorry you were worried, darling.' Dom attempted a smile, but it was a weak effort as I'm sure was my own.

I don't think I slept at all, my mind turning over everything that had happened, speculating about Dom's accident. Had

Scott really forced him off the road? Why would he do that? I didn't come up with any answers.

It was hard to wake Dominic this morning, and for a few moments I worried that my plans for the day were about to be scuppered and I would be forced to take the children to school. But at the last moment he had pushed himself wearily from bed. 'Go to work,' he said. 'We'll talk later.'

The temperature has dropped by at least ten degrees overnight, and as I drive to my destination – my rendezvous with Scott – pedestrians are huddled beneath umbrellas that struggle to stay open against a fierce wind, dark macs are back on, and there are no more bright summer dresses on display. And yet, cold as it is, I feel clammy. My chest is tight, my breathing shallow, and I dread to think what today is going to bring.

I have told Jennie that I need to be with my mother and will be in Cumbria until Sunday but have promised to be back at work on Monday. That assumes I am still alive, of course. There is a vindictiveness about Scott's actions that is so unlike the boy I used to know. He made mistakes, he let me down badly, but he wasn't evil. If he has changed so much that he is prepared to seek revenge by taking two lives, what might he do to me? I shiver at the thought.

Even if I escape unharmed, how can I persuade him to stop preying on my family, watching our every move, and from revealing my crimes on the radio for all to hear? If I can't, I'll be working on my letter of resignation on Monday and very possibly moving out of the home I share with my husband and children. I know Dom won't let me stay.

All night I have been going over my decision to go to Wales today, but I don't know what else I can do. How else can I stop him? Scott seems intent on taking revenge on everyone who ever hurt him – Cameron, Jagger and now me. My hands grip the steering wheel a little tighter. I should feel glad he's alive – it means I can stop thinking of myself as a killer – but for the first time I regret the fact that I haven't brought some sort of weapon with me today, and right now I wish I *had* killed him fourteen years ago, as I always believed I did.

I have no idea how he survived, but I think I understand why he never came home – why he wanted the world to believe he was dead. He would have been in debt to Cameron for the rest of his life. Instead, he left me to that fate.

I take a deep breath to try to slow my breathing, but I can't shift the solid ball of terror from my chest, and despite the cold blast from the air conditioning as I pull onto the M56 to head for north Wales, I feel a bead of sweat slither uncomfortably down my back.

In spite of everything he's done, though, a tiny treacherous piece of me wants to see him – the boy I loved with such fierce passion, who I would have done anything for even though it meant breaking the law and ignoring every value I held dear. At least, that's how I felt until the very end – that last day – when he let me down so badly that I was prepared to watch him die.

58

Becky turned at the sound of Tom's voice as he said good morning to the team, all of whom had come in at the crack of dawn. She had been looking forward to giving him some good news about the CCTV results, but one look at him and the smile slid from her face. He looked dreadful. There was an unhealthy pallor to his skin, and he had deep, dark circles under his eyes. He was smiling at everyone, but she could see it was an effort. What on earth was wrong with him?

He must have sensed her gaze and he lifted his eyes to hers and shook his head very slightly. 'Don't ask,' his expression said.

With slightly less of a bounce in her step, she approached him with her news. 'Hey, boss,' she said quietly, 'have you got time for an update?'

'I certainly have,' he responded, rubbing his hands together with more enthusiasm than was absolutely necessary.

'We think we know who our man is. Lynsey was here all night, checking through CCTV from the car park our suspect disappeared into.' For a moment Tom looked as if he hadn't got a clue what she was talking about. 'If you remember, after he left the scene of Jagger's murder we managed to track him until he went into Manchester Central car park. Well, we think we've got him!' Becky pointed to her screen. 'We're as certain as we can be that this is him, leaving in a car.'

Tom peered closely. The man still had his hood up, but the hoody had distinctive branding on the shoulder.

'Lynsey's a smart girl. I presume we got the registration?'

'We did indeed. Keith's on it now. It's registered to a Dorothy Matthews, who is obviously not the driver, but he'll find out who was driving it last night. It's still early, so hopefully we'll catch her before she starts her day, and the registration number's been circulated nationally on PNC. Shall I come and find you in your office when we've got something, bring you a cup of coffee?'

'Please. And I presume we're checking where the car went?'

'Of course. We're trying to trace where it was headed on ANPR.'

Tom gave Becky what passed for a grateful smile and made his way out of the incident room, looking as if he were a million miles away.

Becky started to plough her way through all the other intelligence that had come in overnight, deciding what was important and what wasn't, but less than ten minutes later Keith came to her with a sheet of paper.

'Interesting,' he said, looking very pleased with himself. 'Mrs Matthews sold her car last week to someone she described as a nice young man with a Welsh accent. She keeps meaning to post the registration document but hasn't got round to it. But we've got the new owner's name and address. We're seeing what intelligence we can gather on him now.'

Becky took the piece of paper from his hand. 'Well done, Keith. I'll go and brief the boss.'

She hurried along the corridor to find Tom, forgetting the promised cup of coffee. His door was closed – never a good sign – so she knocked lightly before pushing it open. He looked up from his desk; the haggard look had returned to his face.

'Tom, are you okay?'

'I'm fine. What have you got?'

Tom hated sharing personal matters – even with Becky, who had known him for years – and now wasn't the time to push him, so she slapped the piece of paper down in front of him.

288

'The person seen in the vicinity of the murders of Derek Brent and Roger Jagger is a man called Scott Roberts. He bought the car from Mrs Matthews a few days ago. Keith's working through anything we can find on him.'

Tom frowned and, saying nothing to Becky, picked up his desk phone and pressed a button. 'Keith, can you bring Edmunds' ledger in, please?'

'What's up?' Becky asked.

'We'll see.'

They sat in an uncomfortable silence. If Tom didn't want to talk, she wasn't going to try to make him. Fortunately, it was only a minute or two later when they heard Keith's brisk step in the corridor.

With a sharp rap on the door, he pushed it open and handed Tom the ledger. 'Sir.' He stood awaiting further orders.

Tom flipped over the pages until he found the one he wanted.

'I thought so,' he said. '"S. Roberts". And Edmunds called him Scott. He is, or was, one of Cameron Edmunds' clients – which gives us motive. His name's crossed out in the ledger, though, because according to Cameron Edmunds, Scott Roberts is dead.'

'Looks like he got it wrong, then,' Becky said. 'Maybe Roberts wanted Edmunds to think he was dead if he owed him money. I can't say I'd blame him. Anyway, dead or alive, he gave an address in north Wales, and we're getting it checked out right now.'

59

Tom told Becky and Keith that he would join them in the incident room in a few minutes. First he wanted to get his thoughts together. The memory of last night and Kate's revelation was difficult to put to the back of his mind.

'Does Lucy know?' he'd asked.

'No. I want some time with her before I tell her.'

'What's the prognosis?'

'I have an operation on Monday. It's stage two in one of my kidneys, so it's not great. But it could be worse.' Kate had given a short bark of laughter. 'It could be stage four, and at least I have a spare kidney.'

Tom had said nothing. He wanted to go and put his arms round her, to offer some comfort, but she didn't look as if she would welcome that.

'My plan was to tell you on Sunday and then suggest you pick Lucy up from school on Monday, take her back to your place and tell her for me.'

Had the news not been so awful he would have been irritated with Kate for leaving him to tell their daughter, knowing that more than anything Lucy would want to be with her mum and talk to her, hug her. But he could understand that it might be difficult to say the words.

'I think the best thing for Lucy would be to hear it from both of us, now, together. Even though I'm not her favourite person at the moment, I'm sure she isn't happy keeping me at arm's length. We can explain it all and tell her how we're going to make sure she's looked after.'

Kate hadn't wanted to agree, but in the end had seen that it would be for the best. She and Lucy could have some time together, and Lucy would move back in with Tom next week while Kate was in hospital – with the air cleared.

It had been so difficult to break the news. Kate wasn't able to say a word, just sitting mutely at the table with tears in her eyes, so it was left to Tom. But at least they were all in the room together. Lucy was devastated, of course, but Tom talked positively about the future, about the amazing care Kate would get and the success rates now being achieved with cancer treatment. He felt it was what Lucy needed, but it left all of them feeling wrung out with emotion, and now he had to somehow push it to the back of his mind and focus on this double murder. Finally they had something concrete to work with, and he had a feeling that the solution was within touching distance.

With a deep breath, he pushed himself out of his chair.

'Keith,' he called as he walked into the incident room, 'get on to Cameron Edmunds and find out why he thinks Scott Roberts is dead. Also, get someone to check if there's a record of his death and see if the address he gave the seller matches the record of his driving licence, please.'

Tom walked over to the board and scanned the evidence they had collated up to now. It all seemed to have started with the moneylending fifteen years ago. Despite Cameron's protestations to the contrary, Tom knew they were going to find enough evidence from his so-called friends to prove he was nothing better than a loan shark. He had to admit, though, that they could have spent days interviewing every person in his ledger and still failed to find their killer. Thank goodness Lynsey had such a sharp eye.

'Sir,' a young detective seconded to the team called to Tom. 'There's no registration of the death of a Scott Roberts that we can find in the timescale.'

Was Becky right? Had the man faked his own death to avoid repaying his debt? Whatever the truth was, they had to work on the assumption that Scott was alive until the moment a death certificate was in front of their eyes.

Tom could hear Keith speaking on the phone, his voice raised, and guessed he was talking to Cameron, a man it seemed no one in the world liked – except maybe Jagger, who was now dead.

Keith slammed the phone down and marched across to Tom and Becky. 'Irritating prick.'

Tom surprised himself by wanting to laugh. 'What's up?'

'He was difficult, that's all. I won't bore you with the details. He's a smug bastard, and frankly I can't see what he has to be smug about. All he knows is that Scott Roberts died many years ago. He can't remember exactly when, as we've had the audacity to take his ledger, and he doesn't know how he died either.'

'Well, it looks as if he's wrong. I quite enjoy the thought of someone getting one over on Edmunds.'

Another young detective handed a slip of paper to Keith, who looked at it and said, 'Dead or alive, his driving licence is apparently registered to the address Mrs Matthews gave us, although the photocard is out of date.'

'Nothing unusual about that, sadly. Becky, you said the local force are on their way to pay him a visit so Keith, let's make sure they know what they're dealing with.'

Keith nodded and marched back to his desk.

'I'll be back in my office when you have an update.'

Tom heard Becky's voice behind him. 'What are you doing here?' He glanced over his shoulder. A tired but wired Lynsey had just walked back into the office.

'Sorry, but I couldn't sleep. Too much in my head.'

Tom knew exactly how she felt.

60

As luck would have it, for the first time this week the traffic seems to be in my favour, and I realise I am going to arrive at Scott's parents' house way too early. With only ten miles left to go I spot a roadside café and pull in. I can't stay in the car – every muscle in my body is twitching – so I get out and pace backwards and forwards, up and down, my umbrella only just managing to defy the wind.

I glance at my watch every thirty seconds, but no amount of pacing reduces the tension that is building, layer upon layer, and I decide a cup of coffee might make me feel better. I push open the door to the café and am greeted by the welcoming smell of bacon and toast, but the thought of food makes me want to heave.

As the time for me to leave draws near, I feel torn. Half of me wants to stay, huddled in the warm comfort of the café, while the other half is eager to get on with it – get it done. I drag myself to my feet and head out into the wind and rain.

The nausea remains with me, and the back of my tongue feels swollen, filling my mouth. My stomach is churning, turning over and over, but I have to do this. Whatever Scott is trying to do to me and my family, it has to stop. I'm taking the biggest gamble of my life, but this is one hand I have to win.

The world has turned darker. The clouds press down, crushing me, dirty water splashing onto my windscreen from the tyres of every lorry that I crawl behind on the narrow lanes that lead to my destination, until finally I find myself at the bottom of the street leading to Scott's family home, remembering the house with the FOR SALE board that the woman in the shop pointed out to me.

I'm still a few minutes early. I don't pull up directly in front of the door – I don't want him to know I'm here, so I park halfway along the street and watch, hoping to see him go in or come out. But nothing happens. I leave it another ten minutes, well past the agreed time, but he doesn't arrive.

He must already be inside.

I pull a tissue from my bag and wipe my sticky hands, my top lip and the hollow above my chin. I need to appear confident and in control, so I search for a lipstick and try to keep my hands steady as I apply it.

The rain has stopped, but the sky is the threatening purple-black of ripe plums, the clouds rolling and jostling each other. There are lights on in the neighbouring houses, even though it's mid-morning. But not in the Roberts' house. That remains in darkness.

Delaying the inevitable isn't going to help, so finally I unbuckle my seat belt and open the car door. The house is a mid-terrace, rendered in grey pebbledash with bay windows at the front. It is uphill from where I've parked and my breathing is fast and shallow, so I steady myself on a gatepost before walking up the path. The place looks run-down, with green paint peeling from the door and weeds sprouting from cracks in the path. The windows stand empty, behind them a black void.

Straightening my back, I lift my hand and knock firmly on the door. As my fist meets the wood for the second time, the door moves, nudging inwards by an inch. I give it a gentle push. It opens a few inches more. I take a step forward and push the door bit by bit until it is half open.

'Hello?' I call, annoyed by the tentative sound of my voice. 'Hello?' I shout again with more authority.

There is no answer. I push the door fully open and call once more. Still nothing. My voice echoes, and the house has an empty feel to it. I peer into the dark hall and reach for the light switch, but when I press it nothing happens. I look up to see there is no bulb in the fitting.

The hall is dreary, its flowery wallpaper peeling in places. It must have been there for years. A dark-red patterned carpet runs the length of the hall and up the stairs, and there is a stale, unused smell to the house, as if food has been left to rot. It hasn't been completely cleared of furniture, but I'm sure no one is living here. There's a hall stand with coats still hanging on it, a couple of umbrellas in the rack and, bizarrely, an old cricket bat. It reminds me of how Scott moaned when we were in Nebraska about missing his cricket. Maybe it is his.

The door to my left is closed but I take a step towards it. The muddy brown paint is cracked and flaking and I turn the tarnished brass knob. It's locked.

The hall bends slightly to the left beside the stairs, and I find myself walking on tiptoe for no reason that I can explain, because I'm sure no one is here. The presence of another person would change the way the air moves, or lighten the stench of decay. I glance nervously at the staircase. Am I wrong? Is he hiding up there?

The further I move away from the open front door, the darker it gets. As I inch my way around the slight bend, I can just make out another door. This one is standing slightly ajar, and I call out again: 'Hello?' I'm not expecting a reply, and I don't get one.

Using my foot, I gently push the door open. Although there is a window, a thick curtain obliterates most of the light from outside, and all I can make out is what seems to be a lighter patch of wall ahead of me. There appears to be something pinned there. I reach out for the light switch, but again, nothing happens. I step into the room and walk cautiously towards the far wall.

Suddenly the room is flooded with light.

Swivelling towards the source, I'm almost blinded. I raise my arm to shield my eyes from the harsh glare of three spotlights on stands. I must have triggered a sensor as I walked into the room. Spikes of fear dance on every inch of my skin. Is there someone lurking behind the lights? But nothing moves, and as my eyes adjust I make out shadows, but none in human form. There's nothing there other than some pieces of furniture pushed back against the wall.

I want to run – to get as far from here as I can. I feel exposed, certain this whole set-up has been designed to scare me. And it's working. I can hear my own breathing – short sharp gasps – and I try to slow it down as I turn back to see what the lights are illuminating. The wall is covered with papers, photos, a map. This is intended for me, and I take a tentative step forward.

I stare at the pictures and immediately I recognise Scott – the Scott that I met fifteen years ago and last saw less than a year later. Next to that photo is one from just after we met, of me with spiky hair. I remember Scott taking it. Next to that is another one from when my hair was a little longer. He uploaded them onto my computer, but I have never looked at them since. There is a more recent photo of me too, one I recognise from Facebook, and I am shocked to see there's also one of me as Saskia in my blonde wig, leaving the apartment in Manchester. I have no idea who took that. Someone knows everything about me – knows all the secrets I thought I had guarded well. There is a photo of Cameron too, and even one of Jagger, unaware of the camera as he walks out of a bar.

Beneath the photos are documents. The first is a sponsorship form that I remember creating, headed with an image of someone leaping from a plane. Then there's a poster for a raffle, offering a holiday in Crete, with minor prizes of pizzas, cinema tickets, book tokens, supermarket vouchers. It's all there. The history of my schemes and deceptions with Scott, and I feel an all-too-familiar stab of remorse.

I'm working my way along the wall, wondering what this is supposed to tell me, when I hear a footstep behind me. I want to look round, but I can't. I can't imagine how I'm going to feel. Will I still know him?

Then I hear a shout, a voice, a Welsh accent. 'Hello? Where are you?'

I don't answer. I turn towards the door, the lights in my eyes making it difficult to see. Into the doorway steps a man. I can just make out the thick, dark curly hair that I loved to run my fingers through.

'Scott,' I say, my voice shaking. 'My God. It really is you.'

61

Tom had intended to stay in his office and use the time productively, but they were getting close to finding this killer and he was struggling to focus on anything else. So within half an hour he was back in the incident room.

'We've picked up the car on ANPR, sir,' Keith said. 'After leaving the central Manchester area on Wednesday night, Scott Roberts drove around Manchester and then disappeared. We've not been able to find a mobile registered to his name, so there's not much else we can do to track him.' He pulled up a map on his screen and pointed to a retail park. 'We lost him here, but it would have been difficult for him to leave without us picking him up again. Which suggests he dumped his car.'

'There's a big DIY store there – a massive one,' Becky said. 'He could have swapped cars. What do you think?'

Lynsey grabbed her jacket from the back of her chair. 'They're bound to have CCTV. I'm on it.'

'If you find it, Lynsey, don't let it out of your sight until we can set up surveillance,' Tom said as the young detective headed for the door.

'We had a call back from the north Wales police,' Becky said. 'They arrived at the address on Roberts' driving licence just before eight a.m., but the house was deserted. It's up for sale. Apparently the son doesn't live there either, and hasn't for a while. They spoke to a neighbour who said the mother has been moved to a nursing home in Colwyn Bay. An officer is on his way there to see if they can supply an address for Scott.'

Tom stared at Becky, who looked as disappointed as he felt. He flopped down into a chair in front of her desk. 'I thought we had him.'

'We're a hell of a lot closer than we were yesterday, boss. At least we have a pretty good idea who we're looking for, so it's only a matter of time.'

'Yes, but if he's on a killing spree, he might well already have someone else in his sights.'

It suddenly seemed to Tom as if the weight of the world was on his shoulders, and he closed his eyes for a moment. He could feel Becky's concern and knew he had to summon up some mental energy from somewhere. He couldn't let events in his personal life drag him down, and he had to be positive for the team. Taking a deep breath, he pushed himself upright and turned to Becky with his best attempt at a smile.

'My turn, I think.' He picked up the mug from her desk and made his way towards the kitchen.

They didn't have to wait long for a response from north Wales. Tom had just put a cup of coffee in front of Becky when Keith told him an officer from West Conwy Coastal Police was on the phone and put the call on speaker.

'The son hasn't been to the hospice today, and they don't have an address for him, just a phone number,' he said. 'But here's the thing. According to them, the son goes by the name of Brad – short for Bradley. Not Scott.'

Tom glanced at Keith and Becky, who both looked as bemused as he felt.

'Apparently Mrs Roberts always calls him Scott – that's the name of her son who died and the only name she seems to recognise.'

Thanking the officer and leaving Keith to get details of Bradley Roberts' mobile, Tom turned to Becky.

'So was Cameron right? If for some inexplicable reason Scott's death was never registered, his driving licence will still appear to be valid, but I'm not ruling him out yet. Could this be Bradley passing himself off as his brother? Let's get what intelligence we can on him too.'

'The owner did tell Keith that the guy who bought it had a Welsh accent, although as evidence goes it's hardly compelling.' Becky shrugged.

Tom grabbed a photocopy of the index page of the ledger from Keith's desk and ran his finger down the list of names.

'There's no other Roberts on here, just Scott, so if it *is* Bradley – and let's face it, that's a massive if – why would he want to kill Cameron and Jagger?'

'Maybe Scott's alive and they're in it together. Or perhaps Bradley found out about the loan and the debt. If his mother thinks he's Scott she might have revealed old secrets, and now he's taking revenge on behalf of his brother. Or possibly Cameron found out the house was being sold and tried to get Bradley to pay off Scott's debt. I don't know. A bunch of theories, but based on nothing much right now.' She shrugged again.

Tom was about to ask Keith to start an investigation into Bradley when he realised the sergeant was still on the phone to the police in Wales. 'Anna Franklyn,' Keith said. 'Yep, got that, thanks.'

Becky's mouth dropped open, and Tom looked at her as Keith ended the call. 'What?'

'Keith, what was that about Anna Franklyn?' Becky called.

'According to the visitors' register, a woman called Anna Franklyn called to see Mrs Roberts earlier in the week.'

Becky slammed her hand down on the desk. 'I *knew* there was something about her. Lynsey mentioned her to you yesterday, boss. She's the woman who has the apartment in the building where Jagger was murdered.'

Becky reminded him of what they had discovered about Anna Franklyn and Saskia Peterson.

'She told us she was visiting the apartment block to see this Saskia. It's on the list of things to check today, because we're pretty sure Saskia Peterson and Anna Franklyn are the same person. But we couldn't find anything to link her to either of the deaths, other than the fact that her car came into the car park about thirty minutes before Jagger was killed.' She banged the desk again and muttered an expletive. 'All we had was the fact that we were sure she lied about being Saskia Peterson. It seemed unlikely she'd killed Jagger, but we knew she was hiding something, as was her husband, because he said she'd been in all night. I just didn't see her as a priority. Sorry, boss.'

'So let's get hold of her now. If she's been visiting Mrs Roberts, there's clearly a more significant connection than we thought, and if she knows the mother there's a chance she knows where we can find Scott or Bradley – even if only to rule either of them out.'

There was no point in Tom going back to his own office. He had the sense that things were going to be moving quickly, so he pulled off his jacket and threw it on the back of a chair. He could hear Becky on her phone, and finally she waved him over.

'We've tried Anna's home number. There's no answer. I tried the school. The bursar says she's taken a couple of days off as her mother has had a fall. She lives in Cumbria, apparently.'

'Check it, Becky.'

Becky smiled. 'Already did. The mother's surname is Osborne, and Keith's trying to reach her now.'

Osborne. Tom grabbed the copy of the index page again and laid it on Becky's desk, flattening it with the palm of his hand. He pointed to the entry.

'"S. Roberts" – Scott – with a line through his name apparently to indicate that he is deceased. Another name on the list – "A. Osborne". Similar dates, although she started paying

Edmunds again over a year ago. Would that be Anna, do you think, Osborne being her maiden name?'

Becky raised her eyes to his. She should have pushed harder against the wall of resistance put up by Anna Franklyn.

'Sir,' Keith called. 'I've tracked down Mrs Osborne and spoken to her. Her daughter isn't with her, and she hasn't had a fall. She used her own mobile to call her daughter's, but there's no answer. According to Mrs Osborne, that never happens. Anna always picks up when she sees it's her mum.'

'Right.' Tom raised his voice so the whole room could hear. 'We need to find Anna Franklyn. Let's get her car registration and see if we can discover where she is.'

'We've already got it,' Becky said. 'Her car was in the car park where Jagger was killed.'

'Of course, so track her. She may be on her way to visit her mother, whether or not she's had a fall. But let's see, shall we?'

Tom felt a burst of elation. Anna Franklyn was paying money to Cameron Edmunds, so there was little doubt she knew Roger Jagger. And she was linked to Scott Roberts, so by default to Bradley Roberts. She may not have been strong enough to kill Jagger herself, but it didn't mean she wasn't involved. They needed to find this woman now, before anyone else died.

62

Tom paced the incident room as Keith continued to try Anna Franklyn's phone and Becky spoke to Mrs Osborne, who it seemed was now becoming slightly hysterical.

'It's okay, Mrs Osborne. There's no problem, I'm sure. Your daughter might be driving so she won't be able to answer. We're just trying to find her in relation to someone she once knew, that's all. Nothing for you to worry about,' she repeated.

Tom signalled Becky to put the phone on speaker.

'Who? Who did she used to know? I know everything about my daughter – if she knew him, I would know him too.'

Tom nodded to Becky.

'Scott Roberts.'

There was no mistaking the gasp from the other end of the phone. 'He's alive then? Anna said she didn't think it was possible. She swears he died in Nebraska.'

Again, Tom's eyes met Becky's. This was new. Cameron had said Scott was dead, but not that he died in America.

'Do you know when this was, Mrs Osborne?'

'Yes, it was this time of year. I remember that. And it was a week or so before Anna's twentieth birthday, so that would make it fourteen years ago. They met when she first went to university a year before that. He died in Lincoln, Nebraska.'

That would explain why there was no record of Scott's death in the UK. There was no obligation to register the death of someone who had died overseas.

Tom made winding-up signs to Becky, but Mrs Osborne

wasn't finished. 'That's why it was odd when I heard him on the radio on Monday. Anna was certain it wasn't him, but he said his name was Scott and his girlfriend was Spike, which is what he called my Anna after she had that silly haircut.'

'What programme was this?'

'Local radio. The bit they call "The One That Got Away" on Monday morning. Scott said he was going to reveal everything that had happened on next Monday's show. But Anna said I was daft believing it was him. I wasn't though, was I?'

Just then Keith waved his hand at Tom and mouthed, 'ANPR'. Leaving Becky to Mrs Osborne, he moved over to where Keith was sitting at his computer screen.

'Lots of hits on Mrs Franklyn's car in the last couple of hours. And look where she was heading.'

Tom stared at the screen. 'She's going to north Wales,' he said, stating the obvious. 'When was the last sighting?'

'Half an hour ago. We lost her here.' Keith pointed at the screen. 'She must have moved onto the side roads.'

Becky had finally managed to extricate herself from the call, and Tom signalled her to join them.

'Get onto the radio station, Keith. Find out if they have any contact details for Scott Roberts.' He picked up his jacket and slung it over his shoulder. 'Grab your things, Becky. Anna Franklyn is somewhere in north Wales, and the question is...'

'I know,' Becky said. 'Is Scott Roberts alive, or is it Bradley? If so, is Anna Franklyn in cahoots with one of them, or is she about to be his next victim? I don't like the sound of this. Whose car, yours or mine?'

'Yours,' he said. 'And for God's sake, drive like you used to!'

63

I can't speak. I peer into the doorway, waiting for him to step into the light. But he stays where he is.

'What did you call me?' he asks, his voice suspicious.

'Scott,' I say, more tentatively now.

Then he moves forward and my heart races. He's too young to be Scott – mid-twenties, probably, but so very like him. Who is he?

'Scott's dead,' he says, and my fear ratchets up a notch. If he's not Scott, what does he want with me?

'What are you doing in my house?' he asks, his words clipped.

I take a step back, trying to hide my confusion. He's angry, but surely he asked me to be here? Is he pretending to be Scott?

'I had a message – from Scott – to meet him here. Who are you?'

He laughs, and he is so like Scott that I guess the answer the moment before he tells me.

'Brad Roberts. I'm Scott's younger brother. You're lying about the message and you'd better tell me why before I phone the police. I got a call from the estate agents to ask if the builder I'd employed had managed to get into the house with the keys they gave him. Except I hadn't hired anyone, and you don't look much like a builder to me. So I'll ask you again. Why are you in my house?'

I don't know what to say. Scott never told me he had a brother. None of this makes sense. I shake my head as he takes another step towards me.

'Who are you, and for the third and final time, why are you trespassing on my property?'

I look at his dark hair again, so like Scott's. Brad can't know that his brother is alive and that any minute now he's going to walk through that door.

'I went to see your mother at the hospice. It was you who ran away from me, wasn't it?' I can hear the accusation in my voice, and for a moment my conviction that Scott is alive wavers. But he has to be. Only Scott knows the truth.

'Ran? What, from you?' He laughs. 'I ran because I'm always late when I go there. My mother thinks I'm Scott. She gets upset and it takes ages to calm her. He was her blue-eyed boy, you see, and I'm just little Brad.' I can hear the bitterness in his voice. 'Why did you go to see her?'

'I was looking for Scott. My name's Anna Franklyn and I was his girlfriend at university. I thought he was dead too, but he's not. I told you – he sent me a message and asked me to come here.'

He shakes his head wearily, as if it's not worth arguing. It's only then that he seems to notice the papers and pictures attached to the wall behind me.

'What the hell's this rogues' gallery all about?'

He walks to the photo of Saskia and turns to look at me through narrowed eyes, as if trying to work out if she and I are the same person. Then he sees the photo of Scott with the smaller one of me next to it, and he stands for a few seconds staring at it, then glances at the map of Nebraska and spins round to glare at me.

'*You!*' he says, spitting out the word. '*You're* the reason he went to Nebraska. We always knew some girl had dragged him there, but we never knew who it was, or why. We've got you to blame for the fact that he died so far from his family.'

I want to shout that he's not dead, and it wasn't me who wanted to go to America. It was Scott. All of it was Scott. He said it was the only way to solve all our problems, and I had sworn I would do whatever it took to keep him from harm.

In the end, though, there was one sacrifice too many. I should have stopped it before it went too far.

Then

Four weeks after I told Scott I was expecting his baby we still hadn't agreed what we were going to do. By then I was working for Cameron, and even though I detested him with a passion, the thrill of the casino had started to get into my blood. I didn't play, but I took vicarious pleasure in watching some of my favourite poker players win.

There were other players I despised – those who thought they had the right to touch me, to put an arm around my shoulders or my waist and ask for a kiss for luck. They never got one – I always laughed and playfully pushed them away. I became good at flirting, flattering, lying through my teeth about what fun I was having, what great company they were. That was when I learned one of the skills that I have since honed to perfection. The art of pretence.

I didn't know I was being filmed until two weeks after I started when Jagger handed me an envelope of stills taken from the CCTV.

'Buck your ideas up, Anna, or you're out.'

The photos captured my disgust when punters weren't looking my way. I wasn't playing the game the way Cameron wanted me to, so I worked on my performance, laughing, smiling and flattering even those men I found disgusting. The photos got better, and Cameron was pleased. But I learned where the cameras were and – over time – how to avoid them.

I knew I couldn't keep the job for more than a few months. At some point Cameron would realise that my shape was changing, my waistline expanding, and he would sack me. Because my decision was final. I was going to have my baby.

Scott didn't like it. He had tried to persuade me that a

termination was the sensible option, but I couldn't do it. This was my baby, and I wanted him or her to live. I was worried about telling my parents, but I was going to need their support. I wasn't concerned that they would be appalled or ashamed of me – I could do no wrong in their eyes. But my mum would want to bring up my baby, and I didn't want that. My parents were already in their early sixties and would be eighty before the child reached eighteen. It wasn't the right solution for anyone, although it was going to be hard to make them understand what I had decided. And I still had to convince Scott.

I arranged to meet him away from my room, which had begun to feel claustrophobic after all the pain it had seen, and as I sat in a café waiting for him, sipping a cup of coffee, I caught a glimpse of him in the distance. Despite all that had happened he was bouncing along, looking as if all was well with the world, and I had to admire his resilience, although the mood swings from elation to despair could sometimes be wearing.

He strode towards me with a beaming smile. 'Come outside. I don't want to talk in here.' He held out a hand and pulled me to my feet. It was freezing, but he dragged me over to a bench.

'Have you decided?'

I had promised to give him my final decision today. Not that I had wavered even for a moment.

'I have. Look, Scott, I know it's not what you want, but I can't have an abortion.' I expected a look of irritation at my determination to have this child, and was surprised when I didn't get one. 'I'm going to go home at Easter and tell my parents, and then I'm going to have the baby and put him or her up for adoption. Some lucky couple are going to get a gorgeous child to bring up in a happy home.'

Scott's face didn't drop as I had expected; in fact he positively beamed. 'It's due in early September, yes?'

He knew that. I also wanted to tell him to stop calling our baby 'it'.

'Okay, and you're not showing at all yet, so you can probably hide the fact that you're pregnant from your family, especially if you don't go home again after Easter.'

I had no idea where this was going. 'I need to tell them. I'm going to go home to have the baby.'

'No, you're not. I've got a plan, Spike. A plan that will solve all our problems.' He grabbed both of my hands in his. 'We're going to America.'

Now

Scott's brother walks away from me, hands shoved into his pockets. As he reaches the door he turns. 'I don't know why you have it in your head that Scott's alive. Do you think he would have let us suffer the pain of losing him, of not being able to bury him, if he was alive?'

In a moment of clarity one word comes to me: *Yes.*

Scott was desperate, and he was a planner. Apart from the sponsorship scam, all the money-making schemes were his. America was his idea. He broke both the law and my heart to escape the clutches of Jagger and Cameron. So what else might he have done?

Brad is by the door now, indicating the way out with his arm.

'I want you to leave. I don't know what this is all about, but please get out of my house.'

As I look at him, not sure what to say, I see a shadow move behind his back. It seems to loom above his head, then suddenly there is a crash and he staggers forward and crumples soundlessly to the floor at my feet.

The only thing I can see is an old cricket bat, the glare of the spotlights reflecting on the yellowed wood. And then I hear a voice, the voice from the radio.

'Hello, Spike. Thanks for coming. I knew you would.'

64

Tom had been hoping that some of Becky's old driving habits had survived, but despite his request that she should drive the way she used to, for the first few miles she was the new ultra-careful driver that he didn't recognise.

'Why don't you let me drive?' he asked after fifteen minutes.

Becky glanced across at him. 'What? Tom, you have moaned non-stop about my driving since the day I met you, and now I'm trying to be more cautious you don't like it, do you?'

Tom had to admit she was right. 'I'm missing the fear-induced adrenaline rush of a journey with you at the wheel.'

Becky glared at him, then the corners of her mouth twitched up into a grin. 'You're right. This is tedious, isn't it? And anyway, you're the boss!' With that she put her foot down.

Tom sat back in his seat and called Keith in the incident room to check what the team had discovered about Bradley Roberts. The answer was not very much, but it was early days. Whether or not he was involved, if anyone knew if his brother was alive, it would be him.

'One more thing, sir,' Keith said. 'DC Whitely volunteered to go back to the casino late last night and ask around again about the woman seen with Cameron Edmunds.'

'Ah yes, the woman he has since denied all knowledge of. And?'

'It seems the dealer was being a bit disingenuous. When the picture was shown to the barman he confirmed that he – and just about everyone in the casino, it would seem – knows the woman as Saskia. She isn't always a redhead, though. Sometimes blonde, sometimes platinum. She likes to ring the changes, but he said he didn't need to see her face – if she was with Cameron, it would be Saskia. Oh, and he said she's one hell of a poker player.'

Tom could see Becky's eyes widening as they listened, but she didn't take them off the road.

He thanked Keith and ended the call. 'That confirms her links to Edmunds, Jagger and Scott Roberts. What else are we going to discover about her?'

'Talk about a multi-layered woman,' Becky said, with what sounded like admiration. 'Mother and head teacher – a picture of respectability – combined with a sassy kick-ass poker player with a variety of wigs, a sexy name and a secret apartment.'

'Which is the real Anna Franklyn, though? What did you make of her when you met her, Becky?'

'I found it impossible to tell what she was thinking most of the time. I honestly couldn't get a handle on her, but if she's such a poker ace, perhaps that explains it.'

Tom pondered for a few moments then pressed the screen on his phone and put it on speaker again.

'Morning, ma'am. I need a sign-off on a request for the live-time cell siting of a suspect's phone.'

'Tell me.' Philippa Stanley, as usual, was not wasting words.

Tom laid out the case, explaining why they needed to find Anna Franklyn. 'Philippa, I can't tell you for certain how she's involved, but my gut is telling me she's either a co-conspirator in two murders or she's the next victim.'

'Your gut.' The slight disdain in Philippa's voice was clear. Tom gritted his teeth. She'd always had a problem with Tom's intuition and loved to make it clear that it didn't replace good police work.

'Okay, I'll trust you on this one,' she said finally, with something that sounded suspiciously like a sigh. 'I'll give verbal authorisation now so as not to delay things. Get the paperwork sorted and I'll sign it. And where are you, Tom? It sounds as if you're in a car.'

'We're on our way to north Wales. I'll tell you about it when I get back.'

As soon as he ended the call, his phone rang again.

'Yes, Lynsey. How are you doing at the DIY place?'

'Their CCTV is excellent, sir. I checked the period immediately following the last time Scott Roberts' car was picked up on ANPR. We were right – it was driven in and parked. The driver got into another car, leaving the one we were tracking here.'

'Did you get the registration of the other car?'

'Sorry, sir. It was parked behind the trolley store, and when he reversed out it was at the wrong angle.'

'Bugger.'

'But it doesn't matter. I recognised him. I know who he is.'

65

He steps into the room, and now I see his face clearly.

'Dominic?'

His expression is blank and I shiver. I have so many questions, but right now Brad Roberts is lying face down, unconscious, on the floor, and I fall to my knees by his head. I reach out my hand to his neck, and there's a pulse, thank goodness.

'Why did you hit him? Jesus, Dom, you could have killed him. He wasn't going to hurt me. Call an ambulance, for God's sake. I'll explain to them that you thought I was in danger.'

Dominic crouches down and reaches into the pocket of his hoody. I think he's getting his phone but he pulls out what looks like a piece of black plastic, yanks one of Brad's arms from under his body, grabs the other one and pushes the plastic over his wrists. I realise it's a cable tie.

'What are you *doing*? Dominic, stop it. He's not going to hurt me.'

He ignores me and takes out another cable tie to bind Brad's feet.

I launch myself at him and try to push him away. Has he gone mad? But I'm half his size and he barely registers my attack. I stumble. He stands up and grabs my upper arm, hoisting me to my feet.

'What are you doing here? How did you know where I was?'

Dominic makes a noise that sounds like a sad little laugh. 'I always know where you are. You're never out of my sight for long, no matter what you're doing.'

'What do you mean?'

Then I remember that he called me Spike, a nickname I have never shared with him. I hear again the voice on the radio. My mouth goes dry and I struggle to swallow as I realise why it sounded familiar. How many times has Dominic shown off his acting skills and had the children in fits of laughter with his accents – everything from Glaswegian to Russian? Welsh would have been so easy. He had phoned in to the radio programme and pretended to be Scott, knowing I would hear him. *But why?*

'You're just like my mother, aren't you, Anna? You have to have your secrets. Did you really think I'd never find out?'

I shiver uncontrollably and lift my hands to rub my arms.

He leans in towards me, close to my ear, and for a moment I think he's going to kiss me. But he doesn't.

'I watch you, you know. I stand where you can't see me, and watch. But you know I'm there, don't you?'

I jerk my head away from him. *What is he talking about?*

Dominic shakes his head and walks to the wall to look at the documents and pictures.

'These are interesting, aren't they? Don't you look young and innocent in this one?' He points to the picture that I thought only Scott had ever seen. 'Or maybe not so innocent, eh?' He points to the second photo of me, to the mound that was my stomach.

'Ah,' he says, indicating the most recent photo of me with blonde hair. 'The lovely Saskia.'

I reach out a hand to prop myself up against the wall, unsure if my legs will hold me. He knows my other name, but how? Nothing of Saskia has ever come into our home. How did he get all these pictures?

I have no idea what I should do. Should I run? From my own husband? But I don't recognise him, and a shudder ripples through my body. Is there anything he doesn't know?

'Why did you do this? Why did you bring me here?' I ask,

hating myself for the tremor in my voice.

He ignores me and points to the photos of Cameron and Jagger. 'Such a pity the wrong man died, don't you think? Or, I don't know, maybe you had become quite fond of him. You saw enough of him.' He spits out the last few words.

He has his back to me, and I reach out to touch him. Perhaps I can make him understand.

'Take your hands off me,' he snarls. 'So many lies, so much deception. I have to hand it to you, you play a mean hand of poker.'

How does he know about the poker, about Cameron?

'It's over, I promise.' I can hear the break in my voice but it has no effect on him. 'I only did it so we'd be safe. You have to understand, Cameron's a monster.'

'*Safe?*' He barks out a laugh. 'Is that what you call it? I presume my "accident", as we euphemistically call my mugging – although even that's a misnomer – was keeping me safe, was it? You let me get beaten up, Anna, let them shatter my leg and my kneecap, and yet you said nothing.'

'You don't understand. I did it to save us all. They were going to take *everything*, Dom – our home, my mum's home – and I didn't think you ever needed to know.'

I can feel every beat of my heart, and it's as if Dominic can too. He sneers at me, mocking me for my weakness, and I have to summon the strength from somewhere to keep him talking until I can work out what to do, how to end this.

'Why didn't you tell me you knew about the poker? Why bring me here – to Scott's old home?'

'Because I had to know what mattered most to you. With everything you've done, the lies you told, I was clinging on to one thing – that you love me and not the little shit you did all this with.'

Dominic flicks his finger at the sponsorship form, the raffle posters and the evidence of every other scam I ran with Scott. I have no idea how he found them.

'I do love you, Dom. You're the father of my children.'

'As was Scott,' he says quietly.

Does he know I lied about my baby? I can't ask. I can't talk about it.

'Why would you think I still love Scott? As far as I knew, he was dead long before I met you.'

'Ah yes, my sweet wife. But when you thought you heard him on the radio, saw all the reminders of your life together, it didn't take you long to go running off to find him, did it? To arrange to see him again, to come to his childhood home?'

'To *stop* him!' I shout the words, but they are not entirely true.

I hear a groan from the floor. Brad is coming round, and I turn my eyes to Dominic's.

'Untie him, Dom. Let him go, *please.*'

He shrugs. 'Collateral damage, my love.'

Dominic doesn't care. I can see it now. He is completely indifferent to Brad's pain, and I finally realise that nothing that's happened has been Scott's doing. He's dead, as he has been for the last fourteen years, and I feel a new rush of guilt as I remember his last moments. It's as if I have lost him all over again, and I was a fool to hope. And then the enormity of what Dominic must have done hits me.

'You killed that man in the car, didn't you?' I'm whispering now, as if afraid to speak the words out loud. 'You thought it was Cameron. I should have known it wasn't Scott.'

'Why, because he's so perfect he would never do something like that?'

'No, because he'd have *recognised* Cameron!' I don't know why I didn't think of that before.

'Cameron Edmunds had been bleeding you dry for months. He would have gone on doing it, and you'd have let him. I killed

316

him for you, and I stuffed the bastard's throat with money. I wanted the world to know what happens to greedy shits like him. But the police kept that little detail to themselves, sadly.'

'Did you kill Jagger too? You weren't at home with the children that night, were you?'

'It was a complete pleasure after what he did to me. I couldn't believe my luck when I saw that piece of pipe lying on the ground. I'd followed you into town. I heard every word the two of you said.' Dominic smiles. 'He had no idea what hit him. Just as you have no idea how much Dippy Della, as Bailey calls her, has been paid to keep quiet about my comings and goings. The poor woman is in our home more than you are. She thinks I have a secret job and I'm saving up for a big surprise for you. And here it is! *Surprise!*'

He shouts the word with fake glee, and I realise that he is completely insane. And that maybe I did this to him.

'Ridiculous as it sounds, my darling wife, I did wonder for a while if the radio broadcast and Cameron's murder would make you decide to tell me everything, to be honest with me, to admit to your sins. But you couldn't do that, could you? Just in case Scott really was alive.'

His eyes glint in the harsh light, and for a moment we're both silent. I glance back at the wall, not wanting to look at him. I don't see how Dominic can let me walk out of here after all he has told me. I could run, but I wouldn't even get to the front door.

My gaze lands on the map of Nebraska, the circle around Lincoln. It's as if Dominic can read my mind.

'Of all your sins, Anna – and let's face it, there have been many – what you did in Nebraska is the worst. You lied from the very beginning about the one thing you knew mattered more than anything else in the world to me. You lied about what happened in Nebraska, and after that there was no going back, was there? The lies kept coming – some of them small evasions, others huge deceptions that sat between us in all their twisted ugliness.'

How can I deny it? If I had told him what happened in Nebraska, none of this would have happened. Lie upon lie, all to cover the first, the darkest of them all. But I was too ashamed to tell him the truth. I never wanted anyone to know what we had done.

66

Then

When Scott first suggested we went to America for the birth of our baby, specifically to Nebraska, I hadn't entirely understood what he was thinking.

'We need to find a state with flexible adoption laws,' he said, his eyes bright with enthusiasm. 'It's not like the UK. They understand there that private adoptions work in a way that lets everyone benefit – in our case, financially.'

It had taken me a while to understand what he meant.

'You want me to *sell* our *baby*?'

'Stop being so bloody melodramatic,' he said, but seeing the look of horror on my face his expression softened and he reached out a hand to hold mine. 'Come on, Spike. You were going to have the baby adopted anyway, and this way two people get the child they desperately want, only they'll be paying for it. It means our child will be brought up by parents who really value it, and they'll have lots of money so it'll have a fantastic life.'

There was that word 'it' again, and I had to wonder if to Scott our baby was nothing more than a route to financial solvency.

'Is this actually *legal*?'

Scott looked sheepish. 'The agency finds a family – which they have done already – and all our costs are covered. But we need more out of this arrangement, so I went to meet them, to check that you would approve of them. They paid for me to go – that's where I was last week. Sorry I lied about the football tournament on the south coast.'

I wanted to say 'not for the first time' but it seemed trivial in the light of everything else.

'Anyway,' he said, grinning with self-satisfaction, 'I negotiated a side deal. It's private – just between us and the new parents. The agency doesn't need to know.' He pulled me into his arms. 'As far as the agency is concerned, they fly us out there – Club Class, no less – and find us an apartment and pay the rent until the baby is born. They cover all the medical expenses, and that's it. But this couple really want our baby, so they were prepared to negotiate over and above covering our costs.'

I had struggled to come to terms with giving my baby up for adoption, but had managed to convince myself it was the best choice for my child. It would be hard, but the thought of him or her being brought up in a happy home, perhaps with other children, maybe somewhere not too far away, had reassured me. Scott's logic – that I was going to have the baby adopted anyway, so why not by a family with money – was hard to argue with, but yet it left me with a gaping hole inside. My child would be so far away, living a life I didn't recognise. I wouldn't be able to picture him or her growing up.

With British adoptive parents, I could imagine my baby's first day at school, visualise the classroom, the other children, the swings and slides at the local park, the school uniform, the games they would play, the toys they would have. But in America he or she would live a life I couldn't begin to imagine. I wouldn't be able to picture what each day looked like, understand the pattern of his or her life. Every thread that bound my child to me in my mind would be broken.

It took me a long time to give in to Scott's proposal. I kept believing that a miracle would happen, and another, easier-to-bear solution to our problems would appear, and all the time Scott was begging me to think about it – to realise that our baby would have a safe and happy life, and we could rid ourselves of the burden of debt forever. It wasn't until Cameron sacked me from my job at the casino because my pregnancy was becoming obvious, as I had known he would, that I decided it was the sensible thing to do, convincing myself that Scott was right and it was little different to any other adoption.

The day I went into hospital in Nebraska to have my baby should have been joyful, but I was terrified. I wanted my mum. I needed to hear her voice, to listen to her telling me that it would all be fine, I was doing a great job; to feel her cool hand stroking the hair back off my forehead as she joked about my dad waiting outside, not able to cope with seeing me in pain. Even with Scott there, I felt isolated. The American accents seemed alien, the nurses brisk and businesslike, and I was so alone.

In the end, my beautiful tiny baby boy with his perfect hands and feet, ears so paper-thin and fragile, was mine for just twelve hours. I barely had time to learn every feature of his face, to feel the velvet softness of his skin and kiss his delicate cheeks before I had to hand him over to his Mom and Dad.

I didn't want to let him go. He was *my* baby; he didn't belong to this smartly dressed woman with perfect hair and make-up, although I couldn't fault the tears of joy on her cheeks as she looked at his mop of dark hair and wide blue eyes, a bit of both his father and me. But it felt as if she had plunged her hand into my chest and ripped out my heart.

I was told it was best 'for baby' to form an immediate attachment to his new parents, and the final form for signature was pushed in front of me. I didn't want to sign, but the adoption agent told me everyone felt like this. It was only to be expected, and I would be fine once it was done. I was nineteen, exhausted both emotionally and physically, and Scott was smiling his encouragement while the agent waved her pen, looking irritated with me. So I signed, not knowing then that I would regret the decision for every day of my life.

As his new parents left the room, my baby held close in his dad's arms, his mom leaning over to lift his tiny feet into what she imagined would be a more comfortable position, there was a guttural scream of anguish that I realised was coming from me, and my baby responded with a cry of his own. He wanted me – I was sure of it – and I reached out my arms, shouting for them to bring him back. But they were quickly ushered from the room and I was left to sob alone.

I don't know how I got through the next few days in the cramped stuffy apartment that the adoptive family had provided. It was hot in Nebraska, and there was no relief from the heat on the small balcony. Even the flowers in the big planter out there had become dry and brittle, perhaps because neither of us could be bothered to water them. I was given sedatives to calm me, but I hated the way they made me feel. I didn't want to avoid the pain; I wanted to feel it. I *needed* to feel it.

And then it was time to leave. Scott had packed for both of us – I didn't have the energy – and our bags were by the door, passports and documents on the coffee table in a folder. That was when I realised that I couldn't go. Not like this. I was desperate to tell Scott what I had decided, but he had gone out hours before. He was probably sick of me crying. He knew I blamed him.

What I had to say to him was going to make him furious, but it had to be said. I'd been sitting staring at the door for four hours, my arms still aching for my baby, wondering where Scott was, what he was doing, when finally he walked in. He couldn't look at me. Maybe he was more sick of me than I had realised, or perhaps he knew what I was going to say.

'Scott, where've you been?' He couldn't have missed the tension in my voice.

'Walking.'

It was too hot outside to walk anywhere, but I no longer cared where he'd been.

'I can't do it,' I blurted out, tears springing from my eyes. 'I can't leave my baby here, so far away from me. I want him back. We have to get him back, Scott!'

Scott raised his eyes to mine in horror. 'What do you mean? You can't have him back. They've paid us.'

I could hear the rattle of hysteria in my voice. If I didn't control it, I would lose this argument. I swallowed it down.

'It was a mistake. I'm sure they'll understand. Surely there has to be a period for thinking this through, deciding if it's what we really want? We'll give them the money back, and I'll promise to repay them for the apartment, the air fares, everything. I'll raise the money somehow, but Scott, I want him back. I can't bear to be without him.'

'What about Cameron, Jagger, the debt?'

None of that seemed important any more. I didn't care what they did – they could do their worst. I hadn't known how it would feel to have a baby and then have him torn from my arms. Others might be able to cope – mothers who can't support a child or think they're too young, surrogate mothers, those who don't want children – but I wasn't like them. My baby was part of me and I couldn't let him go.

'Sod the debt. Sod Cameron. We'll think of some way of getting the money. Or maybe we don't go back. We could stay here, get jobs.'

Scott turned towards the window, no longer able to look at me.

'No, Anna, that's not going to happen.'

I couldn't stop the cry of pain that burst from me. 'He's my *baby* – don't you understand? I can't leave him. I can't bear to not feel him in my arms. I want to feed him, hold him against me, touch him, love him. I'm going to go and get him back. We'll have to transfer the money back to them.'

Scott stomped past me out onto the balcony. I leaped up from my chair and followed him.

'Just do it!' I yelled at him. 'Transfer the money back and let's go and pick him up. *Please*, Scott. I've done everything I can to help you, but this is too much. *Just give them the fucking money back!*'

I was screaming, but Scott still wouldn't turn to look at me. And then I knew. I shivered in the heat of the day. For what felt like minutes, neither of us spoke.

'How much did you take?' My voice was surprisingly calm.

He still didn't face me. 'It doesn't matter. We can't pay them back.'

'You've lost it?'

He nodded and dropped his head. 'I took some and thought I could maybe double it and that would be a nice bonus. But I lost, so I took some more.'

'We already had a bonus. Including interest, you owe Cameron forty-five thousand; I owe him six. We got a *hundred and fifty!*'

Scott shook his head. 'Dollars.'

'So? It's still more than we need.'

Scott looked at the floor.

'What?' I said, although I already knew. 'Jesus, Scott, you didn't?'

His voice took on the pleading note that I had come to despise, as if I were too controlling and he was just trying to be reasonable.

'Cameron offered me some cash to tide us over. He said we'd probably find it useful.'

'And you took it.' It wasn't a question.

Scott finally turned towards me. 'I'm so sorry, Spike. I shouldn't have borrowed more, but I thought I could win enough to cover it – and more. It felt as if all the stars were aligned today and finally I could make you proud of me.'

I felt nothing but disgust for the boy standing in front of me. Any love I had felt for him was subsumed in a blazing ball of hatred. My voice rose again, and he backed away, turning to lean over the balcony to stare blindly at the patch of dead grass four floors below.

'I don't care about the money! I just want my baby. I *need* my baby!'

I was choking on my sobs by then. I spun round to go back into the apartment, banging into the huge planter full of nothing but dead flowers.

'You selfish, thoughtless *bastard!*' I screamed as I ran into the room, the pain of my loss obliterating all thought. I closed and locked the door behind me. I didn't want to see Scott or look at him for a second longer. He could roast out there for all I cared.

I moved around the room, getting the last of my things together. I could hear Scott banging on the glass, but I didn't lift my head. I didn't want to see him. He called out, but I wrapped my arms over my head and ignored him. Too bad if he was hot.

67

Now

Dominic is waiting for me to say something, maybe to apologise. But it's too late for excuses.

'I didn't tell you the truth about my son because I was ashamed. Giving him up was the biggest mistake of my life. You told me how you felt when your mother left, and I couldn't think how to explain it to you without telling you the rest – everything I'd done.'

'I asked you for honesty.' His voice was tight with anger.

It was wrong of me to lie, even though it had never seemed that simple. But right now I'm not sure it matters at all. Dominic has all but admitted to killing two people, and I have to get out of here so I can take my children and hide until Dominic is locked up.

'I wanted a perfect family, you know, Anna, but I knew something was wrong when your mum had no idea about your first child – the one you told me was stillborn.'

I say nothing. He's watching me for my reaction, but I'm going to do what I'm best at – bluff. I'll let him think everything is okay and that there isn't a fire raging inside me, feeding off my fury at what he's done and terror at what he might do. Slowly, slowly, I will find a way to escape.

He's still talking, and that's good. He's engrossed in his own thoughts, his own resentment of me, and I let his words wash over me.

'I knew there was a lie somewhere in that story, because your mum said something about how calm you seemed for a woman having her first child. She was right. You *were* calm. Too calm for someone who'd had a stillbirth – and why would your mum not know about that? It took me a long time to piece it all together.'

I'm not really listening. Escape is all that matters, and I realise that Dom dropped the cricket bat after he hit Brad. It's lying on the floor. It's too far away though, so I turn my attention to the wall of documents and pretend to study it, moving step by step to the left, towards Brad, looking at each sheet of paper. I have no idea how Dominic got all this information, but right now I don't care.

My eye is caught by the words on one of the sheets. I know what this is – it's an email I sent to Scott when he was here, at home with his parents after Jagger had beaten him up the second time. Some of the words have been highlighted with a bright yellow marker:

> My body aches for you…You have brought so much light into my life…I get butterflies when you smile at me, tingles down my spine when you kiss my neck.

I can feel Dominic's eyes on me as I read.

'You never said or wrote words like that to me, Anna.'

For a moment I want to try to make him understand that every love is different, that ours was solid, built to last a lifetime, whereas Scott was my first love and our passion burned fiercely. But it no longer matters what he thinks. If I die here and Dominic gets away, my children will be brought up by the madman standing beside me.

I inch further to my left. I have nearly reached Brad now, and the cricket bat is right by his side.

'And finally, let's talk about Scott's death, shall we? His mum wasn't totally gaga when I came to see her.'

My body jolts. I'm not able to control it. What does he mean? 'How did you know where to find her?'

'You had his passport, sadly now out of date. And his driving licence.'

Where did he find them?

'The licence was handy – it had his address. I pretended to be an old friend from university. When I asked how Scott had died, she told me what the police in America had said when they phoned with the news. It explains a lot about you, Anna.'

I drop my head to look at my feet. What can I say? The truth about what I did has haunted me for fourteen years.

I had left Scott on the balcony, locked outside in all that heat. He was shouting at me, begging me to let him in. But I ignored him.

Then he screamed.

I turned and looked and was horrified to see that Scott was surrounded by yellowjacket wasps. More and more of them were rising from the planter that I'd kicked. There must have been a nest in it. He was waving his arms around, trying to bat them away, but was only making them more angry. He'd been terrified of them since he was stung two weeks previously. His leg had swollen badly, and the doctor told him to take care in future.

Scott banged on the glass, begging me to open the door, but I was frozen to the spot. If I let him in, the wasps would come in with him. Not just one wasp, but hundreds of them. I had always hated wasps, but not so much as I hated Scott at that moment. He had allowed my precious baby to be taken from me, and I would never see him again. The agony he was feeling was physical. To me it was nothing in comparison to the emotional torture I was suffering. I didn't move.

I saw red welts rising on the surface of his skin. He clutched his throat. He couldn't breathe, and still I didn't move.

When I couldn't bear it any more, I rushed to the coffee table, picked up the folder with our tickets and passports and grabbed Scott's wallet with the meagre remains of our cash and our useless credit cards. I heard something fall to the floor. I knew what it was but didn't pause. I ran out of the apartment.

It's a memory that has never left me. I can still hear Scott, feel the heat of the day, smell the stale air of the apartment. And hear the clatter of his EpiPen as it hits the tiled floor.

Dominic is laughing. He can sense how much the memory is hurting me. I killed Scott, and I've always known it. It was foolish to hope I had been wrong. I lift my head, unable to stop myself asking one question. 'If Scott's dead, who's been watching us? Who drove you off the road?'

He laughs louder. 'No one. I wanted to see how you would react if you thought he was close by, threatening us.'

I want to scream at him for frightening my children, but I need to focus. All that matters is that I get out of here. What he did and why he did it isn't important right now.

I'm so close to Brad, and conveniently he groans. I drop to my knees at his side, not knowing what I can do to help him other than get out of here and call for help.

'Can we not roll him over so he can breathe more easily? Or maybe you could get him some water. Please, Dominic. He's done nothing to hurt you.'

Dominic doesn't move.

I'm going to have to time this carefully. I can reach the bat now, and if I can grab it with both hands and spin round on my knees I could hit Dom's bad leg and—

I cry out as I feel a fierce pain in my head. Dominic yanks at my hair and wraps a length around his fist to pull me to my feet.

'Come with me, *wife*.' There is nothing but bitterness in the word.

Taking my arm in a cruel grip, he pulls me round to face another doorway and pushes me forward out of the room.

The doorway leads to a kitchen. It's a while since it's been cleaned – perhaps since Mrs Roberts left – and there are flies everywhere.

Then I see a wasp and I freeze. My breathing is coming in gasps. It is too close. I need to get out.

Dominic twists my face round so he can look at me, and he must be able to see the terror in my eyes. This is one fear I can't disguise, and he knows that as he pushes me forward again. I can barely walk, but when my knees collapse he pulls me upright once more with my hair.

Ahead is another door with a pane of dirty glass in the top. A section has been scrubbed clean, as if to allow someone to look into the room. He pulls open the door and pushes me inside. It's dark and I can hardly see a thing, but there is a dank smell, as if this is an outhouse. The floor feels like earth. A chair sits in the middle of the room.

'Sit.'

I ignore him, but he pushes me down.

'Arms behind your back.'

Again I ignore him, and this time he reaches out and cracks me across the face with the back of his hand. I shriek, unable to believe this is my Dominic. He lets go of my hair and uses both hands to pull my arms behind the chair. I feel the plastic of the cable tie as it cuts into my skin.

'Don't do this, Dom,' I say quietly. 'For Holly and Bailey, don't. Please.'

He reaches into his other pocket and pulls out a roll of parcel tape, ripping off a piece with his teeth and wrapping it over my mouth and around my head.

'You deserve this, Anna,' he whispers, close to my ear. 'Not only for what you did to me – to our family – but maybe even for what you did to Scott.' He laughs nastily. 'It's amazing what you can source in the deep dark recesses of the Internet these days.'

I don't know what he means and I want to beg him to stop, to let me go, but I can't speak.

'Goodbye, my love. I'm going now to pick up our children, who are better off without you, to take them somewhere you'll never find them. It's all arranged.'

He has backed up towards the door, and I see him point a long pole towards something attached to the wall. He hits it once, drops the pole, then the door slams.

I struggle to try to free my hands, grunting for him to come back. And then I hear it.

It starts as a low buzz and builds to a crescendo as more and more wasps pile out of their nest, angry at being disturbed.

68

Becky pulled the car into a lay-by. They were at the point where the last ANPR camera had picked up Anna Franklyn's car, and they still hadn't received the requested telephony information. All they knew, thanks to Lynsey, was that Dominic Franklyn was the man in the hoody, driving a car that had been bought in the name of Scott Roberts. It seemed almost certain that Franklyn was the killer, but how was Anna involved?

'Where do you reckon she's heading, Becky?

'I've got no idea. She could be going to see Mrs Roberts again, of course, and it's all perfectly innocent.'

'Or indeed she could be taking a day trip to Caernarfon Castle,' Tom said, drumming his fingers on the dashboard with frustration.

They had driven here hoping that Anna would lead them to either Scott or Bradley Roberts, but now that their prime suspect was Dominic Franklyn, the priority had to be finding him. They had learned he was a stay-at-home dad, but although a team had been urgently despatched to his home, Franklyn wasn't there. The children weren't at school either. A neighbour was looking after them because she had been told they were going away for a surprise trip that afternoon, and their dad would be picking them up later. The children and neighbour had now been taken to a place of safety, and both houses were under surveillance.

Tom was about to suggest they find a café and grab a cup of coffee while they decided whether they would be more useful back at the incident room, when the call came through.

'We have an approximate position for Anna Franklyn's mobile phone, sir. It's currently situated in a small country town, and there aren't too many masts in the area. I can't give you a precise location, so the coordinates will only provide a starting point. The phone's stationary at the moment.'

Tom took down the details and thanked the officer. 'Let me know if she's on the move again.'

He turned to Becky. 'It's the town where Mrs Roberts' old house is, but the local officers said there was no one there this morning. Why would she go to an empty house?'

Becky slammed the car in gear and pulled quickly out into the traffic. 'Not a clue, but then I haven't got a clue about much right now. So let's go and find out, shall we?'

As they sped down the country roads, Keith called again.

'Sir, we got the details of Dominic Franklyn's car so I ran his plate through ANPR. He followed the exact route taken by his wife, but about forty minutes behind her. The car disappeared from the cameras at the same point as hers, which might suggest they were heading towards the same destination.'

Tom felt a pulse of excitement. Now it was getting interesting.

'Thanks, Keith. Text me the registration number, and well done.' He ended the call. 'What do you make of that?' he asked Becky.

'No idea. Are they meeting somewhere, or is he following her?'

'Just what I was asking myself. The evidence at the casino suggests she led a double life that involved Cameron Edmunds. So the question is, did Dominic attempt to kill Cameron out of jealousy? Is he an angry, vengeful husband? We mustn't forget that he took a beating eighteen months ago too – was that Jagger? Anna owed Edmunds money, so are she and her husband in it together for revenge? And where the hell does Scott Roberts fit in?'

Becky pointed out Anna's car the minute they turned into the street.

'And there's her husband's car,' Tom said.

Becky tutted with frustration. 'How do we know which house? There must be twenty along this stretch of road.'

'Didn't the local guy say Mrs Roberts' house is up for sale? There's one up there with an estate agent's board,' Tom said, pointing to a house about halfway up the road. 'It was empty this morning, but that was nearly three hours ago. Give Keith a call to check the address, but I've got a feeling that might be the one.'

He didn't wait while Becky made the call, getting out of the car and walking along the pavement to check that Anna's car was empty.

'You're right,' Becky said, catching him up. 'It matches the address on Scott Roberts' driving licence, so I asked Keith to call the local force to let them know we've arrived.'

'Did you tell him we're going in?'

Becky gave him a look. If she'd said that, they would have advised her to wait for backup. And Becky had worked with Tom long enough to know that he had no intention of waiting for anyone.

'Come on then,' he said.

69

I feel a wasp on my face – just the barest, lightest touch, like an itch that I would scratch if my hands were free. My body is rigid. Every joint is locked and my eyes are squeezed shut. My mouth is covered by the tape, but will the wasp investigate my nose? I'm scared to breathe in. There are wasps in my hair. I'm desperate to shake my head, but their buzzing is close to my ears and I can't risk making them angry.

There have been times in my life when I have thought I wanted to die, almost all of them connected to the fact that I gave away my baby. But now, as I sit in this room, surrounded by hundreds if not thousands of the creatures that I hate and fear the most, I just want this nightmare to be over, one way or another. Maybe like Scott, one sting will be enough. It will be a terrible death, but it will be quick.

I don't think I can endure the threat of the first sting for another moment. My throat has closed. I can't breathe. Every inch of my body is dripping with sweat. I can feel it running down the backs of my legs, down my arms, and I wonder if wasps are attracted to the smell, the taste, of the salty liquid. Some have settled on my face now – I can't tell how many. Their touch is soft, almost a caress. I don't know if I'm allergic to their sting, but neither do I know how much fear I can stand.

Will Dominic leave me here – walk away and never return? Will anyone find me? If I die here, what will become of my children? I think of Holly's silky hair, Bailey's sticky little hands, and as these images paint themselves onto the backs of my closed eyelids, I know I mustn't die. I have to dredge up the very last of my willpower and resist the temptation to move. That's what I've always been told. The wasps won't bother me if I don't bother them. They are angry because their nest has been poked, though, and I feel the first sting on my chin, as if a red-hot needle has burst the flesh. I squeal under the tape and shake my head, but for that I get another sting so I hold myself rigid. I don't open my eyes and I don't move. The stings are painful, but I'm not dead. My throat, swollen with fear, hasn't got any worse, and I force myself to breathe slowly and evenly.

I try to focus on my other senses – but I can't see through closed eyes, can't taste through my taped-up mouth, and the only sound I hear is the angry buzzing of the wasps. Their touch is the worst thing – so gossamer light but so threatening. I can smell nothing other than the damp ground beneath me.

Another sting on the back of my hand makes me yelp, but that's only three. Maybe they'll calm down now. I force myself to remember that only the females sting, so probably only half of them can hurt me. I try to push out of my mind the fact that each wasp can sting multiple times. I must be still. I mustn't move.

I know he's watching through the window, and I summon up every last ounce of courage. I will not let him see me crumble.

Becky watched as Tom approached the front door. It was open – just a crack – but enough for them to realise that someone must have gone inside since the officers had called earlier. She was right behind Tom as he pushed the door. It swung open. They listened, but neither of them could hear a thing. He turned to Becky and gave her a questioning look. She knew what he was asking. Should they shout out to warn that the police had arrived, or should they go quietly to avoid alerting whoever was inside?

She was about to suggest that they called out when they heard a faint noise. A door closing towards the back of the house.

Tom stepped into the hall, Becky on his heels.

Moving silently, they followed the sound and then heard what sounded like a bolt being shot into place.

The short hairs on Becky's arms bristled.

As they rounded the bend in the hall they saw bright light spilling out from a partially open door. Tom pushed it gently with his toe. Stretched across the floor, preventing the door from opening fully, was the body of a man. As Tom quietly stepped over him, Becky crouched down to feel for a pulse. She looked up and raised one thumb in a silent signal. He was alive. They would phone for an ambulance, but first they had to see who else's life might be in danger.

There was no sound for a few minutes, then they heard footsteps. Someone was coming from the room beyond this one. Seconds later, a tall man filled the doorway.

Becky knew who this was. 'Dominic Franklyn.'

That was all the confirmation Tom needed. 'My name is Detective Chief Inspector Tom Douglas—'

Before Tom had the chance to say more, Dominic spun on his heel and dashed back into the room he had just come from, slamming the door in Tom's face. Tom barged it open with his shoulder. Franklyn had reached the back door and was tugging frantically on the bolts, but Tom was too quick for him and was on him before he could open it, Becky right behind. Pushing him hard against the door, Tom grabbed his arms and Becky stepped forward to flick handcuffs onto his wrists.

'He's secure, Tom. Dominic Franklyn, I'm arresting you—'

But Tom had turned away and was no longer listening to Becky. He was standing in front of another door. Set into the door was a filthy pane of glass with a small clean square in the middle. His shout interrupted Becky reading Dominic his rights. *'Jesus!'* His head swivelled towards the other man. 'You barbaric bastard.'

Becky didn't know what Tom could see, but his eyes turned

briefly to hers before he began to cast them furiously around the kitchen.

'Wasps,' he said as he swivelled round, clearly looking for something. 'Hundreds of them. And Anna Franklyn is in there, gagged and tied to a chair. They're stinging her – I just saw her wince.'

Dominic was looking at the floor, refusing to meet Becky's eyes.

'Move him away from the back door and open it, give them an escape route,' Tom said. 'Then get yourself and this tosser out of here, the other side of a closed door.'

'What are you going to do?' Becky asked.

'Get her out. There's no option.'

'Shit. Protect your eyes as best you can, Tom.'

'There's nothing here I can use. I'll just have to risk it. Go, Becky!'

With one last anxious look at Tom, she turned and pushed Dominic Franklyn from the room.

The stings are throbbing now, the individual nerve centres joining to create a harmony of pain throughout my body. I don't know how many times I have been stung, but I'm surviving. I can live through this. I have to for my children.

I hear the door open behind me, but I don't turn towards it. I don't move. I daren't. I don't know why he's come into the room. Maybe he doesn't think they're active enough and he's going to stir them up some more. A sob comes out as a muffled moan.

Then I hear a deep voice, speaking quietly. 'It's okay, Anna. My name's Tom, and I'm going to get you out of here. But no sudden movements.'

It's not him. It's not Dominic. Thank God. He's right about no sudden movements because I can still feel the wasps crawling all over my skin. I know that just flicking a wasp away is enough to cause it to sting, and I have no idea whether they are able to communicate – to tell each other they have an enemy and should strike as one. I hear the sympathetic voice of the man called Tom again. I can tell that he understands my fear.

'Anna, I'm going to reach out and touch your left arm. Don't open your eyes – I can see for both of us. I'm going to bend down to cut the tie, then I'll slowly guide you out of the room. Try your very best to stay calm. I know it's difficult.'

There's a sharp intake of breath. He's been stung but he's playing it down. I hear myself whimper and hate myself for the weakness.

When his hand touches my arm it is warm and somehow reassuring. His grip is firm, and he talks to me quietly, calmly, telling me to stand up, which way to turn, which foot to move. Slowly but surely. I feel another sting and then hear Tom suck in his breath again. We are both being stung, but it's not killing us.

It seems to take forever, but then I sense that the air around us has changed and I hear a door slam.

'You can open your eyes now, Anna. You're safe.'

Saturday

70

It's over. My children are safe. I'm safe. I should feel relief, but the horrors of the last twenty-four hours and the stress of the previous days are going to take time to ease.

Dominic has been arrested and charged with two murders and a string of lesser charges. Bradley Roberts is in hospital, recovering.

I can't believe that Dominic is the architect of everything that has happened this week. I feel sick at the thought that I have lain in bed next to him as he plotted cold-blooded murder.

For now the children only know that Daddy won't be coming home for a while. I will have to work out what to tell them and how to explain. Maybe they will have to change schools. Maybe we all will. But the worst of the nightmare is over. At least, I hope so.

I was interviewed by the police for four hours after a kind paramedic gave me something for the painful stings. I told them everything I knew about Cameron and Jagger and what I believed had driven Dominic to kill two men. I have no doubt Cameron will be arrested for his sins too, and I'm sure it will be a relief to many of his victims. I couldn't explain it without admitting to the things Scott and I did when we were at university, but they said it's unlikely that charges will be brought, under the circumstances. The case of our baby, though, is different. They want me to provide evidence that the adoption was legal – that we didn't traffic our own baby. I feel sick that they would think I might have done that.

I can't remember the name of the adoption agency. All that

burns bright in my memory is the sight of my son; the rest is a blur. But I do know where the details are. Hidden in my mum's loft.

She knows I'm safe, but I haven't told her what happened yet. I have to before she sees it on the news, and I want to speak to her before the children are awake, so I pick up the phone and take a deep breath.

'Anna! Oh my darling. Are you okay? I know you said not to worry, but I've been frantic.'

I want to be calm, but this is my mum and I don't need to pretend. I burst into tears and sob down the phone to the one person who won't judge me.

When I finally calm down, I stutter through an explanation of what happened yesterday, leaving out any mention of me being hurt, but I can feel the waves of shock and horror coming down the phone line when I tell her what Dominic has done. The why will have to wait, because it's a much longer story. I need to see her face to face for that.

'Mum, there's something I need you to do for me. Do you remember when I left university in Manchester I boxed up everything and put it in the loft?'

'Of course I do. It was after you came back from America. You were in such a state.'

'I know, but there's something I need from the box. I'll explain it all to you, I promise, but there's an envelope in there—'

'I can stop you right there, love. I don't have the box. I gave it to Dominic.'

The breath is knocked out of me.

Now I understand. The box had everything, including my old laptop with every email ever sent to Scott, love letters, sponsorship forms, basic spreadsheets calculating what each of us owed Cameron, photos I had taken of Scott's injuries. Even his wallet was in there.

And the adoption papers.

I want to scream at my mum, ask her why the hell she did that, but I already know. It would never have occurred to her that Dominic didn't know about every aspect of my life. Why would it? I don't believe she and my father ever had secrets from each other.

'When, Mum?' I ask as soon as I can speak.

'It was after your dad died. I decided I was going to have a clear-out so that if anything happened to me, there'd be less for you to do. Dominic brought the children up to stay during one of their holidays. I think you had to work. I asked him to help, and when he saw the box he said he'd take it back with him. It's not a problem, is it?'

Mum wasn't to know it had been full of secrets. She probably thought it was just books, lecture notes and maybe some photos of friends. I had taped it up, knowing she would never look inside it. But Dominic had. But if he's known for that long, why now?

'No, no. But he didn't tell me, and I've never seen it.'

'That's perhaps because I told him how devastated you were by Scott's death and you might not be ready yet to look inside. He seemed to understand, Anna. He said he would hide it until he thought you were ready. Have I done something wrong?'

My mum's voice is beginning to wobble and I know she's about to cry.

'Of course not, Mum. I'm just wondering where he's put it. Don't worry – I'll find it.'

71

I have searched the house – turned it upside down. I've even been up into the loft, but there is no sign of my box.

The children are up now, confused and wondering when Daddy will be back. I need to spend time with them, prepare them in some way for what I have to tell them. But how do I tell my daughter that her father has killed people? Bailey is less likely to understand the enormity of his father's crimes, but I need to be ready for everything. I can't make excuses for Dominic and must explain that he did a bad thing, and when someone does something they shouldn't, there are consequences.

It's every bit as painful as I expect it to be. The children cry, and I cry with them. I avoid telling them one thing – that if their father is convicted they will almost definitely be adults by the time he is released. Finally, they lie cuddled together on the sofa under a blanket and watch a cartoon on TV. They will be asleep within minutes, worn out by all the emotion. I can't bear the pain they're going through.

I wander aimlessly into the kitchen and gaze out of the window. After yesterday's storms the weather is overcast, but at least it's not raining. I go over to the back door and pull it open, wanting to smell the wet earth, to be reassured of the beauty and continuity of life by looking at my garden, knowing that the plants dying back now will again spring to life in a few short months.

Then I see it. The shed!

It's the one place I haven't looked. An ideal spot, because I never go in there.

I grab the key to the new lock and, leaving the back door open so I can hear if the children shout, walk down to the shed and open the door. My gaze immediately goes to the spot where the photo of a young Scott was propped up. Of course it's not there now. It's upstairs, hidden in a drawer under the lavender-scented paper that my mother had carefully lined all our bedroom drawers with when we first moved in.

I scan the shed with no idea where he might have hidden my box. It wasn't large, but it was too big to fit in a drawer. The children's bikes are at the far end, propped against the wall, but I can't see a box behind them. I randomly open cupboard doors but see nothing.

Suddenly I realise where he will have put it.

In the far corner is an old chest freezer we don't use. We keep it locked for fear that a child will somehow get inside and suffocate. I reach up to the shelf above, lift a rusty paint can, and the key is there.

I stare at the freezer for a long moment. The box in which I so carefully stored all my memories was never meant to be opened again, and the fact that Dominic has been through it makes it feel dirty, defiled. Some memories are precious, some I want to forget.

Before I can think about it any more, I push the key into the lock and turn it, then with a deep breath, I lift the lid.

The box is there, the flaps pulled back and open. Inside, on top of the rest of the contents, is a pile of envelopes, a few of them quite large with hard backs, as if to protect the contents from being bent. I don't recognise these. I don't think I have ever seen them before, and to my surprise I notice that all of them are addressed to me. I pick one at random, feel inside and pull out a photograph. It's of the same boy – Scott, I'm sure – but a couple of years younger than he was in the picture left in the shed for me.

Why would someone post me an old photo of Scott?

I open another envelope, and this one has a cardboard

mount inside it, but the picture is missing. A small corner of the photograph paper is still attached, and I remember that the photo I found in here a few days ago was torn slightly. *Who sent me these photos?*

I realise there is something else in the envelope and I upend it. Several sheets of paper covered with handwriting fall out onto the bench. I pick them up and start to read.

Hello

I'm sorry but I still don't know what to call you, so I thought maybe Hello would be okay for now?

I know that after you got my first few letters you wrote to say you didn't think it was a good idea for us to be in touch, but I guess I want to try again, in case you changed your mind. I'll probably keep trying because it matters to me.

Mom and Dad know that I'm writing to you, and they're okay with it if it's what I want. And it is. So I thought that each year I would mail you a letter to tell you about me and my life, just in case you're a little bit interested.

It's strange for me to have a mother I've never met, and I'd really like to know about you too, if you can spare the time.

I feel every nerve in my body tingle, and a massive surge of emotion threatens to drown me. I turn to the last page before I read on in case I'm wrong. But I know I'm not.

It's signed:

Your son Stephen, (if it's okay for me to call myself that?)

I drag out a stool from underneath Dominic's workbench and collapse onto it. *Stephen.* My son is called Stephen.

I quickly pull all the letters out, one by one. There are four of them, three with photos, and one with the empty picture mount. I know now that the photos aren't of Scott; they're of Stephen. My boy.

The postmarks are Florida, so the family must have moved

there, and with trembling fingers I sort the letters into order and start with the first, written when he was twelve, two years ago. He tells me how much he would like to get to know me and how happy he has been with his Mom and Dad. He says he plays soccer because it's English and he knows he is a bit of a Brit. He sounds funny and sweet, and the words keep blurring in front of me as the tears spill from my eyes.

And then I read the fourth one again. He writes about the letter I sent saying I didn't want to be in touch with him, and my heart breaks for my child. I fold my arms on the bench and lay my head there, not even trying to control the sobs that are tearing me apart. That poor, poor boy. How rejected he must have felt, and what resilience he must have to keep on trying.

Now another emotion rises, almost dwarfing the sadness I feel at how my son must be hurting.

Rage.

Dominic has read these letters, seen these photographs and even left one where he knew I would find it – all to scare me into trying to see Scott. Of all the dreadful things he has done, writing to my son to tell him I don't want to have anything to do with him is the worst. It is unforgivable. Why would he do that to a child he doesn't know? *Why?*

I notice some scribblings on the back of one of the envelopes. It's Dominic's writing.

Happy with my life…secure family…don't want to disrupt my children's lives…explanations would be difficult…no space for you in my life.

I know what these are. They're ideas for what to put in his reply, the one Stephen believes came from me.

'No space for you in my life.'

If I didn't hate Dominic before, I do now.

I know exactly why he wanted to keep Stephen out of our lives. He is the son of a man I loved, and based on all he had

349

discovered Dominic concluded that I loved Scott more than him. So his child could never be part of my life. He would upset the balance, and Dominic would no longer have had his perfect family.

Judging by the dates on the letters it seems he made this decision a while ago – before he decided I was no longer worthy of his love. Maybe when Stephen's last letter came, just a couple of weeks ago, Dominic finally realised that my brave son wasn't going to give up, and I was bound to find out the terrible thing he had done. Maybe the last letter was the catalyst – the moment he decided it was time to end it, when the lying had to stop.

Sunday

72

Tom glanced sideways at Louisa, who was sitting next to him as he drove, a brightly coloured box resting on her lap.

'Are you sure you're okay with this?' he asked, not for the first time.

'Of course I am, Tom. As long as you think the invitation was genuine.'

Lucy had phoned the day before asking if her dad and Louisa would come for a barbecue as it was her mum's last day at home before the operation. Fortunately the weather had turned warm and sunny again, although it wasn't expected to last.

'Are you sure she wants me there?' Louisa had asked, so Tom had phoned Kate to be doubly certain.

'Yes, of course,' Kate had said. 'It's what Lucy wants, and as Louisa is going to be looking after my daughter, I want to get to know her. And no, before you ask, it's not to vet her.'

Tom hadn't been entirely sure he believed her, but for Lucy's sake he'd accepted, and Louisa said she was more than happy to come. She could do the cooking, if Kate would let her.

'What's in the box?' he asked.

'Oh, just some bits and pieces that I thought she might like to take with her into hospital. There's no point bringing flowers; she's not going to be there to enjoy them. And she might not fancy chocolates even when she's allowed to eat them, so I thought of some other stuff.'

'Well, we're here now.' He pulled up outside Kate's house. 'Thanks for coming, darling. Just so you know, I love you.' He leaned over to kiss her gently and thought how lovely she looked today. Her cheeks were glowing and her eyes were bright. He hoped it wasn't going to be too depressing.

The atmosphere felt surprisingly relaxed as the four of them sipped pre-barbecue drinks. Lucy had teased Tom about the stings on his face, but everyone could see she was bursting with pride in her fearless dad.

'Becky phoned to see how I am, and she told me about you how you yelped every time another one stung you,' Lucy said with a giggle.

'Very funny, I'm sure.' Tom wrapped his arm round Lucy's neck and pulled her close.

Lucy had hovered between them all for the first half-hour, clearly wondering how this was going to work out – whether the adults in her life were going to get along with each other – but she finally seemed to have relaxed.

'Can I tempt you with a glass of wine?' Kate asked Louisa, who was watching the father–daughter interaction and thinking how great Tom was as a dad.

'I'm driving so that Tom can have a drink for once, but thanks. I'm fine.'

'Right. I'll get the food ready. Tom, you can light the barbecue.'

'Okay. Lucy can help, can't you?' Tom said to his daughter, who nodded enthusiastically.

Kate turned to go into the kitchen, Louisa close behind. 'Why don't you sit down, Kate? I can do this. Enjoy some time with Lucy.'

Kate shook her head. 'I want everything to be as normal as possible today. Lucy's told me you're a good cook, although how you've managed to persuade Tom to give you access to his precious kitchen, I don't know. He never thought much of my cooking, but today I've kept it simple. I need to get the chicken that I marinated out of the fridge, and the prawns need some lemon zest and garlic. Perhaps you could do that.'

Louisa looked at the raw, grey prawns and swallowed hard. She hoped Kate hadn't seen her, but she had.

Kate looked at her for a moment before she spoke, and then seemed to decide to be kind. 'Actually, Louisa, forget the prawns. Would you mix up some salad dressing, maybe?'

The two women worked side by side for a few moments.

'Thanks for the box of goodies,' Kate said finally, as she saw to the prawns. 'Very thoughtful of you. I've packed all the obvious stuff to take in with me, but the lavender pillow spray, the lip balm, the extra-soft eye mask – and all the rest – I wouldn't have thought of myself.' She put the spoon and fork that she was using in the bowl and turned to Louisa. 'I hope it's not going to be too much for you, taking care of Lucy with your job and everything?'

'We'll make it work. Don't worry. Lucy's a lovely girl, and I think we get on okay.'

'I have to say I'm glad she's not being looked after by Tom's ex, Leo. Lucy liked her enough, but I thought she was a bit of a cold fish.'

'She was okay.' Louisa laughed. She had been Leo's anaesthetist when her arm was badly injured and had quite enjoyed spending time with her.

Kate transferred the prawns onto skewers, threading them carefully. Louisa tried not to watch.

'Have you told Tom yet?' Kate asked, her voice crisp.

Louisa lifted her head and looked at her. 'Told him what?'

Kate checked out of the window. Tom was at the end of the garden with Lucy. 'That you're pregnant.'

Louisa froze.

'Oh bugger. How did you know?'

'No wine, even a small glass hours before you have to drive?

Not to mention the fact that you nearly turned green at the sight of the prawns. Oh, and you keep touching your tummy.'

For a moment Louisa wasn't sure what to say, but giving the oil and vinegar a final vigorous whisk, she decided to tell Kate the truth. 'He doesn't know. I found out the day you told him you were ill, and it didn't seem an appropriate moment. Now I'm worried about Lucy. She's going to need all the attention we can give her and I don't want her to feel in any way less of a focus.'

Kate stopped what she was doing and leaned on the worktop with both hands.

'I wouldn't worry about that. Lucy will love the whole idea of being a big sister, and it will give her something to be excited about.' Kate dropped her gaze. 'Tom will be thrilled, of course. He always wanted more children and perhaps if I'd stayed with him we would have had another. But I made one bad decision, and I've paid the price. Funny how the threat of death hanging over you can make you realise what's important and what isn't.'

Louisa was searching for an appropriate response, but at that moment Lucy came racing up to the back door and leaned in. 'Come on, you two. What's taking so long? This might be our last chance for a barbecue.' Lucy said it with a smile, but then her eyes went round with horror and her mouth dropped open.

Mother and daughter stared at each other for a second.

'You're right, Lucy,' Louisa said with a smile. 'They're saying the weather won't last more than another day, so this is likely to be the last barbecue of the summer. Take these out to your dad, would you please?' She handed Lucy the marinated chicken.

When her daughter was well out of earshot, Kate turned to Louisa. 'Thank you. That was very tactful.'

Louisa nodded. 'She's obviously going to find it difficult over the next few weeks, but we'll take care of her. I promise.'

Kate took a deep breath. 'I know you will. Now come on, let's go and feed them. And I'll keep you away from the prawns until they're cooked.'

Walking out into the garden, the two women shared a brief laugh.

Tom lifted his head to give them a quizzical look. Louisa grinned at him without offering an explanation, and with a smile he turned back to the barbecue.

73

Every minute seems to bring a new rush of emotions, and I fluctuate between fury, fear, guilt and profound sadness. I don't know how the children and I managed to get through the whole of today, or how we will cope with what next week is bound to throw at us. I've taken a leave of absence. I haven't even been able to bring myself to talk to Jen yet, although I must and I know she will be supportive, but I'm not sure about the trustees. I don't think the wife of a murderer fits with their vision and values, and I can hardly blame them.

We *did* make it through though, helped by the fact that my mum arrived. She's become quite blasé about catching trains since we moved here, and I was glad to see her, falling into her arms for the hug I needed so badly.

Finally the children are both in bed. I kiss Bailey's plump cheek softly and say goodnight just the way I have since he was baby. I'm striving for normality and I need to get them back into a rhythm.

When I get to Holly's room, she is lying with her sore leg on top of the bed. It has been healing well since her accident, but each evening I clean it to make sure it's not infected. It's not just the injuries to my poor little girl's leg that I'm worried about, though.

'You know, Holls, whoever you heard talking that afternoon when you hurt your leg, he was just a man playing golf. There's no one watching the house, I promise. There's nothing to be scared of.'

'I know. That's not why I ran.' Her little face screws up as if she's going to cry. 'I'm sorry, Mummy. I was hiding from Bailey. He was being a pain, and the shed door was open so I ran in. I told a fib. I shouldn't have, but I thought Daddy would be mad at me because I'm not supposed to go in there.'

I stroke her leg gently.

'It's okay, sweetheart. You mustn't worry about that now.'

'It was Daddy's fault anyway. He dropped the shed key down the drain and had to break in. He thought you'd say it was his fault I got hurt, so it was our secret. But you said no more secrets, so I've told you now.'

I swallow and try to smile at Holly. I now knew that no one had been watching the house, but I hadn't worked out how the lock had been broken. I kiss her gently and go to my bedroom before she can see the new wave of rage building behind my eyes.

Whatever I've done, I always believed I was protecting my family. I may have been foolish and misguided, but I never wanted to hurt anyone. Dominic has followed me, spied on me, scared my children by telling them that someone was watching them, and told a teenage boy that his mother didn't want to know him. Every time I think of Stephen, a knife pierces my heart, and I struggle to imagine how he has been able to deal with the rejection.

I sit at the dressing table and pull out the photo that Dominic left in the shed for me to see. I can picture him comparing Stephen's photos with those of Scott that he found in my box of secrets, knowing I would mistake my son for his father. They are so alike.

What would Scott make of me if he was still alive? I wonder. Which version of me would I want him to see? He would be amused that I became a teacher after all my wild dreams. But it turns out that I love my job, and I'm going to fight to keep it. I shouldn't be held responsible for my husband's actions. And what about Saskia? Saskia is the part of me that learned to fly, and Scott would love her. She is competitive, confident, a woman who loves excitement, who thrives on the rush of adrenaline when she plays poker.

I think back to that last game and know that I lost my focus. Too much was happening. If I play again – no, *when* I play again – I will feel the power flood back and I won't make the same mistakes.

My heart beats faster at the knowledge that I don't have to say goodbye to Saskia. I no longer need to play to pay Cameron, but poker is part of me, and anything I win that we don't need I'll give to charity. After all, it was a charity raffle and the bad choices I made that brought us all to where we are now.

Best of all, I no longer have to ask myself who I am. There are no separate versions of me. I'm a steady, sensible head teacher who also happens to be a thrill-seeking poker player, and I'm good at being both. Then there's the other part of me – the most important part. I'm a mother and will do everything in my power to keep my children safe and happy. All three of them.

I look down at the photograph that I'm still holding and realise there is one thing I need to do while my two youngest sleep. Whoever is to blame – me, Scott, Dominic – Stephen has been hurt enough. I don't know how I will ever explain everything, but I have to try to be honest with him. No matter how I'm feeling now, I can't bear the thought of my child believing for a moment longer that I don't love him, don't want to know him.

I open a drawer to pull out notepaper and pen. At first I don't know what to say, but then the words are there, in my head, in my heart, and I begin to write.

Dear Stephen…

Monday

74

I've let the children lie in this morning as none of us will be going to school today, but I wake early after a fitful night and stumble down to the kitchen for a cup of coffee. Images of Dominic, the wasps and Stephen have tumbled over each other in my dreams, and I feel numb with lack of sleep.

Mum is already up and in the kitchen, the radio playing quietly in the background. She looks startled to see me.

'You should have stayed in bed, love. I'd have brought you some breakfast.'

I shake my head slowly. 'I'm fine, Mum. I'm going to make a cup of coffee. Do you want one?'

'Sit down. I'll make it. The kettle's just boiled.'

I don't argue as she pours water over granules and hands me a mug.

She reaches out to switch off the radio, understanding that chirpy music might not be what I'm looking for, but as her hand touches the button, she freezes.

'It's the day you've been waiting for, folks. Scott will be here in four minutes to tell us all about Spike and what tore them apart in "The One That Got Away". We thought we'd lost him when he didn't answer his phone, but he's travelling and has called in. Hang on in there. He'll be with you soon.'

Confusion washes over me. I breathe slowly in and out, trying to calm myself.

Neither of us speaks. Mum knows as well as I do that it was Dominic on the radio last week, but it can't be him now. So who is this? She looks at me with horror as her hand falls away from the button. I want to tell her to turn it off, but I can't. We gaze at the radio as if willing the presenter to tell us it's a huge mistake, but we have to sit through Ellie Goulding singing 'Love Me Like You Do', which does nothing to calm me.

The cheery voice invades my kitchen over the dying notes of the song. 'Here we go, listeners! Just to recap: Scott told us last week about him and Spike and how things had gone badly wrong in Nebraska. Well, I won't say any more, I'll leave that to Scott.'

For a moment all I can hear is the background noise of a busy location – the sound of people talking, an announcement over a tannoy, but I can't make out the words. Then a man speaks: 'Good morning, especially to Spike, who I do hope is listening.'

My coffee mug crashes to the floor, spraying my legs with hot liquid. I feel nothing. How could I have ever believed it was Scott on the radio last Monday? Even with the fake Welsh accent, Dominic sounded nothing like him. But there is no mistaking this voice, even after fourteen years. I know for certain that this time it really is Scott.

I'm barely listening to his words. I grasp the edge of the table with my hands, wondering whether the events of the last few days have made me delusional.

How can it be Scott?

But it is. I have no doubt at all.

Gradually his voice penetrates the fog in my brain, and I realise the story he's telling isn't ours. He's making it up – something about stealing a car, being arrested but being let off with a warning. It's a total fabrication.

Why? I can only imagine he doesn't want the truth to be aired any more than I do.

'Do I detect a hint of a North Atlantic twang in your voice?' the presenter asks.

'Well spotted. I've lived in the US for a long time now,

but I still listen to Manchester radio – mainly for the football. You always do a great run-down of the weekend's matches on a Monday morning. I wouldn't miss it.'

It's true. It's the segment just before this one. *Oh God – he heard it last Monday!*

'And I keep an eye on what's happening with my old friends, of course. The joys of social media, eh?'

Scott laughs, but he's telling me he's been watching me online. I recognise the warm chuckle, but maybe there's a bitter edge to it.

'I thought this would be my chance to reach out to Spike, who I believed back then was the love of my life.'

The presenter goes a bit over the top after that, and I can feel my mother's eyes on me. But I'm staring blindly at the worktop.

'Are you going to tell us her name?'

'Do you know, I've decided that's not fair. Sorry, everyone. I bet she's married to some safe, reliable guy and has a couple of kids – a little boy and an older girl, I reckon. She was always destined to be a teacher, and I've no doubt she's a head by now. It wouldn't be fair to disrupt her life.'

He knows.

His words are too accurate and, much as I love my job now, I never wanted to be a teacher back then. *Remember, Scott, I wanted to reach for the stars?* I had imagined myself as a movie screenwriter, or the editor of *Vogue*.

'So do you have a message for Spike, if she's listening?'

'I do. I just want to say that I will never forget the day you left, Spike. I have never felt such pain. I stood on the balcony of our apartment and honestly believed my life was over as I watched you walk away. Fortunately for me, a neighbour witnessed my distress and reached out to me – saved me, helped me to rid myself of my old life and start afresh. But you nearly killed me, Spike. I never got over it. I'm not over it now.'

I hear a gentle 'Aah' from my mother as the presenter begins to speak.

'That's one of the most romantic things I've ever heard, Scott. There won't be a dry eye in the house. Beautifully said.'

Neither the presenter nor my mother has understood at all. They don't know how it ended, the agony he must have endured as he sailed so close to death, and I know what he's telling me. It's nothing to do with the pain of losing me. He's telling me he's not forgotten. I'm not forgiven.

But then neither is he.

'Thanks for calling in, Scott. Especially as it sounds as if you're in a busy place right now. An airport, from the sound of it. Somewhere in the States?'

'No,' he says, the excitement clear in his voice. 'I've just arrived in Manchester. I couldn't stay away a moment longer, so I'll be seeing you soon, Spike. We've got so much catching up to do.'

A letter to my readers

Dear Reader,

Thank you for reading *The Shape of Lies*. It all started with a glimmer of an idea nearly two years ago – the thought of a woman hearing the voice of someone she once loved on the radio threatening to expose her for the person she once was. I knew no more than that – until Anna Franklyn was born.

I have grown to love this woman, in spite of her obvious flaws. She made mistakes, but she made them in the name of love, and I had to ask myself many times what my nineteen-year-old self might have done. I know not every decision I took at that age was wise!

It is always so good to write about Tom Douglas too, especially as in this book we see more of his relationship with his daughter, and with Louisa. Some happy news, some not so happy, and I'm interested to explore what comes next in his life.

One of the joys of writing is the relationship that I have with you – my reader – and I am working hard to improve the ways in which we can communicate. I have set up a special Facebook group – Rachel Abbott's Partners in Crime – so that my readers can chat not just with me, but with each other about all things thriller-related! If you have never visited the page, you should take a look. The members share some great ideas for books, and are always happy to express opinions about what next to read.

I also send regular newsletters to readers, and try to feature some of my favourite books as well as tell you about my life as a writer; letting you know when I might be at a venue near to you, or when one of my books is on special offer. If you'd like to subscribe, just go to www.rachel-abbott.com/contact and submit your details.

And, of course, I'm on Facebook and Twitter. I haven't quite got into Instagram yet, but please let me know if that's where you prefer to hang out and I will do my best to come up with something interesting to post.

I'm going to be out and about at festivals in 2019 – details will appear in newsletters and on the website– and if you get a chance to get along to any of them, please make sure you come and say hello.

I'd love to know what you think about *The Shape of Lies,* so feel free to tweet me, leave me a message on Facebook or a review on Amazon. Every author loves getting reviews, and I'm no exception.

Thanks again for taking the time to read *The Shape of Lies.*

Best wishes,

Connect with Rachel Abbott

If you would like to be notified of any new books
by Rachel Abbott in the future, please visit
www.rachel-abbott.com/contact/ and leave your email address.

Twitter: twitter.com/RachelAbbott
Facebook: www.facebook.com/RachelAbbott1Writer
Website: www.rachel-abbott.com

Acknowledgements

As always, I have many people to thank for their kindness and generosity in helping me to shape this book and to make it as accurate and exciting as possible.

Top of that list is ex DCI Mark Grey who never seems to be fazed by my increasingly bizarre questions. He is truly a star. I must also thank Mike Gibbs, who read the first version of the poker game in this book and gently pointed out that, as a poker player, I had a lot to learn. I hope that I have it right now, but as always my interpretation of the expert advice may have been modified to suit the story. All errors are entirely mine!

My nephew, Alex Hall, took me to a couple of casinos in Manchester. It was a great way to get a feel for the atmosphere and, along with Rachel, Judith and Dave, it was a good night, so thank you all. And no, I didn't win anything!

Alan Carpenter of BYXP has excelled himself with the book cover. It wasn't an easy process, but I am absolutely thrilled with the result – so a massive thank you to Alan for his creativity and endless patience.

A special mention must be made of Jennie Lucas, who won the right to be named in this book as part of an online launch party. Thanks for the name, Jen – it worked perfectly for my bright, bubbly character.

As always my agent, Lizzy Kremer, has been amazing. I know she can be relied on to tell me the truth (even if it's not what I want to hear) and her advice and guidance has done so much for me over the last seven years. There are some people I just couldn't do without, and Lizzy is top of that list. Together with the ever-helpful Maddalena Cavaciuti and Harriet Moore, I know that I have the best possible support.

Huge thanks must, in fact, go to the whole team at David Higham Associates, in particular the translation team, headed by Alice Howe, for selling my books into over twenty languages.

Other stars in the line-up are Maura Wilding, publicist extraordinaire, who does a fantastic job of getting people to talk about my books, and Tish McPhilemy – to call her a PA is to significantly undervalue what she does for me. I can't thank these two wonderful women enough.

I am lucky to have a great team of editors: Clare Bowron, Hugh Davis and Jessica Read, plus early readers Judith Hall, Mark Grey and John Rodgers. Each and every one of you has added to the story.

And of course, where would I be without my fabulous readers? I am overwhelmed by your fantastic support, and thank you all for not only reading my books, but for reviewing them, talking about them to your friends, and for joining me online whenever the opportunity arises. You are the best!

Last but not least, my husband John – who looks after me, reads everything several times, and puts up with yet another set of strangers becoming part of our lives. We talk about my characters endlessly, always as if they are real people – which to me, of course, they are.

Come a Little Closer

They will be coming soon. They come every night.

Snow is falling softly as a young woman takes her last breath.

Fifteen miles away, two women sit silently in a dark kitchen. They don't speak, because there is nothing left to be said.

Another woman boards a plane to escape the man who is trying to steal her life. But she will have to return, sooner or later.

These strangers have one thing in common. They each made one bad choice – and now they have no choices left. Soon they won't be strangers, they'll be family…

When DCI Tom Douglas is called to the cold, lonely scene of a suspicious death, he is baffled. Who is she? Where did she come from? How did she get there? How many more must die?

Who is controlling them, and how can they be stopped?

'Clever, creepy and compelling.'
– Sharon Bolton, author of
The Craftsman

'Come a Little Closer is a brilliant crime read. Rachel Abbott is already one of the Queens of Crime, but this dark tale of manipulation, danger and lies adds to her reputation for outstanding storytelling.'
– Kate Rhodes, author of *Hell Bay*

Also by Rachel Abbott

DCI Tom Douglas Series
Only the Innocent
The Back Road
Sleep Tight
Stranger Child
Kill Me Again
The Sixth Window

Novella
Nowhere Child

Sergeant Stephanie King Series
And So It Begins

CPSIA information can be obtained
at www.ICGtesting.com
Printed in the USA
BVHW031620110319
542310BV00011B/1237/P

9 781999 943721